PICTURESQUE AND IMPOVERISHED Largo Bay is the background for this explosive novel about love and fear, the second in Gillian Royes's mystery series featuring Shad, a Jamaican bartender-detective.

With the arrival of Joseph, estranged son of Eric, the bar's owner, hopes for the village's future come alive but are soon to be threatened. Janna, who has returned to the island, falls for Joseph's good looks and charm, but she isn't the only one with an eye for this mysterious man.

As questions about Joseph's sexuality arise, Shad struggles with protecting the survival of his beloved birthplace amid the deeply ingrained culture of intolerance that surrounds him. What it means to be a man and a father raises questions within the bartender's own home, as his longtime love, Beth, pressures him to make a commitment.

In a land where religion is strong, but life is cheap and violence is often the answer, what will it take for Shad to protect Eric and his family? In this truth-telling sequel to *The Goat Woman of Largo Bay,* the village must confront its own darkness or lose a bright future.

Also by Gillian Royes

The Goat Woman of Largo Bay

Business Is Good

Sexcess: The New Gender Rules at Work

THE
MAN WHO
TURNED BOTH
CHEEKS

A Novel

GILLIAN ROYES

ATRIA PAPERBACK

NEW YORK   LONDON   TORONTO   SYDNEY   NEW DELHI

ATRIA PAPERBACK

A Division of Simon & Schuster, Inc.
1230 Avenue of the Americas
New York, NY 10020

First Atria Paperback edition December 2012

ATRIA PAPERBACK and colophon are trademarks of Simon & Schuster, Inc.

For information about special discounts for bulk purchases, please contact Simon & Schuster Special Sales at 1-866-506-1949 or business@simonandschuster.com.

The Simon & Schuster Speakers Bureau can bring authors to your live event. For more information or to book an event, contact the Simon & Schuster Speakers Bureau at 1-866-248-3049 or visit our website at www.simonspeakers.com.

Designed by Kyoko Watanabe

Manufactured in the United States of America

10 9 8 7 6 5 4 3 2 1

Library of Congress Cataloging-in-Publication Data
Royes, Gillian.
    The man who turned both cheeks / Gillian Royes.—1st Atria Paperback ed.
       p.   cm.
    1. Bartenders—Jamaica—Fiction.   I. Title.
    PS3618.O92M36 2012
    813'.6—dc23   2011052423

ISBN 978-1-4516-2743-5
ISBN 978-1-4516-2744-2 (ebook)

*In memory of a gentle man and
courageous leader, Brian Williamson*

To be nobody-but-yourself—in a world
which is doing its best, day and night, to
make you everybody else—means to fight the
hardest battle which any human being can
fight; and never stop fighting.

—E. E. CUMMINGS

CHAPTER ONE

October 2011

With each passing mango tree filtering sunshine onto the asphalt, with each aquamarine bay spreading before him, Shadrack Myers became gloomier and his forehead more crumpled. The things that usually delighted him—a mongoose scooting across the road, children waving as he drove past—went unnoticed on this trip, so set was his mind on the man he was about to meet.

The bartender's anxiety had started shortly after ten o'clock that morning, when his boss, Eric Keller, had approached him holding the keys to the Jeep.

"Joseph's plane comes in at four fifteen," the boss had said. "I need you to go. I can't take the long drive, not with these . . ." He'd lowered to a chair as if it were hot, one hand waving toward his rear end. Distracted by the thought that a white American could have hemorrhoids like any black Jamaican, Shad had kept his face expressionless and nodded, and it was only an hour later that he realized the import of his mission.

"I going to Montego Bay airport to pick up Mistah Eric's son," Shad had explained to Beth, the mother of his four children, while she was stirring pigeon pea soup for his lunch, a sleeping baby Joshua on her left hip.

"You mean . . . the *batty boy?*" Beth answered, looking at him sideways with a wrinkle between her brows. Shad had cringed inwardly. If the first thought Beth had about Joseph was that he was gay, it would be on the mind of every other villager.

"Why he coming to Largo?" she asked.

"To write a *business proposal*—so they call it. The investor man who going into business with Mistah Eric want to see one, and since the boss don't have no money to pay a Kingston consultant, he call Joseph. He say he send him to a fancy university in America to learn all that kind of thing, and he must be able to do it. If you ask me, what he *really* like is that he don't have to pay Joseph until the investor man give us the money."

Beth had only sighed and returned to her stirring. The quivering of her wide nostrils and the pursing of her mouth told it all. Shad moved behind her and put one arm around her plump waist and the other around Josh's stumpy legs, feeling the rhythm of her stirring and smelling the Scotch bonnet pepper in the soup. They were both silent, remembering the other young man, the one named Gideon.

It was ten long years ago now, but he knew she was thinking about that terrifying night, when he'd come home at one in the morning to find her hugging a pillow in their tiny living room, the lights still on. When he asked her what had happened, she'd looked at him with huge eyes and told him how Gideon, Miss Elsa's sixteen-

year-old son from down the road, had come over earlier in
the evening to take another sewing lesson and how she'd
given him a piece of fabric to start pleating.

"Then I hear the voices," she'd said, and started crying, the words squeezed out between sobs still fresh in his
mind all these years later. "I hear them—coming closer
and closer. And Gideon and I just—freeze, and the boy
stop sewing, his hands—he still holding the cloth I give
him to stitch. And—and he turn his head, and his long,
narrow face just get longer—and he lean over the sewing
machine, listening." She'd stood up, needing to act it
out, a young woman of twenty-two who'd never known
such fear. "The people get closer—until they almost
outside, only the wall separating us. So many people—
making noise at the same time and sounding wild, wild
like animals—like they just braying and cackling and
crowing—all kind of noise, and a woman shouting out
that Leviticus—that he say this and Leviticus say that.

"And I go to the window and I peep under the curtain—I careful they don't see me. I couldn't see the faces,
just hands and feet. They walking with machete and
stick—and one man carrying an ax. And I look at the
youth, tall like his dead father, and the two of us know
that they coming to kill him, just because—because he a
batty boy and they say he come from the devil—the poor
boy who can't help how he born. Just because he act—act
girlish sometimes, they coming to kill him. I look at him
and he stand up.

"*I going to Mama,* he say—and like he start to cry—
and I hush him." She put one finger to her lips, the horror

3

of it drying her tears. "They pass us, all the people—and I hear them stop outside the boy's house up the road. I hear them—call out to his mother, telling him to come out, and calling him a sodomizer. I hear them shouting to each other to—to watch the doors, don't let him escape. And I go to the boy and I—and I put my hand on his shoulder—and he shaking, shaking, and I say to him in his ear: "*I give you some money and you take a taxi now-now. Go to Port Antonio, to your aunty.* I tell him they not going to trouble his mother—is not she they come for. And I tell him to hide in the bushes on the side of the house—and run behind them to the main road. And I let him out of the side door, and I tell him—I tell him to go to his aunty."

Shad had held her on the love seat afterward, and he'd rocked her to calm the terror when it bubbled up again. Before daylight, he'd crept out of the house and gone to Miss Elsa's to tell her that her son was safe, that he was in Port Antonio with her sister.

"Thank you," was all the small Indian woman said before quickly closing the door.

After gulping down his bowl of soup this noontime, Shad had kissed Beth and set off west in the old Jeep along the coast road toward Montego Bay. And since he was both Largo's unofficial sheriff and a praying man, he spent much of his time during the drive having a little chat with God about Joseph.

Please, don't make him gay, was the gist of the prayers. *Make it that he was just going around with funny friends when he was younger, and he grow out of it now. Because if he still gay, is me that have to protect him. It don't matter that he white as snow, or that his father been living here fifteen years and own the best bar in town. Some of these heathens just going to be after the boy's blood if he like men. I just asking you, please keep him safe while he here, God, whether he a batty man or not. Please.*

And another time he reasoned, aloud this time, "Not that gayness frighten me personally anymore, you see, God, but you know it frighten Jamaica." Because God and everyone else knew that to be a gay man on this island was to court death, with a trail of beatings and murders to prove it. Even in Largo, a small fishing village with fifty families, a community too small to have a hospital or a police station, there were people who thought that every homosexual was a sinner and should be wiped off the face of the earth. Since the near lynching of Gideon, there'd been another incident in Largo with an outsider who'd suddenly appeared, an older man who kept to himself and who'd built a shack at the end of the village. After it was rumored that he'd made an indecent remark to a teenage boy, somebody had burned down his house and he'd never been seen again.

The country's obsession with gayness, Shad was sure, had started two decades before with the ugly dancehall songs.

"The musicians cause the whole thing," Shad told Beth after Gideon's departure. "They do anything nowadays to make money. So they start selling fear to poor people who hate their own life, I telling you, poor people who need to hate other people more."

In years gone by, there were no songs, no beatings,

no murders that he remembered. The English composer man Noël Coward had lived in peace with a man friend not far from Largo, had even had parties with important people from Kingston, according to Granny, and nobody had said anything. But this new hatred, it was like a modern invention, this poison erupting out of the dancehall singers, a venom full of injustice, as far as Shad was concerned.

Crawling through the town of Falmouth, past the decaying Georgian buildings, Shad reflected on Joseph's only other visit, eleven years earlier. At nineteen he'd been polite, like he was walking on eggshells. Two friends had come down with him, and the three had kept to themselves, driving around the island in the Jeep. The receptionist girls at Eric's old hotel had nudged each other, whispering that Joseph and his friends must be batty boys. Only gay men would ignore them like that, they'd said. Shad had discouraged the talk, because Eric was a decent man who treated his employees well, and he didn't deserve to have them gossiping about his son.

"You can't take Mistah Eric's money one day and talk about his family the next," Shad had chastised the tittering front desk cashier.

Inside the airport's parking lot, Shad sent up his last prayer and screeched the Jeep to a halt opposite the IMMIGRATION sign.

CHAPTER TWO

Airport doors had always been magical portals to Shad, because they opened to airplanes and runways and horizons unlimited. It wasn't that he wanted to leave the country of his birth forever. He knew he belonged exactly where he lived, but one day, he hoped, one day he would step through those doors onto an airplane, feel his breath taken away when the plane lifted off—and know how it felt to be in America. But today was not that day. Today he'd have to be content, yet again, to stand in the covered area outside the airport's immigration hall, watching the tourists and returning locals struggle out with luggage and children in tow, their faces lit with hope.

Leaning on a trash can, Shad took a bite of his patty, the minced-meat pastry he'd loved from childhood, and ran one hand over his freshly shaved scalp. He liked himself bald because it made him stand out a little. People ignored him if they didn't know him or need him, and he had a tendency to melt into crowds like most small men.

He wondered if Joseph would recognize him with the new haircut, because he was otherwise—according to his own thinking—an unremarkable thirty-five-year-old Jamaican man, his skin dark as midnight (his grandmother's description) and his body lean and compact. In Shad's favor, and something he never considered, was his trademark smile that stretched from cheek to cheek, the endearing gap between the teeth earning him the childhood nickname of Bugs Bunny and later of Smiley. What made the smile appealing in adulthood was that Shad usually kept his mouth slightly open, even when he wasn't speaking, assuring the speaker that he was listening carefully or preparing an agreeable answer. So it was seldom that he appeared as serious as he looked today, and the cheerfulness of the throng at the immigration door only made him look and feel more somber.

"Helga! Helga!" shouted a white woman across the barrier from Shad. She hurried forward and threw her arms around an elderly woman.

His patty finished, Shad threw the greasy bag in the trash. He already regretted eating it, and he should have known better, the way his stomach had churned all the way from Largo Bay. He wiped his hands carefully with the paper napkin, threw it away, and pressed his neatly ironed shirt deeper into his jeans. Peering intently at the arrivals, he tried to imagine what Joseph would look like at thirty.

A plump young man emerged from the doors, between the honeymoon couples. Shad started forward. The man walked into the arms of a woman and Shad shrank back, wishing he'd brought a sign like some of the drivers. Eric or Beth could have written *Joseph Keller* on it.

Three pale women under sun hats emerged from immigration, and a man twice Shad's size elbowed him aside.

"Taxi, taxi, ladies?" the man sang out in a sweet voice, nothing like the rough patois he'd used a minute before with the other taxi drivers.

A few yards behind the women walked a muscular young man, about six feet tall, wearing blue jeans and a white cotton shirt. He was pulling a large black suitcase and carrying a briefcase. Slowing to a stop, he squinted into the sunlight and out of his shirt pocket drew a pair of sunglasses, which he placed on his nose.

Shad refreshed his smile and stepped forward. "Joseph?"

The man turned at his name. "Shad, is that you?" They fumbled through handshakes and laughter.

"I thought Dad was going to pick me up," Joseph said, looking around hopefully.

"His back hurting him, so I come in his place." Shad grinned, wide enough, he hoped, to gain forgiveness for Eric.

Joseph nodded. "You look great, man."

"Thanks, you too. Any more bags?"

"Nope, this is it."

Grabbing the handle of the suitcase, Shad murmured that eleven years was a long time, but it was good to see Joseph again. "The car over there," he added, pointing with his chin to the car park, and he led the way across the road, between the creeping cars full of expectant families.

Headed out of Montego Bay, they puttered along the new highway, a straight gray zipper stretching to Ocho Rios. To their left was the sea—sapphire blue and glittering, white waves foaming at the crusty reef a mile out. To their right were ungainly strips of shops and bars, disowned by the emerald-green mountains sweeping upward behind them.

"Montego Bay not Largo, that for sure," Shad commented, sucking his teeth in disgust. What would have been a tranquil drive on the eastern end of the island was noisy and competitive here on the tourist end. Cars filled the four-lane road, screeching from one traffic light to the next, the more impertinent ones hugging the bumper in front. Tired passengers in crowded route taxis looked homeward to their concrete-block houses squatting on the hills. A few miles farther on, the traffic thinned and Shad relaxed his grip on the wheel, his eyes still on the back of a police car.

"We soon be there, only four hours to go," he said. It would be pitch-black by the time they passed through Port Maria, and he'd have to look hard to see the corners in the dark. "I got you some patties if you get hungry."

"I have nothing but time," Joseph said, waving one hand. He'd grown into a good-looking man, big like his father, with a bristle of gold around a square jaw. His brown hair looked boyish, the way it curled over and around his ears, and when he smiled his teeth were almost as straight as cricket pads. It was hard to see his eyes, but the sunglasses made him look classy in the dirty old Jeep, and Shad made a note to buy himself a pair.

"Shad, remember how you taught me to make rum punch?" Joseph's laugh was easy, normal. Not the laugh of a man who had sex with other men. "I went back to college and started making rum punch for my friends. I've been making it ever since. I bet I can make it as good as you now!"

Shad glanced at his strapping passenger for a second before swinging around a twelve-inch-deep pothole, imagining Joseph serving drinks to his friends. Some of them must be women now, because he had a body any woman would love, his arms and legs thick, like he exercised a lot, and he had a nice way about him, warm, but not too warm, relaxed, but not too relaxed—a man who was careful.

"I'm telling you," Joseph was saying, "I've even been making vodka punches, tequila punches, you name it." He broke off and pointed to a construction site with a multistoried building that towered up behind a long zinc fence. "What's that?"

It was a huge building of six or seven stories, raw and unfinished, the squares of future doors forming an open quilt of ocean and sky. Scaffolding and antlike workmen covered two sides.

"Spanish hotel, man, a thousand rooms." Shad shrugged, reminding himself to speak good English so Joseph could understand. "Everybody is worried that the big new hotels going to take business away with cheap prices, but tourism booming on this side of the island. Jamaica have all kind of drama, drug lords and everything, but tourists still love us." He turned to Joseph. "What we have to do now is develop Largo Bay, get some of that tourist money, true?"

Later, with dusk slipping into the cab, Joseph wiped his mouth after finishing his second patty and stretched his arm along the back of Shad's seat. He'd put the expensive sunglasses on the dashboard, and Shad could just make out the dark gray-blue of his passenger's eyes when he looked at him.

"So who's this investor Dad's talking about? Have you met him?"

"No, not yet," Shad answered, and turned on the crooked car lights. The right one lit up the road immediately in front, the left lamp showed the road twenty feet ahead, an arrangement the boss refused to fix. "His name is Danny and he live in New York. He want to build a hotel next to the bar and go into business with your father, since he have experience in running a hotel and everything."

"A hotel," Joseph said, and shook his head. "I couldn't believe it when Dad told me. Why would he want to start another hotel—at his age?"

"Your father not old, only sixty-five!" Shad cried, pressing down on the squeaky brakes for a second, needing to stop Joseph in his tracks, right here, before they got to Largo. "And he excited about it. I don't see him excited like this for a long time." Nothing about Eric moping around the bar grieving another lost lover.

"I suppose if he wants to—"

"Yeah, man, he want to."

"He always loved the hotel." There was an edge when Joseph said *hotel*.

"It in his blood, you mean. And guess what? Your father say he want me as a partner. Imagine that!" Shad whinnied and hit the steering wheel.

"A *partner*?" Joseph said, like he was caught off guard.

"Yes, man, a partner. Imagine, me, just a little bartender, born poor in Largo, not much education, struggling to support a wife and four children. I never even think it was possible—a partner in a business!" Shad ran a nervous hand over his scalp, aware that he might have said too much. "Surprised me, you see?"

Joseph slung his elbow out the window. "You think *you* were surprised? I hear from Dad, what, twice a year at the most? He only invited me to come once, never invited me back down, and all of a sudden I get this call saying he needs me to write a business plan, and he'll buy me a ticket down. Really surprised me, man. I started to say—"

"You know how long he wanted to call you? He said he was going to call every day for a month. Even got your number out and put it by the phone. Then one day he just walk up to the phone and call you."

"He's lucky, that's all I can say. If I hadn't been laid off, I wouldn't be here."

"What you mean *laid off*?" Shad said, shifting to a lower gear to make the deep curve into Oracabessa.

"A few months ago the company I was working for in DC told me, and three hundred other employees, that it was time to leave. That's what it means."

"I sorry to hear that," Shad said, imagining a white man losing his job. In Jamaica, white men fired people,

13

never got fired. It was a terrible job, anyway, firing people. He didn't know how anyone had the heart to do it.
Like how the bus driver had fired him seventeen years
back for not counting the fare right one time, one time
only. A person shouldn't have the right to fire a man for
a foolish reason. That's how a teenager becomes a thief,
Shad thought, because nobody can sleep with his stomach rumbling. His foot slipped off the accelerator and he
slapped it back on. Oh, Lord, he sighed quietly, if he and
Eric were going to be partners in a hotel, he'd be firing
people one day, because the boss wouldn't be able to do it.

"That's what's happening in the States now," Joseph
was saying. "A lot of people are getting laid off. Maybe
it's for the best, I never liked the place I was working.
It was a big corporate place. They expected you to jump
hoops, work long hours. This could be a blessing, I don't
know." There was a softness to the way he ended the sentence and wagged his head back and forth.

"He have a lot of faith in you."

"It's a job, let's just say that. Bills don't get paid by
themselves."

"Amen."

The big man slicked back his hair with one hand like
his father. "To tell the truth, it's not really my thing, putting real estate packages together. I think I can handle
it, but—the problem is Dad not having a computer. He
doesn't even have an email address, so I can't email him
the stuff as I go along. I have to stay here until the whole
thing's done. Who ever heard of a business today without
a computer or email, man?"

Shad stared out at the trees jumping to life in the car's left headlight, being swallowed by the darkness behind them. There'd been computers in the old hotel, five of them, two at the front desk and three in the office behind. After they'd been swept away by the hurricane, the boss had refused to buy another computer, said he'd lost enough money on computers.

"It will be a cold day in hell before I buy one of those machines again," he'd said and slapped the counter with his palm when the real estate guy had suggested it.

It didn't matter to Shad anyway. He and computers had no business together, like reading books and the fine-print articles in the *Gleaner*. Dropping out of school at ten had meant that the reading, the writing, the geography taught by Miss Mac in her singsong voice had been left behind while he went fishing with his uncle, since his grandmother couldn't work anymore. Beth had promised to help him with his reading and writing, but there was never enough time with the children and work and church. So there was no newspaper reading, no driver's license. He could manage, though, as long as he could keep the bartender work—paying two and three times what fishing paid—so his children could learn to read the paper and work the computer.

"How long you think it going to take you?" Shad said. "To write the report thing, I mean."

"I figure a couple months at most."

"We have to do it quick, man. We don't want to lose the opportunity. It mean the world to your father. When the hurricane destroy his old hotel, it was like it took the breath out of him, and he never been the same since. Even the little bar we have now, it don't lift him up, you know? He hardly ever come in at night, like he ashamed of it. I running it for him, a nice place, but it losing money, and I worried sometimes that we—" His voice turned husky and he cleared his throat. If he didn't talk about it, it wouldn't happen, because there was no way he was going back to being a fisherman.

"Anyway," Shad continued, "all of a sudden, this woman move onto the island—the island where the old hotel is—and she start paying us a good rent to stay there. She put up a tarpaulin over the lobby and used to sleep there. She didn't have no water and no toilet, just renting the place and living there. We would take her whatever she need to eat and drink. Simone was her name, she come from Atlanta. She say she want to be alone on the island. Then her brother, Cameron is his name, a man who sell real estate in New York, come looking for her. And before they left, Cameron tell us that one of his clients want to own a hotel in Jamaica, and he come up with this idea that the man should go into business with your father, and give your father the money to build the hotel and run it. That was two months back, middle of August. The man say he need to see a—"

"What d'you mean, there's an island where the old hotel was?"

Shad blinked, thrown off the train of his story. "Well, when Hurricane Albert hit us eight years ago, it mashed up your father's hotel. You know that, right?"

"Yeah."

16

"Your father never told you that the place became an island?"

"Nope."

Shad's small, slim fingers stabbed the air, drawing out the site. "Remember the hotel was on a piece of land that jutted out into the sea? And there was a narrow strip of land with a driveway between the hotel and the main road? Well, that gone now. Hurricane Albert washed away the road, even the land it was on. So all you have now is the hotel—what left of it—sitting on an island all by itself. Nobody live there until the woman come."

Outside the car windows, total blackness had descended, no streetlights to relieve it. The bass call of frogs rumbled through the dark, accompanied by a thousand crickets screaming. Shad dug two fingers into the lids of his eyes and massaged them. It had been a long day driving, two more hours left to Largo. He placed his hand slowly back on the steering wheel.

"This investment business, this hotel offer, it come like a godsend to Largo," he sighed. And you the only man who can get us there, he wanted to add, or we all as good as dead.

CHAPTER THREE

J anna opened the laptop on her knees and turned it on. Waiting for it to boot up, she slipped off her sandals and rested her feet on the dripping verandah rail. The damp of an early morning rain hung around the garden, the air still cool and smelling of earth. It was her first day back on the island in a couple of years, and everything seemed sharper and more serene than she remembered— the pale sunshine washing the garden, the birds calling from the mango trees, the light breeze blowing up the driveway from the ocean.

She hugged her arms, running her hands up and down the long sleeves of her father's blue shirt, stolen from his closet minutes before. Tall like her father, slim like her mother, she'd inherited their café au lait complexions and springy hair, which today sprang out from the rubber band at the back of her head. *Pretty,* people usually called Janna, a description she thought anemic but generous. If anything, she was *pleasing,* she thought once, like a Jane Austen heroine who wasn't really pretty. Her best feature, she'd decided, were her eyes: big and brown, the lashes curling. Her worst: the nose, which was a little too round. The full lips she could live with, now that they'd become fashionable.

Both pretty and pleasing, the twenty-three-year-old had had the fortune or misfortune to be brought up in the protective gauze of being an only child. To her credit, however, she had also become self-analytical, aware that she lived cautiously and irritated that the wary choices of her mother had become her own. Her limitations became annoyingly clear to her every time she listened to a peer's description of traveling far from home or when she avoided her boss instead of asking for a promotion, and she'd now reached the point where she'd had enough of her milquetoast self, and gave herself daily reminders (as she did now) that it was time to tread the untrodden, even if she wasn't sure how to go about it, especially in Largo Bay.

The musical chime of the computer snapped her back to the present. She connected to the Internet, checked her email, saw nothing of consequence since yesterday, and started a letter.

Lorraine:

Safe and sound in JA. Flight down a little rocky, especially over Cuba.

A flight attendant complimented me on my feet. She asked me if I was a foot model. Not a model, mind you, a foot model. Had a flirtation (alas, eyes only) with a guy across the aisle.

House is quiet with Jennifer and the kids gone. Daddy is like a lost soul. What is it with men when the woman leaves them on their own? Anyway, he keeps asking me if I'm okay. When Jennifer is here, he goes about his business and hardly sees me.

It's peaceful here, very tasteful house—cool blue linen on the sofas, big rooms with high ceilings, hardwood floors kind of tasteful. There's not much to Largo Bay itself, but the scenery is amazing. The bay is about a mile long, slightly curving, and the main road runs the length of it. The waves are constantly pounding the beach (no gentle lapping here, sorry), and the sand is powder white. Most of the houses are toward the western end of the beach, which is where Daddy's house is. The road through the village is lined with fishermen's cottages—very cute, like the tourist posters, with pastel colors and gingerbread around the roofs. (Lots of action in those little houses, though, adorable children everywhere.)

Behind the picturesque cottages, towers of bright green bamboo and mango trees give way to the lush foothills of the Blue Mountains. In luxuriously scenic and sadly impoverished Largo, Nature flaunts her beauty but life pays the price. (Nice, huh? Maybe I should take up travel writing.) Over the whole village there hangs an air of ennui, a hopeful melancholy, a feeling that the twenty-first century has passed the little fishing community, has left it to the thundering surf and the eternal breezes that bathe the town and its people. (The end.)

Back to reality: the job search. I'm going to start with Miami and broaden out. Who knows? Maybe I'll find something in Atlanta, but I doubt it. Too much competition. I don't want to stretch too far north, if I can help it. A guy in my class just got a job working with George Lucas's operation in San Francisco, but that's too far for me. Like I have options, right? Here I am starting all over again, savings gone, fresh out of school (again) with no experience (again), and only a certificate—hardly recession proof.

How's life in MIA? Did Sammy finally ask you out? What's happening in the office? No social life here, of course, and definitely no men. You have to drive thirty miles around a million corners, I swear, before you come to civilization. I'd love to go to the beach and work on my tan, but I'm afraid that the new breasts are a little too much for this conservative (we're talking nineteenth-century) population. Nightlife I can forget. The nearest thing to a club is a little bar across the road that a friend of my father's owns. Looks like I'm in for a quiet time, unless I make nice with the locals.

J

As she pressed her initial, the defining letter she'd carved into many a school desk, Janna heard a sound she hadn't heard in years. A haunting sound, it was coming from somewhere in the garden—the soft cooing of a dove seeking its mate.

CHAPTER FOUR

H e must have gotten his mother's looks, Shad decided when Joseph emerged from the shadows and approached the bar, because the curly brown hair and high cheekbones didn't come from Eric. The new arrival was walking slowly, almost sauntering, looking more relaxed than when Shad had delivered him to Miss Mac's boardinghouse the evening before, and the peachy sheen on his cheeks said he'd lost no time in hitting the beach.

The bartender had already decided that Joseph was a likable guy, even if he held himself off a little, didn't look you steady in the eye and smile at the same time. He was a complex man who kept his thoughts to himself, not as straightforward and plainspoken as his father. And although he had his father's height and nose and his father's smoky blue eyes, he looked like a classy guy. He'd sat in a few limousines already, you could tell, but he could still make himself comfortable in little Largo.

"Hey, man!" Shad called. He turned down the radio, Don Drummond's trombone wailing "Eastern Standard Time," and took two beers out of the fridge. "Saw your father today?"

Joseph slid onto a bar stool opposite. "Yeah, I saw him. He came over for a few minutes. We're supposed to meet tomorrow morning." He gave a curt nod at the end, lips pulled back dutifully.

"So, what can I get you?" Shad said, waving to the two shelves filled with bottles behind him. "We have everything, well, not everything, but we have beer, whiskey, rum, vodka—"

"One of your famous rum punches." The man hit the counter with his big hand, the flat ring making a clink. "I want to see if they're still as good as I remember."

"Give me a minute, I coming right back." Shad placed a third beer on his tray and walked it around the counter to a distant table. Business was slow tonight, with a light breeze weaving its way among the few customers and bringing the smell of seaweed and the screeching of crickets from the darkness outside. Behind Shad, the building housing the Largo Bay Restaurant and Bar stretched some seventy feet. Squatting between the coastal road and the edge of a cliff, it was made up of the bar-cum-restaurant on the eastern end, Eric's small apartment on the other, and a kitchen in the middle. A rough structure, it was open to the elements like most North Coast bars, the thatch roof held up by telephone poles that had "fallen off the back of a truck," according to the boss.

"Four hundred and fifty Jamaican," Shad said, setting down the drinks on the round wooden table where two men and a pretty woman were talking languidly. While one of the men dug into his pocket, the woman swung her eyes to the bar.

"Who the new guy just come in?" she said. Janet was a regular, a woman in her late thirties, of some talent with a sewing machine, mostly to sew herself short dresses with tight waistlines. Her openly stated aim, for as long as Shad could remember, was to marry an American and get a green card, and the Largo Bay Bar was her fishing ground.

"Lord, stop being so inquisitive," said one of the men, sneaking a peek himself.

"I just asking who the man is," Janet said. She swirled the beer in the bottle like ice in a soft drink. "Since you can't take care of me, I have to see what out there, not true?"

"Mr. Eric's son," Shad replied, counting the worn bills. He gave them a warning glare meant to stop any discussion, and one of the men shuffled his shoes on the concrete floor.

"Isn't he—?" Janet said.

"Thanks," Shad said, nodding to the men and starting back.

There were a dozen locals in the bar that night, all known to Shad. He knew their pasts and sometimes their futures. Triumphant Arch, defending his favorite political party, had gotten his name from a dream his mother had when she was pregnant. He was arguing with Heresford, a fisherman who came to the bar only when his brother took their boat out to transport weed along the coast. Nakisha at a side table was too young to be out on a weeknight with a grown man, but her mother had never known how to mind her, and the way Jethro was kissing up on her, the child was going to get pregnant and the man was going to leave her. Everybody had a story, Shad believed, and it was his business to know their stories.

In a village with a few dozen fishing families, a forgotten dot on the northeastern end of Jamaica, someone had to keep track of things, had to be the problem solver, and Shad was the man—in his own mind, if not in everyone else's. A *sniffer and snuffer,* Miss Mac had called him once, and although it made him think of a dog, he liked how it sounded. But even better than that, he'd decided, was being Elliot on *Law & Order: SVU,* which he sometimes watched on his afternoons off. Elliot was a man who found small clues that everyone else missed, and made connections. That was his role, too, Shad had decided. Bartending was his income, but *investigating* was his true vocation, and in order to fulfill his role in Largo, it was important—more than that, essential—that he knew who was who and what was what, and how to make the connections.

Even so, there were times like tonight when the size of Largo Bay, the closeness of the faded pink and blue houses, the sameness of the population, and the knowledge everyone carried of everyone else (age, health, family illnesses, relatives, sexual history embedded on mental files) all raised a red flag for Shad. Because, as caring as Largo was, it was also a place of intrepid, unrelenting gossip. In a village where few could read past a fifth-grade level, the grapevine was king. And even though much of the gossip was harmless—Abe moved in with Marcia; Jethro bought a new boat—sometimes it caused havoc.

Back at the bar, Shad smiled at Joseph. "I don't forget you, man. One rum punch coming up!" He removed a jug of orange juice from the refrigerator and placed two cans next to it.

"Let me give you a test," he said. "You remember the ingredients?"

Joseph laughed his easy laugh. "With my eyes closed. Orange juice, pineapple juice, fruit punch, and white rum, of course. How's that?"

"Not bad, not bad, but guess what?" Shad gave a whinny, spun around on one heel, and clapped in triumph. "You forgot the bitters!"

"Bitters? You added bitters last time? I don't remember anything about bitters!" Joseph leaned back on his stool and slapped the counter again. "You're cheating!"

"No cheating, man, I go to church." Shad dropped three ice cubes into a glass and punched open the cans of pineapple juice and fruit punch. He poured both into the glass at the same time, holding the cans opposite each other, watching the twin spouts of pink and yellow merging to peach.

"Try again," he said. "What kind of white rum to use?"

"Hell, whatever I can find, man." Joseph chuckled. "I even tried Bacardi a few times."

"What?" Shad opened his mouth in mock horror. "It have to be Jamaican rum, seen?"

"Seen?"

"That's what we say here now. Like *you know*? You been away too long, man." Shad laughed.

He opened the rum bottle and poured three capfuls into the peach-colored mixture, topping it off with four drops of brown bitters. After stirring the brew, he placed it in front of Joseph, slipping a coaster underneath.

"Talk the truth," Shad said. He spread his legs and cracked his knuckles. "Don't this taste better than the ones you make?"

Joseph sipped, squeezing his eyes shut in concentration. He put the glass down and licked his lips. "You're the man." They bumped fists across the counter and were still beaming when a voluptuous voice interrupted them.

"Good evening."

"Hi," Joseph said, nodding to Janet, who was thrusting her hips onto the stool next to his, the low neckline of the yellow dress offering up her breasts as special deliveries for passing Americans. Shad rolled his eyes up to the thatch.

"A Coke, please, Shad," she said. She dumped her large silver bag on the counter and looked Joseph up and down.

"I thought you were with Eustace tonight," Shad said, pursing his lips. There was no deterring Janet when she was casting her line, but he could try.

"He have to go home early to his wife," the woman replied with a perky smile. The new gold star on her incisor winked at the two men. It would have been just a matter of days, anyway, before the whole village found out about Joseph's arrival, and the time was about to be made shorter by a woman who liked to sew fact and fiction together. True to form, within five minutes Janet had found out what Joseph did for a living.

27

"A *financial analyst*," she said, and crunched a piece of ice. "What that mean?"

"I look at—" Joseph glanced at Shad. "When a company wants to buy or sell their shares, they call on somebody like me to help them."

"Explain what a *share* is for me," Shad said, settling on his own stool behind the counter. He'd wanted to know ever since Eric had told Cameron he wanted Shad to have shares in the company. A share sounded like something good, like a generous serving of food, but he hadn't wanted to ask the boss what it meant in case it made him sound ignorant.

"A share is a part of a company. When a business starts, it has a certain number of shares divided between the owners." Joseph picked up five straws and laid them on the counter. He was trying not to look too proud, Shad could tell, but he liked explaining. "Say this is the total worth of a company, five shares. I invest in part of the company, meaning, I buy shares in the company." He removed one straw. "I pay one-fifth of the value of the company to the owners, so I buy twenty percent of the company's shares. And they now have my money to help run the business. When they make a profit, they pay me dividends on my twenty percent ownership. Like how a bank pays you interest on your savings account. Understand?"

"Sort of," said Shad, who didn't have a bank account. "But how does *your* work come into it?"

"If a company decides they want to invest, or buy another company's shares, I can do research for them and tell them if it's a good idea. I write a report telling them whether they're likely to make money or not. That's a financial report, like the one I'm doing—"

"I get you," Shad said, cutting him off. Janet had enough information for the night. "You went to school to learn it? You must be good with numbers."

"I have a couple degrees."

"And you have a nice job in America doing that—that money business?" Janet said, smiling like she thought the gold tooth would buy her shares. Shad almost sucked his teeth.

"Well—" Joseph said.

"He doing real well," Shad said, hopping off the stool, "just taking a little holiday."

"Nice, man, nice," Janet said, staring at Joseph's thick arm. "He sweet, eh, Shad?"

"You want another rum punch?" Shad said to Joseph.

"Yeah, thanks. So what do you do—Janet, you said your name was?" Joseph was trying to be polite, the way Americans were, ignoring Shad's lifted eyebrows, with their warnings about women and this one in particular.

"My true name is Janet Ann," the woman said, "but is Janet they call me. I am a dressmaker, and if you need me to do any little thing for you, you call me, you hear?" She slurped the last of her drink and stood up. "I have to catch the early bus to Port Morant, but is nice meeting you."

Strutting out of the bar, hips swinging, the bag thrown over her shoulder, Janet left her bill unpaid. Another rum punch later, Joseph took his leave after a laughing debate with Shad, who'd refused to accept a tip. Joseph looked happier than when he'd arrived, eyes twinkling, and when he walked away, he was swaying a little.

He'd have to keep a close eye on Joseph, Shad decided, because he didn't seem to understand that this trip wasn't about rum and sun. It was about writing a report that would get a better life for every struggling body in Largo, and Joseph was the only, only person who could take them there.

"I thirsty." A deep, parched voice broke into Shad's thoughts as he finished washing the glasses. Under his elbow appeared a set of prehensile toes hanging over too-small flip-flops. Solomon, the bar's part-time cook in the tiny kitchen, was towering over him, a tall column of white, from the too-short pants to a chef's hat that had seen better days. Solomon's rough chocolate features hid a man disappointed by life. Lord of the old hotel's stainless steel kitchen, he'd enjoyed calling out orders in his bass voice and terrifying the apprentice cooks. Tonight he was a tired alcoholic on starvation wages, his eyes red and pleading, the smell of white rum oozing from his pores.

"I give you a soft drink," Shad said. "You still have work to do, dishes to wash."

"Pshaw, man, just a little something for the cold?" Solomon gave a dry cough and rubbed his chest.

"After you done working, I give you a white rum," Shad said, and popped open a can of soda.

"The boss's son come and gone," Solomon said, taking the drink. He frowned at the can as if he could read the ingredients, still hoping for alcohol, or at least caffeine. "Handsome, eh?"

"True," Shad said, vigorously wiping down the bar counter.

"You think he still a batty man?" Solomon had never been one to waste words or spare feelings.

Shad spun around. "What you talking? He not a batty man. Don't start spreading gossip around the place." He wanted to wipe the man's smirk off with the dishrag.

"I see him swimming today," Solomon said. "He take off his T-shirt the way a woman do, one arm at a time, and he swim like so, like a girl." He circled his arms, sweeping the can through the air and spilling a few drops on the counter.

"What you know about Americans, eh?" Shad demanded. "Maybe American men take off their shirt one arm at a time. Maybe they swim like that! You wouldn't know. You ever been to America?"

Solomon took a long sip of the drink. "Largo not a place for man-man business."

"Don't let the boss hear you talking stupidness about his son, if you want to keep your job."

"Mistah Eric? He know how it go already. You don't see all the women he sleep with? He know how it go in Jamaica. He know we hear from early what the Bible say. Man not supposed to lie with man because it unnatural. It not the natural order of things. You don't agree with me?" The big man was warming up, burping, blinking, ready to prove his point.

"No man can have baby with man," he persisted. "God create us in his image, and he make it so that the only way we can create is for man to have sex with woman. All this man-and-man, woman-and-woman thing, we must stop it coming to Largo, because if we don't stamp it out, the village gone to hell. Next thing all the young boys will be sexing up each other." Solomon paused and dug his tongue into something in a back tooth. "God say it wrong, and we say it wrong. So it go since Adam and Eve. It can't go any way else. You don't see what I mean? If we don't have children, the whole place going to mash up, not true?"

Heading back to his dirty dishes, he pointed two fingers at Shad like a gun. "*Boom, boom, batty man.* You know the song?"

CHAPTER FIVE

Eric slid the last of the money into the last envelope and licked the flap. On the front of each of the three envelopes on the counter was the name of an employee—*Shad* on one, *Solomon* on the second, and on the last *Maisie,* Solomon's wife and the bar's cleaning lady. He placed the envelopes under an empty rum bottle. *Myers's Rum,* said the faded label on the bottle of twelve-year-old rum he used every week for only this purpose, the bottle that Shad would lift to distribute the envelopes when he came in later.

The salary payments had been on Eric's mind as soon as he woke up that morning, and he'd decided to get them over with first thing so he could focus on his meeting with Joseph. He felt some guilt about pressing his son into work right away, but he'd reasoned with himself that there was no harm in getting him started on the report. The less time Joseph spent in Largo, the lower Miss Mac's tab would be.

Above him, the thatch roof, newly replaced with Simone's rental income, still smelled like cut grass, clean and green in the morning air. The smell reminded him of her, made him grateful to her, along with the thought that her rental payments had also paid his property taxes for the last two years. With her departure from the island, the extra income had ceased, the last of it used to pay for Joseph's airline ticket and these salary payouts. With Christmas coming in a couple of months and four parties booked already for the restaurant, there'd be just enough cash coming in to get through until January, maybe February, when business would be slower than ever.

Eric poured himself another cup of coffee, adding the canned condensed milk he'd become addicted to, and walked to the side of the bar overlooking the cliff, his flip-flops slapping the concrete floor. It was an odd sight: this aging, slightly paunchy Caucasian with freckle-reddened skin and shoulder-length white hair, leaning in old shorts and T-shirt against the post of a bar in the middle of nowhere. It wasn't as if he had a choice. The truth, and what few people guessed, was that Eric was anchored to the spot, or rather to the moldy buildings on the island in front of his bar. A quarter mile offshore, stranded in the middle of turbulent ocean water, sat the love of his life—the remains of the hotel he'd built fifteen years earlier. Seen from the shore, the roofless buildings looked almost romantic, not like Eric's retirement dream in tatters.

It had taken him twenty-nine years slogging at a Manhattan paper company to realize his dream of building the hotel. First he'd envisioned it—a slow churning up of what he wanted to do and where he wanted to live—then the piling of every available penny into his retirement savings. In the years after his divorce, he'd doubled his savings, moving to a cheap apartment in Chinatown, avoiding restaurants, and buying his clothes in thrift stores. In a scrapbook that he kept on his desk he'd glued articles from travel and hotel magazines, planning his inn, awake and asleep. He had had three requirements for his hotel: it had to be on an island, it had to have scenery that would startle him every day with its beauty, and it had to be in the Caribbean. The original idea had come to him in a hammock in Ocho Rios, and thereafter he'd taken an annual trip to a different island (Barbados, St. Lucia, Grenada, Jamaica), and stayed at small hotels to see how they ran things, wondering if he could live here, or there, or there.

When his retirement finally came in 1996, and after the retirement luncheon with Arnie and a bunch of people whose names he'd forgotten now, he'd lost no time in moving down to Largo and buying the long, narrow property that was on sale, cheap, at the end of the bay. That was followed by one year of building the inn block by block with a few workers, Shad among them, and under the direction of a toothless contractor named Old Man Job whom he couldn't understand. It had culminated in the best years of his life, being the owner, manager, and salesman of his own creation: the Largo Bay Inn.

Today the abandoned hotel looked dreary after the rain, as desolate as it had been since the hurricane destroyed it. For the two and a half months that Simone had occupied it, the place had lost its ghostly feeling—to him, anyway—and just the knowledge of her presence had given him hope that the island's life, his life, was not yet over. Now that she had gone back to the States, there was a more lifeless feeling to the place than before, even though the flat-topped almond tree still ruffled its leaves and the lemongrass still bent in the breeze. But her departure had sucked out the life she had brought, because there was no hope of seeing her wild black hair bobbing above the bushes now, no hope of hearing the shrill bark of her little dog, no hope of making love to her with the ocean roaring in his ears.

Eric returned to the kitchen and took another mug out of the cupboard for Joseph. Things were about to get better. He wouldn't have time to think of Simone, because there'd be distractions with the planning of the new hotel. There'd be business meetings, calculations to be made, visits to government offices to get approvals.

Half an hour later, his arms folded, Eric watched his son draining his coffee cup. The small talk had been completed yesterday, with the updates necessary to close the long stretch since they'd seen each other (*It's been, how long, man, five years, six years?*)—an embarrassment Eric had needed to paper over with talk of being busy with building and running the bar. To his relief, Joseph had replied that he'd been busy, too, and nothing had been said to make him feel guilty.

"Where do we start?" Joseph said, wiping his mouth.

Eric leaned his elbows on the table. "Let's start with how you're going to get paid for doing this, this—this business proposal thing. I pay your expenses for the trip. Airfare, lodging, food, everything. If and when we get the investor's money, we'll pay your fee. Remember to include it in your report, by the way."

"Fair enough."

"This is the situation today," Eric said, bending back one scaly finger for each fact. "We have an interested investor in New York who wants to build a hotel here. He has no experience and he doesn't want to run it. I guess that makes him a silent partner. We have this bar here on an acre of land. That would be my stake in the deal—no money, just the land and my expertise.

"Then we have Miss Mac next door, where you're staying. She has nine acres of prime beach land she wants to sell. I mean *prime*. You should walk down and take a look at it. I think she wants to move to her son's house in Port Antonio—he's my lawyer, Horace McKenzie. We might need him. And last but not least, we have Lambert Delgado, an excellent contractor for big jobs—originally from Kingston, has years of experience on the island. He lives across the road. He knows all about it already."

"Sounds like you have everything sewn up," Joseph said, and lifted his chin in a minor challenge that his father didn't miss.

"Your job is to put it together on paper, the whole deal. The investor, Danny somebody—I can't remember the last name—says he wants a business plan from me with all the figures."

"What's the deadline?"

Eric twisted his jaw to one side, thinking. "I don't remember if he gave me one. Should I ask?"

"Absolutely. It'll show that you're serious and give us

something to shoot for. I'd call him as soon as possible, today even."

"Right. What else can we get started?"

"When can we go see this contractor friend of yours?"

"He's expecting us today."

The sun was getting high in the sky when they walked up Lambert's steep driveway, a comfortable arm's length apart. They didn't walk in time with each other, Joseph's stride faster and Eric's longer, but they managed to stay side by side, climbing the road between the fruit trees to the large white house ahead. A welcoming one-story, the home was a modern replica of a plantation house, with its steep shingle roof and wide verandah lined by rocking chairs.

"This is where I came in the hurricane," Eric said, starting to get winded halfway up the drive. "A port in a storm, literally."

"You didn't stay at the hotel?"

"I stayed for the first part. I was alone—I'd sent the guests to bigger hotels and let the staff go—go home. Soon after the hurricane hit—waves started—" Eric's hand slashed through the air, telling the story he never tired of. "They just swept over the cliff and came right through—washed everything out. All you could see were—the walls standing in water. I ended up—on the reception desk through the first part of the storm, watching the roof blow off—one section at a time. And—during the eye of the storm—I realized the second part was going to be—worse than the first, and I decided to make a run for it. More like a swim for it. I didn't know—the driveway had been—washed away—until I got to the cliff. Nothing but water. Waves like—like eight, ten feet. I just jumped in and headed for shore. And the—the backside of the storm hit while I was swimming. I barely made it." He scraped away the film of sweat gathering on his forehead and wiped his finger on his shorts.

"Sounds terrible," Joseph said. "Good thing you made it." He sounded concerned, but kept looking straight ahead in his aviator sunglasses.

"I came here—branches flying in every direction. Crawling on my—hands and knees onto this very verandah—naked as a baby. The water had—torn off all my clothes—and they pulled me inside—Lambert and Jennifer." They mounted the steps to the verandah, and Eric flung himself into a rocking chair.

"You want me to knock?" Joseph said evenly, clearly not winded.

"Yes, knock." In front of the verandah and beyond Eric's bar, curving bays stretched one behind the other, low green hills at the end of each bay keeping them separate. It was a view Eric would never forget. In shock, then in anger and sorrow, he'd sat here and looked at the island opposite for a full year before taking Shad's advice and building the bar.

The deep barking of a large dog followed by footsteps answered Joseph's knock; then the door opened. "Hi, is Lambert here?" Joseph asked.

"He is," a young woman informed him. "I'm his daughter."

"Hey, Janna!" Eric said, heaving himself out of the chair and lumbering toward her.

"Uncle Eric!" the girl cried. He bent down and planted a kiss on her cheek while she kept one hand on the agitated dog beside her. "I didn't see you."

"My God, you're looking more gorgeous every time I see you. Your father makes some pretty children, I'm telling you. How long are you staying this time?"

"I'm not sure. I just finished another course—changing careers, I guess." She looked a little sheepish when she said it and bent down quickly to pat the dog. Long brown hair fell over her face, hair that came from a healthy mix of backgrounds, wavy and wild. She straightened slowly, her eyes darting up to Joseph, down at the dog, up to Eric.

"Would you let your dad know we're here, Janna?" Eric said. "Oh, and, Joseph, this is Janna." He waved. "My son, Joseph."

Joseph removed his sunglasses and stuck out his hand. "Hey, Janna. Did I get it right?"

They shook hands. "That's it—Janna," she said with a bright smile. "Pleased to meet you." Releasing his hand, she held the door wide. "Come in, come in, both of you. Sorry, I shouldn't have kept you standing there. We're only keeping the door closed because of Sheba. She just had puppies and she's still kind of nervous."

In the living room, Joseph let the dog sniff his hand and patted her head. "A chocolate Lab, right? How many puppies did she have?"

"Four, I think. I just arrived last night," the girl

said over her shoulder as she started walking toward a corridor.

"Daddy!" she called. She was barefoot, a tall girl with long, thin arms and legs that swung easily in the frayed shorts.

Eric's best friend came striding up the corridor, making the wooden boards creak. He was a big, well-padded man in khaki shorts with a receding gray hairline and a bushy black mustache that stretched beyond his smile. His ancestry, as he'd said to Eric once, could be read in his face. The beige skin came from Spain and India, the hawkish nose from his Jewish grandmother, and the wiry hair from the African woman whom some white man had impregnated along the way. A commanding man, Lambert left the impression that he went after whatever he wanted. All he needed to look like a hunter in Africa, Eric had always thought, was a pith helmet.

"Welcome, welcome," Lambert said, extending a hand to Joseph. Janna excused herself, saying she had to work. As the men sat in the verandah chairs—Joseph exclaiming at the view—Lambert pointed out the multiple bays in front of them: Poco Bay, Manchioneal, and Happy Grove, Hector's River in the distance.

The housekeeper appeared for drink requests, and Eric lit the pipe he always carried in his pocket, sucking hard and sheltering the match from the sea breeze. A few minutes later, the drinks arrived on a silver tray, Red Stripe beers for Joseph and Lambert and lemonade for Eric—made with brown sugar the way he like it, Miss Bertha said with a laugh.

After taking a sip, Lambert wiped his mustache on a napkin. "Your father and I've been talking. I hear you're preparing the business plan."

"I'm it, I guess," Joseph said with a cautious smile.

"This is going to be fun, man!" Lambert said, giving a sudden booming laugh—his *guffaw,* his wife called it—and slapping his knee. "Ready for action?"

"As ready as I'll ever be."

"Do you have office space, a desk, a computer to work at?"

"None of the above." Joseph tossed his head, flipping a curl back in place. "I have a laptop, but no Internet."

"What about a phone?" Lambert asked. "Your cell phone isn't going to work here, I'm sure you know that already."

"I need a phone, you're right."

"Well, would you like to set up an office here? We have Internet, a landline, everything you need. I was thinking about it this morning. It makes sense, don't you think? There's space enough here; my wife Jennifer's office is free."

Eric leaned forward and exhaled a cone of smoke to one side, wishing Lambert had run the idea by him first. "You can work in the bar any time you want, you know that, and you can have your meals there."

"I tell you what," Joseph said, his voice certain, even a little arrogant. "Why don't I set up an office here, and come over to the bar for lunch? How about that?"

"That'll work," Eric said, and leaned back.

"What do you need from me first?" Lambert urged.

"We need the projected costs of the land, the buildings, the services. All the fees, legal fees, architect's fees, evaluator's fees—"

"They call them quantity surveyors here," Eric put in.

"Quantity surveyors, whatever, everything that's going to be a cost up front and at the back end. And if there's no design yet, we'll just have to estimate how much it'll cost based on square footage and the number of rooms, I guess."

"Twenty rooms," his father said, rubbing his chin. "The old one had fifteen, but I think this one would do well at twenty." Fifteen hadn't netted much profit after the staff was paid. He'd had to forego his own salary a few times.

Joseph frowned. "Let's find out what the break-even point of small hotels in Jamaica is before we settle on that."

While his son talked, Eric looked at this young man with intelligent eyes, heard him throwing around jargon and concepts unknown to his father, and he knew it was Claire who'd done this for Joseph. It was Claire who'd defended him, who'd left Queens and moved to Virginia so she could get him into a decent school, Claire who'd fought for him to go to Georgetown over Eric's objections, Claire who'd parented while he'd gone on with his life in New York and Jamaica.

Joseph ran a hand through his hair and turned to his father. "And you need to give me the cost of running the hotel for the first five years."

"No problem."

"And the income, of course."

"From guests?"

"From everything, guest rooms, bar, restaurant, receptions, weddings—," Joseph responded, and it seemed for a minute that all the years of absences and difficult visits and missed PTA meetings had never existed, that they were just three men talking business, men at last together.

CHAPTER SIX

Lorraine:

There is life on Mars! Met the cutest guy—right here in Largo! His father owns the bar opposite and they both came across this morning. ☺

Picture this: I am in oldest shorts possible, haven't bathed yet, smelling I-don't-know-how, open the door to this AMAZING man, thinking it's one of the construction guys, some plumber or carpenter come to see my father. Can you imagine? I almost died right there. I was trying to hold down the dog, trying to be cool and trying not to get too close so he wouldn't smell anything. (I wish I'd known he was coming!!!)

Moving on: I open the door. Drop-dead is standing there in sunglasses. About six foot. Longish brown hair and the sweetest smile!! Nice little tan, could be from tanning salon or beach, not sure. Arms like a wrestler. Looking good all the way around. His father introduces us. The guy has a kind of shy way about him, genteel, well brought up. Not like his father, who's pretty rough around the edges. Age? I don't know. Maybe 28, 30. (Too old for me? Don't say it.) I call my dad and they all go to sit on the verandah. I retreat to living room . . . to eavesdrop.

Turns out that the guy (Joseph) is here to work on a financial plan for his father's hotel. Probably here for around two months. And guess what? My father invites him to set up an office RIGHT HERE IN OUR HOUSE, since he has no Internet where he's staying. So I'll be working away on my laptop in the dining room while my boy is working in Jennifer's office ten feet away.

He's probably not into younger girls or he's only into white girls or he has a girlfriend already. I promise you I won't be fantasizing about him, the way I did with Alfredo, the guy in Aruba. You were right, I hate to admit. Alfie was probably married with four children. I guess it's easier for me to deal with an online heartthrob than the real thing. I promise you I won't get carried away this time. We probably don't have much in common, anyway. I might never even get a chance to get close to him, since he's only here for a short time. (Breathe, breathe.)

Anyhoo, I've started researching jobs and broadening out. (I'm actually getting something productive done.) Not much in Miami, Atlanta, the big cities in the East. Everything is either online or of uncertain income ("create your own schedule"), or in towns I've never heard of (Lublaw, Arkansas?).

I'm trying not to settle for web designer. It's a beginning, but I don't want to take a dead-end job that's going to have me working on tiny websites every day, hearing complaints from the client about hating the colors, adding a link we never discussed, etc.

Sammy came through, huh? He has a weird sense of humor, but I think he's a good guy deep down. Just go with the flow. I'm not sure what that means, but what I mean is, don't over analyze, like you did with Adam.

J

She clicked Send and smiled to herself, pleased that she'd resisted the temptation to describe Joseph as a *young god,* the phrase that had come to mind while she was typing, because Lorraine would have teased her mercilessly. Nothing wrong with being a romantic, Janna thought in her own defense, because someday, somehow, it would pay off. *You should have grown up in the hood like me,* Lorraine would have shot back, *and you'd know that gods play with gods and have romance in the celebrity columns. The rest of us end up together, looking for sex or money.*

They'd had the argument before. The accusation that she was living in a dream world had been fired at Janna often enough when she and Lorraine had worked and lived together. On many an evening, after they'd thrown themselves in front of the TV, or walked over to Hermanos for fish tacos, Lorraine had tried to enlighten her about the dangers of the rosy approach to life. It keeps you spineless, Lorraine had warned.

"That's why men take advantage of you, girl," she'd said one night after Damian had called Janna with another lame excuse. They were watching a DVD of *Lady Sings the Blues* since Janna's date was canceled. "You come over all sweet and blurry around the edges." Lorraine had laughed, reaching for more popcorn, her short legs suspended over the edge of the beanbag. "They know they can manipulate you. You're like putty in their hands, and they adore you at first. You laugh at their corny jokes and you agree with them when they come up with a ridiculous reason why niggers shouldn't be in politics or some shit. I've never heard you contradict one of these sorry men, not ever."

"That's not true," Janna retorted, doubting it even as she said it.

47

Lorraine answered with her cynical smile. "Name *one* time when you stood up to a man."

When nothing came to mind, Janna had started thinking about it (without telling Lorraine), had started observing herself and her behavior with men. And she'd noticed that, yes, she was always agreeable, never asking the hard questions, making few demands—all in an effort to turn the relationship into a decent romance, something that had yet to occur. On the other hand, Lorraine enjoyed tossing insults at the men around her, laughing at their pickup lines, and commenting on their every fault, and they seemed to love it.

"How come you're so different?" Janna asked her roommate once while they were walking on treadmills at the gym. "I thought all West Indian women grew up with a mother telling them what kind of prince to look for."

"Girl, my mother was too busy working two jobs and keeping my crazy father from losing his," her friend had answered. "She just wanted to know I was still breathing and still in school. She didn't have time to tell me about any prince. She'd come home, see me doing my homework, and breathe a sigh of relief."

They'd laughed, knowing they'd come from different homes, different income levels, different attitudes, different fears. And Janna knew that, despite all her promises to herself, at their cores they'd always be who they were now. Her friend would always be the cynical independent and she the naive romantic, or, to quote one of Lorraine's favorite sayings, one the wit and the other the witless.

CHAPTER SEVEN

"Turn down the music, please!" Shad called while he wiped his feet on the doormat. "You want to make a person deaf or what?"

"Dadda, the music don't sound good when you play it soft," Joella answered above the dancehall song, her arms aloft. The smell of nail polish invaded the small living room. The teenager sat up slowly in the single armchair, making the plastic creak, and turned off the radio with two chubby fingers.

"I could hear it all the way down the road, man." Shad walked into the empty bedroom and returned. "Where's your mother?"

Red-tipped fingers fanning, Joella shrugged. "Dadda," she said, the hands still for a second, "can I go to a movie this afternoon? Portia and Ciboney are going—"

"You mean to Manchioneal? You joking, right?" Shad squeezed behind the dinette table and opened the refrigerator door. Inside he placed a bag with the three fresh snapper Abel had given him.

"No, I not joking," she said, eyes wide.

"And I bet your homework not done yet."

"I going to finish it now."

"Who else is going?" Shad pulled out a chair and sat down. Joella was good in school, an A-B student who could read anything you put in front of her, but something smelled fishy to Shad and it wasn't coming from the fridge. He knew what it meant to be a teenager and the same age that her mother was when she started taking his bus every afternoon in her school uniform, looking coy when she handed him her bus fare.

"Portia and Ciboney—and a couple other people," Joella said, her voice light with innocence.

"What other people?"

"Barry . . . and Winston."

Shad stood and pushed in the chair. His stomach was starting to send warning signals and he rubbed it a few times. "Stop right there. You can kiss that plan good-bye, let me tell you."

"Dadda—" Joella started.

"And don't backchat me, you hear?" Shad stalked into the bedroom and pulled off his shoes.

It was one thing to have done wrong himself, and to still feel ashamed for things he'd done, but he wouldn't let his children make the same mistakes. It was only by the grace of God that he and Beth had got it right, that when he got home late from the bar he still reached for her, still loved her full mouth and satin skin—the roundness of her body welcoming his small leanness—but it hadn't been easy. He'd had to pay for it. There was an irritability to her that came and went since she'd had their first child, an edge to her voice that let him know she would never forget that he'd talked her into meeting him after his conductor shift, talked her into going to his room behind the butcher shop and lying in the sagging metal bed, and been the cause of her dropping out of school because of a big belly.

Shad lay down, sure that sleep wasn't coming for the nap he needed before his evening shift. Just wait, he told himself. Joella had a stubborn streak, but he could match her. Beth accused him of being too strict, but you had to be firm with children. They had their tricks and you had to watch them, especially teenagers. They could turn bad just from the company they kept, yes.

When he woke up, Beth was standing over him with her arms crossed. She lifted one side of her lip and put it down, the way she did when she had something to say and couldn't wait to get it off her chest.

"Hey," Shad said, struggling to sit up. "You were out."

"Down the road at Martha's. You fall asleep in your work shirt. You going to need a fresh one."

"Oh, God." Shad pulled at the shirt, damp with sweat. "I was tired—and vexed."

"I heard about it." She sat down on the end of the bed, her hair newly permed, smelling of sulfur. A small child started crying outside and her head followed the sound.

"If you want to beg for Joella, she not going, so don't even try to talk me into it," Shad said, swinging his legs to the floor. At least he'd taken off his shoes before he lay down. She wouldn't be able to complain about that.

"Shadrack," she said, lowering her voice, "the child is fifteen already and her head on straight. Is a Saturday and

51

they celebrating Ciboney's birthday. Ciboney's big sister Giselle is going with them, the nineteen-year-old. Why she can't go with them, just this once?" Someone hushed the child, and the crying slowed, then stopped.

"Next thing you know," Shad said, unbuttoning his shirt, "they start drinking in town, and they don't catch a taxi back—"

Beth recrossed her arms and pursed her lips. "Oh, ye of little faith," she said. "You don't trust your own daughter?"

"You want to hear the truth?" Shad held her plump arm and shook it gently. "Is not her I don't trust, it's Winston. Something about that boy just rub me the wrong way."

Beth walked to the window, the baby hairs he stroked when they made love lying flat on the back of her neck from the fresh perm. She turned to him and started to laugh in the way that always tickled him, even when she was laughing at him. Shaking with hardly a sound, she clapped her hands, bent over, and hooted.

"What's so funny?"

"You want to know what rub you the wrong way?" Beth said. She straightened, her hands on her hips, her face still twitching with laughter. "Winston is the exact stamp of you when you was his age!"

"What you talking about? The boy tall, not like me at all."

"True, he not your child, but he act like you, he walk like you, he cocky like you was, he know everything. Just like Shad when he young." There was nothing for Shad to do but screw up his lips in denial and shake his head, but they ended up laughing together as they usually did.

On the street outside, music approached, the dance-hall song coming in waves, carried by someone walking with a radio. The music stopped in front of the house, was carried up the five steps to the porch.

"Who is it?" Shad called, sticking his head out the bedroom door.

"Is Winston, Dadda," Joella answered. She liked this boy, he could tell from the lift in her voice. The day had come. Shad looked at Beth and sat down on the bed, his hands on his knees. He took a deep breath and closed his eyes.

"She has to do her homework first," he said, wishing he could swallow the words. "And if she comes home one minute after eleven, she not going anywhere for the next year."

After Beth left the room, he took a shower, working his mind, thinking of six things that could go wrong by the time Joella got home that night. Rubbing the washrag under an armpit, he worried that the taxi driver could drive too fast and the young people might enjoy it and encourage him to drive faster. Scrubbing his left foot, he saw the boys buying the girls drinks and, working on the right foot, saw Winston placing his hand on Joella's breast, felt a stab to his own chest. When he'd almost finished dressing, he called his eldest into the bedroom. Joella entered with little Joshua asleep in her arms while the radio played on loudly outside.

"I want you to listen to me," Shad said, putting one

sneaker on the footboard and tying the laces. "You want to be a dentist's assistant, right? You say you hate to see rotten teeth and you want to help people, and you want to make good money. You know what it take to be a hygeen—" He waved and broke off. "Whatever it called. You have to go to high school in Port Antonio next year to finish up, so you can get a scholarship to the Kingston school, right? And when you finish, you say you want to help me with your sisters' and brother's education. And you know I'm busting my ass—sorry, but is true— working morning and night at Mistah Eric's to keep you in school, right?

"We not rich like the white people and brown people." He tied the laces on the other shoe. "So we have to use our minds and our hands to get ahead, you hear me? I have to say *Yes, suh* and *No, suh* to all these big people, because that is the best I can do and that is how it go in this place. I need the job and I trying to make a way for my children. This is a country where a few people on top, some in the middle, and most of us on the bottom. If you have education and become a dental assistant, you will move up to the middle, and you won't have to say *Yes, suh* and *Yes, ma'am* to nobody. You will have a nice house and a car. You might even have somebody saying *Yes, ma'am* to you." Joshua lifted his head and Joella bounced him a few times, not taking her eyes off her father.

"Are you listening to me?" Shad said, and slipped his belt through the loops of his pants. "Listen to me good, because one time having sex, one pregnancy, one baby, will kill everything you want and everything your mother and I want for all of us. It going to drive us into debt—because, remember, a baby is another mouth to feed, and you can't study and work while you feeding a baby. Dental assistant work gone out the window, and what kind of work you could get around here, anyway?"

"But, Dadda—"

"Think before you do anything foolish or let some boy take advantage of you is all I'm saying, girl. You have a chance to do better than me. Don't throw it away, you hear me?" Shad left her standing in the room, rocking her baby brother from one side to another, and walked to the kitchen.

Beth rolled her eyes up at him from the scallions she was slicing. "You finish with her?"

"And I love you, too," he said, and kissed her on the cheek. "Later."

On the front porch, a young man was sprawled in one of the two plastic chairs with a radio playing on the floor beside him. Shad stopped in front of him and the boy sat up.

"Your mother never teach you to turn off the radio when you go to a person's house?" Shad said.

"Sorry, suh," the boy said, turning down the radio, "but I going to be a deejay and I need to hear what sound good now." He smelled like he'd never heard of deodorant.

"What *good* now?" Shad lowered his head and looked at him hard. He felt Joella standing behind him in the doorway.

"Yes, man. Is plenty deejays out there, and I need to keep up, you know?"

"Boy, you don't go to school?" Shad asked, frowning. There'd be no lollygagging boy hanging around his daughter.

"Yes, suh, but I leaving soon. I planning to learn the trade."

"Since when," Shad said, "is playing a record a trade?"

"Plenty dances every week, all round the country," Winston said, and cocked his head, knowing it all.

"I see. You're a *smart-man*."

The boy smiled up at him, proud and full of ignorance. Shad nodded and put his hands in the pockets of his starched gray jeans. This was a new generation of young men with little education or training in a country too busy surviving to create jobs for them tomorrow, boys for whom music and crime seemed the only options. Shad hardly knew what to think of them, these hard and shiny boys to whom a violent death meant a celebration, who talked about women as if they hated them (the same women who had fathered them), who put down everybody they envied and who thought they knew everything.

"So, tell me, Mistah Smart-Man, you making any money now?" Shad said.

Winston shook his head. Shad walked to the edge of the porch and descended the first step. Sunlight through the mango tree in the front yard warmed his face and arms and left spots of light on the narrow verandah. Turning to face the youth, Joella standing in the doorway tapping the baby's back with her red fingernails, Shad smiled.

"When I was six, seven, I was making money already. You know how?"

Another shake of the head, the boy more alert.

"I used to run errands for people." Ignoring Joella's pursed lips, looking just like her mother, Shad nodded at the disappointed Winston. "I'm telling you, any little message they needed to send, it was me they call. When people planning a party, when there was a letter to take to the post office window, when they need the nurse from the clinic, is Shad they call. And they pay me ten cents, fifteen cents, a dollar every time. And it help us at home, let me tell you, little saltfish here, little bread there."

"Times different, suh."

"And you know what? You know the best part, Winston? Largo needed it. They needed *me*. I was doing something good for people, something that help people." Shad narrowed his eyes, trying to keep the young man with him. "That is when you will make money, son, when you doing something worthwhile and serving a need. That's how the big people up top make money. They find a need and they fill it. True, most of them born rich and get richer, but we can get ahead, too. We can learn from them and get ahead by filling a need."

"Dadda, Winston don't want to hear—" Joella chimed in.

Shad waved at the radio. "What good you can do for people playing stupidness like that?"

"Is a new song, suh. People want to dance and they need good music."

"You ever listen to the words, boy? You really think about the words to your *good music*? That song you listening to now, the people in Largo don't need it. You know what it's about? You understand it telling you to kill people?"

"Yeah, man, batty men. I see two of them in Port Antonio once." The teenager laughed.

"You see two gay men, not harming anybody, you hear one song, and you believe—what?" Shad waved his fingers in the air. "That they taking over the country, taking over your mind?" He descended to the bottom of the steps, shaking his head. "You don't even start to live yet, star, and you talking about killing innocent people!"

"Batty men deserve to dead, that's what all the singers say, suh," the boy said, more uncertain this time, saying it like a question.

"What I know is, if you mess with my daughter, *you* deserve to dead. You don't know that?" Shad clicked the garden gate closed. "Before eleven o'clock, you hear me?" As the bartender strode away, the singer hurled his dancehall drawl over the fence at his back.

> *"They bringing us down*
> *And destroying the nation,*
> *Taking their time and*
> *Storing up riches.*
> *Boom, boom, batty men,*
> *Shoot the bitches!"*

CHAPTER EIGHT

"You doing okay, have everything you need?" Eric sat down with his coffee mug, slopping a little over the side. Joseph looked up from the magazine he'd been reading, his metal-rimmed reading glasses flashing in the afternoon sun, a ham sandwich half eaten in front of him.

"I'm good," he said, slowly taking off his glasses.

"When did you start wearing glasses?" his father said.

Joseph twisted the glasses in his hand and looked at them. "I've been wearing them for a while. I was wearing them when I came down last time."

"You were? I don't remember that."

The tightened mouth spoke for Joseph.

"Anyway," Eric said, "good to see you're relaxing, haven't shaved in a couple days." He chuckled, eyes skittering, unsure of how familiar he should be.

Joseph rubbed his chin. "It's the style, what can I tell you?"

"Looks good, suits you," his father said. He knew he was striking out and felt the years of unfamiliarity all of a sudden. "How's the report going? You've had a few days to work on it now, eh?"

"I'm getting the construction costs together. Lambert is doing that for me."

"Great. And what was it you wanted me to start working on?"

"The hotel's operating costs for the first five years. I thought you'd started—"

"How many rooms are we going for?" his father said. "Twenty, right?"

"I did the research and twenty would work. Anything over eighteen is good, according to the stats. We can base it on twenty rooms. Fifteen rooms wouldn't make it."

Eric scratched one ankle, irritated by the implication that the old hotel had been inadequate. "Exactly what costs do you need?"

"Maintenance costs, salaries, marketing, you name it."

"Landscaping? I always liked a nice garden, with fountains and lawns, a few gardeners—"

"Everything."

Eric looked over his shoulder, out to sea. "What about the island?"

"What *about* the island?"

"I don't know. I thought we should either build a bridge—that's probably too expensive—or take hotel guests out in a boat for picnics or something. Maybe turn it into a theme park. There must be something we can do with it." The two men stared across at the island, both with folded arms. It was a fine day, sunny with a breeze ruffling the almond tree in the island's center.

"It's dramatic, I'll give you that," Joseph said, a bit too reluctantly, Eric thought.

"Looks like a movie set, don't you think?"

"It could be a kind of motif."

"A what?"

"A symbol of the hotel. You could use it as a logo, you know, like on your letterhead, on the gateposts, in your ads. Anyway, I'd hold off on that until you meet with your investor. He might rule it out, depending on what he wants to do."

"Rule it out?" Eric crossed his legs and swung the top foot in its toe-worn sandal. "Just how much power does he have to make those kinds of decisions?"

"It depends on the arrangements you made with the guy. Didn't you say you'd talked about shares?"

"Yeah."

"Did you discuss percentages?" Joseph picked up his glasses and started tapping them on the magazine. "We have to include that in the package. Did you talk about share split? Is he going to have controlling shares? What did you agree on?"

"He'll come up with the money to build the thing. We never discussed anything else."

"You never discussed it." Joseph nodded, his upper lip curling just a little. "Well, you'd better. I have to take that into consideration for the report. You have to do it right away."

"Do what?"

"Calculate your part of the deal, and if Shad is going to have shares—so he told me, anyway—you need to get an agreement on his percentage. And, by the way, if you haven't done it already, you need to get this property valued, the bar and the land—and the island," Joseph said. He set the glasses on the table and brought down the side of his hand on the magazine. "*Everything* you can think of that's going to add value for you and Shad we've got to include. That means this building and even what's left of the buildings on the island—the walls and foundation are still pretty good, I'd think. And you're going to be supervising the construction phase, right? That's sweat equity, unless he pays you to do it. Then there's your experience and goodwill. You've run two businesses here in Largo, both with the hotel and the bar, there's got to be some goodwill we can include in the figures."

"Goodwill?"

It was too damn complicated, Eric decided, enough to make him want to throw in the towel. While Joseph talked his financial talk (this boy whose diaper he'd changed in a park once, who had curled up beside him, crying, when he had chicken pox), he decided he would call Cameron Carter, who'd set up the venture, and tell him to forget it. He was too old for this hassle. Plus it would tie him up with a partner, or more than one, for the rest of his life, and that was not what he wanted to do. It was one thing to run his own place, but another to be partnered, *married*—because that's what it was, a damn business marriage—to a partner he'd never met, to be accountable to some man for every decision he made. As if to punctuate the thought, the phone in the bar started ringing.

"Boss, the phone." It was Shad at his elbow, raising his almost hairless eyebrows.

"Who is it?"

"Miss Ferguson."

It took only five minutes talking to the bank manager, the conversation about his overdraft kept low given the public nature of the phone, for Eric to understand that he had to go through with the hotel deal. An image of himself, impoverished, holed up in Miss Mac's boardinghouse, waiting for his social security check, began to appear, and he brushed it away by assuring the woman that he was making long-term plans to do away with the overdraft altogether. He would update her next time he came into the bank, he added. After he hung up, he walked back to the table and picked up his coffee cup.

"Well, looks like we're on," he said, more to himself than anyone else.

While Shad cleared the plates away, Joseph stood and stretched, his T-shirt pulling up to reveal taut abdominal muscles.

"You going for a swim?" Shad asked. "I hear you swim real good, nice and strong."

"Yeah, man," Joseph said, smiling at Shad. "It's great exercise since I can't get to the gym. I'm waiting for Janna, though. She wanted to start swimming with me." Pocketing his glasses, Joseph picked up the green towel he'd thrown over a chair and turned toward the road.

"That's good, you have company," Shad said.

"Great girl," Eric said. "Here she comes."

A sunglassed Janna walked up to the group, towel draped over one arm, and Eric tried not to look through the transparent white cover-up. He looked instead at the sweet face, the skin tone lighter than Simone's, the hair not as wiry. She'd be a few years older than Simone's daughter would have been, probably a few inches taller.

"Shad!" Janna went straight up to the bartender and hugged him, ignoring the dishes in his hand between them. "How are you doing? How are Beth and the kids?"

"Good, man, good!" The gap between Shad's front teeth made him a happy rabbit again.

"Miss Bertha told me you have a boy now. That's three girls and a boy, right?"

"Yes, Joella almost sixteen now, and Rickia, she eleven but like she forty, Ashanti is four, and the baby, Joshua. He get plenty spoiling from the girls, you see?" Shad laughed, enjoying her attention. Janna smiled at him warmly, her musky coconut oil smell enveloping the men.

Eric took the pipe out of his pocket, needing to stay busy, fighting the urge to join Janna's hand with Joseph's, to bond them somehow. She was a nice girl, *a church girl,* as Arnie would say—the kind you had for keeps.

Janna looked around at the three men, her smile suddenly self-conscious, and stepped back. "Finished your meeting?" she said to Joseph.

"All done—for today anyway."

Eric gestured to the beach with his pipe. "Watch the current, you guys. It can be vicious."

Shielding the pipe from the breeze as he lit it, Eric followed the pair with his eyes, through the parking lot, until they disappeared around the hedge.

"They look good together, don't you think?" he said.

"They two good-looking youths, if that's what you mean," Shad said, wiping the table.

Eric laughed, his teeth clamped around the pipe. "You know what I mean. It was perfect timing that she came down now, just when Joseph is here. She hasn't been down for a while."

"She a woman now," Shad said.

"Yes, indeed," Eric said. He pulled on his pipe and exhaled, fishlike, through one side of his mouth. "Her mother must be getting along better with Lambert, to allow her to come visit. She's been bitter for years. The perils of marriage, I'm telling you. Stay away from that institution as long as you can, man. That's my advice."

Shad laughed. "Beth don't want to hear that, boss."

"There are some things it's good for, I guess, but all this mess, with divorces—" He took another pull on the pipe. "I don't know how the children survive it, I'm telling you. Joseph's doing great, thank God, and Janna seems happy enough. She's always gotten along with everybody, even her stepmother."

"How long is Jennifer gone?"

"I don't know." Eric took the dishes and rag from Shad. "I'll take care of this, you go on home. I'll see you tonight."

Starting in on the stack of dirty dishes at the kitchen sink, Eric looked through the open window and over the cliff. Directly across from him was the island, and to his right lay the beach in its empty heat, the children still in school and the fishermen resting up for the nighttime hunt.

A few hundred yards down the beach, Joseph and Janna appeared between the canoes—two golden youths, tall and tight, shedding their outer clothes and towels on the sand. Janna waded into the water, holding her hands up against the waves, pausing before sinking down into the water. Joseph dived into a wave and emerged farther out.

Placing the first dish on the wire rack next to the sink, Eric glanced again at his son in the waves. This is the boy I conceived from my sperm, he mused. And at the thought there was no change in his heartbeat or his digestion, because it was more of a fact than a feeling, but a fact that came with accumulated memories—of the time they went to a Yankees game with Arnie and his son Bobby, of the weekend they went to the Catskills to fish, of mass on Sunday mornings and Claire, Joseph, and he sitting in the same pew every week. Yet, despite the memories, Joseph felt almost like a stranger. He could be another man's child—if there'd been any doubt of Claire's fidelity.

"It's not in my catechism to be unfaithful, Eric," she'd said once, and he believed her.

Eric stacked the last plate on the rack and started on the dirty glasses. He knew he should feel guiltier about his neglect of Joseph. If anything, his guilt always came from not feeling guiltier. He'd never wanted children. Claire knew it from day one, when she broached the subject of having a child, standing in the corridor of the Queens apartment. The second time she'd mentioned it, she'd been crying over a chicken in the kitchen. He'd laughed it off uneasily and avoided the subject—until she made the announcement of her pregnancy. She'd stopped using her diaphragm, she said, because it was against the Church's doctrine. They'd reached an agreement: she was to be the primary caregiver for the child. Despite her initial resentment of the arrangement, he'd kept his part of the bargain and given her the money and space she needed to raise her son.

When Joseph was four, he'd thought better of it, because Arnie had started talking about teaching his son to catch a football, and Eric had made an effort to talk to Joseph when he got home in the evenings, even arranged a couple of father-son outings with Arnie and little Bobby. But it was too late and nothing seemed to bridge the gap. There was always an excuse: the game lasted too long or the fishing rod was too heavy. Sometimes Joseph tried to endure, wearing a patient smile when his father tried too hard, like the time Eric played a Beatles record and made a few steps around the living room strumming an imaginary guitar, and Joseph had sat looking at him, his boredom making the Beatles irrelevant. By the time Joseph was nine, they'd started dancing around each other, trying to avoid contact.

Eric put the last glass down on the rack and dried his hands on the dish towel. Thank God the boy had turned out to be one hell of a handsome man, normal as apple pie, making time with a beautiful girl. Below the window, a large wave broke over the young people and they struggled to the surface, their laughter floating up on the salty trade wind, survivors of broken marriages—their scars, if any, not visible to the naked eye.

CHAPTER NINE

Breathing hard, Janna threw herself stomach down on the outstretched towel, her feet to the ocean. Facing her was a row of colorful canoes, the names *Jah Love* and *In God We Trust* painted on the two closest to her, and above her the coconut tree leaves made clicking noises in the breeze. She rested her chin on her arms, inhaling the sand's long-buried sea life, a smell that reminded her of childhood beach trips. In her peripheral vision, she could see Joseph's feet approaching and stopping beside her, the fine brown hairs plastered down on his wet calves. His feet were impeccable, the nails well cut, white sand wrapping each perfect toe. She reached across to his towel and picked up his sunglasses.

"Do you want these?"

"Thank you," he said, and took them from her. When he put them on, he looked like one of the guys who strolled down South Beach on a Friday evening, laughing with their buddies, passing her table, making her heart beat faster.

"I thought we were going for a swim," she said, putting on her own sunglasses. "That was more like a survival test!"

"If you want, we can go for a run on the beach."

"Let me catch my breath first."

"Take your time." He sat down on his towel, facing the water, and she was free to peek over her shoulder at his body, every bicep and tricep knowing the gym, having its own machine to define it, glistening with the water dripping down his arms and off his elbows. He seemed comfortable with his own silence, making her feel younger all of a sudden.

"You really have to know what you're doing in that water," she said.

"I know what you mean."

"The current is crazy, like your dad said."

"Nobody around here swims, you notice? Maybe they know something we don't," he said, and laughed, not a loud laugh, not the obnoxious laugh of a tourist who knew more than the locals. It was the laugh of a man who didn't mind admitting he didn't know something, who still had room for doubt.

"Daddy doesn't like me swimming here. He keeps telling me about people who drowned." She lowered her voice, mimicking Lambert. "'This guest in Eric's hotel, she just disappeared beneath the waves. Her husband didn't even see her go down.'" She wiped the beaded drops on one arm. "He'll pitch a fit when I tell him I was swimming here. I'll just tell him you're a great swimmer."

He turned to her with a pucker above the sunglasses. "I hadn't even thought of that," he said, "that one of the hotel guests could have drowned. Oh, God, what a nightmare that must have been!" He made a weird face for a second.

"You didn't know about it?"

"No, I didn't," he said. He looked back at the water when he shook his head. He wasn't like most of the white boys she'd known in college or at work, the ones who either ignored her or had a black-Venus infatuation or were too uptight to approach her. He sounded like he enjoyed talking to her, listening to her, even though she could see his eyes behind the sunglasses swoop down to examine her breasts under the bikini's white triangles.

"What city were you studying in?" he asked when she turned over on her side.

"Tampa." The new breasts felt odd, heavy, and she was learning how they felt at different angles. They looked like half cantaloupes, Lorraine had said when she came up to visit, and they'd both cracked up.

"Tampa, nice town." He nodded. "I went there once."

She sat up on one elbow, the cantaloupes lolling toward the towel. They were a combination birthday and graduation gift from her mother. Phyllis had brought up the idea of a gift, a trip to Europe, maybe, to see Aunty Mags and Uncle Bill in London. They were having tea in the condo the afternoon before Janna's graduation from Tampa's Institute of Technology.

"You've never gone to Europe," her mother had said. "I could meet you over there."

"I want a boob job," Janna replied, her mouth full of cheesecake.

"A *boob job*?" Her mother had repeated it like she was

holding the disgusting words at a distance. "Why would you want something like that? You're beautiful just as you are!"

"I think it would help my self-esteem, don't you?"

"Do you know what would happen to your self-esteem if it goes wrong?"

"I'll use the rest of my savings if I have to."

Although the idea had popped into her head a second before she said it (leading her to wonder later if it had come from too many celebrity reality shows), Janna hadn't backed down, remembering how she'd apologized to both of her sexual partners the first time she'd undressed. She hadn't expected victory, but had seen her stand as separating her from her ever-cautious mother, who would never have done anything as drastic as that. Lorraine, on the other hand, had thought it a great idea. She might do it herself, she said, when she got some dough together. Three weeks of online research later, Janna's mother had agreed to the *breast enhancement procedure* (Phyllis's name for it) and had even gotten mildly enthusiastic.

Five months after the surgery, Janna wasn't so sure they'd been the best idea. The breasts still didn't feel like a part of her. She kept thinking of the silicone sac in her hand in the doctor's office, kept seeing them as foreign objects rolling around inside her swollen chest. It had been worth it, she frequently reminded herself, because they did justice to a bathing suit and she felt sexy for the first time in her life. This is what celebrities feel like, she told herself, women who had their photographs taken in Zagat-rated restaurants.

She straightened her bikini top, shrugging her shoulders to fit the breasts better. "Tampa was a bit boring, though. The whole time I was there I was thinking, *If I was in Miami, I'd be doing this or that. Or if I was in New York, I'd be at a museum or in Bryant Park watching a movie or something.* I was there last summer, visiting my cousin, and I loved it. Anyway, the Tampa school was cheaper than Miami or New York, and I was close enough to my mom to go home on weekends if I wanted to—not that I did that much. Anyway, the good news is that I'm a certified geek." Her ideas sounded childish to her ears, her expressions immature, and she fell silent.

"What were you doing before?" Joseph said. He was wiping on sunblock, and when he turned to her, water was sitting in the well of his top lip and she wanted to reach over and wipe it off.

"I was a copy editor with the *Miami Herald,* mainly did proofing, correcting the reporters' articles before the paper was printed. I did journalism at the University of Miami, and—" She sat up and shook her head. "I was going to be this crazy, groundbreaking, globe-trotting reporter. But papers are going online now, you know, and they don't need as many journalists. The paper wasn't hiring any more reporters, and there are a lot of experienced journalists looking for jobs, so I was stuck. My editor was pretty cool—but I was bored."

"Not enough growth?" he said, leaning back on his hands. He was smiling like he thought she was spoiled.

"You don't approve."

"I was just thinking you were lucky to have the option to quit, that you weren't laid off."

"Okay, I'll accept that." She leaned back on her hands, then shifted positions when she realized she was imitating him. "I was frustrated. The reporters were running around, total big you-know-whats, setting their own schedules, bylines with their names, and I had to work twelve to eight, reading their words, checking facts, adding a comma here, changing a semicolon there. I wasn't asking for executive treatment, just a little freedom, a story, something! I felt like I was in prison, and I remember one day the words on the computer suddenly meaning nothing to me—they could have been Arabic—and I thought, *Is this what I went to school for four years to do?*" She fluffed up her hair to dry in the breeze. "I knew I had to do something else."

"So you reinvented yourself."

"I have to invent myself into a job first."

"Did you go back to school full-time?"

"Yeah, I wanted to get it over with in a year, not drag it out."

"Daddy stepped up, again." There was a tinge of sarcasm in his voice. He was putting her down, she could feel it. Being a prick, Lorraine would have said.

"The joys of being an only child," she said.

"Tell me about it." He stood up and looked toward the end of the bay. "Ready to run?"

"Mind if we walk?" She was still irritated and not in the mood to micromanage her chest without a bra. She shook out the sand from her towel and tied it above her breasts.

They walked the length of the beach hardly talking, wading through the foam that swept up toward the dry seaweed. At the end of the bay, almost a mile, they greeted a group of fishermen mending their nets with plastic thread. On the way back they asked a teenager to cut holes in two coconuts they'd found and he obliged, chopping the tops of the fruit off in one slice of his machete. She drank the water from hers, throwing her head back to drain it. Joseph swallowed his in slow, grimacing gulps.

"It's an acquired taste," she said, and took the coconut from him.

"A taste I don't plan to acquire," he said, laughing.

"So, let's talk about you." She threw the coconut husks into the bushes, and they started walking again. "You're working on a report for your father, I know that. You live in DC, my dad said. Is that where you were born?"

"No, I was born in New York, left when I was nine, that's when my parents split up. My mom and I moved to Virginia, been there ever since."

"Did you see much of your father after that?" she said.

"He came down a few times, and I'd go up for a couple weeks in the summer and he'd put me in a Y camp or something while he went to work. I was in high school when he moved to Jamaica, hardly saw him after that. To be fair, I know he was busy building the hotel, but he kind of disappeared on us. I came down once when I was in college and stayed in the hotel. I wanted to see how it looked, you know, what he'd created."

"You saw the hotel?" She pulled back, hugging the

towel. "I only heard about it after it was gone, but I heard it was cool."

"It was kind of cozy, not big. It had a bar with orchids, I remember that, a couple small beaches, a nice garden. The food was really good." He was saying it with his usual coolness, but he said it in bursts, like he was grabbing at memories of the place, like he approved of his father's creation.

"How long did you stay?"

"Just a week. I brought some friends." He looked out to sea and his eyelashes sparkled with gold in the overhead sun. "We drove around a lot, saw the island, went to a few beaches, up into the mountains. We never got over to Kingston, though." The surf washed up and covered their feet as they walked, then drained away.

"Where did you go to school?"

"Georgetown."

"And you work in DC."

"Not exactly working right now. I was laid off a few months ago."

She felt embarrassed for him and didn't know if she should apologize or sympathize. "But you like DC."

"Yes, I do."

"Anyone special?"

"I have friends, yes." He was looking at his feet when he said it, putting up a barrier she couldn't pass through. They started back on the path to the road, stepping over fallen coconut boughs. Walking behind him, she stared down at her flip-flops, wishing she could take back the question. It wasn't any of her business if he had someone.

She shouldn't have asked. He was a private person, with a life.

The silence between them, the crunch of their footsteps on the path, seemed to signal that whatever ease they'd had was slipping away. *Fuck* (she liked how the word sounded inside and repeated it), she was hopeless at this business, especially with great-looking guys. And she had no experience with older men. She shouldn't care, was furious with herself that she did. Another disaster in the making, that's what it was. When they got to the road, he held her arm and swung her to his right so he could walk next to the traffic, and his touch sent a wave of warmth from her elbow up her arm, into her body, and down to her toes.

Maybe they could just be friends, she thought, glancing at his profile, and she wouldn't fall too hard.

CHAPTER TEN

"Swing low, sweet chariot,
Coming for to carry me home.
Swing low . . ."

Michael was trying to sing like the black American singer they played on the radio sometimes, trying to get his voice down deep, although he was really a tenor, and not a good one at that. It scraped on Shad's nerves, and when Michael sat down, he let out a quiet breath of relief.

Pastor McClelen stood up, his black robe caught under the chair leg. He kicked it loose and swung it with him to the podium, and it floated for a second like the cape of a superhero before settling around his small frame.

"Magnificent! Thanks and blessings, Brother Michael." He turned to the congregation, ten rows of folding chairs filled with fanning ladies and sweating men. "Show him some love, brothers and sisters," he said, spreading his arms. Tepid applause followed. Pastor beamed at his wife and son in the front row and gripped the podium.

"Children of God," he called out suddenly in his penetrating nasal tone, "today is a *wondrous* day, a day of praise and gratitude." McClelen's preaching voice came out of amplified windpipes in what always started as a loud whine and ended with screeching. Shad had often wondered if there were classes in seminary where ministers were taught how to speak in a voice that carried to every corner of the room, out into the street, and past several houses, or if Pastor had just chosen his own speaking style.

Beside Shad, Rickia—Miss Prim, he liked to call her—whispered a loud instruction to little Ashanti to stop shaking her leg. Joella hushed her, and Rickia returned to the library book she'd brought, something about a boy wizard, she'd told her father the afternoon before.

"A wizard?" Shad had said, his hand on the fridge door.

"A person who can do magic."

"Like the obeah man on the hill?"

"*No,* Dadda." The ten-year-old shook her head. "This boy in England, he going to a school for wizard children, and he don't do any *obeah*." Rickia frowned as she said it, bent on separating her hero from the village magician. "He can cast spells and he can fly, he and his friends, but he always working to help people."

Shad patted the book on the dinette table. "Same thing, sweetness. In England they call it *wizard,* in Jamaica we call it *obeah man.* Everybody want to control things, for good or for bad. Some people try to do it by praying, some people by controlling other people, and some people by magic. But it all come from being afraid and wanting to control things. Fear can make people do all kind of craziness."

He'd taken a mango out of the fridge and started peeling the end with his front teeth. "Enjoy your book, you hear? Tell me about it when you finish."

Pastor's sermon this Sunday was about heroes, what with Heroes Day coming up. He talked about his father as his own personal hero. Shad thought of the father he'd never met, and wondered if he was dead or alive now. And he thought of his mother, now deceased, whom he remembered vaguely, only that she'd bend down to give him a quick kiss when she arrived from Kingston, and that the rest of her short visits were spent talking nonstop to his grandmother, ignoring him leaning on the kitchen door, one bare foot on top of the other.

"And we should remember our national heroes, brothers and sisters," Pastor continued, "because that's where our strength lies, our heritage, our *his*-tory."

Granny was a hero, Shad decided. Granny, who smelled of bay rum and old people's stench, Granny with her arthritis and large, flat back, which she would turn to him when they used to lie together in the iron bed at night. Granny, who would hug him and whip him and quote Jesus to him, Granny, who would forget to wash his school uniform, so he had to live in it every day until the teacher sent him home with a message.

Pastor pulled a handkerchief out of his sleeve and wiped his grooved face. "One of our national heroes, Paul Bogle, now there was a *man*." His voice got sharper and louder, climbing with pain. "A man, ladies and gentlemen, who suffered and died because he led a rebellion. . . ."

Beth was Shad's other hero, because she'd stayed faithful to him when he'd gone astray after he lost his conductor job. Only sixteen, she'd been the one to scold him when he started to pick pockets and snatch purses in Port Antonio, and when her father threw her out of the house because she was pregnant, she'd moved in with her sister and come to visit him every week in Kingston Penitentiary while he was serving his one-year sentence. After he got out, it was Beth who'd insisted that they move to Largo and move in with his grandmother, which was a good thing because the old lady was sick while he was in prison and he hadn't known. It was Beth who took care of her and cleaned the house like it had never been cleaned (Joella hanging on to her neck), while he was building the hotel with his grandmother's friend Job. And it was Beth who'd sewn a blue taffeta dress for Granny and laid her out in the pine coffin in the same house they lived in today, where you could still smell Granny's bay rum coming up from the bedroom floor.

"Last but not least of our national heroes, brothers and sisters, lest we forget," Pastor said, and gave a chuckle that sounded more like a heckle, "there's Nanny, our only woman hero, who is said to have caught bullets in her rear end."

Shad twitched his shoulders up and let them drop. How come, when women ran most of the homes and all of the markets in Jamaica, there was only one woman hero—and they had to make fun of her? When so many men were invisible, like his daddy, and the women were left to raise the children and bring home the money, how come they got only one hero? Shad leaned over and nudged Beth, who looked at him sideways.

"You're my hero," he whispered, and rolled his bottom lip out so it wouldn't go to her head. She turned back to Pastor, the corners of her mouth twitching.

"And not a one of our heroes"—Pastor was at full screech now—"not one of them flinched or *turned away* from the dangers before them." He paused dramatically. "They sought the presence of the Most High and called for strength. No sissy men or women, no cowards among them." There were the usual cries of "Yes, speak!" from Sister Arida, murmurs of agreement from others, and Shad clenched his teeth, counting the minutes until the collection.

As soon as church was over, Shad took little Josh from Beth and started edging toward the door, straightening chairs with his foot, stopping for a minute to chat with Miss Maisie, who reported that Solomon had stayed in bed to "rest up," as usual. Behind Shad, Beth greeted all with chirpy good mornings, even though it was past noon. Pastor met them at the door and held Beth's hand for a second, then two and three.

"I like the talk, Pastor," she said and smiled.

"Yes, yes," Shad said, patting Josh's diaper-padded bottom in his little blue jeans. "Good sermon. All of my heroes are women, though." Pastor said nothing, just gave a dry smile and turned to the next person in line.

Outside the church, a row of boys sat on the low stone wall surveying the shuffle of people exiting.

"Winston." Shad nodded to the last in the lineup. "I never knew you come to church."

The boy stood up and started walking alongside. "I come sometimes, suh, when the spirit move me." He greeted Beth with a respectful nod and looked over his shoulder at Joella.

"You brought Joella home on time," Shad said.

"Yes, suh."

"And you coming to church," Shad continued, letting the boy know he had a checklist.

"I like to hear what the minister have to say," Winston said, and Shad thought better than to mention the girl-watching on the wall.

"Sometimes the sermon is good." Shad nodded, rubbing Joshua's back. "But is not every sermon you must follow, you hear?"

"What you mean, suh?"

"You must learn to think for yourself. Every time you hear a sermon, ask yourself if it make sense to you."

"The sermon about heroes? What wrong with that?"

"I mean, take this sermon. While you listening to it you have to think about *your* heroes."

Beth leaned across. "You have a hero, Winston?"

The boy pulled up his baggy jeans. "You mean like— Mojo Man, that my hero," he said.

Shad sighed. Mojo Man, a hero. How to reach these youth? How to reach Joshua when he was old enough, show him what real heroes were made of? Maybe, he thought, looking down at Winston's sparkling white sneakers, if he could get through to this young man, he could get through to Josh when the time came.

"Mojo Man," Shad muttered. "I hear on the radio that America not allowing your hero into their country anymore. You hear that, Winston?"

"No, suh."

"Yeah, man. They won't let him perform for American audiences, come on television to talk."

"He can't sing in America?"

"He can't even enter the country, can't even get to walk out the airport doors in New York. You know why?" Shad raised his eyebrows and waited, but Winston looked back blankly. "Because of his lyrics. Your hero sing about women like they dogs, he glorifying gangsters, and he talk about killing homosexuals. And America don't want him and his negative songs." Shad reached back with his free hand and tucked his shirt deeper into his pants. "You must keep up with the news, man."

Winston said nothing, just kept walking and looking down at his shoes.

"You ever hear about Bob Marley, youth?"

"Everybody know about him, suh."

"You ever hear him say we should emancipate ourselves from mental slavery?" Shad patted the squirming baby's rump, felt the damp coming through. "What he really saying is that you must rise up and not think small. You mustn't be a small man, Winston. The jails full up of small men with ignorant ideas, small men trying to destroy other people."

"I not going to be a small man, suh," Winston said, pulling up his trousers with a wide smile. "I going to be a hero."

Beth looked around Shad. "I like that, Winston," she said. "You keep wanting to be a hero, you hear?"

"Well," Shad said, "if you going to be a hero, you must learn how to be a hero. You have to learn how to be a *champion* for other people. You know what a champion is?"

"Like a boxer?"

"Yeah, but not one who fight for sport. A real champion is a man who fight for justice, who defend people when they need help. A champion is a man who aim high, who aim for the stars, even if he hit the clouds, seen?"

"Like Spider-Man?"

"Exactly."

"But they don't teach that in school," the youth said, stepping over a pile of goat dung.

"That not something you learn in school, star. You learn it from life and wisdom. I show you. I will be your *mentor*—you ever hear that word, boy?"

"No, suh."

"A customer taught me the word and I love it. A *mentor* mean a person who show you certain things, you know, like a teacher of life. So I will be your mentor. Stick with me, man, I show you how to be a hero."

"But I don't too much like the fighting business."

"No fighting, Winston, no fighting," Shad promised, and guided the family down the lane to their home.

CHAPTER ELEVEN

Hi Lorr!

Went swimming with you-know-who in some wild waves in the bay. He swims every afternoon, so I invited myself. You're always telling me to be bolder with guys, so I thought I'd go for it.

We had a great talk about where we are now in life. He learned more about me than I did about him. I was so nervous I chatted too much. He's a Georgetown grad, majored in finance or economics or something. Lives in Virginia. Between jobs. (Sound familiar?) I asked if he was involved with anyone. I know it was a bit early, but it's been bothering me. Hate to get all into a guy and it turns out he's not even on the market. He doesn't say yes, but he doesn't say no, either. He says he has "friends." What does that mean? What do you think? Sketchy, or too soon to tell? Am I ahead of myself, or over my head? I never know with guys, can't read them, especially a total-package kind of guy. It's either young ragamuffins or fantasy men for me, it seems.

No news on the job front. Less inclined to really push for it. Even found myself looking for stuff around the DC/Virginia area. Am I sick or what? Food here is great. I'm going to put on weight if I don't watch it!

J

CHAPTER TWELVE

S tanding with his hand resting on a loaf of bread, Eric stared at the bread knife and knew it was finally over. He had no idea why it should faze him, but it had come as a complete shock, and he couldn't understand why, after all these years, the news should wind him like a blow to the chest.

Lunch had started normally enough for a rainy afternoon, a light drizzle settling over Largo, and the hills at the end of the bay veiled by a gray mist that made them look far away. The bar was quiet and the only customers were a man and woman eating curried goat at the back of the restaurant. Joseph had come in with a damp T-shirt and sat down with his father at the round table where Eric ate all his meals, paid the bills, did everything. Maisie had served tuna sandwiches and come back a few minutes later with one of Eric's shirts and insisted that Joseph change. Outside, the rain had gotten heavier, and gusts of wind started blowing it into the restaurant. After moving the table to a drier spot, the two men had settled down to finish their sandwiches.

"So, is your mother retiring soon?" Eric had asked

with his mouth half full. It was meant as a question to make conversation and he wasn't really interested in the answer. He hadn't seen Claire since Joseph's graduation from business school. They'd held a celebratory lunch at an Italian restaurant in Georgetown where he, Claire, and her sister and brother-in-law had made light conversation, focusing on Joseph's upcoming job with a firm everyone had heard of except Eric.

In answer to his father's question, Joseph put down his sandwich. "Mom's getting married," he said, brushing crumbs off his fingers, looking uncomfortable, the messenger of bad tidings.

"Getting married?"

"Yeah."

The food turned into a hard ball in Eric's stomach. He thought of Claire, cool on the phone the month before when he'd called to ask for Joseph's number. There'd been no mention of a marriage. He saw her standing in a cocktail dress with a bouquet of flowers in her hands, a shadow of a man beside her, maybe someone from the store. Thirty-five years ago she'd worn a long white dress that she'd gotten on sale (plus discount). It had taken her forever to get the dress up the narrow aisle of St. Bart's in Syracuse, the church she'd attended as a child. From the altar, he'd watched her on her father's arm, tugging the dress and trying to smile at the guests, almost all of whom were her friends and family. Arnie had been the best man, and although his parents said they couldn't afford to come, his brother had made it, a nervous Midwesterner among fast-talking New Yorkers.

The thought had never entered Eric's mind that there'd be a second wedding in Claire's life. He'd always pictured her going to church on Sundays, working as a Macy's manager, and coming home to an empty town house in Virginia, because he'd always thought of her as a very Catholic woman who would be married only once in her life—to him.

"Who's she marrying?" Eric had managed to ask.

"A surgeon from Maryland." Joseph picked up his Coke, his eyes glued to the table.

"A surgeon? Where did she meet him?"

"At a party, I think."

Eric put down the sandwich. Claire at a party—slim and graceful, holding a martini—slipped through his mind, followed by a surgeon in an operating theater, in scrubs and a mask, attentive nurses at his elbow.

"Have you met him?"

"Yeah, I have."

Eric wiped his mouth and threw the napkin on his plate. "Well, I hope she's—they're very happy. Please tell her that for me when you speak to her."

Joseph looked distractedly out to sea. "They're in Europe. They should be getting to Rome sometime this week. The last I heard from her, they were leaving London and headed across the continent, taking the train."

Picking up the plates, Eric walked to the kitchen and placed them in the sink. He'd stood there staring at the knife, his hand on the half loaf of bread. Claire married. The thought formed in his head like broken pieces that he couldn't patch together, his mind not permitting him to experience it whole. Betrayal washed over him. He was alone, and she was getting married. It was just another of her revelations, one of a series of surprise attacks that she used to keep him off balance, like he was an enemy she had to ambush.

The first time she'd caught him off guard was when, months after laughingly dismissing his proposal of marriage, she'd suddenly announced she was ready. The second had come with the announcement of her pregnancy with Joseph, and the third when she decided, unilaterally, to divorce.

"It's over, Eric," she'd said as soon as he entered the house that evening in 1990, his briefcase still in his hand. She was standing in her pajamas in the hallway. It was a little after nine, he remembered, because he'd checked his watch under the porch light.

"I've been thinking about it for a while now, and I'm done." She could have been saying that the plumber had to replace the pipes under the sink, but he could tell from the little tremor in her voice that she was nervous. "This is not a marriage, it's a farce. You leave early in the morning, before Joseph gets up. You get home after he goes to bed. You work Saturdays, and even when you're home, your mind is somewhere else. It's like you're a boarder or something." It sounded well rehearsed, like she'd been practicing, maybe on the phone with her sister.

"You're not with me, with us," she'd said. Her eyebrows were high, her eyes steady. "I don't know where you are most nights. I'm not even sure if you're working, like you say."

"I'm working, Claire, I just don't answer my phone

after hours," he protested. That he would be left alone, abandoned, had been his first thought, followed by a flash of relief that the tiring charade of their marriage might be coming to an end. Claire actually smiled, as if she could read his thoughts, and reached up to straighten a watercolor on the wall. That was Claire, always controlled in a crisis, turning it into a test of character.

"Who *isn't* working?" she said. "But they're still part of a family."

"We can work this out, Claire."

She jammed her hands hard into her pajama pockets. "If working this out means what it's always meant, then we can't. How many times have you said—have you said there'll be a change, and nothing happens? I'm done, I'm through." She'd turned with finality and walked away from him, up the stairs. And there in the hallway, his briefcase hanging from the well-worn curve of his right palm, his left hand still on the doorknob, he'd thought of his father, remembered how glad he'd been when his father was away from home, and how his mother had never left the hard bastard who beat his sons with an old belt (that had belonged to his immigrant father) and hit his wife when he'd had one too many, and how she'd never left him, even though they'd quarreled constantly, because they didn't know any other way.

"But we have a good marriage, Claire, we never argue," he'd called behind her. "And we're Catholic, in case you've forgotten. We're not supposed to divorce."

From the top of the stairs came her answer. "Then if we don't remarry, there's no problem."

Raindrops were making pinging sounds on the windowpanes, making it harder now to see the beach below. She'd lied; she was remarrying. He wondered if she'd told her priest. She'd probably been having sex with the man already, a professional man with money (God, she must be laughing at him with his little bar), who'd taken her to Europe, where he'd make love to her in Rome, right next to the Pope.

"Mr. Eric, you want baked bananas for dessert?" The voice beside him was high and squeaky, raised above the pouring rain outside the window. Maisie's face with its flat features hovered like a brown moon above his elbow. As short as her husband Solomon was tall, she was taking his place in the kitchen because he was home again with *a little indigestion*—the couple's code for a hangover.

"Not for me, Maisie, just for Joseph," Eric replied, slapping the loaf of bread. He waited until the woman spooned out the bananas and coconut cream and followed her outside. The rain was making a soothing shushing sound on the thatch straw above. Maisie placed the dessert before Joseph and stood back with a little smile, waiting, checking that her cooking was as good as her husband's. Joseph took a forkful and nodded his approval, and happiness spread over her face. In the same moment, Shad came running in, wet splotches on his clothes.

"What a rain!" he called out. He fanned his shirt away from his body to dry and went off to the kitchen, one arm around Maisie's shoulders.

Eric put his elbows on the table, keeping his voice casual. "When is the wedding?"

"End of December, twenty-eighth, I think. I said I'd be back in time."

"So why are they going to Europe now?" his father said, blowing a laugh out the side of his mouth. "Shouldn't they save that for the honeymoon?"

"Kurt says Christmas is his busy season, so they're taking the honeymoon first."

Eric sat back in his chair and folded his arms tight. Kurt, a damn Viking. He'd be a big guy, trim and athletic, hair gray around the temples, cut just right to inspire confidence in his patients.

Shad came out of the kitchen, patting his arms with a paper towel, and approached the table.

"You know what I just heard?" he said. "A big party's coming up at Marlin Bay Hotel in Port Antonio this Saturday. They bringing two deejays from Kingston, having a clash, they call it. Maurice Barnett putting it on, a friend of mine, and I know it going to be good. He put on parties all the time, from Port Antonio to Negril, and plenty people come. You have to pay, but it worth it, and you get one free drink when you go in."

Joseph was eating the last of the dessert, scraping the creamy sauce off the plate.

"I thought Joseph and Janna could go," Shad said.

"Do you think it's safe?" This from Eric, his thick black eyebrows raised. "Some of these dances can get kind of—"

"Yeah, man. Solomon can work my shift, and Beth and I can go with them. Joseph and Janna safe-safe, don't worry."

92

"How are you getting there?" Eric said.

"Can we use the Jeep?" Shad said with hopeful eyes.

"You thought it out already, I can tell."

"Of course," Shad said, and looked at Joseph. "What you think?"

"Sounds like fun," Joseph said in a lackluster voice.

"Yes, man, plenty fun."

"I'm not a dancer, not for that kind of dancing. And all this reggae dancing—"

"I show you," said Shad. "You can't come to Jamaica and not dance, no way."

"I'm telling you, I have two left feet, man," Joseph said, the boy who'd refused to dance to his father's records, even to foot-stomping Creedence Clearwater Revival.

Shad went behind the bar and tuned the radio to an old-time reggae song. "We going to do this," he said, rushing back to the table. "Come on, stand up, stand up." They were all laughing now, even Maisie, who'd come out of the kitchen to clear the table.

"You gotta be kidding!" Joseph said.

"Let's see you, boy," Eric said, clapping, getting back at the messenger. "Up you get. I want to see this."

Still protesting, Joseph pushed his chair back and stood up slowly. He straightened his shorts over his bulky thighs, his first day not wearing jeans.

"I don't know. It could get ugly."

"Over here." Shad motioned the big man to a space in front of the bar counter and started the lesson, pointing at his feet and bending his legs in time with the music. At first Joseph shuffled, his flip-flops getting in the way, his feet unwieldy. Turning red, he looked at his father as if asking for an excuse. Eric nodded encouragement and patted one arm to the beat of the song. He wondered if Claire had ever seen her son dance to modern music—and if he'd dance at her wedding.

The words of the song rang out above the rain, words about praising Jah, praising the God who grants all good. Halfway through the song, Joseph started moving hit-or-miss to the rhythm, his eyes glued to Shad's loafers.

"That's it, keep going," Shad said. Rainwater was blowing in at the side, forming a stream between the men, and they moved out of its way.

"I suck," Joseph said, laughing. The boy couldn't dance a lick.

"No, you're not terrible," his father said, nodding to his son, letting him know it was all right, the dancing, Claire getting married.

Shad and Joseph rocked to the music and smiled at each other, switched positions on either side of the water. "You got it, the hands now," Shad said, and started a scissors motion with his hands, shrugging his shoulders up and down, showing off.

"Hey, man, that's not fair!" Joseph said, chuckling even while he tried it, messing up the beat with his legs.

"Nothing ventured, nothing gained," Eric yelled above the music.

"That's it, you got it." Shad nodded. He let out a whinny and spun around on his heel, a fancy step. Joseph protested but kept moving, kept rocking, his face pink with pleasure.

A pat on Eric's shoulder. Maisie was standing there, beckoning him to dance. She refused to be waved away and pulled him up by the hand. He blushed, feeling foolish, and slowly got up. And there he was, shuffling, dancing, Maisie laughing and pointing at him. It had been a long time since he'd danced, eight years since the last New Year's Eve party in the hotel, and he'd always loved to dance. Now he was clumsy, his legs and arms jerky, but it felt so good, so visceral moving his body in time to a beat. Beside him, Joseph nodded, pumping his arms, missing a step, trying to catch himself. Then the couple that had been eating at the back joined them, a short, fat man and his short, fat wife who moved fluidly, holding hands, looking down at their feet. They were all dancing, friends and strangers, smiling and dancing while the rain pounded down on the thatch.

Eric pulled his hair back with one hand and looked up at the new roof, not leaking a drop.

"It's all good," he said, nodding in time to the music, dancing with his son for the first time.

CHAPTER THIRTEEN

A small crowd had already started gathering when the two couples arrived at the party. On the raised stage a deejay was spinning a record, a dancehall song with a throbbing beat that tore through the scent of night jasmine coming from the hedge around the hotel garden. Shad ushered the ladies in front of him to the drinks tent, Joseph on his heels.

"Janna, you want a shandy?" Shad asked. "We have a free drink ticket."

"What's a shandy?"

"Beer and ginger ale," Beth said. "It's a drink for the ladies, so Shad says." She was looking good—*looking hot,* Joella had teased her before they left home—wearing a bright pink dress with a wide neckline. She'd gotten the style from a new fashion magazine, she'd announced, and Shad had felt proud of his woman, who could manage four children and still look good.

"Do they have mojitos?" Janna inquired. She was decked out in high heels and a black minidress with a low back.

"How you make that?" said Shad. They'd worked

their way through the crowd and now stood next to the bar.

"I like mine with citrus rum, and you have to put mint leaves in it."

"Sounds good," he said. "You have to teach me to make it. But I don't think this bartender can do that, though. He look too young."

"I'll take a Red Stripe, then."

Shad turned to Joseph. "Rum punch?"

"You got it, man," Joseph said with a broad smile, his teeth and tight white T-shirt standing out against his tan.

It took a while to get the drinks, what with the loud music and Shad being the smallest man vying for the bartender's attention. Eventually, drinks in hand, the four wound their way around to the back of the crowd. The young deejay was killing time until the Kingston guys arrived, late as usual. On either side of the stage, giant black speakers blasted out the voice of the singer and the booming bass. The deejay wore headphones and kept staring at the records he was working, his hands darting to the two turntables, and in between records he would rhyme a couple of phrases, letting the audience know what was coming up next. A medley of locals and a few curious tourists stood below looking on, half of them dancing, bobbing on the spot, some partnered off, others talking, drinking, men inspecting women, women pretending to ignore them.

"What's the song about?" shouted Joseph.

"You ever heard of Shaggy?" Shad said. "He's one of

my favorite singers, man. He's saying that his girlfriend caught him in bed with the next door neighbor, but he's swearing it wasn't him."

"He's a smart one." Joseph laughed.

"He too smart for his own good," Beth said. "He think she believe him."

Janna turned and put her hand on Joseph's arm. "Want to dance?" She blinked a few times after she asked, like she was worried he might turn her down.

"Yes, man," Shad said, nodding at Joseph. "You know how to do it."

"Why not?" He shrugged. "I'm not very good. I only learned ballroom dancing, but Shad's been teaching me." Janna began moving rhythmically to the beat, her partner shuffling beside her.

Shad took Beth's hand and pulled her in close. "Let's keep them company," he said. She slid her arm around his shoulders, the other arm, with the purse, by her side. He reached up and stroked the curly hairs on the back of her neck, the baby hairs that turned him on.

"Don't worry, *boonoonoonoos,*" he said, laughing, in her ear, calling her by the name Granny called him when she was in a good mood. "I not going to lie about the neighbor in the bed."

"Neither will I," she replied, and pretended to bite him on the cheek. He kissed her full on the mouth, her spunk turning him on, her lipstick tasting of strawberries.

The crowd was getting thicker, anticipating the arrival of the experts onstage. Singles were connecting, couples were dancing, everyone was in motion. The robust aroma of sweat had won over the scent of jasmine. Inches from Shad, Janna moved smoothly to the music, rocking back—showing off her long bronze legs—and leaning forward, affording a quick view of full round breasts. If that didn't turn Joseph on, thought Shad, then nothing would. But Joseph was sneaking glances at other dancing men, mimicking their steps, not looking at Janna unless she said something. Coming in the Jeep, Beth had sat on the brake and Janna had sat on Joseph's lap, her bare back inches from his chest, and never once did Joseph touch the curving brown spine with its subtle indentations, and it had crossed Shad's mind that Joseph was too polite, or in his own world like his father.

"They match, don't you think?" Beth said. "They both so tall and pretty."

"True, they look like people in a magazine."

Beth curved her hand around her mouth, whispering, "He look like the man on *General Hospital,* the man who—"

"Let's talk later," he said, and spun her around.

When the song finished, the deejay started packing up, making way for the big guns. The crowd relaxed and socialized, some moving closer to the stage and the big speakers, others measuring the competition. A woman in a short leopard-skin dress, her hair braided intricately, turned around and stared at Joseph, then at Janna (from head to foot), and said something to her girlfriend.

"Look at that dress," Janna said to Beth.

"Some people have no shame." Beth shook her head in contempt.

"Too little cloth, too much torso," Joseph agreed.

"That's a pretty one over there," Janna said, "the yellow dress with the straps. I would wear that, I love yellow."

Shad knocked Joseph's arm with the back of his hand. "Time for another drink. Ask Janna what she want."

"She wants another beer," Joseph said after conferring with her, and Shad motioned him to follow. At the bar, customers were standing three deep.

"Tell me," said Shad after they joined the back row, "what happening with the report business? Any help I can give you?"

"I'm good, man." Joseph nodded. "But Dad could use some help."

"Doing what?"

"I need an estimate, as accurate as possible, of all the money that's going to come in—from guest rooms, bar, dining room, weddings, everything. I need it for a five-year period." Joseph's easy smile had gone and his chin had gotten firmer. He looked like an American business-man all of a sudden.

"What about money going out, the money we spend to buy food and beverage, for paying staff and so? Don't you need that?"

"I need that, too. Whatever's coming in and going out for a twenty-room hotel. Income and expenses, that's what we call it."

"Income and expenses, I like that. Anything else?"

"That should do for now. Lambert's been giving me the construction costs, start to finish, and his wife, in the

States, has been giving him figures for the furnishings, laundry and kitchen equipment, that kind of stuff."

"Glad to hear," Shad said, and inched forward, aiming to take the place of a man who'd left the bar. Despite Shad's protest in brisk patois, a man in a green hat pushed into the spot, and Shad and Joseph took up positions behind him.

"It *real* important that you write this thing for us," Shad said, trying to look like he was stating a fact, not just begging.

"I know, I know." Joseph nodded, but he had that distracted look about him that said he didn't really understand what was at stake.

"Listen, I want you to promise me something," Shad said.

"Like what?"

"That you're not going to run off and leave us, that you going to finish the report."

"I'll finish it, don't worry."

"You have to promise."

Joseph gave a questioning smile. "Sure, I'll promise."

"You have to understand, this is bigger than a little hotel," Shad said. He pressed his lips together. It was time for truth, the reason he'd suggested they come to the party. "This isn't just for me I'm talking, seen? This hotel is for Largo, because the sea getting fished out, the fishermen can't find a lot of fish now, and the whole town suffering. The young people can't find no work, nothing for them to do but fish little bit and they getting into trouble, selling weed, moving to Kingston and getting into crime. We need a hotel, even a little hotel, to bring in some money. If we have a hotel, we going to have guests who want water sports, so a few Largo youths can make money off that, and they going to need taxi drivers, and we can find men to drive, and we can train some of the young men and women as waiters and cooks. The people need it, because—"

"Dad needs it, too," Joseph said. Shad glanced at him, realizing he'd misjudged the man, had thought him unable to see the cul-de-sacs facing others.

"True, the boss need it, too." Shad patted the back of his pants and took out his wallet. "He tell you about his situation?"

"What situation?"

"Between you, me, and the gatepost—he can't even pay his overdraft. It was only when the woman was on the island paying rent that things eased up and the bank woman stopped calling. But she start calling again, and she sounding vex, like she tired of calling. I don't know how long he can hold out, you know. It don't mean anything to you, but to us—"

Joseph spread his hands, looking vulnerable, his eyes anxious. "Hey, man, it means a lot to me, too. I need this job, trust me. I had to let my apartment go before I came out. I didn't know what I was going to do until Dad called and sent the ticket. I'd been looking for work, but I haven't been able to find anything, there's nothing in my field right now. So this is a no-brainer for me. All my expenses are paid, I'm working, and I have some money coming in if this thing takes off." He looked down, turning his hands over, passing his thumbs over his finger-nails. "I don't have much choice, either." Shad saw that the man had been holding back, had been putting on his cool-guy look to pretend he was fine, but he was a man who was struggling, even in America, who was afraid, like everyone else.

"Good, I'll pay for this round," Shad said, and pushed into a space that had opened up.

"Shad, Shadrack Myers!" A man in a white suit and a Panama hat stood behind them, his fingers full of gold rings. He bounced fists with Shad, who tried not to wince when the rings made contact.

"Maurice, how you going, boy?" Shad said. He introduced Barnett to Joseph. "He running the party. Remember, I told you?"

"I know this guy plenty years," said Barnett, nodding to Joseph and laughing with Shad. "From we used to play canoe-jumping, and he still in Largo. What you having, man? Let me order for you, on the house."

By the time Shad and Joseph got back, the headline deejays had finished setting up their equipment on opposite sides of the stage. The women were hemmed in by the thick crowd, with their backs to a tree trunk.

"What took you so long?" Beth said.

"We was talking—"

Music wailed out of the speakers, the volume higher than before, drowning out all conversation. To the right of the stage, Deejay Lion had an arm up high, hips swinging to his own music. Men and women roared their approval, shouted the chorus, and started dancing. Shad bobbed on the spot, bending his knees, taking a sip from his beer bottle, and Beth did the same. Beside them, Joseph was frowning at the stage while Janna swung one arm in time to the music.

"Pretty loud, don't you think?" Joseph shouted, his eyebrows peaked in the middle.

"That's why we're standing at the back," Shad yelled. "You should hear it near the stage!"

An hour later the rival deejays had warmed up, and they were alternating every couple of records, rhyming and rocking when their turn came at the table. Everyone was bobbing on the spot with drinks in hand. The women were expressionless and the men had hand towels dangling from their back pockets, which they used to wipe their faces when the perspiration got unbearable.

"My time now," boomed one of the entertainers. "I play the best for you, seen? I play what hot, not what's not." He was building to his own monologue above the music. He sang out,

> *"I, Deejay Getover, know what best for the nation,*
> *Telling you all to avoid temptation."*

Oh, *raas*, thought Shad, here it comes. He'd had a feeling they would play that ignorant song.

Getover called,

> *"Don't get caught up in woeful sinning,*
> *Make any man come with any twinning."*

A familiar song started from the turntable. Another roar arose from the onlookers as they joined in the chorus, started rocking again with hands in the air.

"They bringing us down
And destroying the nation——"

Shad turned to the couple beside him, shouting above the singer. "This is different from where you come from, right? You have anything like this?"

"They bring shows like this to a lot of American cities," Janna yelled, delight in her smile. "I went to a clash once before."

"I've never been to anything like this," Joseph said. "I have to admit it's intriguing." The word sounded sophisticated, made more so by the way Joseph pulled his head back and gave a quirky kind of smile, like he had private thoughts. *Intriguing.* Shad repeated the word to himself so he could ask Rickia to look up the meaning tomorrow in the dictionary. Words were like magical keys to boxes that fit inside each other, Shad had always thought, each larger than the last, each expanding his world. A person might drop out of school, he'd told Joella once as he stood over the stove with a spatula in his hand, but if you knew words, you could speak English so foreigners could understand you, listen to the news on the radio, talk to people, even important people.

"We not going to stay much more," Shad said. "We have a long drive back and we have church in the morning . . ."

He kept the patter going until the song finished and the cheers died down. The next song was by a singer who sang about women and how a man had to have a lot of money to get a nice woman. What was the country coming to? Shad complained to Beth.

"These songs just bringing Jamaica down, man," he said in her ear. "Sometimes I just shame for my own country. These young people don't care what they sing, or what? What happen when they go abroad and people hear the lyrics? Foreign people going to think that everybody in the country is vulgar like that, that we think of nothing but sex and hate."

"But the same foreign people must be buying the records," Beth said. "The singers making plenty money, selling plenty records abroad, Winston says."

"Because they don't understand the words," Shad muttered.

The next deejay shifted the mood, started playing a Skatalites song, its slow, rough sound reminding Shad of jukebox music in bars he'd passed as a child.

"You ever hear of *ska?*" shouted Shad to Joseph, who shook his head. "It's Jamaican music from long time, like the fifties, sixties. It came before reggae, from before we all born!"

"Daddy can dance it," Janna announced.

"I can dance it, too," Shad said, and started bringing his knees together and separating them, scissoring his arms in time.

"You did that in the bar!" Joseph said, and they all laughed and mimicked the moves, even Joseph.

A slow reggae was fading into the background when the four Largoites called it a night and started back to the car. In the dark parking lot, Shad examined the cram of vehicles, winding his way around the first few, leading the group. He thought he remembered where the Jeep was, that it was near a large tree, but in the dark it was almost impossible to spot among the dozens of cars, trucks, SUVs, motorbikes, and scooters now jostled together. When a tree loomed ahead, he started toward it, Janna and Beth chattering behind, Joseph bringing up the rear. Sure enough, there was the familiar pickup in the shadows—but someone was standing beside it. Shad peered into the dark, until he was certain it was the right car—and that this person had opened the door, was now bending and doing something inside the vehicle.

"Hey, stop!" he yelled. He started sprinting toward the pickup, dodging around the intervening cars, banging his arm against the side mirror of one.

"What you doing?" he called angrily. There wasn't anything to steal because they'd left the Jeep empty and the radio was already missing. The tall man—it looked like a youth but he couldn't be sure—slammed the car door and darted in the opposite direction. Shad was about to run after him, but when he got to the Jeep, he glanced inside to see what mischief the fellow had been up to. From the mirror hung a thin white rope with a loop at the end, and beneath it on the dashboard was a piece of paper. Shad jumped into the driver's seat, shoved the paper into his pocket, and was already pulling at the noose by the time Joseph came alongside.

"Who was that?" Joseph panted. "What was he doing?"

"Some fool messing around," Shad said. "Didn't get anything, though."

An hour later, under the swinging bulb of the bedroom, their shadows looming left then right, Beth and Shad bent over the note. It came from a lined notebook, the page torn in half. On it were a few words written in pencil.

"'*Your friend in danger,*'" Beth read out loud. She straightened and looked at him. "Who you think they talking about?"

Shad rubbed her shoulder. "Don't pay it no mind, sweets. Must be the wrong car."

CHAPTER FOURTEEN

Lorr:

The good: had a date with The Hotness. Yes! He invited me kind of last minute, but a date is a date, right? We went to this very chill dance, one of those deejay clashes like that thing we went to in Atlanta, remember, on North Hairston? This was outdoors on a lawn, though, which was great because it would have been way too hot inside. Only problem was that my heels kept sinking into the ground. No mojitos, but Red Stripe. Good enough.

Anyway, we went with Shad, the bartender from across the road, and his wife. Thank God, because Shad knew his way around. Hotness looked uncomfortable. I don't think he's ever been around that many black people before! LOL.

The place was crammed, lots of sweaty bodies, very authentic. Great music, all the latest. The clothes were amazing—not on the men, the women! Everything tight, shiny, short. Cutouts, diamonds down the leg, bellies out, you name it. There were a couple of real dancehall queens they brought onstage, and you should have seen them dance, girl! They did some grinding that should only be put on coffee.

The not-so-good, but definitely workable: My guy can't dance. He can bounce a little, but not always on the beat. But it's only a minor hiccup. Nobody's perfect. Anyway, these dancehall things aren't for couples-dancing, as you know, so he managed to pass. He didn't embarrass himself (or me) too much.

Got a little kiss at the door. Oh, God, he smelled so good—funk on top of aftershave. I wanted to grab him, but I just thanked him for a lovely evening. My mother would have approved.

Love ya, back to work,
J

She dropped her hands from the keyboard. She'd forgotten to tell Lorraine about somebody breaking into their car. No, she wasn't going to write another email. She had to start keeping some things to herself, even little things.

She entered "computer graphics positions" in the search box and waited. A kiss on the cheek. Not quite how she saw the date ending. He'd been quiet walking up the road to the house, even after she'd taken off her heels and made a joke about saving them for a rainy day. He'd only agreed, like he didn't get the joke, and there hadn't been any talk, any last-minute flirting at the door, only the peck and a thank-you before turning and walking away.

A government labor website popped up.

COMPUTER GRAPHICS
Important Points and Trends

Employment is expected to grow about as fast as the average, particularly in interactive media. (Yes!)

A bachelor's degree in graphic design is usually required. (Groan. At the institute, they'd said it took an average of four months for their graduates to land a job after getting a certificate. It had been eight months for her already. She must be on the other side of the bell curve.)

Keen competition is expected in this field; website design and animation experience is advantageous.

Back to the search engine and a job site.

Position: Assistant Professor, Computer Graphics. No.

Position: Functional Game Designer. Experience absolutely necessary. Sounded great. No experience.

Position: Web Designer, Las Vegas. Too far, even if she settled for web design.

The work was coming, she knew that. It was just a matter of time, a matter of finding the needle in the haystack. Somewhere in the garden a bird squawked loudly like it was quarreling, the sound making her look down the dining table to the living room, with its sofas and hardwood floors, the open double doors a frame for the stunning view. This was the kind of house she wanted one day, her own house, where you could feel the warmth in the walls and the wide-open doors. Her father and Jennifer had done a good job designing and decorating it, even if her mother was still irritated at the idea.

"Why on earth is he building such a big place?" Janna still remembered Phyllis frowning into the phone upon hearing about the house from a friend. "The woman is half his age, eighteen years younger at least. He's going to die of a heart attack working to pay for it, you know that, right? Bad enough he has these little children to take care of. They could have just lived in the house in Kingston and he would have saved himself all that trouble. Most of his work is in Kingston, anyway."

Janna had been tempted to remind her mother that it was none of their business what her father and Jennifer did, because it had been her mother's idea to leave Lambert, not the other way around. It shouldn't matter that her father had remarried, or that he and Jennifer had built a beautiful home. Instead, Janna had kept her mouth shut, knowing that Phyllis wasn't open to ironies.

Refreshing her search, Janna went to another website. She'd had to push herself this morning to do another job search. The house didn't help. It wiped out the sting of unemployment and reduced her incentive. Everything else seemed like a struggle compared to this. She'd be starting at the bottom wherever she worked, earning the lowest salary, working long hours to make a good impression. And she'd spend her weekends toting laundry to the Laundromat and cleaning her little apartment. None of it could compare to life in this house, to having her bed made, her favorite meals prepared, her pajamas ironed, and never having to clean anything but herself.

Her father had been right not to migrate, as much as she missed him in Florida. Had he done so, he would probably have ended up working some dead-end job in his middle age, living in a little suburban house with no view. She couldn't see Lambert's expansiveness fitting into a small life. It wouldn't have held a candle to his comfortable lifestyle in Jamaica, the lifestyle she loved. And to think she'd almost not come, had had to give a few days' thought to the offer.

The phone call from Jennifer had come six months to the day after she'd become certified—and unemployed. She'd been sitting at home in her mother's condo reading a trade magazine, trying to ease the frustration that had been building, beginning to feel it had all been a waste leaving the *Herald* and slogging through the whole Tampa thing. Jennifer's idea had been like a frosty lemonade on a burning-hot day. She'd been thinking, her stepmother had said, that Janna could keep Lambert company while she was away in Orlando. She wouldn't even have to do any babysitting like the last time, because Little Wayne would be with her in Florida and Casey was in boarding school.

"I'm looking for a job," Janna had protested, although she was tempted to say yes right away. "I can't leave now."

"You can apply for jobs from here, right?" Jennifer said, her bracelets jingling over the phone. Janna could see her tossing back her golden-blond hair. "We're on the Internet."

"I don't know," she murmured. "Suppose they call me in for an interview?"

"Phone interview." Jennifer's answer came quickly, like everything she did. "They do them all the time nowadays. Honestly, Janna, your father would love it. He hates being alone, and he's going to call me every day to ask when I'm coming back if you're not here. And the truth is that I have no idea how long I'll be gone. I love your father to death, you know that, but my mom is going down and I just need to spend some time with her."

"What's the matter with your mom?"

There was a pause, a change in tone. "Your dad didn't tell you?"

"I guess he forgot. What's happening with her?"

"She was diagnosed with spinal cancer last year. It's terminal. We don't know—"

"Jennifer, I'm so sorry."

Her stepmother had brightened a little. "She's doing pretty well right now—as well as can be expected—but I haven't spent much time with her for years. A few months should do it. You never know, right?" And despite Janna's mother's muttered protests when she mentioned the call (*she's just using you, you realize that?*), Janna had accepted the invitation.

Having no luck with her search, she stood up, bent over to the left, over to the right, arched her back. It was lunchtime, time to see what was next on Miss Bertha's menu, to enjoy the good life while she had it.

Joseph was on the phone in Jennifer's office when she passed. Through the closed French doors, she could see his back, broad and muscular, dominating the room. He was hunched over the desk making intense gestures with one hand, his low voice bleeding through the panes.

"—kind of freaks me out, man." It sounded like he

knew the person well, another man, by the sound of it. There was an intimacy about the way he said it that made her footsteps falter for a second. But he was silent afterward, as if the other person was giving him advice and he was listening carefully.

In the kitchen, the black and white tiles were cool under her bare feet. Lambert was sitting at the breakfast table, his head bent over a plate, the gray-and-white hair opening to a bald spot she'd never seen before.

"Hi, Dads, what you doing at home?"

"Hey, Sweet Pea." His name for her when she was little, before the split. "We were waiting for the cement truck to arrive at the site, and I'm tired of eating patties for lunch. Thought I'd come home instead for the good stuff." The word *home* made her lean on the chair opposite his, her heart swelling a little in her chest. She hadn't lived alone in a house with her father since she was six, nowhere they could both call home.

"What you eating?" she said.

"Stew peas and rice." He gestured with his fork. "Help yourself."

She reached into the cupboard for a plate and spooned the mixture out of a pot on the stove. The house was quiet, no Jennifer, no kids, no Miss Bertha—only Joseph in the office—everything deliciously different. Her father, astute as he was, would be feeling it, too, but would never mention it, she knew. They ate in silence, side by side, their noses dripping from the pepper seasoning the pork. When her father finished, he pushed his plate out of the way and drained his glass of water.

"How's the job search going?" he said after he wiped his mouth.

"Fine."

He reached for a fresh paper napkin and blew his nose loudly. "Sent in any applications?"

"Not yet." She smiled at him through her hair. "I'm working on it. You won't have me living here forever, don't worry." It was meant as a joke, but it came out sounding like she was testing him.

"What you talking about? I like you being here, you know that."

"I just mean that you're not going to lose your investment."

"Investment? All this education, you mean? Naw, it'll pay off. Just marry a wealthy guy who wants a smart wife." He laughed at his own joke and folded his beefy arms. "Hey, speaking of investments, I want to go up to the Blue Mountains to look at some property. I got it a few years ago. It's in the back of beyond. Why don't we take some horses up this weekend? Think you'd like that?"

"I'd love it! I haven't gone horseback riding for I don't know how long."

"I'll arrange with Steve Halpern to borrow some horses. Miss Bertha can pack a lunch, a few sandwiches. Can you organize it?"

"Sure, sure." She picked up a bone and pulled some flesh away with her teeth. "Can I invite Joseph?"

Her father rolled his shirtsleeves farther up his arms, looking at her from under his eyebrows as he rolled. "Yeah, why not? I'll invite Eric to come along, too."

She put down the bone and licked her lips. "So we're talking four lunches, right?"

"Right."

"Chicken salad?"

"Yeah, that's fine. And some sliced roast beef. Tell her to pack them in the small cooler with some ice and thermoses of water. We don't want the meat going off." He crumpled his dirty napkin and threw it into the garbage can next to the counter. "You and Joseph getting along well, eh?"

"He's nice." Keep it offhand, she reminded herself, keep it offhand—the first time in her life she'd discussed a man with her father, the first time he'd been anywhere near when she dated.

"You're right. He's very nice." Lambert stroked his mustache, pulling his fingers along the length of one side and then the other. "It might be a good idea to take it easy, though—if you know what I mean."

"I don't know what you mean," she said quietly, her breath catching. Sheba padded in from the back pantry, nails clicking and teats swinging beneath her. She collapsed on the floor and put her head on her paws. The black and white tiles on the floor suddenly looked like a checkerboard around the tired dog. Below the table, Janna's feet were in two squares, one black, one white, and she shifted them both to the white one. Her father bent over to pat the dog.

"I mean, he's just here for a short time. I wouldn't count on him to do a lot of running around with you. He's working and you're not, you know. He has a job to do for his father and he needs to focus."

"He's focusing," she said, remembering Joseph's words on the phone, focused words to a close friend.

He stood up and pushed in the chair, anxious to be gone. Nearly out the back door, he tossed a few words over his shoulder. "Some guys you just stay friends with, you know."

Overhead, the fan was making a groaning noise she hadn't heard before. She scraped the remains of her plate into the dog bowl and called Sheba over. Leaning against the granite countertop, she rinsed the plates in the sink and placed them in the dishwasher. He was a good man, her dad, but he was always trying to rescue her, to be her safety net. Typical of him, wanting to protect her from a guy he thought would dump her.

Joseph was bent over a notebook when she passed Jennifer's office. She knocked on a pane and he looked up and took off his glasses. He gestured to her to open the door, brushing his hair back, the eyes—oh, God, the sweetest blue-gray color she'd ever seen, like rain clouds on a summer day—and his eyelashes so long they drove straight into her heart when she stepped into the room.

"Sorry to disturb you," she said, suddenly worried that her lips were greasy.

"What's up?"

"If you want to come horseback riding, we're going up into the mountains, having a picnic. Daddy suggested it."

He ran a hand through his hair, his skin the color of glazed doughnuts. "Riding? When?"

"This weekend sometime. What day is better for you?"

"I don't care. . . . Sunday?"

"I'll tell Daddy and let you know."

"Fine." He tapped the pen on the notebook.

"If you don't like horses or something, no problem," she said, opening her eyes wide and nodding to let him know it was okay, really, if he didn't want to go.

"Actually, I'd like to go," he said. "It should be fun, riding in the mountains. I used to ride in Virginia, quite a bit."

She leaned against the door frame. "I'm not very good myself. I only rode when I was little, and once when we went to a farm in Georgia. There was this pecan farm where you could pick up pecans from the ground, and my mother loves pecans, so we went up there. Turned out that the pecan season was over, so we rented horses instead." He wanted to get back to his work, she could tell. He kept tapping the pen and looking at her with a patient smile.

Walking down the corridor to her room, a corridor lined with black-and-white photographs of Jennifer and Lambert, Casey and Little Wayne, she arrived at a thought, a thought with capitals and periods. Each word had come by itself, dropped into her mind between her footsteps.

Men. Are. Crazy.

"You never know what's going on in their freaking heads," she said to the bathroom mirror before she pushed her toothbrush into her mouth.

CHAPTER FIFTEEN

S had squatted down under the lignum vitae tree, the only shade near the field where Winston and some youths were kicking a ball around. He was tired already and it was only three o'clock. This wasn't how he liked to spend his day off. There'd been nothing but work today so far, not one minute of relaxation, and he kept remembering a television doctor saying that a person should rest at least one day a week, to *de-stress,* the man had said, but it hadn't gone that way today, and he'd be back to work tomorrow.

His plan had been to sleep late because he'd stayed up doing inventory the night before, but Beth had woken him, tugged him by his big toe under the sheet until he couldn't ignore her any longer. Joshua was hanging from her arm with his bushy hair, his diaper soggy.

"Sorry to wake you, but remember you promised to weed today."

She talked on, placing Josh on the bed to change his diaper. Shad struggled awake to her chatter about the vegetable garden. "The tomatoes don't like it when the weeds choking them," she said. "And the lettuce need weeding, too."

Shad reached out and held Joshua's pinkie, the two giving grudging smiles across the sheets.

"Josh, what your mother talking? Waking a man who want to sleep?" The ten-month-old gurgled, and Beth swept him up and out of the room.

So instead of lounging in bed, Shad had spent his morning sitting on a plastic crate, moving it inch by inch as he tugged at the weeds in between the vegetables. It was a hot day, and the only thing between him and the sun had been his grandmother's old straw hat, the one with half a brim. The weeding business took longer than he'd expected, because the beds hadn't been cleaned in weeks, and the weeds had had a chance to dig down deep and twine around the plants. He'd had to tug and chop to get the roots out.

"You done?" Beth had asked when she put his lunch in front of him on the dinette table.

"Done," he said. "Until they grow again."

She turned on the television and settled onto a chair beside him, Joshua on her lap. She pulled out one breast and the baby nuzzled into it.

"When *you* going to be done?" Shad asked, and took a slurp of his split pea soup.

"What you mean?"

"When you—when you done with the breastfeeding, man?" he said, his mouth full of soup. "The baby nursing for one year now, and like how I'm off today, if you weren't nursing, we could—"

Beth had sucked her teeth and turned back to the TV, which was showing a handsome older man standing at a desk. "You too rude. In front of the child, too."

Shad gestured toward the TV and rubbed her arm, its round softness feeling inviting. "What? You don't think Victor like sex, too? Why you think they call it *Young and Restless*? I young and restless, too, you know." They laughed and she turned back to the TV.

There'd been no time for an afternoon nap, either. He'd made up his mind last night that he was going to find out more about Winston today, see if he knew anything about the youth who'd put the noose and the note in the Jeep. The words on the note had nagged at him all week, since the dance. He was sure they referred to Joseph, but who would know they were at a dance so far from Largo? And who would want to threaten Joseph? And why would he be in danger? He was a muscular guy, didn't go anywhere but Largo, and even there he only went between the boardinghouse, Lambert's house, the beach, and the bar. His only friend was a girl, and a hot girl at that.

The noose business was even stranger. Nobody threatened people with nooses in Jamaica, and the mobs that killed gay people chopped or stabbed them. They never hanged them. (He thought of a television program he'd seen where they showed old photographs of black people in America, hanging like sacks of rice from trees, and he wondered if they'd been hanged because they were gay.) There were so many unanswered questions to the whole episode that Shad almost didn't know where to begin.

Apart from investigating the incident in the Jeep, deep down in his gut Shad had a feeling that he had to know more about Winston, and he always followed his intuition. He never knew where it would lead him, but it was usually somewhere he needed to be. Shad had planned, therefore, that while the boy was still in school, he'd find out who his friends were and what he did with his time.

After lunch and a few inquiries, Shad had walked to the outskirts of the village where he heard the boy lived, a shabby area of unpaved roads and wooden shacks with pit toilets in the rear. A woman hanging out laundry waved him toward a bridge when he asked about Winston. Two young men were sitting on the stone wall that ran across the bridge, and he approached them. He'd seen them before but never spoken to them until now.

"He lives over there, that house at the end," the taller of the two had said, a fellow with a high forehead and short dreadlocks sticking up around his head. "Why you ask?" The smell and smoke of a marijuana spliff was drifting up behind his back, where one hand was hiding.

He live here long?" Shad asked.

"Yeah, long enough," the short one said, the mole on the side of his nose crinkling when he smiled. "He born here." Another smart-man.

"You guys know him?"

"No," they said together.

"I not police or anything, seen?"

"We know who you are," dreadlocks said. "You the bartender—"

"Right, me, same one. He visiting my daughter, and I just want to know more about him. A father need information, you know, need to protect his family. I just want to make sure that he straight, that he not going to mess her up or nothing."

The one with the mole pulled up his big shorts. "Winston cool, man. He going to school and learning a little trade."

"Like deejaying?" Shad had said, and tried not to sound judgmental.

"He doing little work at Mas Zeb's shop."

"The mechanic guy?"

"Him, same one," the tall fellow said. He was squinting, probably worried the joint would burn out behind his back before the questions stopped.

The house they'd pointed out was at the end of the unpaved road, surrounded by more weeds than Shad wanted to think about. It was a rotting, abandoned house that had never been painted, its old wooden boards bleached by the sun. Shad mounted the warped steps and knocked, and, without lock or handle, the door gave under his knuckles and creaked open. There was one room to the house, a room that was empty except for a dirty foam mattress on the floor. A sheet was folded at the foot of the foam and a half-burned candle sat in a jam jar beside it. It was the home of a squatter who had nowhere else to go.

"Anybody here?" Shad called. He stepped over a missing floorboard and looked around.

Most of the windowpanes were broken, and rain had

poured in overnight, had pooled on the floor. On one wall there were nails where clothes were hung, T-shirts and a pair of jeans, a woven belt, and some briefs. A kitchen of sorts had been organized in one corner of the room, where a clean dish, a tin of corned beef, and a can opener were stacked one on top of the other. When Shad retraced his steps, the young men were missing from the bridge. He'd wanted to ask them where Winston's parents were and who bought him the clothes and the radio, even though they probably wouldn't have told him.

There was, as usual, a row of beat-up cars in the lane outside Mas Zeb's house, and the mechanic was deep under the hood of an ancient Toyota.

"Hey, boss," Shad called. The two men bounced fists, Zeb with a wrench in his hand.

"How it going?" Zeb said.

"Like I keep telling you," Shad said, "one of these days I going surprise you and buy a car from you."

Zeb laughed and spun his wrench between his greasy fingers. "And like I keep telling you, if you only need a car to go to church and work, you might as well save your money."

"No, man. Like I went to Barnett's party in Port Antonio, and I could have used the car, you know. I could take the children to Reach Falls, take them on little outings in the holidays. I going to have a car one day."

Zeb leaned into the Toyota again. "So you come to tell me you hope to buy a car?"

"I come to ask you about your new worker, a certain Winston Dupree."

"What about him?" Zeb said, and started tugging at a radiator hose.

"He checking my daughter and I just finding out more about him."

The mechanic straightened and let go of the hose. "He come around a week ago and said he need a job. I tell him I can't pay much, a couple dollars an hour, and he say okay. He start working last Saturday and say he can come three afternoons a week. Not today, he say he have football on Wednesday. He don't know nothing about cars, but he ask me to show him, say he want to help people fix their cars. I told him he could just hand me tools for now." Disappearing under the hood, Zeb threw out a final word. "Like how his father gone away and leave him, you know."

Next to the soccer field and a few feet from Winston's radio, Shad stretched out on the ground under the lignum vitae tree. He was still in his old clothes from weeding, and Beth wouldn't complain about the dirt, since they had to be washed anyway. Winston and five or six other boys were kicking the ball, a coach blowing the whistle whenever he felt like. The boys looked like they didn't know what they were doing but had a lot of energy doing it—thrusting bare feet forward and missing the ball, heading balls that darted in the wrong direction, cursing, pointing at each other—nothing like Mr. Stevens would have tolerated in the old days. Mr. Stevens would have shouted, "What are you chaps doing? Get away from the bloody football, Shad!"

Mr. Stevens had been a fat little Englishman who'd

taught the school team a thing or two, brought them into the parish elementary school finals. He didn't teach at the school, and lived in Port Antonio, twenty-five miles away on rough road, and came to Largo twice a week because he loved soccer. Shad wondered where Mr. Stevens was now.

From the coach's shouts, it was clear that the practice match was only half finished, and Shad lay his head back on his arm. A light breeze was blowing across the field. After lumpy fishing nets in his uncle's boat, after concrete floors in the Penitentiary when they took away his mattress, the leaf-blanketed dirt was a joy. There was time enough for a catnap (he loved the word, pictured a cat curled on a chair), like the TV doctor had recommended.

When Shad awoke, the radio was gone and the field was silent and he had to run past the four-room school building and down a couple of streets to catch up with Winston. He saw the boy start when he approached from behind, panting and irritated.

"You couldn't wake me?" Shad said. Winston turned off the radio.

"Nice game. Who the coach?"

"Mr. Gerald, the science teacher."

"Science teacher, I could tell." They lapsed into silence.

"I want to talk to you," Shad said after he'd caught his breath.

"About what, suh?" The boy turned to him, his face a little tired, a little sulkier today. His hair looked rough and uncombed.

"Just a little chat, you know? Like how you coming round—"

"I don't do anything to Joella, Mistah Myers."

"I said you did something? I just inquiring how your life going."

Winston looked down at him, narrowed his eyes. "Fine, no problems, suh."

"Good," Shad said. Old Man Job was walking toward them, carrying his heavy tool box. He waved at Shad, his former protégé in the building of Eric's hotel, the apprentice with promise who preferred to be a bartender.

"Evening, Mistah Job," Shad said. "You need help with the box?"

"Thank you, but I good. Give greetings at home."

When they passed Job, Winston tucked his radio under his arm, and a strong funk drifted up from his armpit.

"Where you living?" Shad asked.

"Over so," Winston said, and waved toward the road with the bridge.

"You living alone?" The boy nodded.

"What happen to your father?"

"He gone to Kingston about—sometime early this year, say he gone to look for work."

"You hear from him since?"

Winston shook his head. The sun dipped below the horizon, sent its last rays over the rooftops, and shrank back. They turned together down a side road leading into the village square.

"Stop here a little bit," Shad said outside Miss Paulette's shop. "Wait here, don't move." Five minutes later he emerged from the shop with a black plastic bag and they continued walking.

"Tell me," Shad said. "How you take care of yourself, like how you bathe and everything?"

"I have a bucket," Winston said. "I fill it at the standpipe at the end of the road and I bathe behind my house."

Shad rubbed his scalp and smiled. "Trust me, star, you going to need two buckets tonight."

Winston cracked a smile, his hand over his mouth.

"Youth, I want to be straight with you," Shad said. "I like you, you understand, but I need to ask you a question."

Winston shifted his radio to the other armpit.

"Somebody, a skinny, light-skinned guy, a young guy—he left a note in the Jeep on Saturday night. You know anything about it?" Winston shook his head.

"Tell me, son, you ever hear anybody say they going to do anything to me or my family?" Shad said.

"No, suh."

"What about Mistah Eric—the man who own the bar—or his son? You hear somebody say they bad people—?"

"No, suh, I don't hear nothing."

"I want you to do me a little favor," Shad said. He stopped walking and turned toward his companion. "If you hear anything at all, hear anybody say anything, anybody going to do *anything* to my family or to Mistah Eric or his son, I want you to tell me. It will just be between you and me, but I want you to help me. I need you to help me look after the Largo Bay people, you know? Like how you going to be a big mechanic and everything."

"How you know—?"

"When you in charge of things, you have to stay *in the know*. You have to have eyes in the back of your head."

"You don't have eyes in the back of you head, Mistah Myers."

"Is just another saying, don't worry," Shad said, looking at the main road, darkening by the minute. "Anyway, I have to go. The wife looking for me."

He thrust the black bag at Winston. "A little something for you, some bread and cheese, a few other things. You have to eat if you going to learn. And if you want to play decent football, make sure you get enough rest and bathe good when you come home, you hear me?" Shad touched the thin shoulder. "Oh, and I put some soap in the bag. Use it before you come to look for Joella."

CHAPTER SIXTEEN

"I'm too old for this," Eric said, looking down at the steep cliff only a couple of feet from his horse's hooves. Thick bamboo branches spreading over the narrow dirt path opened to harsh sunlight. He was already sweating in the heat, his heart racing a little and his bottom getting sore. The four horses plodded on in a line, Eric's horse the oldest of the bunch, its brown coat dull and its belly sagging. Ahead of him Janna and Joseph rode in silence, and behind him Lambert was humming some old Broadway hit. The cliff to his left plunged at least sixty feet, disappearing into bushes and treetops far below, hinting at the awful fate of a misstep by man or animal.

"You could disappear down that mountain and never be found," he groaned, half turning his head to Lambert.

"You're a damn stick-in-the-mud, Eric," his friend said, laughing, his horse's hooves thudding solidly on the path.

"Do you know what it would take to bring me down from here if anything happened?"

"Nothing is going to happen, don't worry. Just relax and enjoy the scenery."

"Easy for you to say. You do this kind of thing all the time."

"You'd stay younger if you did."

"Marrying a younger woman would keep me younger, you mean." Both men laughed.

In front of Eric, Janna rode an edgy horse with scars on its legs. Her back was erect and her head high like Joseph had instructed before they started off. Her hair was pulled back into a fluffy ponytail that the sun shimmered through, forming a halo around her head. She was wearing long earrings and a white gypsy blouse that had fallen off one shoulder—a little overkill for the occasion, Eric decided.

Joseph was in the lead. Lambert had said that the stronger riders should ride front and back. On his large black mare, pointing out the view whenever the mountains opened up, Joseph looked completely at ease, his cowboy boots just right, showing up his father's old sneakers. From the fogginess of the past, Eric dredged up a memory of Claire's voice on the phone, saying something about riding lessons for Joseph. After he asked if it was in the child support agreement, she'd gone silent. And now he knew that she must have paid for the classes herself, because Joseph looked as if he'd been born on horseback, as elegant as his mother.

Claire had always been elegant, not beautiful but elegant, even when she was twenty-five. She'd looked like an aristocrat sitting on the bench in Herald Square, throwing out her sandwich crusts to the pigeons. There'd been something about the way she sat, the way she held her wrist, that spoke to the twenty-eight-year-old sitting opposite, a young man from Cleveland who'd gotten tired of dating giggling girls and sharing a studio with Arnie, and that something had made him ask her the time. She'd looked at him, with her high cheekbones and a piece of bread in her hand.

"I don't have a watch," she'd said, and he'd blushed and felt like a total idiot.

Two days later, when he showed up at the Gimbels cosmetics counter, she'd smiled at him but couldn't remember his name. He was a little surprised when she agreed to go to the movies and dinner. She told him after a few dates that he was the most handsome man she'd ever gone out with, and he told her that she smelled better than any woman he'd known. She wore Lanvin, a French perfume, she said, and she bought it at the employees' discount price. The heady, thick fragrance had followed him for the fourteen years they were married, reminding him that he didn't deserve her. Paper salesmen and supervisors, even middle managers, didn't have wives who smelled like models. A surgeon was more her speed.

He hoped this Kurt guy was obnoxious, a controlling, obnoxious guy, because it made him slightly more palatable. They would probably live in a large house in Virginia or in Georgetown—he saw them entertaining other doctors and lawyers at sit-down dinners—and she wouldn't have to work anymore. She could go shopping for furniture with her sister. He knew he should be happy for her, let go and be happy—twenty-one years was a long time—but it had been eating him up since Joseph broke the news of her marriage, and he hadn't been able to get rid of the image of Claire and this man in Rome, walking among the ruins.

Did she remember the good days? Did she remember having sex for four hours on weeknights and her saying that he gave her just what she needed, even though the church wouldn't approve? Eric recalled laughing and saying that priests knew all about sex, don't worry; they learned it from sinners in confession. Tripping over a small stone, his horse lurched and he gripped the saddle horn to steady himself.

"How much farther?" Joseph called back.

"Not too far now," answered Lambert.

It was an hour already since they'd set out from Halpern's farm. After the rough drive around multiple curves into the foothills of the Blue Mountains—in the middle of which Janna had opened the Rover's window and breathed deeply to get rid of her nausea—it had been a relief to get out of the car and onto the horses. Now all he wanted to do was get off the horse.

"By the way," Lambert said, "how are your projections coming? You know, the five-year projections?"

"We started doing them this week, Shad and I. He's been telling me the new pay rates, and I don't know if he's giving me the right figures, but—"

"The last time you had receptionists and a full staff was how long ago, Eric?"

"Eight years."

"Exactly. Eight years is a long time in Jamaica, man. Inflation, the Jamaican dollar sinking against the U.S., the raised minimum wage, a lot has happened in eight years."

Eric shifted on the saddle. "Sometimes I wonder if it's worth it, you know, this hotel business."

"What are you talking about?" Lambert sounded alarmed.

"You know, the whole responsibility thing. Building and then running the damn place—"

"Hold on, hold on," Lambert said. "You need the money, right? You've been struggling with that bar for years, getting deeper and deeper in the hole. You're always complaining to me that you can't make ends meet. Unless you win the lottery or something, you need to make some more money, my friend. True or false?"

"True."

"And we both know that if you got sick or something, you don't have any extra money to handle it. You don't even have anything to leave to Joseph when you go. True or false?" Eric shrugged.

"The way I see it, you don't have a choice," Lambert said. "Your old age is coming—"

"Jeez, Lam, you don't have to—"

"No, I mean it, man. That's what friends are for, to tell each other the truth."

Mercifully, before Lambert had a chance to drive in another nail, the path opened to a spread of grass encircled by pine trees, the smell reminding Eric of Christmas. Following a track through the trees and around a bend, the party arrived at a small concrete house on a sloping lawn. Twenty feet square with a shingle roof, the house looked abandoned, its white paint peeling, the windows boarded up. The horses ambled through the tall grass and assembled in front of the verandah and, with Lambert's guidance, were maneuvered to face the view. In front of them was a clearing, at the edge of which clusters of yellow daylilies and purple agapanthus waved from what must have once been flower beds. Below them a valley descended at least four thousand feet to a hazy sapphire ocean in the distance.

"This is awesome," Joseph said, and took a swig of water.

"Why'd you buy it, Lam?" Eric asked, still chafing from Lambert's comments. "It's off the beaten track, to say the least. Seems like a waste of money."

"A man owed me for a job and he couldn't come up with the money at the end. We made a deal and he gave it to me. It's not too isolated. There's a truck road, but it's overgrown." The contractor climbed down from his horse and the others followed, tying the reins to one of the verandah posts.

"Let me show you around," Lambert said. He went ahead of them, his boots making a swishing noise in the grass. At the edge of the garden were several thick bushes, and he grabbed a branch with some red berries.

"What do you think this is?" he said, looking like a proud father.

Joseph picked a berry, smelled it. "Can I eat it?"

"Sure."

"Coffee," Joseph announced after he'd chewed on the berry.

"How did you know?" Eric said.

"There's this coffee shop at home, and they had some green beans there one day, kind of a coffee education day or something. I remember the taste."

"Do you know what kind of coffee?" Lambert asked.

Janna shook her head at her father. "Is this one of your tests, Daddy?"

"Of course it is," Lambert said brightly, relishing his moment. "This is important, folks. In Jamaica we have the arabica variety, not robusta, which is the other one. And Blue Mountain coffee is the finest in the world, next to one from Hawaii, Kona coffee, I think it's called. Anyway, arabica is better. Guess where it comes from?"

"Arabia," Janna said, punching the air.

"Right, the Middle East. That's where coffee drinking started."

"You sound like a damn teacher, Lambert," Eric said.

A horse's impatient whinny got their attention. "I bet that's my horse," Janna said dryly, and they all agreed it was.

"Who's up for lunch?" Lambert was off again, wading toward the house. Miss Bertha had packed lunch in the cooler tied to the back of Lambert's saddle. On a blanket on the verandah, they laid out ham, roast beef, and chicken salad, lemonade and ice tea, slices of fruit and—Joseph's favorite—banana bread. After lunch, the four stretched out discussing the scenery, the soaring John Crow vultures overhead, and the possibilities for developing the property, until Lambert started packing up.

"We don't want darkness to catch us driving down

the mountain," he reminded them. "I don't see well at night, anyway."

"And I don't have my night-driving glasses with me," Eric said.

"I'll drive," Joseph volunteered.

"On the left, in the dark? I'll remember that." Lambert laughed.

The ride down the mountain went faster than Eric expected, although his rear end had gone numb by the time they reached the long pasture at the bottom. They remained in single file, Joseph and Janna still in the lead, Lambert behind Eric. The horses neighing, happy to be near the farm. The land had cooled off and an afternoon breeze was blowing in from the sea.

"Janna," Joseph shouted over his shoulder, "race you back to the stables!"

He took off galloping the last half mile, smoothly rising and descending in the saddle like any Englishman after a hound. Janna hesitated for a second, then hit her horse on the rump with the reins. Startled, the horse gave a little neigh.

"Wait for me," she called as her mount started to trot, then to gallop, gathering speed. She bent over the horn and hung on. Still ahead, Joseph glanced back. His hair was whipping around his sunglasses as he galloped. From where Eric sat, it looked as if Janna's horse had come alongside Joseph's, easing its pace, but then it sped up again and raced forward, its rider's bottom bouncing up and down in the saddle. Janna started falling more and more to one side while the lean animal under her was all muscle and thrust—an old racehorse gone mad.

"Not so fast, Janna," Lambert shouted. "Rein him in."

"I can't," she yelled back. Her hair had broken loose and was bouncing wildly around her head. Lambert rode around Eric, trying to catch up with Janna and Joseph.

"Pull on the reins!" Lambert called. He was kicking the horse's sides like he was playing a drum.

Janna started screaming, "Stop! Stop!" like her life depended on it. Joseph was pulling alongside her, extending his arm toward the reins, but her horse was galloping at full throttle, smelling home, trying to stay ahead of its competition. Lambert was not far behind them, riding and beating his drum.

"Joseph," Eric called. "Do something!" His horse started galloping, but the others were getting farther away, their hooves kicking up clods of dirt in his face.

"Slow down, Janna," yelled Lambert. "Slow down!"

"Whooooaa!" Janna shouted. She was leaning dangerously to the side, her legs locked against the horse's belly. "Daddy, make it stop!"

"Joseph, grab the reins!" Eric yelled.

At that moment, Janna's long legs left the horse and sailed into the air, still in the shape of the horse's belly. She released the reins, crashed to the ground, and rolled over. When she came to rest, she lay like a rag doll, her hair fanned out around her head like a dandelion among the weeds.

CHAPTER SEVENTEEN

Some Sunday mornings in church, Shad had a smile on his face even before the service began. Like this morning. Yesterday afternoon he'd asked Beth to make up a pillow bed on the floor beside the girls and put Little Josh there for the night, and when he got home from work—after chasing Tri and Solomon out of the bar when the other customers had left—he'd found her asleep in the black nightgown he hadn't seen in years. When he slid into bed next to her, she continued to snore softly.

"I'm here, boonoonoonoos," he whispered.

Beth moaned. She'd had a busy day, he knew, what with selling in Saturday market and making sure the children's clothes were washed and ironed for church, but she'd put on the nightgown for him. And when he wrapped his arms around her, she woke up and turned to him, her breath a little sour.

"You like it?" she said.

"I love it," he said before turning out the light.

He'd liked it so much that this Sunday morning he was sure there was nothing Pastor could say that would annoy him. Ashanti, always in her own world, sat on her father's lap playing with the edges of her small book. Behind Pastor the choir was singing a hymn that Granny Matilda had loved and they'd sung at her funeral, and Shad's heart was full of gratitude.

"To the old rugged cross I will ever be true," warbled Miss Rose in the choir's front row. *"Its shame and reproach gladly bear; / Then He'll call me some day to my home far away, / Where His glory forever I'll share."*

The last note was hardly blown out the doors by the stiff sea breeze when Pastor McClelen stood up, a grim smile on his face. His hands hadn't even touched the podium when he started speaking.

"Give praise, brothers and sisters, give praise," he said, his frown not praising anybody. "A blessed morning, am I not correct?"

A few *Amen*s greeted him, and he repeated the question, stabbing the air with a skinny finger.

"A blessed morning!" Brother Paul shouted from the rear.

"Aha!" Pastor said, his eyebrows rising with his voice. "But what is blessed for one may not be blessed for another! Am I not correct, my people?"

"Correct!" called someone whose voice Shad didn't recognize.

"Because some are blessed, and some choose, hear me, right?—some *choose* to take the path not blessed!"

The baby started to whine, and Beth leaned over Shad to get a bottle out of the checkered diaper bag.

"What stupidness he coming with now?" Shad muttered, and Beth hushed him with a look.

"And we must be vigilant, brothers and sisters," Pastor hissed, "who we friends with, because if we are friends with people who *choose* to take the unblessed path, we are as guilty as them!" No one in the congregation knew what the man was talking about, but they were all nodding.

"And there are some among us, some who have *chosen* the path of iniquity." Pastor stopped and ran two fingers down the creases next to his mouth.

"They are the *ini*-quitous ones." In front of and behind Shad, folding chairs were shuffled, throats cleared in preparation for some new innuendo.

"There are those among us who indulge in the fruit of the plant called *senseh*," the minister said. "Men and women who choose to smoke that sinful weed, the weed that takes them away from the Lord." He gave several examples of the dangerous life that resulted from ganja smoking, including robbing people and having sex before marriage. Shad rolled his eyes up to the beams, noticing that the white paint he'd applied three years ago had started to peel in the corners. He wondered if Old Man Job still had it in him to paint them again with him next year.

Pastor started coughing. He cleared his throat and plowed on. "Then there are those who covet their neighbor's ass, covet his house, covet his car." Foreheads wrinkled, eyes kept low. Who was he talking about? There wasn't much to covet in Largo.

Shad looked out the window at the waves rolling in, rain clouds gathering on the horizon. *Covet,* now there was a word. Maybe there was a difference between covet and envy, but he didn't know what it was or which was worse, but he preferred *covet* because of the throaty sound of it.

"And some of those covetous people want another man's *wife* and commit adultery, breaking another of the Ten Commandments!" It took him at least fifteen minutes to give detailed examples, no names called, all observed from a distance, he hastened to add. Shad tried to match the examples with names, but got mixed up and stopped. Taking the handkerchief from the sleeve of his gown, the minister wiped his brow, working up to the climax.

He dropped his voice almost to a whisper. "We all know people who do these things. Some of them we may have done ourselves," he said, and flapped the kerchief. Then he paused and looked around at his frozen audience.

"But there is one sin, a demon sin," he roared. "Yes, a *demon sin,* my wife calls it, that we must never allow in this village."

The sound of waves hitting the beach entered the little church. All eyes turned to the back of his wife's head, to the purple hat with the feather that was quivering a little, to the young man beside her with the nearly bald head that nodded at each pause.

"The sin," Pastor said, pulling up to his tiptoes and rolling back down, dragging out the drama as long as he could, "is the sin of sodomy. Yes, *sodomy,* brothers and sisters." He opened his Bible, passing the handkerchief over his mouth and chin. No, he's not, Shad thought, clenching his teeth.

"It says here in Leviticus chapter eighteen, verse twenty-two," Pastor said, his finger on the passage, "'Do not lie with a man as one lies with a woman; that is des-test—'" He paused and started again, his voice sawing the air. "'Do not lie as—with a man as one lies with a woman; that is *de-testable.*'"

"Amen," shouted the faithful Arida. A few murmurs of agreement followed.

Taking a deep breath, Shad shifted Ashanti onto the other leg and looked at his children. Thank God, they were all distracted. Joella was trying to catch Winston's eye, patting her hair, and Rickia was reading, her glasses halfway down her nose.

"And further," Pastor said, his finger in the air, "Leviticus goes on to say in chapter twenty, verse thirteen, 'If a man lies with a man as one lies with a woman, both of them have done what is detestable. They must be *put to death*; their blood will be *on their own heads.*'" The man was almost braying now. Shad cleared his throat, loud enough for Pastor to look down at him and narrow his eyes.

"Let us all heed the word of God," the man said quietly, nothing like his usual loud endings. For a few seconds, he and Shad stared at each other. Then Pastor closed the Bible with a thump.

"Amen, I say, and amen. Let all the people say amen." And they did, everyone but Shad, who suddenly got busy looking for change for the collection.

As soon as the last word of the last hymn had died, Shad handed Ashanti to Rickia and slipped out the side door. He took a few deep breaths of air and looked at the ocean, alive this morning with waves three to four feet high.

"Brother Shadrack," said a deep voice near his arm. It was Mas Cedric, a fisherman who'd known his uncle and fished with them many nights, who'd shown him how to throw lobster pots so they wouldn't catch on the line. He was a small man, still full of stamina, only his face lined and tired.

"Brother." Shad nodded.

"Like you want to avoid shaking Pastor's hand on the front step, or what?" Cedric said with a chuckle.

"No, no, just a little hot in there. How the fishing going?"

"Well, my son doing most of the fishing now. He gone to Manchioneal, living with his girlfriend. I kind of retired, but I go out with him sometimes. But you know how it go. One week you catch fish—next week, you catching hell." Cedric laughed and coughed, the thick phlegm in his chest rattling.

"It not an easy life, I know that," Shad said.

The old man spat and wiped his mouth with the back of his hand. He straightened and turned to Shad. "What you think about what Pastor said?"

Shad glanced at the side door. "Well, it was the usual, you know. Some parts I don't directly agree with, you know?" Beth should be coming out soon. She always stayed too long chatting with the other women.

"You mean the part about sodomy, right? I hear you clear your throat. You didn't agree with him?"

Suddenly feeling the sun beating down on his head, Shad ran a hand over his scalp and squinted at the man. "Brother Cedric, we don't have to agree with everything a minister say from the pulpit."

"You don't agree with the Bible?"

"Some parts of the Bible, yes."

Cedric folded his arms. "But the Bible is the word of God. You don't believe that?"

"Master man, it seem to me that this Leviticus, who-ever he was, used to trouble himself too much with other people's business."

"But is a sin, man sleeping with man, you don't agree?"

"I believe that when a man talk so hard against some-thing, you must look twice. Leviticus, he have so much bad things to say about homosexuals, he might have liked the boys himself. What you say?" Shad tried a smile, but it wasn't going over with Cedric, who drew back and unfolded his arms.

"What you talking, boy? You realize you talking against the Bible!"

"I not talking against the Bible." Shad could feel his temper rising, reminded himself to respect the old man.

"You don't believe that Letivi—what his name, was speaking for God, that God make him say those things?"

"I never meet Leviticus yet, so I don't know if he speaking for God. What I believe is that Jesus say we are to love one another, and I believe that mean all of us, gay, straight, black, white, rich, poor." He couldn't keep his voice down anymore. Ignorance had a way of doing that to him. "And he say we not supposed to judge other people, because all of us is children of God. *That* is what I believe."

Shad nodded his good-bye to an openmouthed Cedric and stalked off to join the family.

"What you so excited about?" Beth asked.

"Just take me home before I get into trouble, you hear," he said. Sucking his teeth, he took Ashanti from Rickia and rubbed the little girl's back. "So, what for lunch?"

CHAPTER EIGHTEEN

The experience was forever remembered by Janna as a dream sequence. In what could only be described as super-slow motion, she saw herself leaving the horse's back, was aware of the coolness of the breeze on her face, knew that one of her sneakers had come off, decided to turn her head to the right to avoid hitting a rock—and blacked out. What they were later to tell her was that Joseph was off his horse first, cradling her in his lap.

"Janna, stay with me, can you hear me?" he'd said. The man's face was stricken, her father said, like he thought she was dead.

She didn't remember but was told by Joseph that Lambert had shouted, "Janna, baby!" and jumped down beside Joseph. Minutes later, Janna opened her eyes and closed them almost immediately.

"That's a good sign," she could hear Eric saying.

She remembered a few things afterward. What she remembered most was being held by Joseph after she fell. She remembered his acrid smell of sweat and deodorant, she remembered the rough touch of his shirt against her cheek and how he stroked her hair away from her face, and she remembered keeping her eyes closed for a few more seconds, because she didn't want him to stop.

It was a blur of noises after that—her father's voice saying something about taking her to the hospital, the jingling sound of keys, instructions to Eric to bring the car around. Then the sensation of being lifted in men's strong arms and placed in the back of a car, her head in someone's lap, and the rocking, soothing drive. When she opened her eyes again, she was lying in a small room, a harsh antiseptic smell pervading everything.

Lambert reached out and took her hand. "Hey, sweet pea, I'm here."

"Where am I?"

"In the emergency room in Port Antonio Hospital."

"I'm good, I'm good," she said, and lifted her head before groaning and lying back down, the pounding coming on.

"We'll tell the nurse you're awake," Lambert said. "They're going to do an X-ray, make sure everything is fine."

"I have a headache, but—" Suddenly aware of the three men hanging over her, looking helpless, all eyes focused on her, she patted the front of her blouse. It had ripped on one side and she pulled it as straight as it would go.

"I'll get the nurse," Eric said, and disappeared.

"Janna," Joseph said, "I am so, so sorry. I got you into this, I know."

She shook her head. "You don't have to—"

"I shouldn't have raced you. That was totally dumb."

149

He stroked her arm, and the adorable lock of hair fell across his eye.

"You have to pay for it," she said, and his frown disappeared.

"Anything."

"You have to keep me company sometimes, while I'm recovering from—whatever I'm recovering from."

"Absolutely."

Eric appeared at the foot of the stretcher. "The nurse is coming. She says to ask you if you remember the accident."

Janna blinked and rubbed one bare foot against the other. "I remember falling off a horse, coming down the mountain after seeing Daddy's place." She stopped, thinking of her shoes. "The horse—I was racing Joseph, and the horse took off."

Lambert clapped with a relieved smile. "Well, the memory sounds good."

"Joseph was in front of me, then my horse passed his—"

"That's right!" Joseph laughed softly in his throat. "You won the race!"

"I won the race," she said, and straightened her shorts.

Lambert moved up by her head. "Do I look a mess?" she said to him when he smoothed back her hair.

"You fell into the bushes and rolled around. What do you expect?"

"Don't tell Mummy, promise me, Daddy. She'd get upset and tell me to come back. You know how she is."

"We'll get you all better and you can tell her yourself,

if you want." Two orderlies wheeled her off to the X-ray department and she waved at the tall men staring after her.

There was a compulsory night in the hospital to observe her, and her father insisted on paying for a private room despite her protests. It was only one night and she wasn't to worry herself about it, he assured her. After the men left, nurses came in and out, checking her temperature, checking her pulse, checking her heart. Dinner was tasteless chicken and mashed potatoes she left almost untouched. Other than visits from the bossy nurses, she spent the night alone, a night filled with noises on the other side of her door. There were constant footsteps, two people sobbing together, a child asking for water, the cries of patients trying to get attention. Her call button didn't work, but she didn't need to call and remained silent herself. The next morning a young Indian woman came in and introduced herself.

"Your X-rays look pretty good," Dr. Ramnarine said after peering into her eyes and listening to her heart with a stethoscope. "You've had a very mild concussion, and we want you to stay in bed for a few days. You're going to have headaches on and off for a while. If they get so bad even an aspirin won't help, you'll need to come back." The woman spoke cheerfully with a clipped accent, each word distinct. "We're going to release you now."

"Can you call my father?" Janna asked, closing her gown.

"Someone is here to pick you up," the doctor said. "He's brought clean clothes for you."

Joseph's head appeared around the door a few minutes later. "My hero!" Janna squealed, and immediately wished she hadn't.

"The villain, you mean." He laughed, holding out an overnight bag. "Miss Bertha packed some clean clothes for you. Your dad had an emergency on the worksite, so he sent me. I think he forgot that I'd never driven on the left before, and I decided not to remind him!"

The drive home in Jennifer's car went too quickly for Janna. Although Joseph was driving tentatively, slowing down almost to a stop around the bends, she got dizzy and asked him to pull over a few times, enough to extend the trip, enough to enjoy his laughter, enough to hear the new tone in his voice, the new friendship he was offering, out of guilt or not. After they arrived at the house, he opened her car door to help her down, and when he placed his arm firmly around her waist, his chest brushing her face, Janna's knees went weak for a second.

Miss Bertha lumbered toward them with Sheba following, wagging her tail. The housekeeper took the bag from Joseph and jabbered all the way through the kitchen and into the house. Didn't Janna know that horses were dangerous and that young ladies were not supposed to ride them?

"Miss Bertha," Janna said as they hobbled down the hallway, the three of them crowding together, rounding the corner to her room, "whoever told you—" And she had to stop talking, because there were no words for what she was looking at. Her bedroom was full of sunshine, the light coming from hundreds of flowers, yellow flowers, branches of shower of gold, orange bird-of-paradise, buttery alamanders. Sitting on the tables beside the bed and the two lounge chairs, on the window seats, on the hope chest at the foot of the bed, on the floor, a memory she'd never forget her entire life, flowers lighting up every corner of the room.

"Oh, my God!" she said in a whisper, afraid of the answer. "Who did this?"

"Yellow, your favorite color, right?" Joseph guided her to the bed, a smile fixed on his face. She looked at him and saw the man she'd always wanted from at least age eight (the Ken to her Barbie), the man who knew how to walk unannounced into a woman's heart, who remembered what she said, who knew how to say he was sorry.

Dropping the bag on the hope chest, Miss Bertha put her hands on her hips. "This gentleman come over this morning, and he tell me to take out all my jugs and vases." She laughed and spread her arms. "You ever see anything like this madness?"

CHAPTER NINETEEN

I t was the summer of the cicadas when they got to the Cape, and if they'd known, they would have spent their honeymoon somewhere else, the noise was so deafening. Only after they'd paid and were unpacking in the dark basement did Claire look up and say, "What's that noise?"

Eric had stopped hanging a shirt in the closet and said, "What noise?" Then he heard it, the screeching-violin sound of millions of tiny insects out of tune with one another. From that moment on, they'd lived with the noise all day, every day, for the two weeks they were there, and sometimes it was so deafening it was hard to hear each other. The path from the basement up to the drive-way was littered with the dead carcasses of the creatures, fallen out of the trees, small, dry shells with red eyes.

"They only come once every seventeen years," the landlady had said. And that was the year.

The wind was coming landward toward the cliff to-night, had picked up speed. A half-moon allowed a vague insinuation of where the island and beach were. Eric lit his pipe again, shielding it with his hand. It was his favorite pipe, the one hand carved by a woman in the Ocho Rios market. When the tobacco was burning steadily, he resumed his gaze at the space in front of his verandah, allowing himself a minute to sink into the old *danzón* selection coming from his bedroom radio.

He'd perfected this staring into darkness over the course of the seven years since he'd lived in the apartment. It was a form of nightly hibernation that he looked forward to before going to bed, providing a comfort he'd never had in his earlier life. The soft Latin rhythms played at night on the Cuban stations distracted him from the strident music in the bar and from the reality of owning a bar. It helped him to forget his own father coming home every night from the Danny Boy after they'd all gone to sleep, waking them up with the rattling of keys and slamming of doors, leaving the stench of cigarette smoke in the corridor until the next morning.

Evenings now, the past would often come blowing back to him on the dark breeze. When Simone moved onto the island, her presence had forced him to stay in the present as he sat and stared, knowing exactly where the island was, even when there was no moon, guessing what she was doing at that moment, feeling her within reach. Tonight was different. He'd allowed himself the flight back three and a half decades, to his marriage and the screaming honeymoon.

They were an omen, the cicadas, the death knell from the beginning, because after the first few years, theirs had become a dry, dutiful marriage, and he'd come to understand that she'd only married him because her friends were getting married. It hadn't been all bad news. Early on, there were occasional moments of laughter, even hilarity, like the time they were apartment hunting and were looking at a place that was truly hideous, snickering, making comments as they walked through, outdoing each other, until they realized that someone was sitting in a dark corner watching them. They'd rushed outside holding their breaths until they got to the street and started running to the subway.

The early years had been the best, the three years before she announced she wanted a baby, even though he'd told her when they were dating that he didn't want children and she'd agreed. While she was pregnant, he'd found it hard to come home. The unborn child seemed to be separating them as it grew in her abdomen. With every purchase of crib and diaper table, he could think only of his own miserable childhood and that he didn't know how to be a father.

Footsteps sounded behind him. "Who's there?" Eric called.

"What's up?" It was Joseph, feeling his way in the dark.

"Hey, pull up a chair."

Joseph felt for the other verandah chair and sat down. "This what you do in the evenings?"

"Most of the time," Eric said, and spread the arm with the pipe. "Welcome to Casa Keller. Want a drink?"

"No, thanks, I just had one."

"What's up?"

"Shad suggested I come see you. This woman called Janet had me in lockdown."

"You're fresh meat, I guess." The two sat in silence looking in front of them, seeing nothing but blackness, Eric puffing on his pipe. It was the first time that his son had entered his apartment, had seen the minuscule living room with its square table and four hard chairs, the bedroom's single lamp and bare walls. His father's descent from a hotel suite. Maybe he needed to see it, Eric decided.

"How's Janna?"

"She's at home. I picked her up yesterday."

"How is she doing?" Eric took the pipe out of his mouth, looked at his offspring in the weak moonlight, at his mother's strong jaw and high cheekbones.

"Seems to be fine, she had a big bowl of soup for lunch."

"That's good."

Below them, waves were hitting the cliff rhythmically, competing with the soca music next door—three discordant rhythms with the *danzón* on the radio. A cricket squeaking in the bougainvillea bush next to the verandah made a fourth.

"Did you know your mother and I spent our honeymoon on Cape Cod?"

"Maybe, I can't remember."

The breeze was swirling Eric's hair around, and he pulled it back from his face. "Yeah, it was quite a trip. One day we took the ferry over to Martha's Vineyard. We ended up on this beach with a bunch of naked people." He laughed and turned to Joseph, who was looking straight ahead. "Your mother was too embarrassed to swim." There'd been this man with an enormous dick walking around. Claire was so mortified she'd lain down with her arm over her eyes and refused to leave until the man had packed up and gone.

"I heard you had a paying guest out there," Joseph said, pointing at the island.

"Who told you?"

"Shad."

"He talks too much, that's his problem." Eric clamped the pipe between his teeth, the embers barely glowing.

"What was her name?"

"Who?"

"The woman."

"Simone, Simone Hall."

"How did she end up there?"

Eric took his pipe out of his mouth. "She'd lost her daughter, her only child, I believe, and she was having a—a sort of breakdown. She was looking for a place to be alone and she ended up on the island."

"Did she have a tent?"

"A tent?"

"Yeah. I was thinking that tents would be kind of cool. Maybe you could use the island to earn extra income, you know, set up a campground among the ruins, take them over in boats. . . ."

Eric frowned, unwilling to picture tents on his property, with cheap guests swarming around. "She didn't have a tent. She'd built a roof, a tarpaulin with wires and whatnot, over the old reception area. When we got there—Shad and I went over to see what was going on—

she'd already set up camp. Quite self-sufficient, actually. She'd created a kitchen under the almond tree like a Girl Scout or something."

"Why'd she leave?"

"A storm came up and tore the tarp away."

"I heard her brother got the investor interested in building a hotel here."

"That's right, Cameron. Nice guy."

"What's his cut?"

"I figured that was between him and his client, the investor guy."

"Not necessarily. He might want a commission for pulling the deal together."

Curling up his toes in his flip-flops, Eric sighed. "I hadn't thought of that, to tell the truth. We never talked about it."

"You need to know if I'm going to include it in the figures."

There was the silence again, the staring into darkness.

"Was she good-looking?"

Eric slid the pipe out of his mouth. "I guess you could say that. She was an advertising executive or something, but she stayed out there for two months, all by herself, so by the time she left the island, she was looking pretty wild. Nothing like when she came. We thought she was a goat when we first saw her. All we could see from the bar was this black hair bouncing around the top of the bushes. Then Shad borrowed Miss Mac's binoculars and saw she was a woman." He slapped his knee and laughed. "Oh, God, we almost had a fit!"

"You liked her, didn't you?"

"Liked her? Yeah, she was nice, is nice, I guess. She isn't dead."

"No, I mean you really liked her, the way you're talking about her." There was a smile in Joseph's voice.

Eric bent down and tapped out the pipe on the chair leg. "I did," he said.

"You had an affair."

It hadn't really been an affair, the kind of sex-soaked event he'd had with a passing tourist on several occasions. In fact, it had taken a long time to develop, much longer than he would have liked. He hadn't preyed on her, nothing like that, but from the beginning, he'd had this compulsion to see her and would count the days until he could row out with some flimsy excuse, taking her fruit or laundry, anything to see her again. There'd been no rushing her, because she'd been so bitter when she got there, their discussions brief and to the point, but over the weeks she'd become lonely and started talking to him whenever he came. It had brought them together, the loneliness. And when she got to the point where she could see a life ahead for herself, they'd become lovers.

"When is she coming back?" Joseph said.

"When did you get so nosy?" They both laughed at the same time, in almost the same way, back in their throats.

"I'm just asking because—because you liked her, still like her. Maybe you could both—"

"Don't even go there."

"Why not? You're thinking about Mom all of a sudden, about a marriage that's been dead for over twenty years, and here you have a nice woman, an attractive woman—you said so yourself—and you're not even doing anything about it. She could be waiting around for your call, you don't know."

Eric sat forward, uncomfortable but still relishing the banter he'd never had with his son before. "Here you are," he ventured, "half my age, less than half my age, and you're telling me how to live my life. I'm the person who held your head on the Staten Island Ferry when you were vomiting your guts out, remember? I'm the father here."

"I just meant—"

"Uttered the longest sentence to me that has ever come out of your mouth, and it's to tell me to call some woman you don't even know." He leaned back in his chair and smiled at the Irishness of what he'd just said.

"Well, are you going to?"

Standing slowly, allowing the circulation to come back to his legs, Eric kicked the ashes left by the wind toward the edge of the verandah.

"I'll think about it," he said.

CHAPTER TWENTY

Being a *full-size woman,* as she called herself, Miss Bertha had trouble reaching across the bed and smoothing the sheet down, and she was puffing by the time she finished. She took a breath and straightened her uniform, the plaid bandanna pattern tight across her wide hips.

"Can I get back in now?" Janna said from an armchair, stroking one of her pigtails.

"Let me plump up the pillows first."

Climbing into bed, Janna thanked her again and reminded her that she could make her own bed.

Bertha blew it aside. "Like how you just come back from hospital, I want to make sure you comfortable, like your father say."

"I think you're missing Jennifer and Little Wayne, and you have nobody to fuss over."

"You right, and your father don't seem to need nothing neither."

The housekeeper looked around the room with her big smile. "I love your flowers." Much as she loved the flowers, it was the housekeeper's firm belief that they should be nowhere near sick people at night. She'd muttered something about plants sucking the life out of sleeping people and taken every vase of flowers out of the room the evening before—lining them up along the corridor wall—and replaced them earlier that morning.

"You know what they say when a man give you flowers." Bertha laughed and clapped.

"What?"

"It mean he sweet on you."

"You think he likes me?"

"So the old people say. When a man bring you flowers—"

"I like how you rearranged them," Janna said.

"I always like things looking nice. Miss Jennifer, she say I is *artistic*."

"And you put them in front of the mirror, so when the sun hits them, the ceiling looks all yellow. The whole place glows."

"Yes, man, brighten up the place. I come back later with your lunch." The woman and her uniform pattered out of the room.

Janna leaned back on the pillows. It was still hard to believe that she was in a mahogany four-poster bed looking out at the ocean like in a tourist brochure, her every need met with meal trays and a bell beside the bed, and it was even harder to believe that she'd fallen off a horse and an amazingly handsome man had filled her room with flowers by way of apology. If the intention of coming here had only been to keep her father company and apply for jobs, the reality was turning out to be a lot more dramatic than the plan. And she liked drama, she decided, because it had an edge to it that was by no means milquetoast.

The afternoon before, she'd called Lorraine and told her the whole story. "And I'm sitting here in this unbelievable *bower*—"

"A what?"

"A bower, you know, like a garden. Anyway, Joseph picked all these yellow flowers and just filled my room with them. You should see them. They take up every available shelf and tabletop around me. I don't know what he was thinking."

"Sounds fabulous. Maybe he was feeling guilty."

"I hope not."

"There's nothing wrong with a healthy dose of guilt in a guy," Lorraine purred. "It makes them notice you."

The words had rung in Janna's ears after she hung up. Even now when she picked up her book, she wondered if she should be playing on Joseph's guilt, or if she already was. When he visited later, appeared with a bouquet of hibiscus, her first thought was that he wouldn't be there if it hadn't been for the accident and she hadn't made him promise to visit.

"You are the sweetest man," she said, conscious that her hair looked childish in pigtails. "I know you have to work."

He waved the red flowers in his hand. "I thought you might need something to contrast with all the—"

"Yellow," she said. "I love it, though. I'll never look at yellow the same way again. It's like a room full of—joy." A room that reminded her of him every minute of the day, the most romantic thing possible. She'd taken photographs of the room and the flowers earlier that morning and text messaged one to Lorraine, and she planned to keep the photos as long as possible to remind herself that a man had done this for her once.

After he placed the flowers in the bathroom sink, Joseph sat down in an armchair near the window. "How are you feeling?"

"A slight headache, but not as bad as yesterday. I'm eating like a horse, though. Not like *that* horse," she added quickly, and Joseph laughed. She liked making him laugh. "What was her name?"

"Carlotta."

"Sweet Carlotta, I'll never forget her."

"Any black-and-blues?"

"A few, none that I can show you," she said, pointing at her right hip. He only smiled this time and placed one ankle on top of the other knee, held the leg with both hands like he was holding on to a fence. The firm way he held on to that fence spoke less of keeping her out than of keeping himself in.

"What are you doing with your time?" he asked.

"Getting a lot of rest, maybe too much. I need to start sending out some job applications, at least."

"Time enough for that, but I know what you mean. I should be applying for work myself." He picked up a small vase of flowers and smelled one. "I was telling this friend of mine that it feels really strange to apply for jobs in Washington, DC, from Largo Bay." He looked up, his eyes now almost green, reflecting the yellow. "America seems like the other side of the moon."

They talked about work, or the work they'd like to have and didn't yet have. She described the animation work she wanted to do in the film industry, particularly in children's movies and cartoons, only there wasn't much of an industry on the East Coast, except in New York. There was nothing going on in Florida, she said. Atlanta had only one film studio, and they didn't do that kind of stuff. New York was far away, and her father and mother weren't keen on her going to the Big Apple or to LA. "They think I'll get kidnapped or something. How about you?"

"I've been looking in DC, Virginia, Maryland. The competition is pretty intense, though." He looked out the window. "I need to add this hotel business plan to my résumé. It'll help, I hope. They say that for every job opening, there are at least five qualified applicants and sometimes hundreds of applications—not very good odds."

"If you start thinking that way, you'll never find anything."

"I'm just being practical," he said, and uncrossed his leg, looking down at it.

"Maybe if you visualize yourself—"

"Oh, don't start that." He shook his head, waving the idea away.

"Don't knock it until you've tried it."

"How'd you do it?" he said politely, like it was part of the visit.

"I made this board and put it in my dorm room in Miami. It had all kinds of stuff on it, all the things I

wanted in the near future, even the banner of the newspaper I wanted to work with—the *Miami Herald,* of
course—and it all came true. I even lived in an apartment
just like the one I had on my board."

He wiggled his eyebrows skeptically, but she kept
going. "I'm telling you, the darn thing works, this whole
vision board thing. I don't know how, but it does. It's
like you draw the stuff to you or something." She knew
it sounded trite. "I had to make a new one after Tampa.
Things change."

She told him about the vision board standing right
now on her chest of drawers in Fort Lauderdale. The
magazine cutouts came back to her as she spoke, and
she described how she'd pasted ads and words onto the
poster board—pictures of the car and house she wanted
to buy, photographs of friends having dinner together,
the cartoon of a young woman sitting in front of a computer with a big grin. She didn't mention the picture of
a couple getting married, standing on a beach kissing,
the hem of the woman's wedding dress getting wet. Nor
did she speak of the large red heart she'd drawn around
the picture.

"A bit airy-fairy for me," he said, his lip curling on
one side.

"What do you have to lose?"

"Nothing, I guess."

"It could be fun."

"If you say so." He clapped his hands and stood up.
"Got to go, work calls," he said, and winked, making a
warm liquid explode in her chest. Watching him leave

the room, relishing every move he made, the swing of his arms, the sauntering walk (a slight bow to the long legs), the flipping of the curl behind his ear, Janna knew she was past the point of no return. She was falling, falling for this man, and, whichever way it turned out, she'd be falling into thorns—and it would be worth it.

Later, when the housekeeper came in with her lunch, Janna asked about old magazines. There were tons of them, Miss Bertha said, and she was dying to get rid of them.

"When Joseph goes to lunch, could you look in Jennifer's office and see if you see some poster board, large pieces of thick white paper? She probably has them for the kids."

"Those in the nursery, with all the art things," Miss Bertha said.

"Great! I'll need two of those, some markers, all different colors, glue, and scissors, two pairs of scissors, if you have them, and the magazines. And when Joseph gets back, can you please tell him I'd like to see him when he's finished working?"

It wasn't a *plot,* as Lorraine called it later. It was something to keep them both on task, she would answer, just a device to help them aim for their higher objective: to get jobs. She'd decided to create another board for herself, this one totally professional. It would describe the perfect workplace and boss, the kind of work, everything, and show nothing personal this time.

When Joseph entered her room that afternoon, she was sitting in one of the armchairs reading, changed into jeans. Her hair fell around her face in waves and she was wearing lip gloss. Atop the white bedspread were two poster boards, each with a rectangular box at the top. *Janna's Future,* she'd written in one, the letters striped with red and yellow markers. On the other board she'd written *Joseph's Future* in black, with green dollar signs on each side. Magazines, markers, scissors, and glue were in a basket at the foot of the bed.

"Oh, my God." He laughed and slapped his thigh.

Janna handed him a pair of scissors. "Your destiny awaits you, sir," she said, leaving him no choice.

CHAPTER TWENTY-ONE

"Did you bring the medicine the last doctor gave us?" Shad asked just after they'd left Largo Bay behind.

"In my bag," Beth said. She was holding Ashanti on her lap, had tied them both in with the seat belt. The Jeep was creaking more than usual, Shad thought. He'd take it into Zeb for a grease-and-spray when he got back. The boss never remembered. The vehicle could be falling apart in the parking lot and he'd never even notice. It was all right for the boss, who hardly went anywhere, but when you lived in a place like Largo, far from things, you needed transportation for emergencies and picking up people from the airport. You had to keep your vehicle alive, had to have pride in the things you owned.

Traffic was light in Port Antonio, and Shad wound his way around the town square. There were major renovations going on in the gingerbread government buildings and old courthouse, and he had to drive carefully around the orange cones and scaffolding. On the way out of town, a detour sign blocked their path and directed them up a hill.

170

"What is this?" Beth said. "They going to make us late."

Shad hit the edge of the window. "Pshaw, man, they always doing this when elections coming up."

The nurse had said they should come early so they could fill out some forms. She'd had a deep voice on the phone, and Shad had pictured her as a mature woman who knew what she was doing, who wore closed shoes and had a bun like Miss Mac. They'd never been to this doctor before and they didn't know how much he would charge, so Beth had brought all her money from last Saturday market and Shad had brought his tip money from the last two nights.

When the detour ended and he swung back onto the main road, Shad pressed down hard on the accelerator and the Jeep sprang forward. Beth gripped the door and turned to him, irritated again. "You want to kill us or what?"

"You was the one said we going to be late."

"Haste make waste, so ease up, man. We going to have a long wait, anyway. Every doctor have a packed waiting room."

"True," Shad said, and slowed down.

They wound around the narrow coastal road, a road with a hundred corners, a road that made all but the strongest stomachs weak. After they passed Annotto Bay, Ashanti was whining, pushing to open the door, going into one of her tantrums. Shad pulled the car over onto the beach side and got out. He took Ashanti from Beth through the passenger window and held her at an angle so she could vomit into the dead leaves on the side of the road. After wiping her mouth with a tissue, he walked with her in his arms toward the beach.

"Breathe deep," he said, and took a deep breath himself to show her. Ashanti ignored him and looked around at the rocky, treeless beach. She liked being here, being in his arms, he could tell. She had the dreamy, peaceful look that sometimes replaced the vacant look or the angry look.

"Sea," she said, almost inaudibly.

"Sea," her father repeated, taking her hand in his and pointing toward the reef.

Back on the road, the child fell asleep in Beth's arms, lulled by the noises of ocean, wind, and Jeep. Beth nodded off once and started awake. There was a peace between them, sitting like this, knowing they would be together forever, a peace Shad liked. She was his best friend, a woman he could trust, the kind of woman who deserved the best he could give.

Years ago, a foreign guest at the old Orchid Bar had asked him one night, "Do you know what a woman of substance is? That's what I'm looking for—a woman of substance." Shad had agreed, liking the expression, knowing that he had what the wealthy guest didn't.

Only a few more miles to Ocho Rios, and the traffic was getting thicker, slowing them down.

"You thought about it some more?" Beth asked.

"What?"

"The wedding."

Shad sighed. He'd had a feeling she'd bring it up. It

wasn't in her to waste a good opportunity like a long car ride. "Not much, everything too hectic."

"If we going to have it, we have to plan it from now."

"We going to have it, I told you. What you want to plan?"

"I have to make the dress, and I have to start soaking the fruit for the cake. And we have to book the church and Pastor and we have to make out the invitation list—"

"I just want to be sure we have the money. It sounding expensive already, dress and cake and invitations." He slowed down behind a large truck. Market women were seated on planks of wood facing them, their baskets of yams, tomatoes, and avocados tied to planks above their heads. "We have to take time, like how Joella going to school in Port Antonio next year—"

"Shad," she said, giving him the same squinty look Granny used to give him when she thought he was lying, "you don't want to get married, or what? You talk about it, but you always backing out, putting it off. You can't keep telling people that we husband and wife. I don't even have a ring." She rubbed Ashanti's tummy and looked out the window. "I don't want to be like everybody else in Largo, just have a common-law marriage. I want the real thing, with a wedding and a ring like Kingston people. Pastor say we to marry in the sight of the Lord. Tell the truth," she said, turning to him, "you don't want to marry me, or what?"

"What you mean? I not marrying anyone else. You are the onliest woman I ever want to marry. I have four children with you—and I not going nowhere. Believe me, we going to marry properly one day, in church like Parson say. You can't rush these things."

She squeezed her lips together and they rode for a while, staring out different windows. "Okay, okay," he said, unable to bear one more minute of cold silence from his woman, "go ahead and look at next year's calendar. Find a Saturday afternoon that free—not Christmas or Easter weekend, or Labor Day weekend, or Independence, and not near end of month, because we busy in the bar. It must be at least six months away, because we have to start saving now, putting little something aside every week, you know? And don't plan anything big, just a few people, family and so."

She turned to him and shook her head. "Shadrack Myers, if you change your mind again, I going to kill you."

"No, man," he said, "we going do this." And he meant it, at least for now.

When they got to the doctor's office, it was, as Beth had predicted, full of waiting patients, mostly women and children. They found a seat and waited, one hour, two hours, with babies crying, people coughing, Ashanti making her hunger noises. Beth fed her some bread and cheese and promised her chicken soup later. The doctor was a woman, not what they'd expected. She was older, with a deep voice, the woman who'd spoken to him on the phone. Her gray hair was cut short in a natural and her eyes looked tired. She took Ashanti's temperature and looked into her eyes and ears.

"She quiet all the time, doc," Shad said. "Sometimes she say a few words, but only one or two words at a time."

"How old is she?"

"Four," Beth said.

"She's healthy enough," the doctor said. "Smaller than normal body size, but no physical problems I can find."

"She don't play good with the other children," Beth said. "She stay to herself most of the time, unless she need something. And she don't listen when you speak to her, like she not hearing you."

The doctor spoke to Ashanti, hit her knee with a little hammer, gave her a plastic tractor to play with. Ashanti stared at the tractor and put her finger in her mouth. She started rocking back and forth on the examination table, sucking her finger and hitting her thigh the way she did sometimes. Beth and Shad looked at each other when the doctor used a word they'd never heard before.

"*Autism?*" Shad said. "What that mean?"

Leaning against the counter with the boxes of syringes and cotton balls, the doctor explained what autism was, using more words than Shad could digest at one time. One fact became clear. It was a brain problem, the doctor said. Ashanti's brain wasn't the same as other children's.

"She always going to be this way, doctor? What we can do about it?" Shad said, the questions Beth was too terrified to ask.

"Not much, I'm afraid," the doctor said, and shook her head. "There are no schools in your area to deal with it, so unless you plan to take her to Kingston or Mo Bay, you have to deal with the problem at home. If you have an Internet connection, you can read about it. Or if you have a nurse in your community who knows about autism, you can ask her what you should do. You going to need a lot of patience with this child." She left the room and returned with some reading material on neon-colored paper and gave them a phone number to call. Shad didn't mention that he had no phone and that the nurse came to the Largo clinic only a couple of times a week and you had to wait a whole day to see her.

"Thank you," he said, knowing Ashanti would be the child who'd never leave home. He pictured a white-haired Beth and himself taking care of a grown, rocking Ashanti. Another question he wanted to ask almost slipped his mind until the woman's hand was on the doorknob.

"Doc, one more thing, please." The doctor turned, and Shad stood up. "Do you know anything about gay people, about gayness?"

"Your daughter isn't homosexual, that's not what's wrong with her," the woman said, pulling in her chin.

"No, I asking about somebody else," Shad said. "What I really want to know is what cause this homosexual business? We have people where we live who say people choose it, and they sinful to choose it. What you say, Doc?"

The physician leaned against the counter again, and Shad hoped that didn't mean she was going to charge them more for answering the question. "Homosexuality," the medical woman said, crossing her arms tightly, "is not a sickness. Neither do most people choose it. They just feel attracted to people of their own sex; they can't help it." There was something about the woman that

176

made you believe her, the firm way she said it, like a teacher or a policewoman would.

"What causes the gayness, Doc?"

"We still don't know exactly. Some people say it's caused by experiences that homosexuals have as children. Some researchers say it's caused by the level of hormones a baby is born with, or the way the brain was formed in the womb."

"You mean, they come out of the mother's belly like that?"

"We're not sure, but it could be that a gay man is born with a low level of a chemical called testosterone, and a gay woman is born with a high level of testosterone. We still have a long way to go to find out exactly what causes it."

"Intriguing," Shad said, stroking his chin, and the doctor smiled. "So, when they grow up, can they decide to become normal people, to stop being homosexual?"

"No, for the most part, although some people say gay people can be trained to become like *normal people*." She said the last words like she was making fun of him. "There are all kinds of homosexuals, you know, even some who can be attracted to either a man or a woman. Those are called *bisexuals*."

"What?" said Shad, and leaned toward Beth with his eyes wide. "You ever hear anything like that in your life? They can sleep with a man or a woman!" He turned back to the physician. "Doc, they have people like that in Jamaica, these bisexuals?"

"Of course, they have them all over," the woman replied, "but most homosexuals prefer to have sex with people of their own gender. It just comes naturally to them."

It was only after they'd paid the cashier—with no fee for the second part—and gotten back in the Jeep that Beth spoke again.

"Ashanti going to get better, or what?" she said.

"It don't sound so, but she not going to get worse, either. We must read the papers she give us."

Beth was quiet for a while, stroking the top of Ashanti's head. The child pushed her hand away and looked down at the lollipop the doctor had given her.

"Why you ask the doctor that question, about gay people?"

Shad shrugged. "Long time now, I want to know what make them different from us."

When they were circling the clock in downtown Ocho Rios to head back home, Beth spoke his thoughts. "I wonder if Joseph is a gay."

Shad turned and looked at her for a second, the woman who read his mind. "I don't know. One day I think he queer, and the next I don't."

"He going out with Janna, though."

"Exactly."

"You think the doctor was a gay?"

"Why you say so?"

"She kind of mannish, you don't find? And she talk so strong about it—stronger than about Ashanti—and she don't have on a wedding ring."

"Maybe she waiting for her man to marry her," he said

with a wink. Beth twisted her mouth to one side while she unwrapped the lollipop for Ashanti. A man pushing a cart heaped with large, green breadfruit caused Shad to slow the car to a crawl, and when he swung around the sweaty man, Shad thought of the doctor and realized something for the first time: gay women also had it hard in Jamaica. Like Florencia, a stocky girl who always wore boy's shorts and had gone to Mandeville to work with a security firm. People had talked about her, had made sneering comments that must have been painful, sometimes made them to her face, although she laughed them off. Still, no one had chased her out of town.

The hunt, the lynching, seemed to be saved for gay men, because, for some reason, they had to be eliminated. They were not to be forgiven, because to be like a woman was supposed to mean you were weak. When the truth was that those women—Florencia, Beth, Granny, and the other heroes—had never been weak at all.

CHAPTER TWENTY-TWO

I t was a quiet midafternoon and the bar was empty. Eric pulled up Shad's bar stool to the counter where the phone was sitting. He was going to call her and let the phone ring five times, he'd decided. If she didn't answer by then, he was going to hang up, because there was nothing more pathetic than the voice of an ex-boyfriend leaving a message, sounding all lovelorn.

Placing his glasses on his nose, he looked at the pink Post-It note. Then he stood up and opened the fridge door and got out an orange. He peeled the orange round and round, keeping the peel intact. Maisie had once told him that if the peel didn't break, he'd have a good marriage. He'd learned how to peel it in one go, but Maisie was still wrong. Eating the orange one peg at a time, he looked over at the island, wishing a goat's head would bob up over the bushes.

It had been three days since Joseph had suggested he call Simone, and he'd pushed the thought away until he was finished with Claire, and he'd been finished with Claire when he realized that every single thing he owned that had reminded him of his ex-wife had been washed away by the hurricane. Every photograph, every letter, every legal document was gone, and there was nothing to bind them together anymore, not even a marriage certificate. That had consumed one night of contemplation. By the next night he'd decided to move on, like Claire had moved on, and started thinking about his future hotel and, yet again, about the woman who'd made it possible.

The number rang once. She might be at work. She could have changed her mind and gone back to work. It rang twice. She might be out shopping. Three times. Or she could be taking a nap.

"Hello." Her voice was warmer, less haughty than it used to be.

"Simone? Hey, it's me, Eric."

"Eric!" She was surprised, he could hear it, and she needed time to accept that he'd called.

"Calling from Largo Bay," he said with a chuckle to hide the fact that he was a romantic old fool.

"It's good to hear from—"

"I thought I'd take a chance."

There was a question in her voice. "It's good to—to hear from you, Eric."

"Just wanted to find out how you're doing."

"I'm well, doing well." He pictured her with her hair cut close to her head, the way she'd had the barber cut it before she left, and his fingertips itched to stroke it.

He cleared his throat. "Back at work?"

"No, I quit. I think I told you I was going to." Her voice dropped all of a sudden, the way it did just before he kissed her.

"That's right, I forgot." He should have thought this through, jotted down some notes. "Cameron gave me your number. I called him to get the investor guy's number and—"

"I'm glad you called."

"Everything okay up there?"

"Yes, fine." A noise in the background like she was doing something else. Maybe someone was with her. Maybe a man. He hadn't thought of that, dammit.

"If you're busy—"

"No, this is a good time. I'm cleaning out Celeste's old room." She paused and he heard her take a sharp breath. "My friend Dorella is helping me."

"Oh, Jeez, that must be tough." He imagined her surrounded by the remnants of her dead daughter, posters on the wall, clothes hanging in the closet, boxes on the floor.

"How's the island?" she said all of a sudden. The noises stopped, like she'd sat down or left the room.

"Still there, still empty. I'm looking at it right now."

"I can hear the breeze in the background," she said. Then she laughed, remembering. "Always the breeze, eh?"

"Always." In the silence, her breath was coming through the phone, right onto his neck.

"My son is here now," he said, regretting it immediately, hearing the boast that his child was alive and hers wasn't.

"Oh, that must be nice for you." She sounded genuinely pleased for him.

"Yeah, he's working up the financial proposal for Cameron's client, for the hotel."

"I'm glad you're going ahead with it."

"He wants to turn the island into a campground or something, I dunno."

"Oh, I can see that."

"D'you think so? I thought—"

"No, totally. I think it could work, I really do."

"I'll have to give it a name."

"What are you going to call it?" He had her attention, saw the twin furrows between the thin, arched eyebrows.

"I thought I'd call it Simone Island. What do you think?" He flushed as if she could see him.

"I love it! An island named after me, oh, my God." She was happy, would be wearing that wide, face-splitting smile he remembered, the one she'd kept for the end of her trip.

"I wanted your permission. Would that be too—?"

"Of course you have my permission. I mean, it's your island."

"I just thought—well, that's good, then. I'll go to the Parish Council and fill out the papers."

"I'll even come back and stay in the camp, bring a few friends to the island." She was smiling again, he could tell, probably planning what friends she'd bring.

"Right," he said. No way she was going to stay there with some man, over his dead body. "Well, I'll let you know when it's official. How about that?"

"Please do."

"Take care, then."

"Thanks for calling, Eric. Call again—if you want to."

"I'll do that," he said. And it was over, just like that, even though his heart kept racing for a long while after.

CHAPTER TWENTY-THREE

J oseph was running backward across the field, his powerful legs and thighs pushing as fast as he could, but
not fast enough. The small orange-and-blue kite refused to rise more than a few feet off the ground, the tail
of bright plastic squares bobbing up and down as he ran,
stroking the grass.

"Pull up, pull up," Janna shouted, her slender arm
high, mimicking his.

"I'm trying, but—" He kept looking over his shoulder,
left and right, trying not to bump into any children tugging at their kites. For a minute his kite rose higher off
the ground, the tail dancing in S shapes. He looked much
younger, almost like a boy, a grin on his face, making her
heart soar. She sat down on the grass, clapping and laughing. Around her there were clumps of people attending
to their kites or admiring those of others. A family on a
blanket nearby struggled to assemble a large eagle kite, the
adults more interested than the kids, who were digging into
a picnic hamper and pulling out treats. At the far end of the
field, Joseph's kite fell to the ground, the kite they'd bought
when they arrived, and he was winding up the string.

"There's not enough wind," he said after he'd run back across the field. She loved how he collapsed onto the grass beside her, the way in which his long legs fell, one on top of the other. One of his Dockers fell off his foot.

"We can wait for the wind," she said. "I want to try next."

"You're not supposed to, that's what your father said. I told him I'd be flying the kite and you'd be watching." He sounded like an uncle, breathing heavily, not taking any nonsense.

"But if there's a good wind—"

"Good wind, no wind, it doesn't matter." She made a face, tried not to look at him the way she felt, all soft inside because he was trying to take care of her.

"Question," she said. "Where did you learn to fly a kite?"

He laughed, his head thrown back, the sun sneaking in behind his sunglasses and lighting up his eyelashes and the light-brown bristles on his chin. It was all she could do not to tell him how amazing he looked.

"Oh, God, confession time, I've never flown a kite in my life." They laughed together, she in her thrift store shorts that showed off her legs, and he in his Banana Republic shirt.

"You ride a horse like a pro, but you've never flown a kite," she said, shaking her head. "You're definitely uptown."

He sat up and fit his shoe back on. "Because I've never flown a kite?"

"Yes, because you've never flown a kite. Kite flying is

an essential element of childhood education, didn't you know that? Making it from old plastic bags, cutting your fingers on the thread, pulling it up until you hear that whistle and you know you're clear—oh, man, that's life for a kid. For me it was, anyway. My father used to take me to the university campus and we'd fight with the kite and the wind. Then he'd take me for an ice cream after. It was great."

"That sounds like fun, but it sure wasn't my childhood."

"Didn't you do stuff with your dad?" She shook her head, laughing.

His face straightened, only the shadow of a smile left. "My father and I—I was just thinking this morning, all this stuff is coming back to me—we're just—different." He'd never talked that frankly before, and she almost stopped breathing, not wanting to cut him off. "He'd— I don't know—he'd want to play touch football in the backyard and take me to games, but he never asked me, never *once* asked me, what I wanted to do. I tried to go along with the stuff he liked, I did, but—I don't know— I just wasn't into football and fly-fishing, I guess." He plucked at some grass and threw it aside. "I never felt like I belonged with him, no matter where we were or what we were doing. I think he tried, sometimes anyway, but I always thought he was kind of—crude, you know. A nice enough guy, I guess, but—"

"So you're closer to your mother, then?"

"I guess so, but she's not a person you can get close to. She allowed me to make my own choices when I was growing up, I give her that, but she's not a touchy-feely type, you know. My mother—my mother never comments much about my life. She allows me to live the way I want to, as long as I don't embarrass her. She doesn't like that. She likes things in their place, people in their place. We respect each other, I think you could say."

"And she brought you up to be a Little Lord Fauntleroy," she said, trying a tease to lighten his heaviness. He smiled at her obligingly with his mouth, not his eyes.

"I'm just joking," she said. "I'm not accustomed to being with—you know, guys who did horseback riding and ballroom dancing. That's pretty high-class to me. I mean, I come from a bicycle-riding, kite-flying background. My cultural training was learning to make some really bad ceramic pots in high school and salsa dancing in Miami." She patted his arm and leaned toward him. "I like being around you, Lord Fauntleroy, that's what I'm trying to say. You make me feel—expensive."

"Don't worry, my skin isn't that thin," he said, but she wasn't sure, because his mouth was still tight.

"I have an idea." She switched on her English accent. "Milord, would you do me the favor of buying me a snow cone?"

"A what?"

She leaned back on her arms. "A snow cone. That's part of your third-world education, so make a note. It's shaved ice with syrup on top. Good stuff, man."

He jumped up and held out his hand. "Oh, I remember those in New York," he said. "My mother wouldn't let me have one, though."

She held on to both of his hands and took her time getting up. When they were standing face-to-face, he released one hand. "Feeling all right?" he said.

"Suddenly got a little dizzy, that's all."

"And you want to fly a kite."

He bent down to pick up the kite, and she turned toward the snow-cone truck, loosening but not releasing his hand, curling her right hand around the fingers of his left to secure them. They were still holding hands when they got into the line at the side of the truck. A little farther away, a deejay in a white tent was playing music; next to him was a table selling T-shirts to raise funds.

Miss Bertha had suggested that they come, arranged the whole thing behind Janna's back.

"Sun just come out and is a nice-nice Saturday afternoon," she'd said when Janna finished eating lunch. "You need to get out of the house."

"I'm going to take a nap."

"You can nap tomorrow. This a good thing to do today." The maid slid a flyer for the disability fund-raiser onto the dining table.

"I can't go alone—" Janna had started.

"Joseph going to take you," Bertha said, clearing the dishes away. "I ask your father already if he can borrow the car. You can't waste a good Saturday afternoon." And Bertha was right. It had been a spectacular afternoon. The air was clean, with sunshine sparkling off the sea, reflecting off rooftops and cars after the morning rain. Down the hill from the high school field, newly cleaned shops and old houses crowded down to Manchioneal's town square and toward the canoes at anchor in the bay.

"A tattoo next," Janna said with a firm nod after they'd thrown away the snow-cone cups.

"Your mouth is still red with syrup."

"Stop digressing," she said, hands on her hips. "Let's get a tattoo."

"I don't want a tattoo."

"Just the spray-on kind, don't worry. Thirty-year-old men can get spray-on tattoos. They'll let you." While they stood in the line with the children waiting for their tattoos, Janna munched on popcorn.

"You eat more junk," said Joseph. "You're like a kid. Look at you!"

"I'm a growing girl," she said, and popped three more kernels into her mouth. She felt high, a different kind of dizzy.

They chose matching tattoos of a blue mermaid and laughed about her true identity. Janna said she was the Little Mermaid, and Joseph said she was the porno queen for a pirates' den. And so the afternoon went, with laughter and nonsense chatter, dribs and drabs about their past and future, filling in the blanks with short bursts of information. At one point, while they were looking at T-shirts, he mentioned that the vision board had really made him think about what kind of work he wanted to do. He'd decided he wanted to open his own consulting business, or maybe join a small consulting firm, he said. And while he was speaking of his future, his mouth open in speculation, she noticed something. He had one tooth that was wrong (it was a canine that lay a millimeter out of alignment, slightly overlapping the one next to it), and just that fact made her feel it was all right to care for him, because he wasn't perfect after all.

"What is the most embarrassing thing that's ever happened to you?" she said when they were walking back to the car, weaving their way between children and balloons.

"I'm supposed to tell you, and get more embarrassed?"

"Don't be shy. I have a ton of them."

"Let's see, probably the time when—" He paused and started again. "I once wet my pants in school."

"No, you didn't!"

"I'm telling you." He unlocked the car with the remote and opened the door for her. "I was a little guy and I had to sing at this concert and I was so scared I peed right in my pants. I almost died." He closed the door to her laughter, opened the back door, and placed the kite on the seat.

"I don't know if I can top that," Janna said, feeling again the warm ache in her chest that came when he did something kind, something as simple as opening her car door.

"Not fair," he said, sliding into the driver's seat. "You said you had tons."

"I do, I do. I wasn't known as Miss Klutz for nothing. Let's see—there are so many to choose from—there was this one time I was in a speedboat with some friends of my mom's, and my bathing suit top blew off. I'd been trying to tighten it and it ripped right out of my hands.

190

Oh, my God," she said, laughing, "I thought it was the end of the world. There was this boy on the boat who I thought was really cute. I had to dive for a towel. Not that there was anything to show. I was only about ten." He laughed and she laughed at him laughing at her, slapping him on the arm.

It was late when they drove up her driveway. Janna invited him to dinner, and when he accepted, she warmed up the curried chicken Miss Bertha had left and served it on the back patio, placing a candle in the middle of the table. Halfway through the meal, her father joined them.

"And a good time was had by all?" he said, plopping his glass and a bottle of wine down on the table. Janna took another forkful and waited for Joseph to answer.

"A great time," he said. "Thanks for lending us the car."

Her father nodded. "You got tattoos, I see."

"At my age, a fake tattoo." Joseph laughed. "She made me do it."

"He copied mine," Janna said.

"No, she copied mine," he said, and they both looked at each other and laughed.

"Wine?" Lambert held out the bottle. "A cabernet sauvignon, good stuff."

By the time she walked Joseph down to the road, they were each floating on two glasses of wine and the hand-holding seemed easier. He insisted on walking her back up the hill, and they joked about walking up and down the driveway all night. Almost at the front steps, she tripped on a stone and he caught her by the arm. She straightened and pulled up, past the muscles of his arm, past his chest with its gentle heaving, up to his wide shoulders. In the dark, she couldn't make out his eyes but knew exactly how they looked, the blue irises she'd looked at all afternoon, with flecks of gray streaming out from the dark middle.

Standing there, not moving his head, not stepping back, not speaking, he seemed to be waiting for her to do something. When she was close enough to feel his breath, she looked up at him—because it had to be his decision to close the deal—and if he wanted her a quarter as much as she wanted him, he would do it, but she wouldn't embarrass herself and regret it later. The seconds ticked by, long seconds feeling his warm breath on her cheeks and forehead, feeling his hands on her arms, and she closed her eyes, because she didn't want to challenge him in any way, wanted him to decide. Waiting for his lips to come down on hers, feeling the touch of his chest on her breasts, she felt as if she were opening a door, felt the light spilling out as the door opened. When she pulled back after a minute and looked up at him, he was smiling like a little boy again, and the kiss he gave her then was a self-conscious one with a dry tongue that didn't last long.

Afterward she moved closer until there was no space between them. She put one hand gently on the back of his head and pulled his face down to hers, kissed him on his bristly chin, on his lean cheeks, on his nose—slow kisses meant to torment. His eyes were shut under her lips, and she heard him moan deep in his throat. When she slid down to his mouth and opened it with her tongue, she gave him the kiss she'd wanted to give him from the first, probing and teasing, sucking on his tongue, keeping her lips soft, the kiss she'd practiced with the frog boys who'd stayed frogs.

It was a long kiss, and when it was over, she walked up the steps alone, nodding to her father at the living room window with his glass of cabernet.

CHAPTER TWENTY-FOUR

F or the year that Shad was in the Penitentiary for stealing a purse, he did pull-ups every morning using the bars of his cell window, which he'd wrapped with soft strips of fabric to make more comfortable. He did it partly because he was nineteen and antsy, with nothing better to do, but mostly he did it because it kept hope alive. He loved seeing the dark blue water of Kingston Harbour in front of the walls, and had even timed it a few times to pull up at the precise moment a plane left the runway from the airport opposite. When he took his one-hour break outside, he would wander with his enamel cup of tea among the weeds in the yard and look at the steep hills above Kingston where the rich people lived, look up to the mysterious, tall mountains behind them that disappeared into clouds, comforted to know that Largo was on the other side.

Since those days, at least a hundred tourists, maybe a thousand by this time, had told him that he lived in a beautiful place, and even though he'd never traveled and had nothing to compare Jamaica with, he'd come to believe it as firmly as he believed in God. He knew there were other countries that were wonderful, had seen them on travel documentaries—countries where there was snow on mountaintops, vineyards with grapes, grasslands full of lions and giraffes—but to Shad there was no sweeter country than his own.

Once he'd gone on a weekend church outing with Pastor and a few other men to Blue Mountain Peak. They'd set out at midnight and hiked, then staggered, the seven miles up the mountain, and later that morning, he'd stood in awe more than seven thousand feet above Largo Bay, on the island's highest point, listening to their guide rattling off facts that Shad still remembered. Jamaica was a hundred and forty-six miles long and fifty-one miles wide, and to the northeast were the coconut plantations of Portland (Largo Bay not visible from this distance), and to the south the million houses and shacks of Kingston, right down to the harbor. Shad had squinted and tried to see the Penitentiary, but couldn't make it out.

"We are surrounded on four sides," the guide man had said, both arms spread wide, "by the Caribbean Sea, our view only blocked by the western mountains and the Cockpit Country." Later, while Pastor was sermonizing about the wonders of paradise to come, Shad had thanked God for the paradise he lived in right now.

Time had taught Shad that beauty came at a price, however, and there were some idiots who didn't understand what they had, who seemed bent on destroying the perfection around them. There was evil everywhere, he'd decided. So a man had to make choices about which side he was on, good or evil, and had to take up the sword sometimes to protect God's creation.

These thoughts came back after drinking Miss Mac's fine pumpkin soup a week after the visit to the doctor. More specifically, they came after the phone call. Up to that point, he and Miss Mac had been sitting peacefully in her kitchen, talking and sipping soup, he and his old elementary school teacher—the woman who still loved to teach. She had rested her head on her open hand, breathing hard from the exertion of cooking. At seventy-five, she was entitled to get winded, she'd said to Shad, and she'd asked him to excuse her if she needed to draw breath for a minute. Since her retirement, Miss Mac had mellowed, giving Shad hope that one day Beth would do the same. The old lady still wore the shoes and plaid dresses of her teaching years, still cackled with laughter when something tickled her, but she'd lost the sternness of her profession and become the wise adviser, Shad's in particular, in matters official and legal.

They'd been discussing autism that afternoon, and between them lay the stack of pamphlets the doctor had given him and Beth. He'd brought the literature to Miss Mac to interpret, because Beth had had trouble with some of the words, and they'd ended up disagreeing about what they were supposed to do with Ashanti. Miss Mac had picked up a leaflet and was reading it, her enormous breasts resting on the tabletop, like they used to on the teacher's desk. Hearing her slow, aging voice, watching her sweaty face with its million moles, sipping her excellent soup always gave Shad a feeling of the rightness of the world—like he used to feel with Granny, even when she glanced at him sternly over her glasses.

"It says that when you have a child with a disability—"

"A *dis*-ability." Shad said the word carefully, broke it down to appreciate it better.

"Yes, that mean the child is different from other children. It has a disability." She smoothed her hair back into its bun, authority in the sweep of her flabby arm and lined hand. "The child is not able to keep up with the others."

Pushing her glasses farther up her nose, Miss Mac continued. "Anyway, it says, 'You and your partner should share your feelings and needs.' So, you and Beth need to talk to each other about Ashanti, whenever anything bother you. Don't keep it inside, you know?"

"It tell you how to keep it inside?" said Shad. "Beth don't have no trouble letting it out."

Miss Mac laughed, the two gold teeth at the back of her mouth winking. "But that's good, means she letting off a little steam," she said. Returning to the leaflet, she read on. "And it say, 'Joining a parents' group is a great way to get information and support.'"

"I don't hear of any group like that around here."

"We can call the number they gave you. Maybe they know something nearby."

After another sip of soup, she returned to the lesson. "'Help your other children to understand the needs of the disabled child. Spend time alone with each of your children every day.'"

Shad chewed on a spinner, one of the long dumplings

Miss Mac made so well. He and Beth barely had time for sex, the whole day was so full. Whoever wrote that you should spend time alone with each child, he reflected, must have had a maid and two children.

Just then the phone rang, and Miss Mac had looked at him over the leaflet. He didn't remember hearing Miss Mac's phone ring before. It sounded shrill and old-fashioned. The woman stood up, almost knocking over the soup bowl with her breasts, and hurried out of the room. It was probably her son Horace, she muttered.

From the bedroom, he could hear her nice "Hello-o," followed by low talk, then startled expressions and anxious questions, her voice raised.

"Who is that?" she kept repeating at the end of the call. Then there was no sound but the cuckoo clock ticking in the hallway outside the kitchen.

"What the matter, ma'am?" Shad said when she appeared at the door, looking old with her spindly legs in the teacher's shoes. She groped her way back to her seat and dropped into the chair as if she were blind.

"I don't know what this world coming to," she said.

"Miss Mac, what happen?"

The woman shook her head and looked up at Shad, the moles on her face seeming to stand up in alarm.

"You never believe what just happen," she said, but she couldn't finish, the stew of her feelings making her struggle for reasonable words.

"It a man," she said finally, surrendering to patois. She sucked in her thick lips and then relaxed them. "He sound like an older man, I not sure. He ask for Joseph. 'The white man who staying there,' he call him. I told him that the man not home right now. 'Give him a message,' he say."

"What he say, Miss Mac?"

"He say, 'Tell him he have to leave, or he going to dead.' That's what he say, 'he going to dead.' I ask who it was, but he wasn't answering me."

"He have to leave," Shad said, and dropped his spoon into the bowl, "or he *going to dead*?"

Neither spoke for a minute, the words sinking in. He have to leave, or he going to dead. The death threat kept repeating itself back to him like dancehall lyrics.

"And no idea who the person speaking?" he said.

"No. It sound a little familiar, but I couldn't lay my head on a block and say is so-and-so."

"He didn't say why?"

"No, but he call Joseph a *batty man*," she said.

A batty man. That was it, then. A fly sat on the rim of her soup bowl, and Miss Mac made a face and pushed the bowl away. "And now I have to give him a terrible message like that."

"No!" Shad said, loudly enough for her to frown at him. He dropped his voice. "Don't say anything to Joseph, whatever you do. Don't say anything."

"Of course, I have to give him the message."

He put both elbows on the table and leaned across it. "If you tell Joseph, he might leave. And if he leave, the whole project falling through, because we don't have the money to pay anybody, and we not paying him until the money come in. If the project fall through, you won't be able to sell your land to this investor man, and you can't retire and move in with Horace like you want to. You have to stay here looking after people in your boardinghouse, scrimping and scraping for the rest of your life. And if the project fall through, we can't build the hotel and have jobs for the young people. We won't get a nice hotel and tourists coming into Largo—and God *know* we need the money."

Miss Mac bit her lip and frowned. "Then we have to tell his father."

"The boss is a funny man," Shad said, shaking his head vigorously. "You never know how he going to react to anything. He don't like to mix up in any confusion, and he don't know how to deal with it. Sometimes he get kind of ignorant, you know, don't think and do some stupidness. Next thing, he tell Joseph the deal is off and send him back to the States, and everything mash up, even his own future."

Meredith McKenzie sat back and wrapped her arms around her breasts. "You see my trial?" she said. "I have to keep quiet and we might have a murder on our hands? Suppose they coming to kill us one night? All these years I running this boardinghouse, how long now, twenty-three years? And I never have any trouble like this. I have people coming from Australia, England, America, coming to stay with me. Never, I'm telling you, have a single person ever had reason to say they were threatened or anything like that in my house." Her eyes above the glasses were fiery. "And to call him—"

"You think he gay, Miss Mac?" Shad said. "You think Joseph a homosexual?"

"Is none of my business. He nice and polite. He don't mess up the room, don't even ask me to make up his bed. He's a decent young man."

"Maybe he a *bisexual*. You think is a sickness, this gay business?"

"I don't know," Miss Mac said, and screwed up her face. "As long as they don't bring it in my house, I don't care. I don't like the idea of two men in a bed in my house. I don't like to think about it, like how a child don't like to think about his mother and his father, you know? These homosexual people, if they do what they want to do, quiet-like, and don't bother me, I won't bother them. And to want to kill people for having sex with another adult who agree to it, oh, my God—I shame for Largo."

Miss Mac continued, pouring out a confused defense of her guest and herself, and beneath the downward flood of her words, Shad swam upstream, thinking of who could be behind this, and why they would want Joseph out of the way. The caller was saying that if Joseph didn't leave, he would die. Someone wanted to warn him or wanted him out of the way. Someone who was jealous, or someone who was afraid, maybe. Probably someone connected to the noose and the note left in the Jeep.

"Miss Mac," Shad said. "Excuse me, but I have to go."

"You can't go, just so. We have to decide what to do."

"I already think about it. Behind something like this is usually just one or two perpetrators." Shad answered the old lady's frown. "That's what my police cousin Neville call them."

"How we going to find them?"

"I want you to think hard about who the caller was and let me know."

Standing, Shad picked up the forgotten papers. "I going to see Neville, but I have a feeling I know what he going to say. Meantime, keep an eye on Joseph. If you hear any sounds at night, make a lot of noise and call the bar next door. We usually there until one o'clock in the morning. After that, call Lambert up the hill, he have a gun. Keep the two numbers by your phone."

Miss Mac nodded, looking distracted, like she was making plans of her own.

"Please don't do anything foolish, you hear?" he said. Halfway out the door, he turned back. "And thanks for the lunch. I always love your cooking."

CHAPTER TWENTY-FIVE

It rained the next morning, and Eric was reading the paper, drinking coffee out of his blue mug with the chip on the rim. He never minded the rain in Largo, because it blew over in no time, not like the dull days in New York that seemed to last for months. He'd made up a little ditty that morning and sung it in the shower to a tune he'd made up.

> *Warm skies, warm rain, take the place of cold and pain,*
> *No more umbrellas, because you know*
> *That when it goes, sunshine will flow.*

It was the most recent of the silly mantras he'd been singing to himself ever since he came to Largo. They were the only souvenirs left of his teenage rock-and-roll stint, created to make him feel better about his fate, stuck behind God's back in a poverty-stricken little village, a place where the temperature seldom varied and people remained in the same houses their whole lives, a place where the only difference between one day and the next was church and the rain.

"Boss, we have to finish the stuff Joseph ask us to do," Shad said. He'd appeared above the newspaper Eric was reading and was carrying some sheets in his hand.

"What are those?" Eric said, lowering the *Gleaner*.

"Some figures I was working on last night."

"When did you find time to work the figures?"

"In between customers," Shad said. He sat down next to Eric, his ruffled forehead and burning eyes looking more intense than usual, and he was holding on tightly to the papers.

"Do we have to do it now?" Eric said, and picked up his newspaper again.

"Joseph waiting for them. The longer we keep him back, the longer it going to take to build the hotel, not true? Joseph have to go back to America, he can't stay here forever."

Eric sighed and heaved his leg off the adjoining seat.

"I hope the figures are lower than the last set you showed me. Let's have a look." After perusing the rough pencil notes, Eric frowned across at Shad. "You've only lowered the salaries by one US dollar an hour!"

"That's how it go, boss," Shad said. He spread his hands. "I already ask everybody what they willing to accept, and this is it."

"What else?"

"Computers. I speak to the teacher at the school and she give me the prices. I put in twelve, enough for a twenty-room hotel, what you think?"

Eric grunted. "What next?"

"The cost of linens for the housekeeping department, a year's worth."

"Why so many?"

"The guests tear them up, remember? Burn cigarette holes in them, get all kind of—things on them, take them home."

Eric agreed, nodding and then shaking his head. He'd never liked the accounting part of running the hotel. "What else?"

"Supplies for the gardening. Hoses, fertilizers, insecticide, all of that."

"What about cleaning products?" Eric said, and pushed the newspaper out of the way.

"I forgot that, put it in."

"Beth help you with this?"

"Yes, man."

"What else?"

"Maintenance costs to keep up the buildings. I ask Job this morning."

"What about liquor?"

"Right down here." Shad pointed to another page with *Food and Beverage* written at the top. Rough and jumbled as the figures were, he'd created an exhaustive list, including entertainment.

"We don't need limbo dancers and a reggae band, for God's sake," Eric said. "Why can't we just have a little *mento* band, like at the old hotel?"

"Naw," Shad said, and leaned back in his chair. "People want reggae and dancehall now. They hear it abroad and when they come here they want the real thing. And they want to dance, you know, and dancing will bring the locals in when they want a little party action. Don't forget, people drink plenty when they dancing. We can save the old-time mento band for Christmas."

"Anything you didn't include?" Eric said, his mouth already sour.

"Your salary, boss," Shad said, laughing as he walked away from the table. "Mind you don't make it too high."

At lunchtime, Eric presented the figures on their blue lined sheets to Joseph.

"These are annual figures," Eric said. "You'll have to multiply them by five for your projections. I still have to get estimates for the utility costs. I'm going out right now to get them." He held up the car keys as evidence.

Joseph narrowed his eyes at the numbers. "This your writing?"

Eric raised his eyebrows. "Does it look like my writing?"

"I don't know how your writing looks," his son replied, scrutinizing the papers, while his father made a mock smirk and played with the car keys.

"Looks like the rain is holding up," Eric said. "I'd better run. If you need anything else, let me know." He walked briskly to the parking lot before Joseph could answer.

The afternoon turned out to be frustrating from beginning to end. When Eric arrived at the Water Commission office in Port Antonio, it was two o'clock and still closed for lunch. He waited for half an hour for the doors to open, was only third on the list, and met with a youngish-looking man in customer services who told him he was retiring the following week, that they were throwing a party for him that afternoon. But the man was helpful and they figured out what the costs of water for a twenty-room hotel would be over the next five years.

"As long as the Public Service Commission don't give an increase of more than five percent a year," the man added.

Hitting the power company next, Eric sat in a lounge with a dozen other people who had come before him. After a half hour, he gave up and drove to the Parish Council to look into naming the island, but it was closed, the old wooden shutters sealed tight with bars. A sign on the door said they'd moved to 59 Church Street. There, in a brand-new building, he found the Parish Council's secretary, Miss Daphne.

"Nice office," Eric commented, making the small talk that was part of any dialogue with civil servants. It had always been a test dealing with Miss Daphne, a thick woman happy to stand in the way of doing business with anybody at the Council.

"We just moved in last week," she said, crossing her short legs in their stilettos. "Didn't you see the opening ceremony on TV?"

"I don't have a TV," Eric admitted.

She sighed and patted her French roll. "How can I help you, Mr. Keller?"

"I just want to name an island. Where do I go for that?"

"What are you going to do with it?"

"Nothing. I just want to give it a name."

"You naming an island you not doing anything with?" She was admiring the design of miniature palm trees on her long acrylic nails. "Have you paid taxes on it?"

"Paid up, four months ago," he said, remembering standing at the property tax window and giving thanks. Miss Daphne sent him back to the property tax window with a wave of her fingernails.

"Where is the island?" the woman standing behind the window asked. Her voice was stifled by the glass and he had to lean in to hear her.

"It's at the end of Largo Bay, in front of my bar."

"What address—?"

"What?" He cupped his hand to his ear. Tall for a woman, she was almost his height, and her frown was directly opposite his eyes.

"The address of your bar," the clerk shouted. She didn't like foreigners, Eric could tell. He gave her the address, and she sat and clicked away on her computer.

"Anybody living on the island?"

"No."

"No tenants or anything? No rental income?"

"Oh, no."

"You have employees in the bar?"

"It's just me and—yes."

"Check the payroll tax window," she said, and looked up at him, smiling. "Your property taxes are paid."

Eric descended the glossy marble stairs to the Jeep. His flip-flops skidded once in the middle and he caught himself on the banister. There was no use checking the payroll tax window, since he hadn't paid employee taxes in years. If he was going to name the island, he'd have to get a lawyer, Horace McKenzie, and that would mean he couldn't call Simone back until Horace had filed the name or done whatever he needed to do. After all the rent money she'd paid him, he couldn't tell her he hadn't paid his payroll taxes. It just sounded too cheap, even though she wouldn't have cared. If she'd been standing in front of him, she'd just have given him that mischievous look that made his groin tingle. But he couldn't do it, admit that he'd failed, so the call would have to wait.

CHAPTER TWENTY-SIX

The petals of the orchid looked like they'd been carved out of icing, the color the palest lavender in the afternoon light. One large central petal was a vivid scarlet, which spilled out like a sulky lip. Lambert turned the pot around for her to see. He glowed with pride when he held it, like he'd conceived and parented the small plant. A man who rarely displayed affection, her father found comfort in touching the plants he grew—it was one of the things she'd come to terms with from childhood.

"Look inside this one," he said. "Tell me if it doesn't look like a nun praying." Janna looked inside the large petals and thought it looked more like a vagina.

"It's called *Cattleya Enidson*," he continued without waiting for an answer. "I got it from a woman in Montego Bay just last month, paid an arm and a leg for it."

"Beautiful," murmured Janna. They'd make the perfect wedding bouquet. She must remember that when the day came.

Walking to the next hanging pot in the greenhouse, he turned another orchid toward them. "*Dendrobium for-*

mosum," he said, rolling out one syllable at a time, "from guess where?"

"Formosa," Janna said. It was a game they'd played over the years, he quizzing, she guessing—a game she was tired of playing. They drifted to another few pots, Lambert telling the species and origins of each plant.

"I remember your orchids from the house in Kingston on Merivale," she said. "I used to love to go out in the early morning with you."

"You remember?" her father said. He looked delighted.

"Of course. I remember following you in my nightgown early in the morning when you were misting them. Mummy would call me to come back inside and put on my shoes."

"God, that's right," Lambert said. He moved on to muse over the progress of another flower. "She never thought I could take care of you." He was touching down, light as a butterfly, on a subject they'd never ventured into—with the expectation of flitting to another.

Decisive moments come with sharpened senses, in this instance with the pungent smell of rotting coconut husks that made up the orchid soil, the noisy crunch of the gravel underfoot, and the image of flower pots with large drainage holes hanging at eye level. This was the moment when the obedient daughter made her decision, fittingly in the orchid house, that she would once and for all stop being *Jannus Jamaicanus,* as her father had once dubbed her, and become whole, at least in his eyes.

"When were you ever careless with me?" she asked.

He shrugged and examined another blossom. "Careless with you, never. Young and foolish, maybe." The affair she'd heard about, the one with a woman named Sophie Lawrence. Her mother still dredged up the memory when she was angry with him. If a check arrived late, it was Sophie's fault.

"Is that why she left, you think?" Saying it, Janna thought of baby steps. Baby steps out of the father-and-child circle they'd created for twenty-three years.

Lambert released the pot he was holding and watched it for a while, the small pink orchids shaking as they swung. "Your mother left me—" He broke off. "I'm still asking myself that question." Picking up a plastic bottle, he sprayed the plant and watched the drops fall off the leaves. "After her friend Ruth was stabbed by the gardener—I think she'd fired him or something—your mother started talking about leaving."

"Was that why she left you, though?"

He touched the leaf of another plant, stroked it between his thick fingers. "It's getting dark."

Ten minutes later, on the back patio, Lambert placed two glasses of wine on the table and sat down heavily. "Your mother is not an easy woman."

"And that's tonight's news," Janna muttered, and they both laughed. "She has her good points, don't get me wrong," she added to offset feeling like a traitor, because there'd be no playing one side against the other. "She's honest . . . and she's a good hugger."

"I know, I know. She's been a great mother, brought you up right, kept you straight. I give her full credit."

He brought the glass to his nose and sniffed, swirled the wine and examined it closely. "But when it came to me, I always felt she had me under a microscope. Somehow we never got past her being older than me, no matter how well I did, no matter how much money I made. It was like I had to report to her all the time." She saw the burly man saluting her mother, still a petite dress size.

"But you married her knowing what she was like."

"Janna, your mother—" He broke off and squinted at her, measuring her, she knew, against what she didn't know.

"—was pregnant," Janna said. It was out, the unmentioned, the subject her mother couldn't bring herself to discuss. Her father took a long sip of his wine and she of hers, eyeing him over the rim of the glass.

"She told you?"

"Oh, no, you know Mummy, but it wasn't rocket science. Your wedding and my birthday are six months apart. I saw it on your marriage certificate. I was digging around looking for my birth certificate when I was applying to Tampa, and found it."

His sudden booming laugh. "And we thought we'd hidden it from you so well."

"You mean by lying about the year you'd married?" It was unlike her, accusing her father of deceit, and he stopped laughing.

"That was your grandmother's idea. In those days when a woman got pregnant, and you were from what we called *a good family,* you had to get married. There was no getting out of it. Our parents decided the whole thing.

213

Marriage had never entered my mind. I liked her a lot, you know, but—" He looked away, alarmed by the truth.

"How did you both meet?" A question her mother had brushed aside. "I know you were neighbors, but I never heard the whole story—the grown-up version, if you know what I mean."

Halting between sentences, Lambert told her how he'd just gotten out of college in London and come back home when he saw her mother again. She was living next door and he remembered her from high school. She used to go to St. Hugh's, he said, his eyes a little dreamy, and she'd wear a green uniform, always starched and ironed like she never sat down in it. She was in sixth form when he was in fourth, and he always thought she was the finest-looking girl he'd ever seen. He was staring at his glass and smiling when he said it. "I used to see her walking to school, and she would look right past me, you know, with her pleated skirt swinging. So when I got back, Mister Big Shot with a degree in engineering, I started talking to her—and she started noticing me. She was working with an insurance company and she used to drive this little red sports car, a Triumph, and she asked me one day if I could take a look at it because something was wrong. I can't remember what it was, but anyway, we went out for the first time that night. The rest is history, as they say."

She took another long sip. "And you slept with her."

His eyes darted around for a moment. "We—dated and—of course, where'd you think you came from?" Sheba waddled out to join them, flopping down on the cool stones at her father's feet, and he bent down grate-fully to pat her.

"Where was I conceived?" She tipped her head back and drank her wine, all of it at once like a shot, making a slurping sound. The question had slipped out before she'd even thought about it, but the wine was making her head buzz, and she might as well ask, even if the idea of her parents having sex repulsed her.

Lambert pushed away from the table. "Oh, God, Janna, you really want to know that?"

"Yes, I do."

"What's brought this on?"

"Probably your cabernet." She smiled so it wouldn't sound obnoxious.

His shoulders slouched down as he leaned over to pat Sheba again. "We were at your Uncle Wallace's house. His grandparents had just died and left him the house, and he invited a bunch of us to come up and spend the weekend." Uncle Wally's house, the squat little house in the middle of the island, the one with all the mosquitoes and the sagging beds. She'd imagined a hotel somewhere, saw them walking on a beach, maybe rolling in the sand in the moonlight.

"We'd had a few drinks, rum or something." He leaned back and stroked his mustache. "That's what happens. You get carried away, do things you might later—"

They looked at each other and he downed another sip of wine. "I'm just glad you were the product of that—you have to be careful, you know. One wrong move and that's your fate."

"Things are different now, though," she countered. "You can have a child without marrying, or have an abortion. You can use protection to begin with."

"Exactly." His eyes looked suddenly worried under the bushy eyebrows. "You must use protection, whatever you do. Hear me, sweet pea?"

"Is this a birds-and-bees talk, Daddy? Because I had that in middle school."

"No, no. I just thought that you're so attractive—" He smiled, flustered. She knew he meant but wouldn't mention that her measurements had grown since he saw her last, even though he'd probably helped to pay for them.

Janna threw back her head, groaning. "I'm a big girl, Dad. I'll use protection, don't worry."

"I don't mean to get in your business, but—"

"I appreciate the advice—really." They looked at each other, the smiles fading. "This is about Joseph, isn't it, Daddy?" Lambert clasped his hands behind his head and looked at her.

"Go ahead and say it, whatever it is," she urged.

"Janna, I know you like him. You'd have to be deaf, dumb, and blind not to see that."

"Yes, I like him. What about it?"

"I'm just thinking of you. Please—I'm asking you— please get to know Joseph well before you get involved." Lambert took his last sip and set the glass down carefully. He put his hands in his lap, twiddling the thumbs.

"You haven't finished, have you?"

When he looked up at her, his eyes were steady under

the patio light. "There are people, Janna, who think Joseph is gay."

Her mouth went dry. Her breath stopped. "What are you talking about? He's not gay!"

"When Joseph came out last, he was around nineteen, twenty. It was his first time in Jamaica. Two friends came with him, two college friends. Well-behaved, good-looking guys. You could see they were from good homes, you know. But one of the guys was really—effeminate, I guess you'd call it. Back in the day, we'd call him a queer. We invited them over for dinner. Jennifer thought it would be a good idea, and Eric brought them over. They were—tight—a definite threesome, Joseph and his friends. You know when you get to the point where you and your friends sort of talk in code? You have certain jokes that you share, but no one else finds them funny? That's how close they were. But they had a kind of closeness that—we never said anything to Eric about it, but Jennifer and I just felt—we didn't have any evidence, mind you—but we thought they might all be gay. Joseph was a little different, though, more masculine, and the other two seemed closer, so we didn't—" Lambert broke off and stroked his mustache.

"He's not gay," she snapped, and Sheba raised her head from the stone floor to look at her, a gaze even steadier than her father's. "I'm sure of that."

There was no sleep for her that night. It wasn't only the result of drinking the wine on an empty stomach. Turning from one side to another, switching the overhead fan on and off, she kept recalling fragments of her father's words and snatches of talks she and Joseph had had over the last two weeks. She thought of the shift to a new intimacy between them since the accident and the delicious kiss at the foot of the front steps. Their conversation had gone past the preliminaries to the personal, about their relationships with their parents and the burden of being an only child. They were diving deeper, allowing more access to their secrets. There was no way he could be gay.

The next morning she waited, gritty-eyed, in the dining room until Joseph finished his phone call. Then she stood in the doorway to Jennifer's office with her coffee cup, looking at Sheba stretched out possessively, barring the door.

"What about a swim later?" she said.

Joseph looked up and smiled. One of his eyelids looked a little droopy today behind the glasses. She'd never noticed that before.

"Feeling strong enough?" he said.

"Yeah, my checkup went well."

"Five o'clock, then." The lock of hair bobbed with his nod. His hair was getting longer. She hadn't noticed it before.

It rained before lunch. She willed it to clear, and by afternoon the sky was again blue with a few clouds. When they got to the beach, it was empty except for three children playing in an old canoe, jumping in and out in some kind of a game. Taking up their usual positions after their swim, lying on their bellies, chins on crossed arms, Joseph continued the monologue he'd started on the walk down the hill.

"I don't understand him—he's—in this world of his own. Like he wants to connect with me, but then he doesn't. I had this insane idea that we could bond or something while I was here, but there's no bonding with him. He—he's separated himself from the rest of humanity. How do you get through to somebody like that?"

"You know what they say." Janna nodded. "You can't change people, especially your parents. Sometimes when you try to change things, it doesn't come out the way you intended." She and her father had ventured out of their circle, only to find themselves on rocky ground. "They still have clay feet."

Joseph snorted and turned to her. "I can't even call him Dad to his face, you know that? I'm thirty fucking years old, and there's still something holding me back that—I don't know, I just don't—don't trust him or something. Technically he's my father, but we don't even shake hands, can you believe that?" He started playing with the sand in front of him. "I don't know why I'm telling you all this. I sound like a kid, and it must be boring as hell to you, so don't mind me." But under the stretching shadows of the coconut trees, she could feel him mellowing with the crash of each wave behind them and knew the worst was over. His mood was shifting, and her father had been wrong.

"This parent-child business sucks," she said. "I used to think Daddy was this knight in shining armor when I was a little girl. Then when they separated, I didn't see him much. I missed him like crazy, but my mother was—still is—angry that he didn't join us." She drew two small circles in the sand with her finger. "But I adored him. He'd show up in Florida every few months and rattle my mother. I'd look forward to his visits so much, count the days, the hours, until he showed up, and he'd take me with him to buy construction materials or go to building shows. What I loved was that he'd ask my advice—and pretend to take it—when he had to choose between tiles or carpet. Then all of a sudden Jennifer comes into the picture." Down the beach, the children jumped out of the canoe and ran away, shouting at each other.

"And when he took me to Disney World, I'll never forget—I thought it would be just him and me, you know, because it was my birthday and he'd promised me we'd go—but there was Jennifer, the two of them looking into each other's eyes and laughing together, and it was like—I wasn't even there. I guess they were in love, but when you're a kid you don't think like that. It spoiled the whole trip for me. I've never liked Disney World since then, and our relationship changed. He was somebody else's, not mine anymore. Being here this time has been different, though. He's—I'm seeing him more as an equal—in some ways, anyway." She turned to him. "It feels good talking about it."

"Any time."

"It's fun hanging out with you. I haven't been around guys for a while. I broke up with my last boyfriend earlier this year, this guy in Tampa named Carlos. Or he broke up with me, I guess. We dated for a couple months, then he stopped calling. Anyway, I've been taking a break."

He said it was probably a good idea, and she smiled

on top of her fist. "I have something to ask you," she said. She flicked the sand off her arm with one hand. "There's someone in your life, isn't there?"

He raised his head and pushed his hair behind his ear, avoiding her eyes. "I guess you could say that."

She turned over onto her back, listened to the waves rolling in and out, to the clattering noise when they dragged pebbles back to the sea.

"Janna, I like you. Really, I do. You're—I don't know, an *authentic* person—God, that sounds corny—and you're gorgeous." She could hear him smiling. "What's there not to like?"

"And I'm too young, why don't you say it?"

"You're young, true, but not foolish—young and deep."

She rolled her lips in and clamped down on them. He had nothing to defend. It had been all her, her imagination, her foolish attempt to play with a god.

"You're a very cool person," he was saying. "I just came down to do a job and spend a little time with my father, you know. That's all I was expecting. And then I meet this girl who makes me laugh, listens to me ranting on. I like hanging out with you. You're fun to be with."

She kept staring above at the palm leaves, and he leaned over her, making her start. He kissed her on the mouth, a soft kiss like she'd given him the last time.

"And I like this," he said. Then he reached across and pulled her closer, kissing her cheeks and her forehead and her eyes, the heel of his hand pressed into her breast— almost by accident. And what could she do, she asked

Lorraine later, but kiss him back? When all she seemed able to do was think about this man, when she felt this incredible, umbilical connection to him, what could she do? He said he liked her, and it had been a real kiss this time, like a man kissed a woman. And did "I guess you could say that" mean he was in a *serious* relationship? It didn't sound that way to her. And was this other person a man or a woman? And he wouldn't kiss like that if he didn't like women, right?

"What would you do in my place?" she ended, and Lorraine, who always had a comeback, had none to offer.

The rest of the time, while she was eating and watching TV, washing her face, putting on her moisturizer, she had arguments in her head with Lambert, told him, *These are different times, Daddy*. The world has changed. Roles and gender and sexuality have changed. And Joseph didn't have to be gay himself; he could have just had gay friends. Maybe he even had relationships with guys, but young people did that nowadays, tried out things, took a break from the opposite sex, even had sex with their own gender—and were still heterosexual. (There was a time in high school when she'd hung out with three girls and didn't even realize for a month that they were gay. After they told her, they'd tried to talk her into sleeping with one of them, just to try it, and she'd thought about it. She'd even gone to a movie with one and held hands, but she couldn't do anything more than kiss. She wouldn't tell Lambert the story, but it confirmed her analysis and made her feel smug.) He wasn't gay, she was sure of it. He was probably just experimenting.

The very next day she decided that, even if Joseph was straight, she was making assumptions, assumptions that he really cared for her, and by the day after that, she'd decided that in the unlikely event that Joseph was gay, they could still have a relationship. They could even marry, and handle it. And with only some slight discomfort, she googled "bisexuality" and found websites called bimarried.org and marriedandgay.com, and she read an online article that said more married couples had at least one admittedly bisexual partner than ten years ago. Another article said that only 20 to 25 percent of marriages with a gay partner survived, and she stopped reading halfway through. But she recalled that one of the editors at the *Herald* had a wife everyone thought was gay, a quiet woman with a butch haircut, and they seemed happy enough. They must have found ways to live together, to satisfy all parts of themselves and even have children.

Besides, she knew she loved this man, every morsel of him, down to his toenails. It had to be love. It certainly felt like it, this change in the very molecules of her body: twenty-four hours a day feeling the blood sparkling through her veins, feeling every cell alert and anticipating, a constant agitation in her stomach. She'd thought that a person had to be in the loved one's presence to feel *in love,* but now she'd discovered that the feelings continued from morning to night, including (and somewhat alarming to her at first) a knowledge that everything was in its perfect time and place. And if it wasn't love, why the pounding in her chest when she saw him, the excuses to herself to go to the kitchen just to look at his back?

The only uncertainty, once she'd thought it through, was that she wasn't sure how *he* felt. He seemed to like her. He'd said she was gorgeous and kissed her, even fondled her breast, which said something, but he hadn't mentioned the *L* word or even hinted at it, and he hadn't said anything about seeing each other back in the States. Then again, men learned to keep their thoughts to themselves. It was the nature of the beast, according to her mother. But even if he didn't love her yet, there was still space for that. She'd be everything he needed, make him laugh, bring him down to earth, help him to stay optimistic, and make love to him like no woman had made love to him before, with her mind and her body and her soul, and he wouldn't be able to forget that easily.

The fly in the ointment, of course, was this guess-you-could-say-that person, the source of his ambivalence, no doubt, but time would take care of that. She could feel it in her bones.

CHAPTER TWENTY-SEVEN

The woman sat with her back erect, a proud woman from the southern agricultural district, always above her husband's fishing folk. She was small and fine boned, with the bronze skin and hooked nose of her ancestors who'd sailed from India on British ships after the slaves were freed, contract laborers for the sugarcane fields. It had been at least ten years since he'd seen her last, and Shad remembered very little of her. She had lived with her son after her fisherman husband died at sea, a woman who hardly spoke to anyone, before or after the incident.

"I don't know where he gone," she said. What little hair she had left had been given a bad dye job long ago and was now pulled back into a bun, which she kept clasping.

"I don't want to know his whereabouts, Sister Elsa," Shad said. "I just need your help, that's all."

"What kind of help?"

"I want to ask you a few questions."

It had taken almost a week to find her, precious time wasted. She had left Largo a month or two after it happened, and the house at the end of their lane had sat empty since then, the zinc roof fallen in and rats scurrying across the floor. Her next door neighbors hadn't been helpful.

"Like she disappear in the middle of the night," Mas Alvin had said. "She was never the same after that night, you know. She didn't even say good-bye or nothing."

The old ladies in the market who usually knew everything had shaken their heads. "One week she here, and the next she gone," Miss Winnie said. She'd tightened her mouth and started counting the change in her money belt.

It was Neville, his sergeant cousin in Port Antonio, who'd helped him to track her down. He'd run his fingernail down a column in a ledger and stopped at one line.

"What you want with her?" he'd said in his bossy policeman way, his finger still on the name, stomach pulsing against his starched uniform and threatening two buttons.

"I have something to give her," Shad told him.

"It say here that the son was arrested for indecency in 2003. He was living with her at 28 Santana Road, here in Port Antonio. You can check see if she still there." Shad thanked him, the cousin who'd never forgiven him for bringing the family name down.

The house at number 28 was nicer than Shad expected, bigger than his own, with a fresh coat of yellow paint on the exterior. He'd knocked, and a large Indian woman had opened the door. Behind her was a living room with neat furniture and a rug with an animal pattern.

"Excuse me, please, is a lady living here by the name of Miss Elsa?" Shad had asked.

"Who want to know?" the large woman said, blocking the doorway.

"Tell her Shad of Largo Bay come to see her." Her sister wasn't at home, she said, but he could wait outside for her. He'd sat on the front step until Miss Elsa, looking much older now, pushed open the gate. When she saw him, she stopped walking. He approached her slowly with his best smile, and she narrowed her eyes while he spoke. Probably out of gratitude, or to save herself the trouble of cooking, she accepted his invitation to eat a meal with him and he'd guided her to a small restaurant at the end of the street.

Miss Elsa wiped her mouth on the napkin and pushed her plate away, the saltfish and rice only half eaten. "I thank you for the dinner, but it don't mean I have to answer your questions."

"No, ma'am, it don't."

"I only talking to you because of what your wife did . . . that time." She looked around the empty restaurant and reached for her bun.

"Would you like a drink?" Shad asked.

She dipped her head, eyes suddenly shy. "I wouldn't mind a rum and Pepsi."

He ordered the drink and a fruit juice for himself. The waiter took his time clearing the dishes, like he was listening, but they said nothing. When the drinks came, she sipped hers right away and pulled a pack of cigarettes out of her purse, her hands steadier.

"What you want to know?" she said after she exhaled and leaned back. The lines on her face had relaxed, opening to him.

"We have a little problem in Largo," he said. "A man who visiting is getting death threats—"

"A queer?" Elsa tapped her cigarette in the ashtray although there wasn't enough ash yet to flick.

Shad took a sip of his too-sweet lemonade. "I don't exactly know."

"Why you come to me, then?"

"The two threats refer to this guy, and one directly called him a—a batty man."

She shook her head, flicking the imaginary ash.

"I want to find out who the people are behind this," he said. "I know it already happen in other places in Jamaica, but I want to stop it in Largo. We gone to hell in a handbasket if we keep allowing a few evil-minded people to control us, you know."

"I can't help you."

"If you can tell me who the people were who harass your son, that would help. I'm thinking, maybe it's the same people. I promise you, I not going to tell anybody where you are or anything."

She was having trouble talking about it, swallowed her drink hard and set it down. With a forefinger, she stroked her elegant nose.

"It was everybody," she said after she'd taken another drag on the cigarette. "They harass Gideon, the children did, even the teachers at school. He start coming to me when he was eight or nine. They call him a *sissy,* make fun of him. He was afraid of his father, so it was me he used to come to. He try to act like the other boys, you know, but he say he can't help himself. You know how many times his father beat him? How many times I talk to him? But he say, *Is so I was born, and is you, my mother, make me so.*" She waggled her head, imitating her son.

"Then after his father die, he went to Mo Bay to his cousin one time, and he come back and say he want to be a dressmaker. I told him he was going to end up in trouble if he don't watch out, and he should start going out in his father's canoe to fish like the other men. But he say he would dead first before he become a fisherman, and he ask your wife, Beth, to teach him how to sew, because he want to be a *designer.*" She made a little face at the word. "He was going to support me in my old age, he say."

"What was the first sign of trouble, before the—?" he said.

"Sometimes people call him names on the street, you know."

"Which people call out?"

"All kind of people, especially all them church people."

Shad leaned forward, tried not to frighten her by looking alarmed. "What you mean?" he said, his heart racing.

"All them people talking about the Bible." Her top lip curled at the memory as she tapped her cigarette. "And when they come to get Gideon—"

"Tell me about it again." He signaled the waiter to bring another drink.

"They never give us any warning, like how they warn-

ing the queer man you talking about now. He lucky. Nobody told us nothing. They didn't talk much to us, any-
how, but you would think if they hear something, they
would say something, right? But we don't have no idea
it was going to happen or anything.

"All of a sudden one night—2001, September fif-
teenth, I never forget the date, right after the American
buildings drop—I hear a crowd of people near the house,
and I look outside the window. Gideon wasn't home,
thank God. He was by your house. They come around
the house with machete and stick, come to take him and
kill him." Her eyes were wide open, staring. "I tell them
he not home, but they stay there half the night, like they
waiting. Thank God, Beth have plenty good sense. She
give him the money to take a taxi to his aunty—my sister you spoke to, she work with the post office thirty-five
years—and he come here right away."

"Who were the people?"

She couldn't make them out, she said, but she could
hear their voices when they came close. Uncle Thomas,
who had died already, and Sister Arida, she knew their
voices. And there were some other people, but she
couldn't tell who they were.

"They come banging on the door, calling his name.
They start to shout outside the house and tell him to
come out. One man was saying Gideon was a sinner and
start to quote Scripture, but it wasn't Pastor. I tell them
Gideon coming back tomorrow, but I didn't open the
door. I put a vanity against the door, then I turn off all
the lights like I going to bed. I could hear them talking

outside, saying they could come back tomorrow night if he don't come home.

"After they left, almost daylight, you come tell me Beth send him to my sister. Later that morning I took a taxi to Port Antonio and he was here, safe and sound. I report it to the police in Port Antonio, but they don't do nothing. They laugh at me." Neville would have laughed, Shad knew, had it in him to make the woman feel worse than a John Crow vulture for having a gay son.

"A week later I went back to Largo, because I was working in the bar, Quality Life Bar, in the square. And I tell everybody about it, because I think the guilty people will shame."

She examined the age spots on the back of her hand holding the cigarette. "But they don't have no shame. I still hear people talking things behind my back, like they want me to hear. And they make jokes, and one man ask me—in front of the customers—if I hear from Gideon, if he turn actress in Hollywood yet."

"So you came here?"

"I move here, yes."

"Your son do okay here?"

She gave a crooked smile. "You could say so."

"He got a job?" Shad looked at his watch under the table.

"Nobody want to give him work." Her eyes squinted at him through the cigarette smoke. "He start to come and go, bring me little money sometimes. I don't ask what he did, and he don't tell me. Then he got arrested."

"But he didn't go to prison?"

"No, a friend of his, an old white man from abroad, bail him out. The man got a lawyer for him and he got off. Then he come to see me and say the old man died and he going to Kingston to learn to sew."

She paused like she was baiting him to ask another question, but he waited, knowing she'd had enough rum to talk until it was done.

"Last I heard, he still in Kingston, but I don't know where, so don't ask me." He assured her he didn't want to know, it wouldn't help him.

She gave a short laugh, sour with resentment. "If I knew, you don't think I'd remind him he was going to support me? I wouldn't have to work till I dead, work cleaning toilets in the hospital. Like how I don't have no child to take care of me, like a son supposed to take care of a mother. And after all I go through for him? He should be ashamed. He don't even write to find out how I going."

It was on the walk home, Shad steadying her on the rutted sidewalk, that she remembered something. "There was a young man—a teenager like—with a high voice. He was among them. I never saw him, but I remember this loud, high boy's voice. He was calling out his name, calling Gideon things when they came for him. I never forget."

When Shad got back to the police station in Port Antonio, Neville was at his desk reading the *Star,* the afternoon gossip paper.

"Cousin Shad," he said in his deep voice, folding the paper. He was clearly displeased with the interruption, but happy to be the authority who would know what was best for everyone, including his wayward cousin. Granny used to say that Neville, Ezekiel back then, was born to be a police. When they were young he used to play "lockup," his name for the game he'd make his younger cousin play when he and Aunt Jasmine visited Largo. Shad was invariably the criminal and Ezekiel the police-man with the stick. Before he enlisted with the police force, he'd changed his name to Neville, because Ezekiel sounded too *fenky-fenky,* weak like a church deacon, he said.

Shad nodded to Neville and sat down in the cheap metal chair opposite. "Thank you, I found the woman, but I have something else I want to talk to you about." He told Neville about the noose and the threatening phone call.

His cousin leaned back and interlaced his thick fingers. "But no crime been perpetrated yet?"

"No, but it looking serious. It sound like a threat, like they coming to do something."

"And the tourist is a batty man?"

"I don't know exactly."

Neville chuckled. "Well, we can't come look when we don't know what we looking for. You say you don't know who the person or persons are. You just have two threats. One of them don't even sound like a threat to me, could be just a youngster playing a prank."

"If you can come—"

"We don't even have decent transport to drive around town here, just five working cars for the whole parish. We can't come all the way out to Largo to run after we-don't-know-who." Neville picked up his newspaper again. "When you get a better idea of who doing what, come back and tell me. Or if a crime perpetrated, call me."

CHAPTER TWENTY-EIGHT

November 2011

"This is where she lived," Eric said, pointing to the corner where her mattress had been, where its civilized sheets had always looked alarmed by its wild surroundings, where she'd surprised him and Shad looking for her that first time, where he'd made love to her. The bed was gone now and he wondered who'd taken it after the storm, soaked through as it was. It was his first trip back to the island since she'd left, one he was making only because Joseph had insisted. He wanted to inspect it, Joseph had explained, to see if a campsite on the island would be practical.

"How long was she here?"

"Over the summer. She left in August, three months ago."

Joseph looked above his sunglasses at the open sky. "The roof couldn't have been very strong."

"It held up for a while, until the last storm. She'd done a pretty good job." She'd been a tough woman from the start, forcing him to stand back, beckoning him one step forward with each need, and he'd done it like a child playing "Red Light–Green Light."

"This was the old reception area, I remember." Joseph stretched out his hand toward the empty space, the tiles bleached and cracked. "And the office was back there."

"That's right."

"I remember you had a bunch of silly women at the desk," Joseph said. "They were always giggling when we came around."

"Silly women who worked hard," his father said, rubbing his paunch. "I'd give my eyeteeth to have them again."

Joseph frowned, a little scorn in his smile. "Where'd you get that expression, *eyeteeth*?"

"Jamaica, Ohio, New York. I don't know anymore."

Outside the old lobby, he recounted the last afternoon when they'd come for Simone, he and her brother, Cameron. It had been in the middle of an unexpected storm, which had ripped off her roof, and they'd had a heck of a time coming over in the boat. They found her sheltering in one of the old guest rooms, her little dog with the white patch over one eye shivering in her arms.

"She must have been terrified," Joseph said.

"She was lucky it wasn't a hurricane like the one that came through here eight years before, I tell you that. But it was still a bad storm, and she stayed pretty calm. She had this smile on her face and she said, 'I'm ready,' something like that."

Eric reminded Joseph of the layout of the hotel. The reception and bar (*remember the high ceiling and the mobiles?*)

had extended into the two stories of guest rooms. North of that was the long one-story building—now just four mildewed walls—that had once housed the dining room, kitchen, and housekeeping quarters. He pointed out the faded mural that Jennifer had painted in the dining room of fish and seaweed, and the view that diners had of the ocean.

"Nothing between us and Cuba," he added. He walked over to the almond tree and pointed to the spot that had once been a koi pond he'd dug himself, but Joseph didn't remember it. They walked down the old driveway, now riddled with potholes and lined by the wind-blown weeds and lemongrass that covered the rest of the island. A colorless hurricane shutter lay across their path, a remnant of the bright yellow shutters that were one of the first things to fly off in the hurricane, the worst hurricane in over eighty years. Near the end of the road, leafless frangipani trees displayed their white blossoms, perfuming the salt air with a fragrance that had once reminded him of romance and now smelled of funerals. It seemed a lifetime since his hands had patted the soil down around their roots. In front of them, the land fell off suddenly. Scraps of asphalt clung to the edge of the cliff, a few pieces still visible under the surface of the water.

"The road was gone by the time I left the reception area," Eric said, waving at the invisible road and the water above it. I had to make the decision, standing right here, if I was going to swim to shore. You better believe I was praying." It didn't take much to remember the taste of salt water in his mouth, feel his lungs losing the battle. "I ended up over there." He pointed to the beach opposite, below where his bar now sat. From here the bar looked shabby with its thatched roof and open sides.

Covering his eyes, Joseph squinted at the bar. "I think we should keep the bar just as it is," he said.

"That thing?"

"I'm not kidding. It's the perfect island bar, has lots of local flavor, great location on the cliff. There'd also be a really upscale bar inside the hotel, of course, close to the beach or something. You could get Jennifer to paint another mural for it."

"So we have to change the figures?" He didn't know if he wanted to see the bar survive, to have it next to the new hotel, mocking him, reminding him of his years of waiting.

"Why not? It'll increase your contribution to the project."

They walked back toward the center of the island, Eric looking down at his old flip-flops, examining his square, dry toes, dreading the moment. He'd have to do it soon, he knew. It was now or never.

"You want to see where Simone spent most of the day?" He showed Joseph a large, bench-like rock close to the water. "She'd sit here and read or write." They'd tried to make love there once, but the rough limestone had chased them back to the striped sheets. "Have a seat."

Eric sat down on the rock without looking back at his son, the full blast of the trade wind in his face. Below his feet, the edges of passing waves washed the rocks and splashed up every now and again. Joseph brushed off some loose rocks before sitting.

"I called her," Eric said.

"Who?"

"Simone. I told her you wanted to have a campsite on the island. She thought it was a good idea. And she liked my idea of naming the island after her."

"Hey, that's cool." Arching his back and stretching, the younger man looked around at the ruined buildings. "Simone Island—that could work. Especially if we kept the story going about how she—"

"I don't know about that."

"Why not?"

"She's a very private person. It's her story, you know."

Pulling hair out of his eyes, Eric turned to his son and then back to the ocean. There was nothing else to do now but get it out.

"She wasn't the first woman I had a relationship with—a serious one, you know," he said, and folded his arms. "Since your mother, I mean."

Joseph looked at him and laughed. "You don't have to—"

"I had a girlfriend a few years back—a Canadian woman named Shannon," Eric said, and Joseph turned away, his discomfort with the conversation as audible as the breeze in their ears.

"We have a child," his father said. A wave churned up against the rocks. Foam gathered around their feet, the bubbles bursting. Eric clasped his elbows tightly. He felt like a boy kneeling in the confessional again.

"A daughter," he added, and held his breath.

The voice beside him, when it came, was low and gruff, the voice of a man who despised another. "You have a daughter and I have a sister. Is that what you're trying to tell me?"

Eric looked out at the bright blue horizon and nodded.

"How old is she?"

"Eleven."

Joseph stood up and climbed the low shelf. When Eric looked back, he was sitting under the almond tree, on the rock where Simone used to eat. His head was bowed, his hands clenched together. It would take a few minutes for him to work up to a well-deserved steam, all the years of politeness between them blown away. The only saving grace was that there was no one around to hear it.

"I knew you were a cold son of a bitch." Joseph's icy voice reached Eric while he was still strolling over to the tree. "But this takes the cake." He flung a small rock into a clump of lemongrass. "My sister was either born or the woman was pregnant when I came down last time—and you said nothing."

"She wasn't born yet, and you had your friends with you. It wasn't a good time."

Joseph's face was as hard as his voice, his eyes narrowed. "When would it have been a good time? When she was one, two, twenty? If I hadn't have come out to Jamaica for your goddamn hotel, because I was trying to *help* you, would you ever have told me?"

"I would have told you—"

Joseph stood up and turned his back to his father. His arms and shoulders bulged under the T-shirt. He shook his head and turned around. "You certainly know how to win your son's trust, don't you? Were you even planning to introduce us?"

When Eric spread his hands wordlessly, Joseph threw his head back with a strangled laugh. "Oh, yes, you haven't changed much, have you? Just drop a child and leave it for the mother to take care of, just go about your business. It's like some part of you doesn't even know how to—to belong or something. I don't even know what it feels like to have a real father."

Here it comes, Eric thought, and sat down on the rock. Joseph's face was turning red, an artery in his neck pulsing. "The only person you ever thought about was yourself," he said. "All our years living together, you only wanted to do what you wanted to do. If I didn't want to play ball in the backyard, you were pissed. If I didn't want to go to the hardware store with you or go to a concert, you didn't talk to me for a week."

He slapped his arm and glared at his father. "My God, what kind of man are you? It's like you're not even in touch with your feelings. If you were, you'd know that people want to know who their relatives are. Didn't it even occur to you that I'd want to know that I have a sister, know that I'm not an only child?" He lowered his voice, barely heard above the breeze. "I bet you hardly see her, whatever the poor child's name is."

"Eve, her name is Eve. I've been up to Canada three times. It's—"

"Three times in eleven years. Boy, does that sound like you. The absent father—that's your claim to fame." Joseph examined his hands, turned the palms over and stared at them. "You have no right to be a father, you know that? You couldn't parent if your life depended on it. Why in God's name you had children, I have no idea. If it hadn't been for my mother—" He pushed his hands into the pockets of his shorts. "Tell me—I want to hear it from your lips—does—Eve *know* she has a brother? Does she even know I exist?"

"Her mother knows."

"And Eve doesn't. That's right, never finish anything that you start."

Eric measured his son, wondering what a punch from him would feel like. He decided he was safe, because Joseph had closed his eyes as if he was trying to calm himself down.

"You want to hear the truth?" the younger man said, his voice raised, the eyebrows high. "I'd be surprised if this whole hotel thing gets off the ground—with your history. You call me to bail you out, because you're so broke you can't pay a regular consultant, and because you're such a cheap bastard you didn't insure your old hotel properly and lost your shirt, all your retirement money down the drain. You hadn't saved a goddamn penny over the years of running the place, didn't manage your money well, didn't invest anything. So, let's face the truth, you failed at running the hotel. And you know what?" Joseph snatched his hands out of his pockets, and Eric started. "I could forgive you for that, even for failing as a husband—if you'd been a decent *father*!"

"I supported both of you," Eric protested, "through everything, I supported you. I helped to send you to school, and I send Shannon—"

"Yes, but you're not *there,* you asshole!" Joseph shouted, pointing at Eric, his face beet red now. "Do you think that throwing money at us takes the place of a father?"

Eric stood up. "But if I didn't—"

"We both know, hell, we all know that you send the checks every month—" he said, and threw a fist in his father's direction. "BECAUSE IT MAKES YOU FEEL BETTER, YOU SON OF A BITCH! BECAUSE YOU KNOW AND I KNOW THAT YOU DON'T GIVE A FUCK FOR EITHER ONE OF YOUR CHILDREN." The words soared with the breeze, echoing in an upward spiral long after Joseph had uttered them.

The truth, the bullet Eric had dodged all these years, had finally hit. And even though Joseph said nothing more and stomped toward Minion's old canoe, it continued to hit all the way back in the boat, hitting in the stillness between the splash of the oars, Joseph sitting with his back to him, rage tensing every muscle in his body. When they got to shore, he leaped out of the boat and walked away, leaving his father alone to drag the borrowed canoe up to the trees.

Eric turned the boat over onto its logs. Breathing hard and resting for a minute on the inverted stern, he looked back at the island. At least one pattern was broken. Joseph had spoken in a way he, Eric, never could have to his own father. Hurtful things had been said that couldn't be taken back, but the sentences, the words, the syllables, coming as they did from his son's heart, were so honest that they'd almost created an intimacy between them that had never been there before. But he hoped it would never happen again; it had been awkward and could have easily turned physical if he'd responded in kind.

Now if *he'd* brought Joseph up, Eric decided, walking back to the bar, it would never have happened, because he would have shown him that a man didn't allow his emotions to threaten the balance of a relationship. Claire had brought the boy up as a woman would, had taught him to delve down below the surface and bring up all the slimy stuff, regardless of the consequences, and you never knew what shit was down there.

CHAPTER TWENTY-NINE

Janna slid into the armchair in her room, the phone clamped between shoulder and ear.

"He's been like a black cloud for days, girl. He and his father had a big blowup. That's all he wants to talk about." There was no need to mention the eleven-year-old sister Joseph hadn't known about. She wanted to keep a few things between them, hug some of his confidences to herself.

"At least he's talking to you about it," Lorraine said. "That's a good thing." She had on her sardonic smile, Janna could tell.

"He talks to somebody else, too. He makes this collect call every morning and talks for an hour."

"Well, you're closer."

"Yeah, but he's gotten so serious. I'm trying to get him to think positively—"

"Stop trying to solve his problems. He's a big man."

"I'm not solving his problems," Janna said, and took a mouthful of Miss Bertha's new creation.

"Leave the man alone. If he wants to talk about his father, let him. All you have to do is listen, be a shoulder for him to cry on."

"I want to be the love of his life, not a soggy shoulder."

"What are you eating?"

"Stewed mangoes in brandy sauce."

"Oh, sweet Jesus. What do you have to complain about? You're living in paradise, eating divine food, dating a superfine man. Girl, don't you realize you got it going on?"

"I want the superfine man to have it going on with me, that's what I want. When it comes to romance, he's like a wheel spinning in mud, I swear."

"Easy does it. That's what you said to me with Sammy, remember?"

"How's that going, by the way?"

"It's not going, to tell the truth." Lorraine sighed and sounded like she was putting her legs up on a table. "He's been doing the disappearing act."

"I thought he was pressing you last week!"

"He was. But of course, get some ass, you're good to go."

"You slept with him, Lorraine? Didn't I tell you to hold off for a while?"

"You didn't tell me that! I don't know what you're talking about. You told me not to overanalyze, remember? So I thought about it and it made sense. I just went with my feelings. My feelings told me I wanted to fuck the guy, and I did."

Janna took another mouthful. "I don't know what I'm talking about. I'm trying to get Joseph into bed and I'm calling you out. I'm the last person you should listen to."

"Totally understandable, you're just jealous," Lorraine

said, and laughed. "Anyway, it didn't pay off. Let it be a lesson to you."

"How are you feeling?"

"Pissed, but worse pissed at myself for waiting for him to call. It's humiliating." A word Lorraine never used.

Janna tilted her cup and scooped out the last of the mangoes. "You know what they say: absence makes the heart grow fonder."

"He knows where to find me."

"Not if you're down here."

"You mean, in Jamaica? You're kidding, right?"

"Serious as cancer. I've been thinking about it. There's lots of space in the house. The children's rooms are empty." She licked the dessert spoon. "Besides, you can scope out you-know-who and tell me if you think he's gay. I need an objective eye, and as an experienced journalist, you're right for the job. I'm biased."

"So you're importing someone with fine-tuned gay-dar, is that it?"

"Just don't take him on, that's all I'm asking."

"Hey, I'm your girl. I wouldn't do that."

"You have enough vacation time?"

"Yes, I think so."

"So, what's the problem?" Janna said, hearing the whine in her own voice.

"The problem is—oh, hell, I'll just say it. I like Sammy. I want to see if he comes through. And I won't have the money for another couple weeks. I went and bought this dress. Girl, you should see it, a red one-shoulder thing. I wore it to a club last weekend with Sammy."

"A *freak-em* dress?"

"Right."

"And you freaked him all right."

"You weren't here to save me from myself."

"If you change your mind or get some money, the invitation is open."

"Thanks, girl, I'll bear it in mind. You never can tell, I might just show up on your doorstep," Lorraine said, the sardonic smile sliding through the line.

CHAPTER THIRTY

Rain or shine, Sister Arida was always seated on her verandah in the afternoons, rocking and doing something with her restless hands. Sometimes she'd be shelling peas, other times reading the Bible and fanning herself, and her glance would be going up and down, from the road to her hands, saying hello to passersby, turning over a page and reading aloud. This afternoon, she was working on a piece of fine embroidery, her glasses smudgy with grease. Shad looked at the half-completed cloth she held out, tulips and daffodils that only grew in England and America.

"Nice small stitches," he commented.

"My older sister teach me when I was little," she said with a modest smile. She was a neat woman, still slim after all the children, and wore a blue housedress, freshly ironed.

"Miss Arida," Shad said, putting down his empty glass and pulling at the creases in his pants. "I really came to see you about something—something to do with a church matter." The woman looked up at him and took off her glasses. "I know you are a rock of Holy Sepulcher Baptist," he started.

Sister sat back, smiling smugly. "'On this rock I will build my church, and the powers of death shall not prevail against it,'" she said.

"And I know you have been at the front of making sure things were—straight in the village, because you love the people, right?"

The woman beamed. "'Faith, hope, and charity, but the greatest of these is charity.'"

"You're a charitable woman, I know that," Shad said, and leaned forward in his chair. "But ten years ago there was a little incident with a teenager. He was acting like a girl. You know who I talking about, right?"

Sister nodded, closing her eyes.

"I understand that you felt that, that he shouldn't be—"

"He was a wicked sinner," the woman said, her eyes popping open. Her hands and fingers twitched on top of the tulips and daffodils. "He was a sodomist."

"Sister, he was a youth who didn't harm anybody, a homosexual boy living with his mother."

"And the Bible hate a sodomist, Brother Shad. 'Do not be deceived; neither fornicators, nor idolaters, nor adulterers, nor effeminate, nor homosexuals, nor thieves, nor the covetous, nor drunkards, nor revilers, nor swindlers, shall inherit the kingdom of God.'" Her eyes were huge with self-righteousness, her head pulled back into her stringy neck.

Shad sat back and sighed. "I going to get straight to the point, Sister. I hear that you was one of the persons, you, a person who uphold charity above all, who went to pull the boy out of his house to kill him."

Sister Arida's eyes flared, and she snarled at him. "We want him to leave, and he left. We was just trying to frighten him. There is no place for the unrighteous in our midst."

Her church brother leaned forward and clasped his hands. "And you know what you did was a crime, right? Attempted murder?" The woman looked down at the embroidery and the hands vibrating on top of it. "And that no one reported it because there was no police around and they couldn't get to Port Antonio. They too 'fraid of you, anyway. So you were lucky that time. You know that, right? And you know that I not going to tolerate that in this town again, right? First sign of trouble, I gone to my police cousin in Port Antonio."

Her mouth drawn up like a purse string, the woman kept staring at her hands. Just then the gate latch clicked. A girl and a boy in school uniform straggled up the path to the house with heavy backpacks.

"Afternoon, Grandma, Mistah Shad," the boy said coming up the steps, a Sunday school regular.

"Matthew." Shad nodded. The children went through the lace curtains into the house.

"Sister," Shad said, "I have something to ask you. Over the last few weeks, you hear of anything, anything like what we was talking, going on again?" Arida lowered her eyes and shook her head, tight curls quivering. "Tell me the truth, Sister, tell me if you hear anybody saying or doing anything that could threaten a person in our village, anyone telling them that if they don't leave, they going to get killed."

Her eyes were still narrowed when they lifted. "Nothing, I don't hear nothing, and even if I hear something, my time coming soon. Is God I have to report to."

"You mean," Shad replied, taking a calming breath, in and out twice, like a guest had once shown him, "for your grandchildren sake, you better not get mix up in anything, because, as God is my judge and your judge, I not going to stand for any stupidness. And if you get mix up in anything, you can take all your charity and practice it in St. Jago women's prison."

Shad let himself out of the gate and headed toward the bar. On the sidewalk, school children were returning home, some arguing, some teasing, others trudging alone.

"Mistah Shad," a barefoot girl sang out, running past him.

"Child," Shad answered. He couldn't remember her name, Rickia's friend.

A few minutes later, a dancehall song approached from the rear and a scratchy adolescent voice came over his shoulder. "Afternoon, suh."

"Winston," Shad said. "How it going?"

"Good." The tall boy slowed down and turned off his radio, clasping it under his arm.

"Making plenty money with Mas Zeb?"

Winston smiled and looked down at his sneakers, turning dirty around the edges already.

"I see you still following the music, though," Shad said, nodding to the radio.

"Like how I can't leave it at home—"

252

They walked for a minute before Winston said, "I went on the computer at school. It said you right, about Mojo Man. He can't go to America."

"The computer give a reason?"

"It said he was *gay bashing*." The boy grinned, his big teeth shining. "I never hear that before: gay bashing."

"What you think about it?"

Winston shook his head. "I don't like the whole sodomy business, you know, and I don't like how they lock him out of America. It don't seem fair."

"But you can see how he losing money and losing fans with his bad mind, right?"

The boy glanced down at Shad. "The Bible——"

"Don't give me none of that 'Bible say' thing, you hear me? I had enough of it today." Shad bit his lower lip and shook his head. "Let me tell you something, Winston, the church is one of the main things keeping this whole hatred thing going in this country. I love my God, but I don't love what the church is doing. They have a real old-time idea about what we supposed to do. They going back to the Old Testament and pulling up things, one quote after another, that not even relevant to us today in Jamaica. This is a world that have all kind of people, where men and women getting equal, where black people not slaves anymore, and gay people speaking out for themselves. If the church would just teach us to respect each other, we would be in a much better place, but they going back to a Bible that don't even mean anything today."

"But like how you is a church man——"

Shad stopped abruptly, and Winston turned back to him.

"Being a church man," said Shad, looking up at the youngster, "don't mean you go along with ignorance, Winston. You ever hear Jesus say anything about killing people—gay, straight, anybody?" Winston shook his head, and they walked without speaking to the corner where the boy had to turn off.

"Youth," Shad said, putting his hands in his pockets, unsure of how to begin and how it would end. "We need to talk."

They sat down in the square under the tamarind tree, on the bench with the fewest slats missing, and Shad described to Winston what had happened to Miss Elsa's son, and the boy listened, frowning.

"But why we want to have batty men in Largo, suh?" Winston said. "What they can do for us?"

"What you mean, *what they can do for us*? We can say that about anybody. The world made up of different-different people, Winston, even you. Think about it. You never going to live in any place with people who different from you? You not going to live in a place with old people, or people with *disabilities,* or people who don't look like you? Let me ask you something, when you travel abroad, you think you only going to see people like you?" Shad stared at the boy hard, needing to get through, remembering his own ignorance. "No, man, they going to be different from you. And suppose those people who different from you say they don't like black people from Jamaica, and they chase you out of town, you think you would like that? You think that would be fair?"

When his companion said nothing, Shad leaned back and folded his arms. "And you know what the doctor say? That gay people can't help it if they gay. Is a chemical thing or it come from childhood, she said. They just attracted to the people they attracted to. You think they would choose the life they live? Because it not easy, I telling you."

Shad looked up at the tamarind pods dangling above his head. "When I used to work in the hotel, it was pure foreigners coming through there, people of all kinds. Trust me, people come in all colors and ages and sizes and shapes. Some fat, some thin, some old, some young, some pretty, some ugly, some gay, and some straight." He laughed and Winston, relieved, joined in.

"And you know what? They all breathe and eat and go to the bathroom like me and you. They all looking for the same thing, a little peace, a little love, a little happiness. And most of the people mean well, and they don't want to hurt other people." He leaned toward Winston. "But you know the real sinners in the world, boy? The people who decide that other people should be just like them, who think they have a right to kill people because they not like them. People like Mojo Man and his friends."

Many words later and Winston started nodding. It wasn't clear if he really understood or just wanted to get away, but, before Shad had finished, Winston promised that if he heard anything about anybody wanting to hurt anybody, gay or straight, he would come directly to Shad.

"Because we don't want no beating, no burning, no raping, none of that in Largo," Shad said, standing up.

"We trying to build a little hotel to bring in some money to this little chew-up-spit-out town, and if we have a murder of any gay people, that is the end of that. If we bring in some tourists every week, is money in everybody's pocket. Mas Zeb have more work, you make more money, because we have more cars and taxis. You see what I saying? No tourists going to come if they hear of violence in Largo. We need peace to make little money and survive. You think Mojo Man a hero? You can be a bigger hero. Keep the peace in Largo and lift up the town. That's what a hero does, he don't pull people down—he lift them up."

Shad brushed off the back of his pants, tired of his own voice. "And don't let me hear you talking any more of that batty-man business. Just because your father not here don't mean you shouldn't learn little respect for people. They want to be call *gays,* not batty or backside anything, you hear me?"

"Yes, suh," Winston said, and turned on his radio again.

CHAPTER THIRTY-ONE

Mundane places—a bathroom, a bus shelter, an office desk—are the places where the spark of insight seems to fire best. And the life-changing moment is marked, leaving the thinker in a slight daze for minutes, sometimes hours, after, seeing the ordinary differently. So it was with Eric, seated on the smooth concrete floor of his business place, surrounded by broken chairs he was repairing, when he had the first thought in what was to be an afternoon of thoughts that changed everything.

He was hammering away, connecting a chair leg to its seat, the nail too big for the job, while thinking about Joseph. He'd been in a funk for the five days since their quarrel or, rather, Joseph's quarrel with him. The words flung at him had stung, partly because he knew they were true, but he'd been hurt even more because Joseph had stopped coming to the restaurant for lunch. The thought that he might be eating lunch at Lambert's or Miss Mac's, that Solomon looked at him funny when Joseph didn't appear, had burned him every one of the five days.

The floor cool beneath his bottom, Eric understood in

a sudden shaft of recognition that Joseph was right. He had never loved his son. More important, he'd never *allowed* himself to love him. He had resented Claire's pregnancy from the beginning, thinking of it as a unilateral decision, and he remembered looking at Joseph in the delivery room with resignation, accepting the duty before him. And at that moment of realization—hammer midair—he knew that he'd never engaged with Joseph as a father with his son because he, Eric, had made the conscious choice to stay aloof—and not to love him.

At that precise moment of acknowledgment, the proverbial lightbulb flashing in his head, the phone started ringing, startling him. He pulled himself up and slowly walked to the counter.

"Largo Bay Restaurant—"

"Is this Eric?" It was a strong voice, fresh and energetic.

"Yes, speaking."

"Hey, Eric. We talked once before. This is Danny, Danny Caines."

"Danny! I didn't recognize your voice," Eric said, and sat down on Shad's bar stool. He imagined the man, his future partner, as a tall, hearty black man of forty-something, a man who always sat at a desk in a shirt and tie. It would be cold outside his window today in New York, on another planet.

"Yeah, it's me," Danny said. "Just thought I'd call, keep in touch, you know."

"Things have been pretty busy around here. Tourist season coming up, you know." The last time they spoke, Eric had told the man he'd call, and he hadn't.

"I was wondering how the business proposal was going. Did your son come down to put it together like you said?"

"Yes, yes. It's going well." He saw Joseph jumping out of the canoe and stomping away.

"How far have you gotten?" Danny's voice was more intense than the last time.

"We've gotten the operating costs for the first five years together."

"That's a good thing."

Eric put his feet on the rungs of the stool and leaned forward. "And he's been working on the construction estimates."

"Great. By the way, I got those drawings you sent a couple weeks ago."

"The contractor drew them up."

"Cameron showed me the photographs, you know, but it helps to see what you have in mind."

"What did you think of them?"

"They're a good start. I'd like to have a swimming pool, though. I hear the water is rough in the bay there. If we have families with children, they mightn't want the kids to swim in the ocean, you know what I mean?" A swimming pool? A small fortune.

"And nowadays," added Danny, "you have to have a Jacuzzi to go with the pool."

"And a lifeguard—" Eric nodded. And chemicals and someone to clean it every day.

"I like the size of the bar. Were you thinking of a place that could convert into a club, with entertainment and all that? If Largo is as isolated as Cameron says, the guests need something at night, you know."

"Yeah, we were thinking of that, singers and limbo dancers, that kind of thing."

"Exactly . . . talking about." His voice broke up like he was on a cell phone. "Sounds like things are moving along, then. How long do you think it should take, I mean, before you get the report to me?"

Eric looked up at the row of bottles on the shelf. "Another month, I think, maybe six weeks." He suddenly remembered Joseph asking for a deadline. "Is that okay?"

"Great, great."

"Any particular date?"

"The sooner the better. Things are getting a little tight again, the economy and all that—"

"I'll tell him we need to get it to you ASAP. How about that?"

"Good idea. I have to run it into the bank, you know."

Awkward silence. "So, how's good old New York?" Eric said.

"Okay, I guess. I'm in Mexico right now, looking at some property."

"Right. Nice talking to you."

Eric returned to the chair he'd been working on, mulling his second revelation. Caines wasn't sitting in New York. He was considering another property—in Mexico. Leaning back on a table leg, he suddenly saw Joseph's work, Shad's hopes, Miss Mac's plans coming to naught, saw his life remaining what it had been for the last seven years—unending blight and boredom—if

Caines changed his mind. He stood up, holding on to his back with one hand and his knee with the other, returned to the phone, and dialed a number.

"Horace," he said when the lawyer came onto the line. "I need you to do something. I can't pay for it now, but we'll settle up when we buy the land from your mother."

A hoarse laugh came from the attorney, who always seemed amused talking to Eric. "I like how you think, man," he said.

"I'll be brief. I have to get back to something I'm doing."

"You mean you don't want me to charge you for the phone call, right?"

"You know that we're going to build—well, it looks like that anyway—this hotel on your mother's land. And we're planning on extending the resort over to the island, you know, the island off of the bar, the one that—"

He broke off, remembering how he'd run to Horace when he first discovered Simone on the island, and how Horace had laughed and told him no self-respecting policeman would row an eviction notice out to a squatter.

"I need to give it a name, the island, I mean."

"What you want to call it?"

"Simone Island."

"Simple enough. You just go into the Parish Council—"

"I tried that already. Nothing is simple at the Parish Council, you know that."

"Oh, the taxes. I get you."

"I paid my property taxes," Eric said quickly. "It's the

payroll taxes—I was thinking that if you filed the name change for me, it would be easier. What do you think?"

"I guess I could do it. I know some guys over there." He heard Horace shifting in his large padded chair, heard the chair squeaking when it swiveled around to the alley under his window. "Why are you naming the island? It doesn't have to have a name, you know."

"We're thinking of turning it into a campground with tents. Added income for the hotel, but less expensive than hotel rooms, you know? Make it appeal to a younger market. Joseph thinks it would be a money spinner."

At the other end of the line a match was lit, a cigarette inhaled, smoke exhaled.

"What about this?" Horace drawled. "If you let me in on the campground deal, let my company lease the island from you and run the camp, I'll handle all the legal affairs for the hotel and this campground, gratis. You're going to need a lawyer to prepare all the real estate documents, the agreement between the partners, the setting up of the corporation, and the closing. It could run you into some money, you know?"

Eric opened and closed his mouth—another moment of wonder. If Horace thought that his services were worth the rights to operate a business over there, the unsightly rock and useless buildings had some value after all.

"Well?" Horace said.

"Let me get back to you on that. It sounds interesting, but there are other people involved, you know, not just me. I'll call you back."

Later, the leg secured, Eric sat down on the chair to

test it out just as a group of customers came into the bar. They were salesmen passing through, they said, and he served them Heineken beers at a table. He was searching for napkins when Shad hurried in.

"What happened to you?" Eric said.

"Had to take care of some business, boss. You having a problem?"

"No, not really." Shad went into the kitchen and emerged a few minutes later, taking his place behind the bar, jumping into his work, opening the fridge to start setting up the bar.

"It's like this, since you're going to be a partner and everything," Eric said, watching Shad's hands. "Joseph told me that we should use the island to make money, for a campground or something, and I've been thinking about it."

"Sound good."

"I asked Horace to give it a name. Simone Island, I want to call it."

"Nice, man." Shad was nodding and slicing limes at the same time.

"Well, that's not all," Eric said. "Now Horace Mc-Kenzie wants to lease it from us. He says he'll handle all our legal work on the hotel, free of charge, if we let his company rent the island and run the campground."

"I love the idea."

"Why?"

"They do all the work and we get steady money flowing in. We don't have to do nothing, like when the woman was living on the island paying rent."

Like when Simone was living on the island. Nothing was like Simone living on the island. "I wouldn't want any of the buildings torn down, though," Eric said.

"You just tell Horace that. Make it part of your agreement thing, you know."

"This is your agreement thing, too, buddy," Eric said, and slapped the counter. "You're going to be a partner. You have to sign everything we agree to."

"True? I have to sign everything?"

In an afternoon of surprises, Eric had his last revelation. If the winds were in his favor, he was about to launch a business of some significance, a hotel with a swimming pool, two bars, and an offshore camping ground. Up to that moment, it had all been a vague idea, more like wishful thinking, and beneath it all the feeling that the whole thing would fall through. But now he had to accept that the vague idea was going to be a reality. The unspoken wish of the last eight years was going to come true, and failing in the venture was no longer an option, because there were too many people counting on him. And now that he thought about it, he couldn't fail himself. Not again. The whole thing would be a pain in the ass, might even kill him, but he'd have to die trying.

He'd be going into business with a man of means in the States, a silent partner who refused to stay silent, and he'd chosen a Jamaican partner who didn't have a lick of experience in business, other than counting cash and placing orders. And there'd be the whole construction process where everything had to be imported or trucked in from Kingston, guaranteed to frustrate the most patient man. But the long and short of it was that he had a chance, a real chance, to own a hotel again, a hotel that would be big enough to be really good.

"Boss, how come you never think of that before?" Shad said. "Think of renting the island to a businessperson, or running a campground? All these years you just looking at the island, not making money from it. You didn't believe it was worth anything, nuh?"

Eric turned on the stool and faced his past, stranded at sea on a clump of rocks. "I never thought of it."

"I didn't, either," Shad said, and Eric felt better hearing it.

CHAPTER THIRTY-TWO

Sheba was lying on the floor of a cupboard in the pantry. Three pups—one chocolate, the others gold—were sucking at her tits, their paws pressing against her flesh. They'd grown fluffier and fatter since she saw them last.

"She lost one this morning," Joseph said, stroking Sheba's head. "Did Miss Bertha tell you?"

"No," Janna said.

"It was a black one. She asked me to bury it, and I buried it under a tree in back." He was looking at the dog like they'd lost a child together.

"You should have told me so we could have had a proper funeral," she said. He smiled a little toward her and the tasteless comment.

"Chocolate Labs are a new breed, did you know that? Only developed in the last century." He seemed to be talking to himself, and she had no answer. While he was washing his hands at the kitchen sink, he told her about his Labrador retriever, Angus, the dog he'd had when they first got to Virginia. "Mom thought it would be good for me to have a dog since I was in a new place, new school and everything. I don't think she realized it would be so much trouble. We were in a small apartment and I had to take the dog out three times a day. If I wasn't home, she'd have to do it. She complained, but after a while we got used to it, though, and we really loved him. Great dog."

Over the six weeks she'd known him, Joseph had swayed through an unpredictable series of emotions, from detachment to guilt to passion to anger, and she had started to think of herself as even-keeled compared to him. And here was yet another side to him, caring for his dog and for Sheba, the sentimental burying of the dead pup. This was easier to relate to, a side that made her want to walk over to him and bury her face in his shiny hair.

"Do you want some chicken salad?" she said, opening the fridge door. "Bertha's gone to the market." She loved that he'd started eating lunch at her house and didn't leave until late afternoon.

"Sounds good."

She placed the food on the kitchen table, adding a jug of iced tea.

"I like Miss Bertha's cooking," Joseph said, munching a pickle. "Not that I'm knocking local food, but sometimes the pig's trotters and curry goat get a bit much."

"Especially with the Scotch bonnet pepper, if you're not used to it," Janna said. "I think she cooks to suit Jennifer, more American. Daddy likes a mix, so Miss Bertha's probably a little schizophrenic. Maybe we all are, all us mixed-up Jamaicans."

"I hadn't thought of that before. Like, you're Jamaican, but you don't come here often. Living in the US, but not really American. How does that feel?"

It felt intimate, that's how it felt, one of the first times he'd asked her a question about her feelings. "It's like being bilingual," she said after a few seconds. "I have friends from Cuba, from all over the Caribbean, and we talk about it sometimes. It's not a big deal, but we just know we're different, that we're divided into two parts. I mean, there's a part of me that will always be Jamaican, that loves the food and the patois and the music, the whole culture. You revel in it, you know. It's yours, even if you don't come back often. Then there's a part of you that's—more international, open to a global way of being. Most of that is American, of course, since I live in Florida, but I'm also aware of the Latin culture, and the African-American culture. I just take from each what I want. I'm lucky, I get to choose."

"Makes being Caucasian seem kind of boring."

She took a sip of tea. "I don't know. You have privileges you haven't even thought of. Anyway, we need all that technology and education stuff. We couldn't do without you." She clinked her glass against his and they laughed. He seemed more relaxed today, like he'd eased up from his rage at his father. It was easier to laugh with him.

"I remember," he said, leaning over the table, "when I was in Trinidad earlier this year—"

"You went to *Trinidad*?"

"Yeah, for Carnival."

"Oh, my God, that must have been amazing. I've always wanted to go."

"It was crazy, I gotta tell you, the costumes, the music, like it was never ending." His eyebrows were twitching, as if he'd been naughty. "I even bought a costume, me and my Trinidadian friend, and there was one time, when I was in the middle of the road in this Speedo bathing suit, glitter on my body and a gold feather thing on my head, and I felt like—like I wasn't American or anything, just some primitive man!"

"Must have been totally insane."

"It was. And once we were watching the steel bands pass by, and I thought, *I've never seen so many black people at one time!*" A look of wonder spread over his face. "It wasn't a scary feeling, just this recognition that I'd never been in the minority like that before."

With her mouth half full, Janna waved a hand. "But you have a Trinidadian friend, right? So it's not as if you don't have friends—you know, friends of color." An exploration she'd been dying to have.

"My closest friend is Raheem, the guy I went to Trinidad with, and he's introduced me to some other folks from Trinidad, one from Barbados. But in DC, I go to work and go back to Virginia. I'm not around a lot of black people or Latin people at one time. But I like knowing people from other cultures. I really do."

"So, growing up—?"

"I was around different kinds of people in New York, at Catholic school, but in Virginia we lived in the burbs. A few internationals, but not much else. I went to school with all kinds of people in college, though, and where I worked, but I didn't really have any close friends who were—you know—minorities." He blushed and looked down at his sandwich. "My mother's a buyer for a department store, so she's had her share of diversity, I guess, probably more than me."

"Has she met Raheem?" She was trying to picture him, needing details.

"Yeah, she said he was good-looking."

"Have you met his family?"

"I did, but we didn't hang out with them much." His voice had drifted off while he wiped his hands on a napkin.

"Who'd you hang out with?"

"Some of his friends. One of them was a film director. I liked her."

"That must have been a baptism of fire, Trinidadian family, Carnival, all the cultural stuff going on."

"It was wild." He stood up with his plate, shaking his head.

"I want to go to Carnival one day," Janna said. She could see herself in a skimpy costume, dancing behind a music truck like her friend Pat had done. "Maybe next year I'll go."

"You better rest up before you do," he said, laughing, halfway to the door. "I don't think I got more than eight hours' sleep in five days."

As soon as he disappeared, a frown replaced Janna's smile, and her unvarnished fingernail began outlining the hibiscus embroidered on the tablecloth. There seemed no end to the surprises coming from Joseph. That he'd gone dancing down the road in Trinidad—in a Carnival costume, no less—was a jarring thought. The loud calypso music accompanying the picture didn't have any area of overlap with a very white, very uptown financial analyst. And to top it off, he'd gone with a man, not a woman, an Indian Trinidadian man who was his "closest friend." Joseph was a man with many unturned rocks. She might never be able to turn them all.

CHAPTER THIRTY-THREE

Almost everyone—with the exception of a few restless youths—liked the predictability of things in Largo. For his part, Shad liked knowing that the steep mountain slopes, with their tangle of bamboo stalks and fruit trees, would rise behind the village for as long as he lived. He liked the water in the bay swelling every minute of every hour, racing toward shore, and he loved to feel the sea breeze lifting the hairs on his arms as soon as he stepped outside. On Saturday mornings, he liked passing by the market to say hello to Beth with her tomatoes and lettuce spread out on their old blanket, and he liked watching the cricket game in the square that afternoon before going to work. And every Sunday morning, he happily put out the folding chairs in church and later listened to the sermon, thinking that he could do a better job at preaching than Pastor did sometimes. He always listened and he always kept coming, because he liked being part of a congregation, liked the coming together over a potluck lunch under the trees for Father's Day and Mother's Day.

There were times, however, when the village's rhythm

got out of sync and nothing was predictable. Those were the days of chaos, and at those times Shad had a mission. Because to him, chaos was a storm—a vicious, blowing deluge that threatened his people, rocking the fishing boats at sea, flooding the farms and gardens, pushing them all a little more toward starvation—and his task was to look for the source and come up with answers. Only occasionally was he stumped for a solution.

A few days after talking with Sister Arida, Shad sat at his dining table feeling out of sorts. In front of him was a teapot and a cup of cocoa-tea, the oily hot chocolate that Beth swore would settle his stomach but seldom did. He was turning over in his mind for the umpteenth time the phone call that had come to Miss Mac while he was there, angry yet again that the police wouldn't do anything to help, wondering who to sign on to help him protect Joseph, and asking himself if he was doing the right thing by not letting Joseph himself know what was going on. He had just started having another logical discourse with his Maker when the front door opened.

"Mistah Shad, good afternoon." Winston stuck his head in the door, his eyes drifting around the room.

"Joella not here, star," Shad said. "They all gone out."

"Is you I want to see, suh."

Shad waved him inside. "Talk to me." Winston slid in sideways and closed the door behind him.

"Excuse me, suh," he said, "but I hear something about the thing we was talking about."

"The hero business or the—"

"No, suh. The ho-mo-*sexual* business you was talk-

273

ing." Probably the first time he'd used it, the word came out with spaces between the syllables.

"What you hear?"

The lanky teenager perched on the arm of the living room chair, and the plastic cover creaked. He had on a new baseball cap with *Ocho Rios, Vacation Paradise* embroidered on it.

"I hear that a man talking, saying that Mistah Eric's son is a batty man."

"What man talking?"

Winston rubbed one eye. "I don't directly like to give people's names."

Shad beckoned him to the dining table and Winston threw his hat on the chair and joined him.

"Why you don't like to talk people's names?" Shad said.

"They could get vex and come after me. Like how my father gone, I don't like to get into any mix-up business, grown-people business, seen." The boy's fingers were twisting and untwisting on top of the table, the fingernails bitten to the quick.

"But you willing to see other people suffer as long as you don't get mix up? Think about it, boy. If you see a problem, and you don't name the person at the bottom of the problem, how people can solve it? People have to be responsible for their words and actions, and if they put out wrong words and actions, they have to pay the consequences. You see what I mean? If you going to be on the side of *justice,* then you can't walk in fear. You must be a man of courage." Shad stirred his cocoa and knocked the spoon against the lip of the cup. "Pshaw, man. You a big man, you can protect yourself."

"But it's just me one alone—"

"Is not you one. I will be there for you, promise you."

Shad got another cup and poured Winston some cocoa-tea. "Tell me, who this man making trouble?"

The youth took a hungry slurp and put down his cup. "Brother Kelvin, suh."

"Wait, wait, wait. You mean—" Shad's stomach went numb. "You talking about the same Kelvin, Pastor's son?"

"Yes, Mistah Shad."

Shad closed his eyes. He saw the man sitting up front every Sunday, nodding on cue at the end of his father's sentences, a fellow who didn't speak much to anybody after service, who stayed busy collecting hymn books while everyone else chatted.

He didn't really know Pastor's son. He'd been an un-attractive, skinny teenager who never talked much and, as soon as he finished school, had gone to Kingston to attend religious seminary. When he came back a couple of years ago, his parents had thrown a party for him after one service and invited the whole congregation, but Kelvin hadn't said two words at the party and had done a lot of nodding. He was neither friendly nor unfriendly, but he didn't seem to have friends or reach out to anyone in Largo.

"Where was he talking?" Shad asked on opening his eyes.

"At Quality, the bar in the square."

"He *drinks*?"

"Drink plenty, and when he drink, he talk. He was talking how you couldn't have batty men in Largo."

"What he say?"

"He talking about how no batty—no gay man should be allowed in Largo. He always saying that—how gay people nasty—and ever since Mistah Eric's son come, Kelvin talking plenty talk, saying how we can't tolerate foreigners bringing evil ways to Largo."

Shad put his head in his hands. The whole town would be talking now. There would be gossip in the market, over fences, in the grocery shop. They would be asking each other if they see the boss's son, Joseph, and if they think he a batty man. They would be comparing notes, watching him and Janna, disagreeing, had probably been whispering behind Shad's back already.

Shad raised his head and leaned in. "Did he say if he going to do anything about it? Anything?"

"I don't know."

"Who tell you this, anyway?"

"A friend of mine, Lebert, tell me."

The two sat fingering their cups until Shad walked to the window in the living room. Miss Livingston's yard next door was overgrown, the bushes needing to be trimmed and nagging at him. "Winston, you done good, boy. You did the right thing coming to tell me."

There was no sound from the table. When he turned around, the youth was staring at his empty cup.

"You want some more?" Shad said. "Help yourself."

Winston shook his head. "I don't agree with the—the

276

whole homosexual business, Mistah Shad, like I was telling you, but I don't like how Pastor's son mash up people life."

"What you mean—he ever done anything like this before?" Shad said, and sat down heavily.

"Kelvin and my daddy—" The youth turned to the living room as if his father were there.

"He and your daddy what?"

"He and my daddy have words. Pastor's son was saying my daddy was a sissy, because he looking after his son. He say no man should look after *pickney,* only women should take care of children."

"When he said that?"

"Last year, in the same bar." His eyes low and shuttered, Winston described how his father had at first mocked Kelvin's words when someone reported them, and how he'd gone to the bar to confront him one night. The two men had quarreled but nothing more. But over the following months, his father had grown distant and irritable, and he'd started talking about leaving for Kingston because he could get more carpentry work there, and he'd given him an American fifty-dollar bill and left six months back.

"Where's your mother?" Shad asked.

"She dead, suh, died of—" The teenager passed his hand across his chest.

"Breast cancer?" Shad said, and Winston nodded. You couldn't make assumptions about people, Shad reflected. You never knew what they were going through, what joys, what sorrows.

"You make me proud, son," he said, and clapped a hand on Winston's bony shoulder. "You know why? You're working to make your own way, learning a trade that people need, and you still managing to stay in school. Who else in Largo doing that?" Winston shook his head and Shad smiled. "You a bigger man than a lot of full-grown men, trust me. When hard times get to people here, they just drop out of school and start fishing. You don't notice that?"

And being the storyteller he was, Shad began to tell Winston how he'd left school, despite Miss Mac coming to his grandmother and begging her to leave him in, but like how Granny had arthritis and couldn't do embroidery for the tourist shops in Port Antonio anymore, he'd left school and gone out fishing with Uncle Obadiah. Half hour later, Joella found her father standing in the middle of the living room, playacting for Winston, the way he did sometimes. She stood at the door, her hands on her hips, and watched Shad whinnying and spinning around on the spot with glee, saw him acting out for the tenth time how he'd fallen out of his uncle's canoe once and been so afraid of sharks that he wouldn't let go of the fishing net to grab his uncle's oar, and her boyfriend, Winston Dupree, had laughed his croaky laugh and had tears running down his face at the end of it.

CHAPTER THIRTY-FOUR

"I can see that Jennifer's not home," Eric called out before his friend reached the bar's counter.

"When the cat's away——" Lambert said, and they laughed, knowing it was nonsense because the burly Jamaican man was still grateful that a pretty young American had married him, and he wasn't about to mess it up by playing around.

"What are you drinking?" said Eric, who'd just finished pouring himself tonic water.

"Cabernet." After Shad had poured the drink, they walked through to Eric's apartment and sat on the verandah, the sounds of a Haitian meringue weaving its way from the bar through the bougainvillea.

"Guess what?" Eric said. "My wife, sorry, *ex*-wife Claire's getting married."

"When did you find out?"

"Joseph told me, a few weeks ago I guess." They sipped their drinks in silence, moonlight bathing their arms and legs.

"Jennifer's mother is getting worse," Lambert said. "They put her in the hospital."

"What's wrong?"

"They're doing some tests."

"Sorry to hear that. How's Jennifer doing?"

"Handling things, as usual. Her sister is there with her."

A minute later, Eric crossed one leg over the other. "How's the project going, with Joseph, I mean?"

"I haven't seen much of him lately. I've been busy with this reservoir job in Manchioneal."

"Well, we need to speed things up. Danny, the investor, seems anxious to have the report. He wants to add a swimming pool and a Jacuzzi."

Lambert looked at him and laughed. "Watch it, Eric. You might have a boutique hotel on your hands."

"A boutique hotel?"

"One of these expensive little four-star hotels, very creative, each guest room different. There's one in Oracabessa. You should take a look." Lambert had stopped laughing, drawn into the possibility.

"Horace Mac wants to lease the island," Eric said, "wants to set up a campground."

"Was that his idea?"

"No, Joseph's."

Lambert exhaled through his thick mustache. "He has a good mind."

"He does, he does. Seems to know his stuff when it comes to women, too." He turned to Lambert, expecting a guffaw.

His friend placed his glass on his knee. "With Janna, you mean. Yes, they're spending a lot of time together, becoming good friends."

"More than that, you think?"

"I think Janna is more interested in him than he is in her, if you ask me."

"I don't know why. I can't think of one red-blooded boy who'd pass up Janna." He might have gone too far. "She's a beautiful young woman, bright, well brought up."

"I don't want her to be hurt, you know?"

"I'm sure he wouldn't—"

"I'm just saying, he'll be here today and gone tomorrow, you know what I mean?" Lambert said, staring out at the silvery ocean or into space.

Eric swiped after a mosquito. This was not a direction he'd have expected Lambert to take. "Maybe you should take this up with Joseph."

"Maybe." A few delicate seconds passed before Lambert spoke again, his tone careful. "Does he have a girlfriend, somebody in the background?"

"I don't know anything about his personal life. Hell, he barely knows anything about mine."

"I was just wondering—" Lambert said, and cleared his throat. "Remember those friends he came down with last time? The two young men, the ones from New Hampshire or Vermont or somewhere?"

"Yes, I remember them, not well, though."

"Did you ever think they were a bit—different?"

"What d'you mean, different?"

Lambert grimaced. "Kind of—feminine, you know?"

Eric swallowed hard. Something acidic was rising in his stomach, bubbling up into his chest. "What are you saying? You're saying Joseph is gay?"

"It's just that—"

"And you don't want him dating Janna because you think he's gay."

"I don't know, I'm just checking with you. You have to see where I'm coming from."

An evening sea breeze had sprung up and was blowing between them. Eric clamped his teeth together, grinding the molars. He started to say something and changed his mind. He wished he'd lit a pipe, had something to suck hard. Taking a deep breath, he reminded himself that Lambert was his man, had saved him in the storm, was saving him now with the new hotel by charging him half his fees, had given Joseph an office to work out of, was always there for him.

"He was always a thoughtful boy, you know," he said after his breathing slowed. "If anything, it was my fault. He blames me, attacked me the other day, saying that I didn't understand him when he was growing up. I didn't. He wasn't like any boy I'd ever known."

Stroking the hair on one arm, he stared across at the island. "I couldn't get through to him. Perhaps I didn't try hard enough, I don't know. He read a lot, I remember, books about werewolves and all kinds of crap. I didn't think the stuff was good for him, and I tried to stop him, but it didn't work. He had a friend at school in the fourth grade, Oscar the guy's name was." He turned to Lambert. "You ever heard of a little boy named Oscar, for Christ's sake? Sounded like a damn hot dog or something. Anyway, they used to share books, weird kinds of books. Once I got him a biography of Babe Ruth, a kid's version, you know? He had that thing on his nightstand, never opened it as far as I know." He nodded, more to himself than anything. "He was different, always different, like he didn't want me to get close to him. And that was fine with me. My father had gotten too close to me with that fucking belt, enough times that I always hated to hear him coming in the house. Fathers and sons, you know? I didn't want that to happen to us, and I didn't know how else to be.

"After Claire left, I'd go down to DC to see them. He never seemed happy to see me. He was always rushing off to gymnastics or something. I never felt that either one of them wanted me coming around."

Stroking the rough skin on his chin, he looked up at the moon, almost overhead now. "When the hotel opened, I told him he could come any time he wanted to, I'd take care of his ticket. I wasn't expecting him to come, mind you, so I was real surprised when he said he was coming."

"What did you think of his friends? You never told me."

"Hell, I thought they were the queerest set of pansies I'd ever seen."

"And Joseph?"

"Naw, he's not queer," Eric said. He stared at the outline of the three bougainvillea bushes on the edge of the verandah. "He was just in the wrong company, lonely in school."

"Why would he hang around the other two guys, then?"

"Probably because he was used to being with his mother, you know. That's what I thought. I hadn't gotten the male-bonding thing with him right."

"What about now?"

Eric bent down and picked up his glass, white hair falling over his red face. Jamaicans had a way of jumping to conclusions, and there would be no listening to it, even from his best friend.

"Hell, he's hooked up with your daughter, hasn't he?" He chuckled behind the curtain of hair. "As red blooded as his old man, if you ask me."

CHAPTER THIRTY-FIVE

S he loved to watch Joseph swim. He had the confidence of a competitive swimmer, and Ocho Rios Bay had the calm water for his crawl, not like Largo with its furious waves. His powerful arms were rotating up and around like a windmill, his legs kicking in perfect synchronicity, his body controlled like an Olympian's. There seemed to be nothing he didn't do to perfection.

Janna lay back in the water and floated, the clouds overhead thin and narrow. She was glad, almost proud of herself, that she'd given Joseph time to make the next move. She'd come to the conclusion the week before that she'd forced herself on him enough, and she'd spent the mornings on the computer in her bedroom, searching for jobs, applying for a few—and waiting. Afternoons, even more aware of his presence in Jennifer's office, she'd kept her distance, reading, giving herself a pedicure, even baking brownies once—and waiting.

He'd finally come forward the day before, cornering her in the corridor. "You've been avoiding me."

"I've been right here."

"Something wrong?" She could feel his hand through her thin blouse, warm on her shoulder.

"Not a thing."

"Good." He smiled, blocking her way, the book-shelves behind her hemming her in. She couldn't have moved even if she'd wanted to.

"What about Ocho Rios tomorrow?" he said. "Go swimming, spend the day?"

"Sure, why not?"

And here she was, floating in her best swimsuit, the black Greta Garbo number that showed off her figure without being vulgar, feeling retro sexy. They'd already stopped at a jerk pork pit for lunch, laid on the beach for an hour, napped in the sun, talked about Jamaicans and a little about sex.

"Can you imagine," he'd said while she was putting sunblock on his back, "Miss Mac told me that every man needs a woman?"

"You're kidding!"

"I'm telling you. She said every man must stake his claim and stake it regularly, something like that. I was so embarrassed I didn't know what to do." They'd laughed and changed the subject.

Floating on her back and looking up at the puffy clouds, she tried to imagine Miss Mac talking to Joseph about sex and failed. Four children swam past her, then swam back under her. They bobbed up around her, laugh-ing, and she laughed with them.

"Can't you swim?" one of them, a boy, asked. She had to lift her ears above the water to hear him.

"Yes, I can swim," Janna said. "I just like to float, look at the clouds." The kids decided to do the same, and they all floated on the water's surface.

Joseph's head appeared next to her face. "May I join you?" He instructed the children to connect, until all six of them were floating, holding hands on the water's surface in the afternoon sunshine, like a sea anemone, she thought, feeling happier than she remembered being in a long time.

An hour later, she was sitting on the deck of a catamaran beside Joseph, heading into the setting sun. The sunset cruise had been his idea, too. After the children had gotten bored and swum off, they'd waded ashore and sat on the beach. Then he'd looked up suddenly. He had an idea, he said, and had her run with him to a concrete pier, at the end of which was a sailboat, and he'd signed them up for a sail.

"Rum punch?" the hostess said, bending down with her tray to where they sat on the deck, their backs to the steering cabin with the captain. They helped themselves to the drinks.

"Love rum punch," Joseph said. "I like making it, too."

"You have to make one for me sometime," she said, licking her upper lip. Soca music, too loud, was coming out of speakers attached to the mast above them. Three couples were dancing, holding tight to their plastic glasses, shuffling on the foredeck.

"Do you sail?" he said, looking up at the mainsail.

"No. Do you?"

"I have friends with boats in the Tidal Basin. I sail with them sometimes."

"I bet your mother had you taking lessons."

"You're getting to know me too well."

The wind picked up as they sailed out into open water, and the boat heeled over a few degrees. Joseph slid toward her until their upper arms were pressed together, and she willed him not to move, because she wanted to keep feeling his warmth down the length of her arm.

Janna looked up at him and winked. "This was a great idea."

"Thanks." He hesitated for a second, then started coming in, looking at her mouth, and she tilted her face up to his.

"Oops, sorry!" A blurry voice interrupted them, a man in a loud floral shirt who had lurched, grabbing Joseph's knee for support.

"Hey," Joseph said. He held on to the man's hand and helped him straighten. "You all right?" The man staggered off on his wife's arm.

"You're a caring person, you know that?" she said.

"What d'you mean?"

"Like with Sheba, and the flowers in my room, and that man falling on you. You're a softie. Most guys would have said something rude just now."

He ran one finger around the rim of his glass. "Anything wrong with being a softie?"

"No, I like it, that's all. It makes you—makes you kind of vulnerable."

"Aren't men allowed to be vulnerable?"

"Of course. I wish more of them were, though."

"Maybe they're not allowed to be themselves."

While the sun was dying before their eyes, she pointed to the pink and peach streaks spread across the sky, and he to the gray-and-orange clouds.

On the way home they pulled over twice. The rum punch was reacting to the twists and turns of the road and the Jeep's rough ride, making them nauseated. They cracked jokes about who would throw up first, but they kept it all down, the jerk pork, the alcohol, and the patties, getting back to Largo later than planned.

"Do you want to come to my place for a while?" he said when they rounded the last corner into the village. She managed to nod. After he parked the pickup in Miss Mac's driveway, they tiptoed in, trying to avoid the crowded furniture in the dark.

"Ow!" Janna whispered when the corner of a table surprised her. She smothered her nervous laughter, and when they got to his bedroom, she patted her way inside.

"Aren't you afraid Miss Mac will—?" she said, still whispering, thinking of the old lady's judgmental eyebrows.

"No," he said, switching on the bedside lamp and closing the door. She sat down on the crochet bedspread, her handbag in her lap. He took her bag and placed it on the floor.

"Don't put it there," Janna said. "Bad luck."

"Sorry." He put it on the chest of drawers and sat down in the armchair. He was looking matter-of-fact, like they were just visiting.

"So, what are we doing here?" she said.

"What do you mean?"

"Are you trying to prove something by sleeping with me?"

He looked startled. "I don't care what people think. They're entitled to their own opinions."

She was silent for a while, looking at her hand running over the cream crochet spread. "Did you invite me here because of what Miss Mac said? Am I a claim, a stake, whatever?"

He stood up and came close, close enough for her to feel the roughness of his jeans rubbing against her bare legs. Crossing his arms, he looked at her hard, his nose inches from her own. "I invited you because we had fun in Ocho Rios." He reached over and turned out the light. "And I wanted you to introduce me to those fabulous breasts."

She fell back on the bed, laughing at his dark presence above her. "Would you like to touch them?"

He lay down beside her on the sagging bed, making the mattress squeak. She removed her beach wrap and bikini top and guided his hand to her breast, telling him to be careful, they were still sensitive. He stroked her breasts, pretending he was a doctor examining her after the fall from the horse, and he was so playful that she joined in the game, acted the silly patient in the examination room who was getting excited. Suddenly his hand slid off her breast like something dark had descended on him, and she could just make him out, smelling of suntan lotion, his energy withdrawing.

"What else would you like to do?" she said.

"Take off your bathing suit." It was a calm instruction, not a suggestion, completely different from Damian, who'd ripped at her clothes without a word.

"Do you have any protection?" she said.

"No. Do you?"

"I'm on the pill."

"How many partners have you had?"

"Two, only two."

"Well, I'm willing to chance it," he said. "I've only had one partner in two—almost three—years, and I got tested last winter. We'll be fine—unless you have something."

"I don't have anything."

Her stomach queasy, wondering if she was making the right decision, trying to remember what she'd read about STDs, not wanting to leave his room, she pulled off her bathing suit bottom while he kicked off his jeans. *In for a penny, in for a pound,* she decided, and kissed his salty, sun-warmed back while he removed his bathing suit. When he rolled over, she kissed his chest and stomach. He lay still, patting the back of her head until she got to his waist, then he turned toward her. His cock was limp and she couldn't tell what size it was. She stroked it, moving up until their faces were close, staring at his eyes in the dark.

He touched her breasts, let one hand fall to her crotch. Her back arched, electricity racing from his warm hand to her clit to her entire body. He slowed down, hesitated, until she guided him in past the outgrown Brazilian wax, used her own fingers to show him, kept her hand on his. He was thinking, she could tell, was concentrating on exploring her folds and fluid with gentle fingers, the rest of his body rigid, his head lying still on the pillow. Her body was throbbing in a way it never had, not ever before.

She felt older than him all of a sudden, felt like she was holding him by the hand and showing him a field—of strawberries or ripe melons, perhaps, something clean and refreshing. She put her face close to his and breathed against him while she stroked him. His eyes were now closed, she could tell, no reflection from them in the half dark, but his breathing was getting faster. She kissed the hair on his cheek, almost smiling, kissed the smooth, taut skin of his shoulder, his neck, his cheek again. He lifted his head then and kissed her hard on the mouth, coming alive, wanting her at last. He stroked her breasts, one after the other, and she, screaming *YES* inside her head, felt him coming alive in one hand while she rubbed the other over his nipples. Wrapping her legs around him like a vine, she rolled over on top of him, his body warm and slick under hers, and reached for his sudden stiffness.

CHAPTER THIRTY-SIX

S had slammed the straw broom down on the linoleum in Miss Mac's kitchen.

"Did you get him, Shad?" The woman's face was contorted in distaste and she was leaning away from the deed.

"Is the fattest, longest cockroach I've ever seen," Shad declared. After he swept the remains into the dustpan and shook it out the sash window, Miss Mac slammed the window shut.

"Pshaw, man, is a pestilence," she said, sucking her teeth, "and I don't have no idea where they coming from. I tired of this old house now." Patois always reclaimed the old lady when she was upset.

The back door's creaking turned both their heads. Still in his bathing suit, Joseph was limping in, holding on to the doorknob for support.

"What happened to you?" Shad said.

"Sea urchin," Joseph groaned, throwing his towel over a chair at the kitchen table. He sank onto the chair and put one foot on the knee of the other, turning the bottom of his foot up. Miss Mac and Shad leaned in for a closer look, their three heads almost bumping.

"A sea egg, man, that what we call it," Shad declared, grimacing. "You step on a grandfather sea egg."

"Poor soul," Miss Mac moaned. "It must hurt bad. The black ones always hurt worse than the white." They all gazed down at the ugly spines covering half the man's sole, from heel to arch. Some spines had broken off and another dozen still stuck out of the foot.

"Do you have tweezers?" Joseph asked. He was making a face like a little boy. Miss Mac rushed to get a pair of tweezers and returned. She poked gently around the pale sole, removed three prickles, broke off a couple, and gave up.

"You're supposed to wee-wee on it," Shad said. "They say they'll come up if you do that."

"The man can't urinate on his own foot," Miss Mac countered.

"Well, I not going to help him." Shad laughed.

"Can't I just go to a doctor?" Joseph said, looking up hopefully.

"Your father gone with the Jeep to Port Antonio to buy food for the restaurant," Shad said. "He not coming back until six, seven o'clock tonight. He always go to a movie first, then he go shopping. So we can't go to no doctor, because the nearest doctor's office in Port Antonio and he going to close at five. You can either wait till tomorrow to go to the doctor, or you can go to the health clinic down the road here. Like how it Tuesday, the nurse is there. Nurse Thompson, she good. She can take them all out, gentle-gentle. When Ashanti got a splinter, she took it out and the child didn't even cry."

"Nurse Thompson it is," Joseph decided. He stood up and limped to the door, walking on the ball of his foot.

"Come, I help you, and I know the receptionist," Shad said. He went to Joseph's side with the injured foot and put his arm around his waist. "Hold on to my shoulder, up here, make it easier. Tell me to stop when you tired." Together the men left the house, Shad acting as Joseph's other leg, the two tied together with arms. They must have looked odd, Shad thought as they progressed slowly—he, the stronger, short and black, dressed in his work clothes, and Joseph, weaker, big and white, still in his T-shirt and blue bathing suit with the palm trees on it.

What started out as an innocent hobble down the main road turned into another lesson for Shad, a lesson, again, that five minutes could end your life, and a reason not to tell Beth about it for weeks, until all the terror and the tasting of blood in the back of his throat had passed. It was too much to relive right away by telling another person who hadn't been there. When he eventually allowed himself to think about it later, he had to go slowly, because his mind remembered everything like it was fresh and shiny, especially the rims on the car.

The rims were so shiny that they almost blinded him when they first passed, the afternoon sun catching them and leaping off straight into Shad's eyes. They were spectacular rims, rare in Jamaica, the kind of double rims with the outer spokes circling in a different direction from the ones behind them, the tire only a thin layer of black around the edge. Must have cost five, seven thousand American, Shad calculated when he first saw them, and they must have been new, and the young men, probably from Ocho Rios, were showing them off. The car's four occupants looked like those guys who'd made a little money from drugs, small-time cocaine salesmen, clean-cut, with brand-new sneakers and long shorts made of shiny satin fabric. One had the number forty-two on the front of his shirt, he remembered, would remember until the day he died.

He and Joseph were making slow progress around the potholes and weeds beside the road when the car approached. Shad heard the music first or, rather, felt the bass pulsing in his chest when it was still a distance off. The music got closer, the car unheard. Rap music with a man rhyming, his insistent voice blasting into the quiet village. Even before he saw it, Shad knew the car would have black tinted windows, a big-town car browsing for small-town girls. The rims cruised slowly past, the car bright red, a newish Japanese car with a spoiler on the back and a big antenna. Thirty feet ahead of them, the car stopped, its flashing rims still turning. There was no one else around, no girl in a skimpy top, no woman coming back from the grocery shop, no one to harass, not even a dog.

They limped on a couple of steps, Joseph breathing harder. Shad suggested a rest. It was a good time to stop, to keep their distance from whoever was behind the tinted windows. They stood on the side of the road, panting. Shad removed his supporting arm and Joseph rested his hand on it, his head bowed, the curly hair hiding his face.

The music got louder, the pounding in Shad's chest stronger. The rims had started rotating, reversing toward them. When the car was beside them, the throbbing of the singer went soft, like somebody had turned him down, had more important business. The window lowered, showing real people inside. A man about twenty-five years old looked out at them from the passenger side. He had short dreads, carefully tended and trimmed, and he was smiling, not with his eyes.

"Brother man," he said, eyeing the duo up and down. "Like the two of you need help."

"We good, we good," Shad said. Joseph's head swung up, like he hadn't noticed them before. The man opened the car door and got out. He was not a big man, medium sized, wearing a blue basketball outfit with the number forty-two, a thick gold chain around his neck.

"You looking good, the two of you, a nice couple." From the car came snickers and muffled comments.

"We just minding our business," Shad said.

"What's going on?" Joseph said, looking from Shad to blue shorts and back again. That was to be his only comment, Shad told Beth later, much later.

"Nothing going on," Shad said to him. "You ready to go now?"

"Hold up, man," the blue youth said. He put up his hands, both with rings. "Not so fast. Where you going? What happen to him?"

"We going to the clinic."

"You going clinic? You fuck the white man so hard, he have to go to clinic?" The men inside the car tittered.

That was the start of it. Before Shad knew what was happening, the other doors opened and three men got out of the car, all medium height, a fat man in a sweat suit in charge, it looked like. The others crowded around him, showing each other they were at the top of their game, next in the pecking order. Sunglasses hid the eyes of the big man.

"Yo, you don't know we don't tolerate any nastiness around here?" sweat suit grunted.

"You come from around here?" Shad said.

"Shut your mouth when I talking," the man said, a bully by the sound of him.

"Shut your mouth," the others chorused.

"Is my town, and I don't remember you, none of you," Shad answered. He crossed his arms and leaned on one leg, mimicking the leader, looking him in the eyes.

"You not only a batty man, but you talk back." The man laughed.

"A batty man, this man," one of the youths said, stabbing his hand toward Shad, the fingers in a V.

"And is a foreign faggot with him," blue shorts said.

"A foreigner come to buy a local batty boy," yellow shorts said. "You think we don't know what going on?"

Shad's heart was galloping in his chest. He glanced at Joseph, who had gone as pale as the sole of his foot. *Don't say anything,* Shad said with his eyes. *Not a word.*

"We want you to come for a ride with us," the leader said.

"We not coming for any ride."

"I not asking you, I telling you."

"And I telling you we not coming."

The man with the biggest chain held on to Shad, his hand coarse and heavy. "We not playing, you know," he yelled, the first to raise his voice.

The others joined in, shouting, stabbing the air with their fingers, calling them ugly names in the afternoon quiet of the village, no one around to call. They got closer. One man pushed into Joseph's shoulder, looked up at him, taunting him. His gold chain kept hitting Joseph's arm, making little clinking noises with the jostling.

"Move away from him!" Shad cried.

"Who you think you are?" said green shorts.

"You just a little shrimp," blue shorts shouted in Shad's ear. "You should be ashamed how you sell yourself to American men. Is people like you need to *dead* in this country."

One man grabbed Joseph's arm and started pushing him toward the car. Joseph tried to wrench his arm away, stepped backward, winced, and bent over. The man laughed and held on with both hands.

"Leave the man alone," Shad yelled. "He sick. You don't see he sick?'

"What wrong with him?" fat man said. "Nothing wrong with him that a beating can't fix."

"He got AIDS. You want to catch AIDS from him?" The men all turned to stare at Joseph, and the man holding him let go, his mouth open.

"He have AIDS?"

"You don't see he can hardly walk? Don't touch him, or you going catch it."

"You can't catch AIDS so." The big man smiled shakily. "You making joke."

"You don't believe me?" Shad said. "He have sores all over his body, and the pus coming out of his clothes. If you have a cut anywhere, a bruise anywhere, and the pus get on you, you can get AIDS, you didn't know?"

"You have it, too?" yellow shorts said, and they all stared at Shad.

Limping on one leg, Shad pulled away from the group. "I have it, yes. You touch me, you going to get it. It too late for us, save yourself."

"You going to dead?" blue man said, his eyes anxious.

"Yes, we going to dead, and is a terrible death. You ever see anybody die of AIDS? Is like a plague from the Bible, I telling you. You get sores on your body, on your cock, all over. You scream for pain."

The men squirmed, and the big man squinted at Shad. "How we know you telling the truth?"

Shad started unbuttoning his belt. "You want to see?" He loosened the belt slowly and pulled it off, kept it in his hand with the buckle loose.

"No!" one of the men shouted.

"Yes, man, I show you," Shad said, and continued to his pants button.

A taxi slowed down beside the group and the driver shouted, "All of you batty man, or what?" The passengers screamed with laughter and the taxi sped away.

"Pshaw, man," the leader said. "Let we go. I don't want to catch nothing, you hear. Is trouble, this."

"You don't want to see?" Shad said, unzipping his pants, pulling his shirt out.

The men dashed back to the red chariot and jumped in. Dust flew up under the rims of the fleeing car while Shad pushed in his shirt and zipped up his pants, his heart still racing.

"What the fuck was that?" Joseph said at last. Although his voice was harsh, his hands were trembling.

"Small men, thinking they big," Shad said, pushing his belt through the loops. "Come, is just a short distance to go. The clinic not far now."

Red velvet, thought Shad, rubbing his hand over the worn velvet arm of Miss Mac's chair, the car probably had red velvet seats inside to match the devil-red paint outside. Joseph came back from the bathroom with his shaving things in a neat brown leather bag and placed it next to the suitcase on the bed. He lifted a stack of T-shirts from a drawer and settled them in the bag, stuffing the leather bag next to them.

"Miss Mac told me you want a ride to the airport."

"Yeah, man."

"Is about what happened yesterday, right?" Joseph kept packing. "It not going to happen again, you know. Is just a one-time thing, we just unlucky that these fools passing by. They don't come from here. You not going to see them again."

Joseph sighed and sat on the edge of the bed. "I can't—" He dragged his hand through his hair. When he looked up, his tanned face was locked with frustration. "This is a fucked-up place, man, that's all I can say."

"I telling you, all you have to do is keep writing the—"

"It's not only what happened yesterday, man. Everything is so screwed up—my dad, the anti-gay thing—"

Shad closed the door and sat on the other side of the suitcase. "Let me hear the whole thing. What really bothering you?"

Joseph laughed, not a happy laugh, more of a groan. "Where do I begin?" He walked to the open window, peered outside into the rain, and turned around. "Did you know my father has a daughter?"

"Is that why you stop coming to the bar? Yes, I know he have a daughter. Her mother—Shannon is her name— a nice lady. She used to come and stay at the hotel, the year before you came out last time. Then she got pregnant, and we never see her again, but every year she send us Christmas cards."

When Joseph only raised his eyebrows and reached for his briefs in a drawer, Shad sighed. "Let me tell you something," he said, one arm out, stopping Joseph with the underwear filling his hands. "Let me tell you about your father. You don't know him like I know him. I know that not right, because a child should know his parent better than anybody else, but let me tell you what I know about him." Shad leaned forward, the better to gesture with his hands. "He was wrong, he was wrong, I agree. But the boss is not a mean man, he don't have a mean bone in his body. He have his faults, mind you. He kind of tight with his money, and he don't like things to change. Most of all, he hate confusion. He don't talk things out all the time, try to avoid talking because he hate confusion. That why he don't tell you and your mother about the baby. But sometimes when you pretend everything all right and you don't talk the truth, it can come back to bite you, yes?

"He not always so bright, you know, but one thing about your father, he treat everybody the same. He treat us with respect. You know what that mean in this little place? We not accustomed to a white man who treat us fair and speak to us nice. And here come Mistah Eric, saying we all equal to him, trying to fix the pipe when it clogged, trimming the hedge himself. That make us all feel proud, that a white man do the same work as we, knowing that we're as good as a white man. And another thing, everybody welcome to his bar. He don't try to keep anybody out, as long as they peaceful. He never say 'I big and you small,' you get me?"

Joseph sat down on the bed, staring at his hands and the briefs. "He should have told me, man. I'm walking around all this time, not knowing I had a sister." His eyes bore through Shad. "All these years, eleven years, I thought I was alone. Suppose I'd died in those eleven years, died not knowing I had a sister?"

"Now you know," Shad said. "What you going to do about it, besides being angry with your father?"

"I don't know."

"You a big man, you must move on. Time to forgive, turn the other cheek."

"He's such an asshole, though," Joseph said, shaking his head and the curls.

Shad leaned against the mahogany headboard and put his sneakers up on the arm of the chair. "You mean, because he not the best father in the world? Suppose you had a father like mine? I don't even know my father. He just gone, *disappear.* He made my mother pregnant and then we never hear from him again. At least your father try to do what he could do, send little money, see you sometimes. You was the first person he think of when we had to write the report. He proud of you. 'Joseph can do that,' he say right away, as soon as the man said to send him a business report."

"He's just using me, man."

"Of course he using you!" Shad nodded. "When he need you, he call on you. That what a family should do. You look first at who can help you in your family, then you look outside."

The man stood up and fitted the briefs around the other clothes in the suitcase. "I'm still leaving, though."

"Why?"

Joseph said nothing, bent over the suitcase.

"I hear you and Janna having a nice time, so Miss Mac tell me. You had a quarrel?"

"No, we haven't quarreled."

Shad lowered his voice. "Is it what happen yesterday?" Joseph nodded. "You understand what they were talking?" Another nod. For a minute, the only sounds were a few passing cars, the sloshing of wet tires on wet asphalt. Shad rubbed a hand over his scalp and looked out the window.

The socks packed, Joseph sat down again on the bed, his back to Shad. "This is a shitty country, man. They could have killed us. I haven't been near any gay people, as far as I know, and yet this thing happens to us. I've been spending time with Janna, slept with her even— and some idiots accuse us of being gay. Suppose I *were* gay?"

"You *slept* with her?"

"Yeah."

"That's good."

"So what am I missing here?" Joseph said.

Shad leaned back in the chair. "They were just idiots, don't worry."

"What about the police? Shouldn't we get them involved?"

"Pshaw, man, nobody going to do nothing to you. I know who all the idiots are in Largo. Is only one or two of them give trouble."

Joseph turned to him, holding on to the footboard. "I know what this place is like, man. If anybody thinks I'm gay, I could end up dead. I've read about it. You and I both know it could get ugly."

Shad ducked his head. "I know, I know, but you a big, strong-looking man sleeping with a fine woman, finer than fine. You don't have nothing to worry about. Nobody going to think you gay."

"I don't know, man. This is some wild stuff."

"You made a promise," Shad said. "Remember, at the party? You promise you would finish the report."

"That was before—"

Shad pushed his hand in his pocket and fingered the little bag with his grandmother's grave dirt, his good luck charm, sending up a quick message to the old woman, wherever she was, asking her to watch over Joseph. He knew he should be encouraging him to leave, but they were too near the end, and it would be worth the risk.

"You not going to leave," he said, standing up. "We going to make sure nothing happen to you. If anybody tell you anything, let me know and I will deal with them, give them some reasoning. That what most people need, a little reasoning."

Joseph looked down at his hands and turned the ring on his finger.

"All I asking you," said Shad, "is to finish the report, like you promised. You almost done with it?"

"About three-quarters finished. I just have to get back some estimates on the architect's fees and some other stuff from the Parish Council."

"Good, good," Shad said. "You just finish up and you will get your money as soon as the investor guy gives us the money." He shrugged, spread his hands. "If you don't finish it, no money for all your work."

"This is still a crazy place, man." His eyes had turned the darkest blue, like the sea way out deep.

Shad opened the door. "You ever use a gun?" he said. Joseph looked at him with his mouth slightly open, a fish out of water.

"I used to be a bad-ass shooter, back in the day. I could knock a bottle top off any fence post. I teach you, man, no problem."

CHAPTER THIRTY-SEVEN

I f he'd had a cap in his hand, he would have been turning it, but he only had the slightly stretched-out band
of his shorts to run his hand over, back and forth. He
stayed standing in the doorway, because Joseph hadn't
asked him to come in and the sleeping dog was barring
the door.

"Just wanted to give you an update," Eric said. "I was
speaking to my lawyer, Miss Mac's son, you know, and I
asked him to file a name for the island with the parish
government. He's interested in leasing the island, in running the campground himself. Well, he and his company,
you know. He'll waive all his legal fees, he says, if we give
him the lease." Eric shrugged his shoulders up and down,
drawing the tension out. "So we'd have no legal fees if we
do that."

Joseph was still sitting facing the desk, his head only
half turned, eyes slanted toward Eric.

"And I heard from the investor, Daniel Caines. He's
in a hurry to get the financial package, something about
the banks tightening up. We set a deadline for a month's
time. That work for you?" Joseph nodded, barely. "He

likes the drawings we sent, and now he wants a swimming pool and a Jacuzzi. Crazy, eh?"

"What size?" Joseph said.

"What?"

"The pool."

"I'd speak to Lambert about that. Something along the lines of the other small hotels, you know. Not too big."

"How much are you leasing the island for?"

"We didn't get to that," Eric said. He stepped into the small office and edged around the dog, which had opened its eyes. The walls felt too close. Jennifer's sketches were still pinned to the wall in front of the desk, pastels of orchids that appeared pale and subtle next to Joseph's hulking frame.

"I thought you might want to see this," his father said. He put a photograph on the corner of the desk. Joseph glanced at the picture of the young girl and swiveled a few inches toward it.

Eric cleared his throat. "That's her, that's Eve."

It was not a moment he'd thought would happen like this. He'd imagined telling Claire one day and asking her to tell Joseph he had a sister, keeping it all distant and calm.

"That's from last Christmas." The child had on a red sweater with reindeer dancing around her shoulders. She was not a beauty, but had the plain, square face and mature gaze of a person you could trust.

"Thank you," Joseph said. "Can I keep this?"

"Yes, it's for you."

Brushing his hair away from his face, Eric started toward the corridor. Outside the French door, he turned around.

"You're right. I should have told you when you were here last time."

He released his hand from the waistband of his shorts.

"I—I'm sorry," he said, and hurried back down the corridor.

CHAPTER THIRTY-EIGHT

"We're kind of parallel, you know?" Janna was trying not to pant, not to sink into the sand, not to fall behind his long strides. She liked running with him, but sometimes he'd spurt forward like he was running away from her.

"Parallel?" Joseph said. A wave crossed their path and they splashed through the foam.

"Yeah, I've been thinking about it. We're both—only children. We were brought up by our—mothers. We have half siblings. We're—unemployed and looking for work, you know." She giggled to hide her embarrassment. "And our fathers—are both divorced from our mothers and live in Jamaica."

"I guess you're right." He kept looking ahead through the sunglasses.

The beach was busier than usual. He'd said he wanted to switch his running to early morning, and she'd run down to meet him like they'd agreed, but they'd been surprised to see returning fishermen hauling in their catch with the first rays of the sun, the shadow of the eastern mountains covering half the beach.

"Morning," a couple of men greeted them. They were carrying a lobster pot between them, two lobsters clinging to the sides of the chicken wire maze.

"Morning," Janna sang out. Joseph's breathing beside her was rhythmic with his jogging. He was bare chested and wearing sneakers and socks for the first time, cushioning his wounds, uncaring that the shoes were getting wet. His hair, longer now, had shaken free of his ears and flew across his face in the light breeze coming off the water. She wanted to reach out and touch his back, his shoulder, anything, but he was encased in his own head and she kept her arms swinging like his. She'd come to terms with his silences, allowing that it was okay that he should keep his thoughts to himself sometimes, because that's what mature men did. And whenever she had any doubts about his feelings toward her, she'd remind herself that they were having sex, and, even though they never mentioned it in the light of day, she was his lover by night.

Farther down the beach, three men were pulling a dark green canoe onto the beach, their bare feet, strong and sinewy, digging into the sand. In the bottom of the canoe was a tangled fishing net and a bucket full of fish. A woman walked alongside the canoe and surveyed the catch, her hands on her hips. All four looked up at them and said nothing when they veered around the canoe.

At the end of the beach, under the cliff, Janna raced into the water, throwing up her arms, yelling that it was cold. He pulled off his shoes and socks and followed her slowly, the bandage still on his foot, a figure eight around the sole and ankle. Diving in, arching his body as he dove, he swam underwater past her. Janna paddled out to meet him. He was shaking the water out of his hair, his head back and the sun bathing his face on one side. A wave hit her in the face while she stared at him, and she ducked under the next one. When she came up, Joseph was laughing.

"What's the matter?" she shouted above the din of the waves.

He pointed to her bikini top. It had rolled down to her waist and her breasts were exposed, two coconuts bobbing on the surface of the waves, the dark brown nipples standing up.

"Oh, my God!" she shrieked, and pulled at the white bra. He dove and came up under her legs until she was riding his shoulders above the water, still pulling up the swimsuit.

"You want the whole village to see me?" She laughed.

He let her fall forward and drop into his arms. "Why not?" he said. He kissed her with a salty mouth, turning her on. He'd never been this affectionate in public before, but she never knew with Joseph. On again, off again. She would let him be whatever he was, whenever he wanted, as long as it was with her. She kissed him back, her legs floating up, until a wave forced them apart, and she held on to his shoulder as he pulled toward shore, the muscles in his back and shoulders working under her fingers, interchanging with each move he made.

On the beach, she toweled off her hair while he pulled on his socks and shoes. "Want to eat at the house?" she said. "Miss Bertha is making saltfish and ackee for breakfast."

"No, I better not. Shad is meeting me at Miss Mac's."

She wrapped the towel around her waist, and they walked along the road to the boardinghouse. She wouldn't ask what he was doing with Shad. He was a thirty-year-old man, and if she was going to date him, she had to learn to keep her thoughts to herself like he did. The oldest man she'd dated was twenty-four, and that was Damian, a brat who always wanted the limelight, was always jealous, tweeting and Facebooking her to find out what she was doing.

"I'll come with you to Miss Mac's," she said. "I don't want her to think I only come to her house after she's in bed." They walked past the bar and her father's driveway. A taxi rushed by, full of gawking passengers, and she felt out of place in her flip-flops and towel. The earliest of the children were off to school already in their crisp uniforms, walking along the side of the road.

"Morning, miss," one said, respectfully enough but staring her up and down.

"Morning," she answered. She pulled the towel higher, wondering if it was the breasts that made the difference and vowing to wear a beach dress next time.

Miss Mac was making johnnycakes when they found her in the kitchen. She was rolling the dough between her hands and placing the balls in hot oil in a frying pan. "You children are up early," she said. She cocked her head when she spoke, her eyes mischievous behind the metal-rimmed glasses.

"Went for a swim," Joseph said.

"And I wanted to come by and say hello," Janna added.

"To my face, you mean," Miss Mac said. She let out a squeaky cackle and lifted some of the fried dumplings onto a paper towel.

Janna smiled quickly and sat down. "How've you been?"

"Me?" the woman said. "You know how it go with us old people, nothing much any day of the week. You young people keep us entertained."

"I'm going to get changed," Joseph said, and headed toward the door.

"Before you go," Miss Mac called, "a friend of yours rang up this morning. He said he's coming down to visit."

He turned around with a frown. "A friend of mine?"

"He say his name is Rahman, Rasheed, something like that."

"Raheem?"

"Yes, that's it."

"Raheem, coming *here*?" Joseph said, pointing to the floor. His face was pulling in different directions, the eyebrows peaked in the middle.

"Yes, he's coming here."

"To *Largo*?"

"So he said. He wanted to make a reservation."

"A reservation to stay *here,* in *this* house?"

Washing her hands at the sink, Miss Mac turned to Janna with a laugh. "He sounds like a deaf person now, repeating everything I say." She looked at Joseph over the top of her glasses, her words precise. "Yes, he is coming to stay *here*."

"When?" Janna asked for Joseph, who was still staring.

"He say this weekend, on Saturday. I wrote the time and flight number down. He asking you to come for him at Montego Bay airport."

When Joseph turned wordlessly, his body didn't seem connected to his mind and he stumbled on the small step up to the corridor.

"Like he in shock," Miss Mac said. She turned to Janna, her eyes big over the top of her glasses. "You ever hear of this *Rasheed*?"

"Raheem. I think he's a close friend."

The woman started breaking eggs into a bowl. She beat them fast, bubbles forming instantly under the power of her arm.

"You think Raheem know about you?" she said. Janna shrugged, tightening the towel again.

Sitting on the back patio of her dad's house later, hardly tasting her breakfast, Janna imagined how it would be with Raheem, the new dynamic that would emerge. If he was Joseph's lover, well, everything would change, but that wasn't likely, because he enjoyed sex like a hetero man, she could tell. Raheem had to be just a friend, even if he was his best friend. But a friend, any friend, would shift the balance. A friend would have expectations and Joseph would have obligations.

It was hard enough to keep his attention since he'd started working furiously at the report again, like he had a time bomb in his head. In the evenings, when they sat on the verandah or the patio, eating whatever dessert Miss Bertha had left in the kitchen, they would chat, she doing most of the talking, but sometimes his answers would be so glib that it was better to sit in silence. Sex seemed to bring him back in a way that was so fierce it made her feel powerful to know she could do that for him. His lovemaking had become that of a man who had to drown himself, eyes shut, in her mouth, her breasts, her belly, her vagina, and after she came, he usually turned her over and drove into her from behind, hard, then harder, until he came, too, few if any words between them. Afterward they would lie on their separate pillows, and he would pant like he'd been running.

Picking up her plate, she went back into the kitchen, Sheba trailing behind her. There was nothing she could do about Raheem coming down. She couldn't make demands on Joseph or have him choose between them, because he'd known Raheem longer than her, had traveled with him and met his family. He was his best friend— and he would be there between them.

She was just stepping out of the shower, talking herself into liking this Raheem, when she heard the shots. At first she thought they were firecrackers going off and couldn't imagine who would be setting off firecrackers on a Wednesday morning. But each explosion lingered, low and hollow, not the way a popping firecracker would. She wiped out her ears with a towel and stood still. Another explosion, and another. A pause, followed by two more.

"Miss Bertha, you hear that?" she called, running

down the hall, zipping up her shorts. The housekeeper was sitting at the breakfast table polishing silver, her wide hips spilling off the chair, the sharp smell of silver polish filling the room

"They shooting off a gun in the back," she said, and put down a large serving spoon next to a serving fork, the spotless utensils lined up for duty.

"Shooting off a gun? Who?"

"Shad ask me if he and Joseph could do some *target practice,* and I tell them to go on, like how your father gone to work already."

"Target practice?"

"Every man should know how to use a gun," the woman said. She picked up a fork and rubbed the cloth up and down the spine.

"Why does he need a gun?"

The woman smiled up at her, two hairs under her chin begging to be tweezed. "Duppy know who to frighten."

Janna walked back to her room, trailing one hand along the wall. A duppy knows who to frighten. A ghost, an evil person, only frightens someone weak. Had Joseph seen a ghost?

CHAPTER THIRTY-NINE

O ff the platform and shirtless, the man looked smaller, his chest undeveloped and childlike without the big black robe, and the usual intensity on his face was now toned down to a tired alertness. He was sitting on the bottom step leading up to his house, taking a rest from cutting the grass, his machete beside him. Sweat dripped from every inch of his body, and bits of grass were stuck to his legs and arms.

"Brother Shad, you looking for me?"

Shad opened the gate, closed it back, and walked up the path. "Yes, Pastor, a little matter."

"You ready to get married?"

"No, another year or two."

"Can't keep the Lord waiting, you know. You living in sin a long time."

"Me and most of Jamaica," Shad replied.

"And we must rise above the sinners." The little man stood up and wiped his hands on the back of his shorts. "Glad you came, anyway. I wanted to ask you if you could take a look at a window frame in the back of the sanctuary. Look like it coming loose."

"Next Sunday."

"How is the little girl? The one that so quiet?"

"She good, good as we can expect. We took her to the doctor. She say she have autism."

"What's that?" Pastor said. He bent down and picked up the machete.

"A sickness. We don't know if she going to get better."

Pastor wiped the blade of the big knife with his finger. "The sins of the father are visited on the children," he grunted.

Shad had never liked the man, plain and simple. In the old days, he would have called him the worst Jamaican bad word he could think of, *a bumba claat,* a sanitary napkin. But since he and Beth had been baptized by Pastor Davis twelve years ago, before McClelen came, he just remembered what he would have called him and felt better. It had been Shad's suspicion from the beginning that Pastor secretly looked down on his flock. Sent by the Baptists in Kingston one Christmas, his first sermon about Mary being a virgin (*unlike the women of Jamaica,* he'd announced) had unsettled Shad, despite the fact that his passionate nasal voice had worked up the congregation quicker than Pastor Davis ever had.

Shad ran a hand over his perspiring head. "Hot day, eh?"

"I hoping for rain," Pastor said, and squinted upward. He was holding the machete flat between his two hands, ready to finish the job.

Shad straightened his shirtsleeves, which were already

straight. "Pastor," he said, "something need your attention."

McClelen lowered the knife. "What happen?"

"It look like your son—your son saying some things—"

"What kind of things?"

"Talking against homosexuals, saying that no gay person should be in Largo."

The minister narrowed his eyes at Shad. His voice got harsh. "I don't know what you talking about, and he don't say anything to me, but if he said it wrong, then it wrong. He study in seminary, and he know his Bible. You should be supporting him, not running to me tattletaling on him."

Shad folded his arms, looking the man in the face. "Pastor, he could be endangering a person's life."

"We have free speech in this country, and he can state his mind."

"Is not as simple as that, suh."

Bending down to swipe at some tall weeds near the step, Pastor muttered, "I don't know why we even talking about this."

"We talking about this, Pastor, because your son trying to get men in the bar to frighten a man, a man who don't do him nothing."

Pastor stood up, angry, his brow low. "What you saying?"

"He talking to people in a bar, not the bar where I working, another bar. He saying that we have gay foreign people in Largo, and they don't belong here. And you

THE MAN WHO TURNED BOTH CHEEKS

know how it go here, Pastor. People will listen and attack, even kill somebody if they think they gay. You and
Kelvin are people we respect in the village, and foolish
people will follow him."

"Who you hear that from?"

"I not exactly free to say."

"So how you know is true?"

"Like they say, suh, if it isn't so, it nearly so. Where
you see smoke, you see fire." The boy wouldn't have made
up the story. He knew him well now, not enough to swear
on his grandmother's grave, but enough to believe him
for now.

"And you passing rumors."

Shad said nothing. He wanted to see what this man
of the cloth would say about his own son who threatened
people's lives, ran off a good father by making him feel
weak and worthless.

Pastor started thwacking away at the tall grass beside
the path, and Shad waited. When the man finished working, the last stalks felled, he straightened slowly and put
one hand on his hip.

"Men talk all kind of foolishness in bars. You as a bartender know that. If anything, I will talk to him about
going to the bar, because liquor is sin, and liquor make a
man's tongue get loose."

"But is the things he saying against homosexuals that
I want to talk to you about, Pastor."

"You know what the Bible say about sodomism,
Shad?"

"Yes, Pastor."

"It say, 'Thou shalt not lie with mankind as thou lieth with a woman.'"

"Well, in Mark something," Shad said, stabbing his finger in his palm, "don't it say that if a man die without a male heir, his widow should have sex with all his brothers so she can bear him a son? We don't follow that today, right?"

"What that have to do with sodomy?"

"I just saying—"

The minister frowned hard, looking serious but not knowing he was looking funny with grass in his hair. "You saying you believe in sodomy, Shad?"

"I just saying, suh, that we can't believe everything we read in the Bible."

Without looking at Shad, Pastor wiped the blade with his fingers and started up the steps.

"Pastor McClelen, suh, if you could just have a word—" Shad said. But the clergyman disappeared behind the doorway curtain before his church member had finished the sentence.

"You ever see my trial," Shad muttered, and sucked his teeth. Walking back along the main road, shooing three goats aside that blocked the path, he was struck by the thought that, when Pastor retired, Kelvin would take over the church. And Pastor was getting ready to do it, like how he'd started calling him "junior pastor," even though he didn't get paid and the Baptists in Kingston probably didn't know anything about it. Maneuvering around a gaping hole in the narrow sidewalk, Shad realized that it wasn't the dancehall singers who had started this whole prejudice business, it was his church. Pastor and his church had failed him, had failed all of Jamaica, because it had fallen backward into all the Old Testament malice. And when violence came as a result, the church wouldn't even talk up against the beatings and the killings. Pure malice and spite, that was what it was, and any religion, Shad was sure, that preached hate was wrong, even his.

By the time Shad arrived at the bar for his evening shift, he had worked himself into such a temper that he had to sit down for a few minutes in the kitchen and fan himself with Eric's newspaper, and he resolved while he was fanning that he wasn't stepping foot in Pastor McClelen's Baptist church until the man and his family were gone from Largo—no matter what argument Beth put to him next Sunday.

CHAPTER FORTY

"I am *imploring* you," Janna said. She wished that she smoked. She would have taken a good suck on a cigarette and blown it out loudly so Lorraine could hear her frustration.

"I love it when you beg," her friend said.

"Don't make fun of me."

"I hear you."

"Are you thinking about what I'm asking you, though?"

"About coming down? What's the big rush?"

"This friend of Joseph's—"

"Yes, I got that part. He's coming down on Saturday." It sounded like she took a sip of something.

"I thought you were giving up coffee."

"Damn, like you can see through the phone. Will you stop trying to be my mother!"

"Give me one good reason why you can't come down."

"Let's do it the other way round. Give me three good reasons why I should come down."

"You've never seen Jamaica, number one."

"True, but it sounds like you don't want me to come

down for a holiday. You want me to work, to keep some man entertained so you can make it with his friend."

"Moving on to number two—it's a cheap vacation. All you have to do is pay for the airfare from Miami to Montego Bay. You'll be picked up at the airport, brought to this fabulous house, entertained and fed *free of charge,* and then, after you've had a wonderful time, deposited back at the airport."

"And all that in exchange for babysitting what's-his-name."

"Raheem, practice the name."

"Just the name—"

"He could turn out to be the love of your life."

"That's a myth, by the way. Love is—"

"Number three. Sammy."

"Did you have to mention him?"

"Whatever works."

"It's not going to make him jealous, if that's what you mean."

"You think I care about Sammy? I'm thinking of you. Sammy isn't that into you. Remember the book, we said we'd always tell each other when a guy wasn't into us? Well, now I'm telling you. You haven't heard from him since . . . God knows when. It's time for a change. You said so yourself."

"And, *hello?* You think setting me up with some gay guy is going to make me forget Sammy?"

"We don't know if he's gay."

"Whatever. What are my duties supposed to be?"

"We'll be a foursome when we go out, sort of keep

things in balance. It's going to be too weird with just the three of us."

"You want me to keep him busy so you can have sex with Joey. Why don't you be honest?"

"Maybe you'll have sex—"

"You're not pimping me out, sweetie."

"I'm just saying that you'll be company for Raheem, and, besides, you're funny and interesting. You got nominated for a state award in journalism, even if you didn't get it."

"And you almost got the award for diplomacy."

"Sorry."

"What does he do?"

"Raheem? I don't know. Joseph hasn't said much about him. I know they went to Trinidad for Carnival."

"Awesome. Maybe he'll take me to Carnival next year."

"You never know."

"Answer me another question. What exactly is happening between you and Joseph?"

"It's all good."

"The sex, you mean."

"No, everything."

"Don't lie, I can hear it in your voice. You think Joseph may not be serious about you and you want to drive deeper—I couldn't help the pun. You wouldn't be trying to distract Ramen—no, those are the noodles or something, whatever—if you and Joseph were tight. Nothing would be able to come between you, not even a friend."

Janna exhaled short and hard. "The sex is great, and almost every night. The days are different. I don't know, he's busy, working on this report. You know how men are." Silence from Miami. "It's at a delicate stage. He's easily distracted and kind of moody, ever since he heard that Raheem was coming. We spend evenings together, although he's a little—*vague* is probably the best word. I'm trying to be patient and not make too many demands, though."

"Did you say something about 'just not that into you'?"

"Well, if you can't catch Quaco, catch his shirt."

"What the hell does that mean? It sounds like some Jamaican shit."

"It means, if you can't hang on to a person, hold on to his shirt. My mother says it all the time."

"Just what—"

"Can you come, Lorr? Do you have the money now?"

"I have the money."

"And you said you had some vacation days, right?"

"Yeah."

"So what's keeping you back?"

"A gut feeling. Something isn't right in Denmark. Why is this guy suddenly coming down? From what you say, Joseph wasn't expecting him."

"Take off your investigative reporter hat. Are you coming or not?"

"Let me think about it."

"Please."

"And if the whole thing is a bust, you're going to reimburse me, right?"

"Oh, stop, it'll be fun," Janna said, and heard her own voice falter.

CHAPTER FORTY-ONE

E ric kept glancing at his passenger. He ran his eyes
down the lean frame, observed the graceful hands
with the long fingers resting on the light brown
linen pants, the soft beige shirt that hadn't wrinkled, the
Italian loafers without socks. And while they were talking, he took a good look at the flawless, heart-shaped
face and the straight black hair smoothed back with a
lift on top. Five minutes out of Montego Bay airport,
Eric had decided that Raheem was a goddamn replica of
Elvis Presley, a honey-brown Elvis, but more naturally
handsome than Elvis had ever been. He was possibly the
best-looking—a better word for him was *beautiful*—man
that Eric had ever seen, on or off the stage.

"Sorry that Joseph couldn't meet you," he'd said at
first when he shook the young man's hand, a firm hand
with a surprising roughness to it. "He's working and he
doesn't know the way to the airport, and the Jeep only
holds two people." He blushed, disliking making excuses
for anyone, even his son.

"No problem," Raheem had said, and smiled like he
meant it. He didn't look much like the photograph Jo-

seph had shown him, but there'd been something about the way he emerged under the IMMIGRATION sign that had alerted Eric. He'd stopped and looked around, stood with his legs apart for a few seconds, unafraid of what others might think, or unaware of his own beauty. No one else had come forward to greet him, and Eric had thought that a man like that would definitely have someone to meet him.

A cringe had come over Eric while they walked to the Jeep, because there was no other place to put the expensive, battered suit bag that Raheem had thrown over his shoulder but the back of the truck—and the truck's flatbed was rusty and muddy. But the fellow had said nothing, just found the cleanest part and heaved the bag in.

"Ever been to Jamaica before?" was Eric's first question after they left the airport.

"No, but I've heard a lot about it. When I was growing up, I used to hear people talk about Jamaica, the big island, you know." He was playing with a gold fish pendant on a necklace that hung a couple of inches under his collarbone.

"You're from Trinidad, right?"

"Yes, sir, I'm a Trini." Raheem ducked his head and turned to Eric, his eyes jet-black. Where had Joseph met him, this exquisite man with good manners? Why was he here? Joseph had seemed flustered when he asked his father to pick Raheem up at the airport.

"I'm at a crucial point in the report and I don't want to stop. Would you mind?" If there was another reason, he wasn't saying.

"Been in the States long?" Eric looked back at the road, aware he'd been staring.

"Seven years. I went up for school and stayed." His words dipped and swayed, the vowels longer than Jamaican ones, almost sounding phony mixed in with the Elvis Presley looks and the slight American accent.

"And you're living in DC?"

"I went to school in Virginia, still live there, but I work out of DC."

"What kind of work do you do?"

Raheem hesitated and smiled. He was looking straight ahead. "I'm a model."

"A *model,* you said?"

A chuckle emerged from his passenger. "I love how people say that!"

"I didn't mean it that way. It's just that—"

"You've never met a model before, a male model."

Eric shrugged. "Any model. I've lived a kind of limited life, I guess. Grew up in Shaker Heights, Ohio, worked with the same company in New York all my life practically, and then came here. I used to see model-type people in New York, skinny women in fur coats, that kind of thing, but I never met any." He pulled his hair back with his free hand. "There aren't a lot of models in Largo, you know?"

"It's kind of an odd profession. I still wonder how I ended up in it." Raheem waved his hand, a sweep of a gesture—his long fingers slightly bent—a gesture both feminine and masculine. He could have been gay or not; he was hard to slot. There was a poise about him that spoke of a life so alien that Eric couldn't capture it, couldn't imagine where he ate, where he lived, nothing. And it was a life that Joseph knew, a life that Eric had never thought about, that suddenly made the distance between father and son almost tangible.

As the afternoon wore on, Eric discovered that he liked the young man more and more. He was easy in his own skin, a man who liked himself exactly as he was. You couldn't help but feel good when you were around him, because there was an internal wholesomeness about the man that seemed to shine through his body. It made him so attractive that everyone, male and female, gay or straight, would want to be close to him—which was probably why Joseph was his friend.

They started talking about the places that Raheem had been in his life. It hadn't been a long life, only twenty-seven years, but he'd started out, he said, in the cane fields of central Trinidad. His father owned a car parts business that had mushroomed into a company with branches in the southern town of San Fernando and the capital, Port of Spain.

"Don't they want you to come back?" Eric said. "I know that—you people—" Eric wagged his head.

"You mean, Indians?"

"Sorry, I didn't mean to—but you folks usually keep the business in the family. I admire that, don't get me wrong, but I notice that—Indians like family to run things, you know?"

"Yes, they want me to come back." Raheem turned to the chalky cliffs they were passing. "I miss them a lot. My mother, my sisters, we're very close. Maybe in a few years, I've been thinking, when my parents—"

"Both your mother and father alive?"

"Yeah, getting older, you know. I have a big family, six sisters. Five of them are married in Trinidad, so they take care of my parents. The youngest one lives with me in Virginia—she's studying dentistry. I'm the second to last." He was smiling and nodding while he talked about his family.

He'd become a model, he said, when he was in college. A woman had come up to him while he was sitting on the steps of the chemistry building, doing a quick read before a quiz. She'd come up the steps and taken out a business card. She was an agent, she said, and if he was interested in modeling, he should contact her. He'd been stunned and hadn't done anything about it for a while, but he kept thinking about the card and called the agent when he needed cash to buy a car.

"Where has it taken you?"

"I bought the car, and then paid my tuition with it. When I graduated I started doing it full-time. I was only going to do it for a couple of years, but one thing led to another."

"Pays well, eh?"

Raheem only opened his eyes wide and smiled. A modest kind of guy, Eric thought. He liked that.

"Gone overseas?"

"I went to Dubai last year. That was crazy."

Eric frowned. "Dubai is—?"

"The Middle East. We did a desert shoot. You should

332

have seen the hotel where we stayed. It looked like a huge sailboat. And earlier this year we went to Bali. It was a lot like Trinidad. I kept thinking I could be at home, you know, with all the coconut trees and sugarcane. Beautiful beaches, though, and great restaurants." He didn't say it with any pretension but described it in a way that made Eric want to visit Bali. They stopped at a garage in St. Ann's Bay to fill up the Jeep's tank. While Eric stood beside the attendant, two teenage girls walked by and one smiled at Raheem.

The journey continued with an occasional comment about the passing scenery, Eric waving to a great house or a beach, giving a name and little more. Raheem said he'd always heard stories about Jamaica when he was growing up, that the island was the most beautiful one in the Caribbean. When they got to the bridge over Dunn's River Falls, with its three-hundred-foot drop, he asked Eric to stop for a minute

"Do you want to take a picture?" Eric shouted over the roaring water. "I can take one—"

"I don't have a camera," Raheem shouted back, peering over the bridge. "I like to remember things in my head."

They got back in the car and continued through Ocho Rios. The spluttering in the engine started afterward, a few miles outside the town. Raheem leaned forward and Eric leaned back, knowing it couldn't be gas. A few minutes later, the Jeep jerked to a stop.

"Oh, shit," Eric said, and hit the dashboard. He jumped out and opened the hood, propped it up with the metal rod he always used. The engine was dirty, the edges of everything dusty, corroded, or caked with salt. Behind the Jeep, a taxi honked and then pulled alongside.

"Why the *raas claat* you have to stop in the middle of the road?" the driver called. "Fucking white man come to Jamaica and can't drive!" Eric gave him the finger and the driver slapped the side of his vehicle and drove off.

Eric shook a few wires and none came loose. The battery terminals were attached, no problem. The engine hadn't overheated.

"What you think it is, Mr. Keller?" Raheem said beside him. He was standing back a few feet, keeping the pants clean, no doubt.

"I don't know, to tell you the truth. It's pretty reliable most of the time."

Raheem came closer. "It can't be the carburetor," he said. "It didn't sound like it." He leaned in, his hands still in his pockets. "Maybe we should push it over to the side—"

Together they maneuvered the vehicle closer to the bank. After a few more minutes of engine gazing, Eric put his hands on his hips and looked around. "We just passed a gas station. Maybe they have somebody."

"I'll go," Raheem said. "If you get it started, you can come back for me."

Eric watched him loping around the corner and out of sight behind the tall weeds. The sun was about to go down and he didn't have a flashlight. He hoped the mechanic would bring one. Half an hour passed and Eric was sitting in semi-darkness when Raheem arrived in a taxi, which screeched to a halt behind the Jeep. Raheem jumped out and it drove on.

"Where's your fuse box?" he asked Eric, turning on a flashlight. Squatting down next to the door, he fitted a new fuse into the box.

"Try it now," he said. "It should work." The Jeep started with a sputter and then cleared.

"I don't believe it," Eric said, his foot on the accelerator, revving.

"Fuel pump fuse."

"How'd you know?"

"The noise it was making, and how it cut off dead like that. And the ignition started, but you couldn't get any fuel."

When they were under way again, the Jeep squeaking around the corners, Raheem started reminiscing about helping his father install car parts. All his teenage years he'd worked in the business, he said, either in the shop or on the cars, and that was all they talked about around the dinner table.

"It started in our backyard. We live out in the country and my mother couldn't stand it, all the cars in the yard. She used to nag my father all the time to find another place for it." He laughed at the thought. "So he moved it into town and we all worked there growing up. My uncle Baba and his sons work in sales, they can sell anything to anybody, and my sisters work the cash registers. They're good with money. He had me working in the back most of the time, doing stocking and inventory, but I liked to hang around the shop. I like fixing cars."

"Why did you go to school, then?" Eric said.

"My father said that his *one son,* that's what he calls me, should have an education. He wanted me to study business so I could go back and take over." He looked down at his hands and spread his fingers wide. "My mother made me bleach my fingernails before I went."

"It must have been a—a shock, coming to America."

"I'd seen Florida before. We used to come up sometimes when my father had to do business. Virginia was different, though, more like the America I'd seen in movies, with all the old houses and neat lawns and stuff."

They lapsed into silence until the outskirts of Largo. "Sorry," Eric said, "but I forgot to ask you. How much do I owe you for the fuses and the flashlight?"

"Nothing, Mr. Keller," said Raheem. He was playing with the fish pendant in the dark. "Joseph is my friend. I couldn't let you pay me anything."

CHAPTER FORTY-TWO

There was more than one reason for Shadrack Myers to feel angry these days, an emotion that was so rare for him that he never knew what to do with it. Apart from his silent fury at the church, he found himself irritated at home, one day after the next, and the double stress had silenced him, because he had no pathway to channel it. The habit of silence he'd learned when he was a little boy, because Granny Matilda didn't tolerate rude children. On one occasion he'd rolled his eyes when she said something, and she'd slapped him so hard that he still remembered seeing the window behind him. In adulthood, he'd learned to talk the truth when he was upset, because it felt better to get it off his chest, but when he was really angry, he reverted to the childhood habit of keeping his mouth shut. It wasn't an act of self-preservation anymore, but an act of defiance—especially in a house full of women.

On Saturday afternoon he arrived home at lunchtime and found himself entering his zone of silence, fully aware that it annoyed Beth. She was sitting at her sewing machine, which took up all the space at the foot of the bed, and he had to crawl over the bed to get to the closet and crawl back.

"Since I don't have anything much to sell in the market today," she said, "I decide to sew." Tight-lipped, he started picking off the pins and the white fabric clippings spread over his side of the bed.

"You taking your nap?" Beth said. When he said nothing, she started working the treadle with her foot again, bringing the machine to life.

Shad lay down and put his arm over his eyes. The roar of the machine shook the bed, his legs, his body, his arms, his head, adding to his upset stomach. It was the fifth day in a row that he'd come home to a cold kitchen and the blasted sewing. Over the years since they'd lived together, she'd sewn the children's clothes and many of her own, but never five days in a row.

"The noise bothering you?" he heard her say. The machine started again. He rolled over, his back to her, and jammed a pillow against his ear. The machine stopped and he felt her crawl over the bed and across his feet on her way out, heard her mutter something about *people who can't speak their mind.* After a short, angry nap, Shad emerged from the bedroom buttoning his shirt. Beth was in the kitchen, Joshua on her hip.

"You want coffee?" she said, and he nodded, still blurry. He knew he was frowning and decided to leave it, to make his point.

He sat at the dinette table and she poured the coffee. After she brought it, she sat down opposite. Joshua stood up on her legs, his cloth diaper hanging low, and started hitting the table with both hands. His mouth was wide open in delight, two teeth shining from his lower gum. Shad took a sip of coffee and looked at his son.

"He going to walk soon, you don't think?" she said. He nodded and looked back at his cup.

"I know what you vex about," she said. "You don't like to come home and find the bedroom messy, nuh? If you want, I can just stop sewing as soon as you come. But during the week I have to go for Ashanti at three, and after we come back, I can't do no more sewing. I have to cook dinner and keep watching them. Evening time you not here, is just me with the children, making sure they do homework and don't kill each other." She sucked her teeth. "You think it easy?"

She raised her voice like he couldn't hear, defending herself. "I work in the garden all morning when it cool, and I have to look after Joshua while I doing it. Then I have to cook your lunch." She plunged on, and he knew she wouldn't stop until she'd let it all out, the way a woman had to. "Saturday I usually have market, and Sunday we have church and I have to cook dinner. You not the only person working, you know."

Shad took another sip, holding the cup with both hands, and waited for her to subside. When she finished, he sighed.

"Is the sewing?" she said, her voice turning anxious again.

"Is not the sewing," he grunted.

"You upset because I don't make you lunch?"

He bit his lower lip and took Joshua's hand. He

bounced the baby's hand in his and Joshua crowed, loving the new game. "Is the whole wedding thing," Shad said.

"What you mean?"

"Like you gone crazy, making wedding gown already, ordering cake—"

"I not ordering the cake, I ordering the fruit. I going to make the cake myself, I told you."

"We don't even settle on a date yet and is like you getting married next week," he said, looking at Joshua's tiny hand making a star pattern in the middle of his.

"July twenty-eighth next year," she said.

"July twenty-eighth?"

"That's when we getting married."

He looked up at her, felt the frown folding in on his forehead again. "You ask me about any July twenty-eighth, though?"

"You told me we would get married next year. I pick July twenty-eighth, the weekend before Independence. It not near a holiday, like you said."

"You ever see a thing like this?" Shad said to the baby. "Your mother just pick a date and don't say nothing to nobody."

"But you said—"

"If we going to get married," Shad said, each word slow and clear, looking at his woman of seventeen long years, "we have to communi-*cate*. That mean we have to agree on things. You pick the date and you ask me what I think. You don't just decide on a date and don't tell nobody. Is two of us getting married, you know."

Beth lifted Josh off her legs and stood up. "If I wait for

340

you to agree to a date, I wait until kingdom come. You tell me we going to get married after Joella was born, not true? I waiting fourteen years and four children now. I done waiting." She started toward the bedroom and paused, leaning a generously padded hip against the door frame.

"And if we going to communi-*cate,*" she said, "that mean you going to have to tell me what is in *your* mind when you get angry." She had on one of those looks she gave the children when they were about to answer her back. "I can't read your mind. You vex one whole week now and walking 'round the house like a duppy, not talking to anybody." She humphed and disappeared into the bedroom with Joshua dribbling saliva on her shoulder.

Shad sucked his teeth quietly as he rinsed the cup in the kitchen sink. The woman didn't even know when to leave a man alone. One day he would teach his girl children that they must leave a man to himself sometimes, let him be vex in peace.

It took him the rest of the afternoon to get back into bartender mode, good-humored enough to laugh at stale jokes, to blow off any problems behind the counter. By the time the sun had gone down and Joseph and another man approached the bar, he was in a reasonable frame of mind. Both were dressed in jeans and white T-shirts, both the same tall height, but the stranger was an Indian with a yellowish-brown color, his hair dead straight, his chest and shoulders narrower than Joseph's.

"What can I get you, gentlemen?" Shad said, leaning into the counter.

Joseph kept glancing at the other man. "Shad, this is my friend Raheem," he said. "He just got here." The man nodded. He was a pretty man with a diamond in one ear, and when he shook Shad's hand and smiled, his teeth were perfect, the straightest teeth Shad had ever seen.

"Welcome to Jamaica, Raheem. Let me pour you something. I like to guess people's drinks." He put his fingertips to his forehead like a fortune teller and smiled at the stranger. "You look like you drink wine at home, but you want a cold-cold beer now, right or wrong?"

"You're good, man. Do you have Carib beer?" The man had big, black eyes, ackee-seed eyes, Granny would have called them.

"Carib? No problem," Shad said. "And rum punch for Joseph, I know." Joseph nodded, his face stony.

Shad gave them his openmouthed smile, trying to relax them a little. "You guys want to sit at the counter or a table?"

They sat at a table facing the view and sideways to the bar, Raheem saying something every now and again, Joseph hardly speaking at all. They kept staring into the darkness toward the island and sipping their drinks, avoiding each other's eyes, and there was a tension so high you could almost see the jagged lines between them. But there was also an intimacy that reminded Shad of when he and Beth argued, when two people knew how far they could take the argument and that they'd work it out somehow.

When Shad served the drinks, Joseph gestured toward the unseen island. "That's where I met Shad, at the old hotel."

"We had a nice bar there," Shad said. "The Orchid Bar."

Raheem craned forward as if he was trying to imagine it. "It must be a ghost town now."

"But not for long," Shad affirmed quickly. "We going to have a hotel again. Right, Joseph?"

Shad walked back to the bar to shift into restaurant mode. Setting out the salt and pepper shakers on the tables, he glanced over at the two men. Raheem was saying something, running an index finger down the side of his nose and holding his other fingers at right angles from his face, a gesture so delicate it made Shad blink. The arrival of four customers distracted him and he hurried to attend to them. Back at the bar preparing their rum and Cokes, he called over the partition to the kitchen.

"Solomon, come!" The gangly cook pushed the kitchen's bead curtain aside and shuffled out. He was looking sleepier than usual, his chef's hat askew.

"The people at number three table," Shad said, "they want to order dinner."

The evening went by, a few customers came and went. Joseph and his friend stayed on, kept staring into the darkness like Eric next door. When they talked it was with voices too low to hear, except when Shad approached from behind with fresh drinks.

"—told you not to come," Joseph was saying, more than irritated, his jaw muscles tensing.

"I thought you would be—" Raheem shot back, and fell quiet while the drinks were being replaced.

"How you enjoying Jamaica so far?" Shad asked the newcomer.

"Very pretty." Raheem nodded with a straight face.

"You must move around, see things. You been to the beach?"

"Not yet."

Shad raised a finger. "Number one for beaches in the Caribbean." They didn't want dinner, they said. Raheem insisted on paying, despite Joseph's comment that it was on the house.

"No, let me pay this time, you always take care of the bill," Raheem insisted. He dug into his pocket for his wallet while Joseph pursed his lips.

"You staying long?" Shad asked.

"A week or two," Raheem said. "I don't know yet. I have an open ticket."

"You going to enjoy your stay, anyway."

"I hope so," the man said, and placed the cash on the tray. He was the kind of person whose emotions showed in his face, and when they left he was looking unhappier than when he came in.

Later, in the lull between dinner guests and nighttime drinkers, Solomon came out of the kitchen wiping his hands on a towel. He glanced around the empty restaurant and smiled, his big lips stretched wide. "I tell you so," he said.

"Tell me what?" Shad said. He was wiping the last of the glasses, his uneasy stomach telling him where Solomon was going.

"I tell you he was a batty man. You didn't see his batty boyfriend with him?"

"The man have a friend come to visit him. What

wrong with that? They just two men having a drink to-gether. We don't know anything about the people's pri-vate business. Leave them alone, nuh?"

"If Joseph might be a batty man, his friend is one from head to toe."

"Your tongue going to get you in trouble." Shad turned his back and started putting the glasses away on the shelf.

"I telling you, the man not just a *friend*. I saw them."

"Saw what?"

"I saw them hold hands under the table, just a quick thing, but they touch hands."

"I don't know what you talking about. When I saw them, they was arguing."

"They must have made up." Solomon came closer and lowered his voice. "You know what they call men who look pretty like his friend?"

"I know you going to tell me."

"They call them a *queen*."

"A *queen*?"

"That's right, a pretty man who look more like a woman than a real woman."

"You always getting everything wrong, so hush your mouth. You better not say nothing about no *queen* to any-body, you hear me?"

"I not going to say nothing, but somebody need to tell them that Largo not a place for batty-man foolishness. Jamaica is not America." Solomon strolled back to the kitchen straightening his hat.

Shad smoothed the towel on the counter and threaded

it through the refrigerator handle. He couldn't fault Solomon for saying what the other villagers would be thinking about this Raheem guy. Joseph hadn't expected him, sound like. Had he come because of Janna? Whatever the reason, he was going to make life more difficult for everybody. It was touch and go already with the noose and the phone call, but at least Joseph looked like a straight man, and he was sexing up Janna. Shad sighed and started putting the mixers away in the fridge. This Raheem could mess up the whole plan, yes, stop Joseph from finishing the report. A batty boy who looked like a batty boy in Jamaica was nothing but trouble.

CHAPTER FORTY-THREE

J anna leaned into the telephone receiver beside her bed. "You've got to come."

"What—?"

"I can't speak long. Daddy is complaining that I'm running up the phone bill. I thought about Skyping, but the whole house would hear the conversation."

"Update me quick, then," Lorraine said. "I'm watching Rebecca choose between two total imbeciles."

"Rebecca?"

"TV."

"Listen, Raheem is here. Joseph brought him over for a quick intro on Sunday, on their way to Ocho Rios or somewhere. Girl, I'm telling you, he is the most amazing-looking guy you have ever seen. He's a model or something, a real, genuine, flying-to-Morocco-for-*Vogue* model. Sideburns, the whole nine yards."

"Oh, my God," Lorraine said in a whisper.

"You have to feast your eyes on this specimen."

"Is he straight?"

"Could be. He has a kind of androgynous way about him, though."

"You *must* be able to tell if he's gay."

"I can't. He's a model. They're not normal, you know that."

"So is that why you want me to come down? To test the metrosexual waters?"

"No, well, yes. Joseph is acting weird. He hasn't finished working, but he hasn't come to the office since Raheem came three days ago. I need you here to—"

"Give you some time with Joseph."

"Precisely."

"What else? There's something you're not telling me."

"You're a witch."

"I always told you so."

"I was thinking that if you came, it would prevent any—I don't know—"

"Spit it out."

Janna put her legs up on the bed and stretched out. "Miss Bertha, our housekeeper, was saying that it wasn't good for two men to stay together all the time. Like they could attract attention if people thought they were gay, you know. Homos aren't cool here."

"Tell me about it. I was doing some research. You can still be sent to prison for ten years for buggery in Jamaica. That's what they call two guys fucking—*buggery.* Funny word, eh?"

"Not so funny when you're here."

"The gay association there says that there've been dozens of homosexual murders in Jamaica since nineteen-ninety or something."

"Will you stop? You're giving me a headache."

"I'm telling you. The leader of the association was

stabbed to death in Kingston a few years ago. Human Rights Watch has written about it, even wrote to the prime minister down there. Not much has changed, though. Most of the murders are crimes of passion, or whatever they call it, one lover killing another, but they've had mob murders, too. Very Middle Ages."

"That's not Largo," Janna said, and closed her eyes.

"Not if I come down and hook up with what's-his-name, you mean, because if the hunks hook up, it would be disaster. That's what you're thinking, right?"

"I don't even want to think about it. Anyway, they might not even be lovers. It could all be in my head—or my father's head. If anything, you'll have a story to tell. Not to write, mind you, just to tell your grandchildren." The wheels were turning in her best friend's mind; she could almost hear them in the silence. "Lorraine, this is not material for an investigative article. Promise me you won't write any of this in the *Herald*."

"Of course not."

"And promise me you'll come."

"As a decoy."

"If you want to put it like that."

"God, what have I come to?" Lorraine said, and sighed. "Okay, I'll come. It'll trump staying home and watching *Bachelorette*."

Janna hung up the phone. Her hand lingered on the receiver before she lay back. It had been the right decision not mentioning the thing that was bothering her most. A sin of omission, not a sin of commission, her mother would have said.

It still upset her to think of that late Sunday morning and the sight of them both sitting in the living room, Joseph looking like he wanted to be somewhere else, Raheem scrutinizing her from head to foot. She'd gotten them something to drink, and when she leaned toward Raheem to hand it to him, he'd pulled back an inch or two, as if he might catch something, but she'd covered it by making small talk with him about Trinidad and Carnival, and pulled up her blouse so she wouldn't show too much cleavage.

Joseph, meanwhile, had said little and kept patting Sheba, at his feet. Their sweaty nights of lovemaking were behind him, she could tell, and she couldn't get him to connect. He'd only glance at her, then look back at his friend to see his reaction. Once or twice a look shot between the two men, and she wondered what Joseph had said about her, and if this visit was only to satisfy curiosity. The funny thing was that she'd liked the newcomer, even if he called Joseph "Joe," which she wouldn't have dared. When he talked of Trinidad and its food, he got animated for the first time, his eyes lighting up and his hands gesticulating. His mother was a great cook, he said, made really good roti, the wrap with curried vegetables or chicken, and he couldn't find any as good in DC.

After they left, she'd collected the glasses and taken them to the kitchen, almost breaking one when she dropped it in the sink, and after she washed them and placed them carefully in the dish drainer, she'd held on tight to the side of the sink and shook her head to stop the memory of Raheem saying "Joe."

CHAPTER FORTY-FOUR

The *G* was always the hardest letter to paint. Eric steadied himself on the upturned pail and leaned into the sign. A car shot by a few feet away and he waited for the dust to settle. Grasping the bottom of the sign, he placed the pad of his right hand on the board, the paintbrush trembling slightly between his fingers. He had to do this only once a year, which he always did after the rainy season, when the red letters on the sign saying LARGO BAY RESTAURANT AND BAR had faded again to a dusty pink, but he liked doing it because it affirmed that his place of business still existed. Holding the sign steady, he started the downward curve on the *G*.

"Mr. Keller—"

Eric's hand jumped a half inch outside the line, leaving the letter with a thorn in its side.

"Shit," he said, and turned around. Old Miss Mac was standing behind him, her hands clasped together under her breasts.

"I didn't mean to frighten you," she said.

"Hold on, just a minute," he said. He wiped the mistake off with a turpentine cloth while the woman stood watching, and after he painted the letter straight, he turned to her.

"You want to see me, Miss Mac?"

"Something I have to talk to you about."

"I'll come by after I finish the sign, okay?"

"Good, I see you then," she said, and went tottering off along the main road to her house next door. It was about buying her land for the hotel, Eric thought, finishing the *O,* a letter he liked painting. She probably wanted to ask when the investor would be coming down, or wanted to talk about the price for her nine acres and beach. It reminded him that Cameron had asked him to look at the prices of land in the area, another thing he'd been meaning to get to.

Funny that Miss Mac should come to him now, just when he'd been thinking of Simone staying at her boardinghouse before she left Largo. He'd been thinking for some reason of her small hands with their short, square nails while he painted the *L* and the *A* and the *R,* thinking of how he'd reached out once and taken her hand and kissed it when she was lying in bed at Miss Mac's, recovering from malnutrition, after they'd brought her back from the island. He'd been aching to hear her voice again and postponed calling her until he heard from Horace, and Horace had called yesterday to say that the papers for naming the island had been filed. And even though he'd felt victorious, he hadn't called her right away, because he wanted to relish feeding her another bit of good news that told her he was a success, not the down-and-out he'd looked while she was here. By the time he arrived at Miss

Mac's back door an hour later, he was feeling exultant, having finished the sign's affirmation and anticipating the phone call.

Miss Mac had cucumber-and-ginger juice waiting in a pitcher with ice. "Sit," she said, and pulled out a chair at the kitchen table for him.

His glass was almost empty when he put it down. "It's been a while since I sat at this table, Miss Mac. Remember how you used to serve me dinner when I was staying here, when we were building the hotel? It seems like a million years ago, eh?"

"It's been a long time, yes." She pulled out a chair opposite him and sat down with a heavy sigh. "Mr. Keller, I wanted to talk to you—"

"About the land, I know," Eric said, eyeing the chocolate cake on the counter that was calling to him.

"Not about the land, no," she said.

"What's it about, then?"

"It's about your son."

"What about him? Last time I saw you, you said he was a 'fine gentleman,' except that he brought home Janna every night. If you have a problem with that, I can talk to him."

Meredith McKenzie put her elbows on the table and cupped her moley face in her hands. "Do you know he has a gun in his room?"

"A gun?" Eric said, his head jerking back.

"Yes, in one of the drawers."

"How do you know?"

"I was looking in—" She started again. "I had a phone call from Simone, Simone Hall, the woman who—"

"I know who you mean."

"Anyway, she said she thought she'd left a necklace here in a drawer."

"Simone Hall called you."

"She asked me to look in the bedroom where she was staying, and go look in the chest of drawers to see if I could find it." The blue bead necklace he'd given her, it had to be that. She'd left it behind, hadn't taken it with her.

Miss Mac leaned back, bracing her arms under her breasts. "She say it was in the top drawer at the back, and she wanted me to send it to her. So I went in the room when Joseph wasn't there, and I searched in the drawer she told me. That's how I found the gun."

"Can I have a piece of cake?" Eric said. "I think better when I'm eating."

She cut a slice of the cake, added an extra dollop of icing, and set it in front of him. After he'd chewed and swallowed a large forkful, Eric started thinking out loud. "I'm not seeing Joseph with a gun. I can't picture it at all. Why would he need a gun? How could he have bought a gun?" Another forkful. "He doesn't even have a car and he doesn't drive the Jeep. He must have bought it in Jamaica—he couldn't have gotten through the airports with it. But what in God's name is he doing with a gun?"

The woman eased herself up out of the chair and smoothed down the skirt of her striped dress. Out of the cupboard she took a packet with a tea bag, which she tore open carefully and placed in a cup. She filled a kettle with water and turned on a gas burner to heat it.

"Mister Keller, I know you love Largo," she said,

choosing her words. She was leaning against the counter with her arms folded, the muscles in her lower arms still sinewy and useful. "Most of the time the people here are nice, and they love you. You treat them good and they treat you good. But Largo people are poor and most of them haven't gone anywhere more than Port Antonio. They spend their whole life fishing and growing vegetables on a little piece of land, just trying to survive one day at a time." She pushed her glasses farther up her nose and turned back to the kettle. Eric rustled in his chair, almost holding his breath. After she sat down at the table with her teacup, he watched her dunking the tea bag in the hot water, in and out.

"They don't have enough education," the woman continued. "When a person don't have education, they think all kind of foolishness. And the leaders of our country don't have no backbone. They don't know how to stand up for what is right, and how to teach the people better. My father was a teacher, and he would say that today's leaders have *moral turpitude*—they have no set of values. They just looking for votes, and they don't stand up for nothing but what is going to get them votes. It suits them when people stay ignorant, little people like in Largo, people who can be spiteful and small-minded." She blew into her cup to cool it. Knowing she was doing her teacher thing, forcing him to listen, Eric waited.

"Anyway," the old lady said calmly, "one of the things they talking now in the village is that Joseph is a homosexual. I don't know where it coming from, but that is the new gossip."

Eric ran his hand through his hair and took another breath, blowing it out hard, feeling the anger rising, making his cheeks hot.

"That's *crazy*!" he burst out. "He's not a homo. You said it yourself—he's having sex with Janna. He doesn't have a queer bone in his body. The whole thing is made up. I don't know if they're remembering those friends who came out with him the last time, or what. There's no truth to it. Right, Miss Mac?"

She blew into her cup again and took a sip. "I know for sure he had sex with Janna, unless they jumping on the bed, but it sound like sex to me."

Eric walked to the window, his back to her, and looked at the deep turquoise water beyond the reef, the part of the ocean that men in small boats tried to stay out of. "Is he having sex now—with—with his friend?"

"I don't think so. They talk a lot, late into the night. Sometimes they argue, quiet-like, but they sleep in separate rooms—Joseph sleep in the blue room, your old room, and his friend in the green room. But I sleep sound, anyway. I don't really hear nothing."

He turned around and looked at this trusted woman, his neighbor and friend for fifteen years. "You think Raheem is queer?"

"I can't tell you. He's a nice young man like your son, brought up nice."

"How you know people are talking about Joseph?"

She told him about the phone call and the older man's voice. She spoke in a flat way, sipping her tea, reporting the call word for word, what the caller said, what she said.

"And he called him a *batty man*?" he asked, having to hear it again, the insult of it, to absorb the kick of it to his head.

"Yes."

"And they said he was going to die if he stayed?" She nodded again. "The whole thing is *horseshit*!" he shouted, and slammed his fist into the concrete wall, making Miss Mac jump. A long minute passed while he recovered from the pain, his eyes closed. It felt like a movie, a horror movie he was trapped in, he and Joseph.

"Somebody made this up, made the whole thing up to get at me, maybe to kill the idea of the hotel." He crossed his arms and squeezed his elbows, held himself together. "I want to know who these mother—do you have any idea who called, any idea whatsoever?"

"I couldn't make out the voice."

"Did you tell anyone else?"

"Just Shad."

He yanked the back door open, needing to get away from this kind woman. "When Joseph comes in, tell him to come see me right away," he said, and shot out.

CHAPTER FORTY-FIVE

"Now!" Shad shouted, and heaved. The freezer seemed heavier than the last time they'd lifted it, but it was well overdue for another servicing at Ketchum's Appliance Center, although they both hated lifting the thing. They pushed it to the front of the Jeep's flatbed, and Eric flipped up the back gate and closed it. Shad bought two orange sodas at the grocery across the street, climbed into the passenger seat, and handed the sullen Eric a drink, a small peace offering. Port Antonio behind them, Shad broke the silence separating him from his future partner.

"I thought it would be better to keep it to myself. Sometimes, what you don't know, don't—"

"Don't know about your own son? Give me a goddamn break, Shad." It was rare when the boss spoke to him that way, if he'd ever spoken to him that way, with that much anger, his voice hard like a stranger's.

"I got the gun from a friend, an old friend in Port Antonio who owe me a favor," Shad said. "I thought Joseph needed something to protect himself, in case of—anything."

"Joseph?" Eric said with a rough laugh. "I bet he'd never seen a gun in his life."

"He know how to use it now. I had him practice already."

"You had him—his mother would die if she knew."

"He pretty good, too. He have a steady hand." Shad chuckled, thinking of how he, a man who had only fired a gun once at a person—the night they were protecting the woman on the island—how he'd taught Joseph how to hold a gun, how to aim it straight and knock the small green mangoes off the fence post.

He could hear Eric inhaling, his breath unsteady. "You knew about these threats, this phone call, and you didn't say anything to me?"

"I didn't want to bother you. And is only foolishness, anyway."

"Why didn't you go to the police?"

"I went already," Shad said, and sucked his teeth, drawing it out at Neville. "You know what it like. They ask you if anybody dead or robbed, and when you say no, they just tell you they don't have no police vehicle to come to Largo. They don't even want to come for a stolen purse or something small. If anybody do *bodily harm,* they can come. You know how many times I gone to them already about things here, and they just laugh after me?"

Eric hit the steering wheel. "I'm *sick* of the damn police in this country. They're supposed to protect us, man. That's their job. They can't treat us like—" He broke off, tears starting to rim his eyes. "It's unfair, just unfair. The boy is not bothering anybody, working hard to write this report for his old man, and this is what they're doing to him, and there's not a *damn* thing the law does to protect him."

"We little people in Largo, boss. We have to take things in our own hands."

Eric wiped his eyes on the sleeve of his T-shirt. "I told him he should leave," he said.

"You told him to leave." Shad ran his hand over his scalp to prepare for the worst. Better to sacrifice a dream than a life, he told himself. Maybe Joseph could finish the report from abroad and they could mail him whatever he needed.

Eric cleared his throat. "He said he wasn't leaving."

"He did?"

"He said he didn't like unfinished business and he wasn't a coward."

"*Rawtid,*" Shad said in awe. "That is a man, not true?" A man or a fool, time would tell.

"He said he was going to finish the job and he wasn't going until he'd done that," Eric said, shaking his head slowly. "I think he's trying to prove something to me. He wants to show me that he finishes what he starts—unlike his father, of course."

"He has much left to do?"

"Something with the Ministry of Works, some estimates for running the water pipes and a few other things. I gave him the five-year projections, and Lambert gave him all his quotes for the construction."

"What about Miss Mac's land? You got a price for that?"

"Not yet."

Shad hit the dashboard. "Boss, stop the car! Stop the car!"

Eric slowed down. "What's the matter?"

"We passed a real estate office in Port Antonio. I saw it. Let we go back and find out how much we have to pay for the land."

"You think so?" Eric said. "If we bring another real estate agent into it, Cameron will have to split the commission."

"He going to have to do that anyway," Shad said. "You think the government here going to allow an American real estate man to do the whole business? We need a Jamaican real estate man. He will know all the laws and be able to do the thing from here. Cameron alone can't do it from New York."

Dunlop's Real Estate on Broad Street was a storefront office with only two desks and one person in the whole big room. Two walls were plastered with flyers for houses and land on the North Coast, and one wall had a large primitive painting of a tropical jungle with a view of the sea through the trees.

"Can I help you?" the woman said. She was stocky with braided hair.

"We need a real estate agent," Eric said. Shad wondered if Eric's shabby old clothes would make the woman think he was joking.

"I'm your man," the woman said—Joy was her name—and laughed a nice, full laugh from her belly. She waved them to the two chairs in front of her desk and they told her what they needed, and she answered that she needed to visit the land with an appraiser. Is it going to cost anything? Eric wanted to know. If she was hired as the agent for the transaction, she would be paid at the end, she said. If she closed with another agent, foreign or local, they'd split the commission according to the amount of work each had done. She sounded like a reasonable woman.

"I'd do the comps for you and everything," Joy said. They made an arrangement for the date and time of her visit and left, nodding to each other on the way out. The return trip went quietly, Eric slowing down almost to a halt around the corners, Shad thinking about the next step he had to take. He'd been trying to find the minister's son, to speak to him away from church and house, but no one had seen him for a week. When he'd questioned Pastor's wife after church, she said Kelvin had gone up to Kingston for a few days.

Halfway back to Largo, taking a sharp corner, Eric said, half thinking, half talking, reading his bartender's mind again, "So what do we do now—about Joseph?" The freezer slid into one corner of the flatbed and back again.

"Question is," Shad said, "how to find the person or persons behind the calls." Neville would have said *persons*.

"Where do we start?" Eric grunted. "Miss Mac said she didn't know the man's voice."

Shad updated him on his visit with Sister Elsa and his warning to Sister Arida. "I have an assistant working on it with me. He keeping his ear to the ground."

"An *assistant*?" Eric yelled. "You brought someone in on this and you didn't even tell *me*?"

"I needed somebody who could move around the village without being noticed, an extra set of eyes and ears."

"You're running a goddamn detective agency, is that what you're trying to tell me?"

"Whatever." Shad shrugged. "You don't have to pay me, though."

"I certainly wasn't planning to pay you, although for Joseph—"

"The hotel will pay us enough when it's built," the little bartender said, and they both fell silent.

Rounding one of the last corners before Largo, Eric shifted to a lower gear. There'd been a rumbling sound for a while and it didn't sound as if they could last until the restaurant.

"Shit!" Eric said. "This damn car." He slowed to a stop. The tire was almost flat. It took them longer to change than Shad had expected, because the jack was shaky and kept dropping the truck until they propped it up with rocks. By the time they finished changing the tire—Eric doing the changing and Shad the lifting of tires, tools, and rocks—the sun had gone down and they were both barely able to talk.

"Boss," Shad said when they were under way again and he'd gotten his wind back, "you included any cars or a truck in the estimate? We going to need a new Jeep soon."

"I thought I'd have to do that on my own."

"If I was you, I'd put a vehicle in there, because you

going to need a car to run up and down for the hotel. If the investor don't like it, he can throw it out. I'll call Caribbean Auto tomorrow and ask them the price," Shad said, because some things he preferred to do himself to make sure they got done.

CHAPTER FORTY-SIX

At the same moment that Eric and Shad were heaving the freezer into the Jeep in Port Antonio, Lambert's Range Rover was rounding the dry fountain in the town square in Falmouth, about eighty miles to the west. Raheem was at the wheel in a gray muscle shirt and jeans that looked old but weren't. He'd assured Lambert he could drive on the left, that he'd driven a lot in Trinidad picking up and delivering cars, and indeed he'd driven like a pro, if a little too fast.

On the ride to Montego Bay that morning, the three of them had chatted, at first awkwardly, with long silences between the short sentences. But as the miles went by, Janna had felt a small opening as conversation became easier, and the two men started including her in their eye contact when they spoke. Raheem asked her about Jamaica and she answered as best she could, and he nodded and glanced intently at her, riding in the front beside him. Before they reached the airport, Joseph suggested a bathroom break, and while they were sipping on sodas in the small bar, Raheem told her about his married sisters who worked in the business and still had time for their families.

"Women manage their lives better than men, you don't find?" he said, holding his fish pendant.

When they got to the airport and were standing by immigration, waiting for Lorraine to arrive, Janna filled them in on how she'd met her best friend.

"We hated each other when we first met at the *Herald,* but by the end of the week we were going shopping together."

Lorraine came off the plane, almost dancing off, with a good buzz from two martinis, she told them, declaring that she was on vacation and intended *to vacate* every minute she was here. She had a new weave, long and straight with a jagged cut, and she was wearing an orange halter top, showing off her graceful brown shoulders and arms, and skinny jeans that made the hours she spent in the gym worthwhile. When Janna introduced her to Joseph and Raheem, the diminutive woman looked up at the two men, lips parted, but she recovered quickly and gave them a huge smile with her teeth clenched together. Getting into the car, Janna opened the front door for her with a wink, and they were off to Largo.

"I got two weeks on short notice," Lorraine said, flapping her hand, the orange nail polish sizzling. "My editor was out of town, and the city editor said it was a good time anyway, not much news before Christmas. It was meant to be, I'm telling you."

Janna wanted to laugh, to tell her to slow down, but it was vintage Lorraine, the I-got-it-going-on girl who couldn't be stopped. She bubbled on about Miami and a story she'd been working on about the rising crime rate in the city, until she broke off and turned to Raheem.

"Have you been here long?"

Raheem leaned over the wheel. "I came in five days ago," he said. "Joe's been here eight or nine weeks already." He flashed a look at the backseat. "Right, man?"

Lorraine examined Raheem with a frown, as if she was just noticing him. "You have an accent. Where are you from?"

"Trinidad."

"You came all the way up here from Trinidad?" Lorraine said, and Janna smiled. Oh, the girl was good.

"No, I live in the DC area. Joe, too. He's working, though."

"Yeah," Janna said. "He's working on a project for his father."

"Has either of you visited Jamaica before?" Lorraine said.

"I have," said Joseph.

"That's perfect, then. Since you know the island, maybe we can hang out a little. I've never been here before. I've heard so much about Jamaica. I swear, everybody has been here but me." She was almost pouting, and Janna had to suppress a laugh.

"It's an amazing island," Raheem said. "Different from Trinidad, you know. Joe's father lent us his car and we've been driving around."

"We climbed Dunn's River Falls yesterday," Joseph said. "That was awesome." He threw back the forever straying lock of hair.

"We're going to drive right over it in a couple hours," Raheem said. "We could stop and you could see it." He liked Lorraine, Janna could tell, smiled at her with his head tilted away from her, a smile worth a few thousand dollars, whatever the magazines paid him, a slow smile, reluctant, and incredibly sexy.

They continued driving alongside wide and narrow bays, over streams and a river or two, around corners, endless corners, Lorraine keeping up the patter, playing the tourist role to the hilt. By the time they reached St. Ann's Bay, Janna realized that the dynamic between the four of them was different, had shifted yet again and become, as she'd hoped, more balanced. Lorraine's playfulness had infected them all and they were laughing every few minutes at one of her quirky comments. By the time they entered Ocho Rios, anyone would have thought they were two couples. Over a late lunch in a Chinese restaurant, they talked about where they were from and how they'd gotten where they were. Lorraine spoke of growing up in south Miami and how she'd fought for a journalism scholarship to Columbia. When they finished, they all voted Raheem's story the best.

"From the cane fields to Cannes," Lorraine trumpeted, raising both arms, and they fell out.

It was, as usual, Lorr's idea that they do something together that night. There was no time to waste, she said, and suggested a bonfire on the beach. They had them on the beach in Miami when she was little, and she'd been hoping they could do it here. Raheem said they had no plans.

"Is it safe, though?" he added.

"We can do it at the end of the beach, near the bar," Joseph said, and nodded to his friend. "It should be fine, don't worry."

Janna adjusted her black-and-white striped top, stretching it across her shoulders. "Are you sure you want to do it?" she said to Joseph. He'd touched her back in the restaurant while they were walking, sent a shiver down her spine, but she didn't want to press her luck and demand too much of his time in one day.

He turned to her, his eyes steady. "I think it'd be fun. We can collect dead palm leaves and light them. It'll be fun."

A few hours later, watching Lorraine unpack her suitcase on the four-poster bed in Casey's girlie bedroom, Janna took a banana from the fruit basket Miss Bertha had arranged. She sat down in an armchair, pushing a stuffed monkey to one side, and started peeling the fruit.

"How are the cantaloupes doing?" Lorraine said.

"I'm still getting used to them," Janna said, and touched one breast. "They got a smash when I fell off the horse, though. I need to go back to my guy in Fort Lauderdale, have him check them out. They've been feeling kind of sensitive since then."

"Maybe it's not the horse, but all that sex you've been having—"

"No sex for twelve days now. The girls are getting a rest, don't worry."

Lorraine put her hands on her hips. "And you aren't, are you? You have those bags under your eyes that you get when you haven't been sleeping."

"Oh, God," Janna said, and leaned over to look at herself in the mirror. "Is it that obvious?" She sat back and took a bite of the banana, chewed thoughtfully for a minute. "I've been having these nightmares, not horrifying things, but just—unpleasant, uncomfortable dreams that make it hard to go back to sleep. I had this dream a few nights ago. I had to do this job, and I had a big, square box that I had to do something with. And there was this disgusting dead rat lying on the top. Half of its face was eaten off—I can see it now—and I had to remove the rat before I could start working. There was a man standing on the other side of the box and he kept looking at me, waiting for me to do something, and I didn't want to touch the rat."

"Maybe the rat was Joseph."

"No, I don't think so," Janna said, and peeled the banana lower.

"You're crazy about him, aren't you?"

"Can you tell?"

"*Hello?* It's written all over you. You're holding yourself back, I can see it, but it's like you can't keep your eyes off him. You're forever looking at him like he's manna from heaven."

Janna took another bite of the banana and her words came out mushy. "Okay, I like him a lot, but it doesn't mean I'm *crazy* about him."

"Then why am I getting the feeling you're not telling me something?"

A heavy exhale from Janna followed. "Maybe because I don't know how he—how he really feels about me."

Lorraine opened her mouth, and Janna held up her hand. "He likes me, I'm telling you. We spent a lot of time together getting to know each other, going all over the place, having dinner together, spending nights together. But once he heard that Raheem was coming, things started to cool down overnight. Then after he arrived— no more dates, no more nothing. He suddenly had no time for me. He was spending all his time either working or driving Raheem around."

Lorraine stood in front of her with arms folded. "Let's call it what it is: you're in love with him and he's not in love with you."

Janna exhaled and let her shoulders drop. "I guess so. I've never been in love before, but you're probably right. I can't sleep, my stomach feels kind of queasy all the time. I thought being in love was supposed to be fun. This is hell." She threw the banana peel in the trash can. "And I don't want to be in love with someone who's not in love with me."

"Did you ever think this could be just a holiday thing for Joseph?"

"You mean—a *fling*?"

Lorraine waved her arm in the air and snapped her fingers. "An affair, a tryst, call it whatever you want. Men are different from us, you know."

"No," Janna said, and hugged herself, rubbing her hands up and down her arms. "He's not the type. I know him."

"Right, me and Sammy all over again," Lorraine said, and turned back to the suitcase. "Wake up and smell the ganja, girl." They were silent while she arranged her bras and panties in a drawer, bras arranged parallel to one another like in Victoria's Secret, where she'd worked in college.

"Well, what's the word?" Janna said, changing direction. It was the opening volley for their usual analysis of every man they met, every occasion they shared. After Lorraine hung a dress in the closet, a green minidress with the tag still attached, she sat down on a footstool.

"About both of them, you mean?" she said, and Janna nodded, loving that her friend was here, that she knew what Janna meant.

"I almost don't want to think about it," Lorraine said. "They're amazing to look at. Joseph is gorgeous, you said it yourself. He certainly doesn't *look* gay, whatever that is, but he's more into himself than into other people, you know. He has a—a kind of distant way about him that makes you want to slap him sometimes."

"I know the feeling."

Lorraine touched a finger to her cheek. "Now, Raheem—"

They looked at each other. Lorraine reached over and took a banana from the fruit basket.

"Raheem?" Janna said.

"—is the finest motherfucker this side of the equator," Lorraine said, staring at the banana so hard her eyes started crossing. They roared with laughter, bending over their legs. When they slowed down, Janna wiped her eyes.

"I knew it," she said. "I knew you'd like him."

"I can't wait," Lorraine declared with a mischievous smirk, "to see his face hanging over mine. No analysis needed this time, don't worry." She stood up and did a little salsa step with the banana. "Can you imagine how it feels to be kissed by those pouty lips—Botoxed, no doubt?"

"Will you stop? Do you think he's gay, that's what I want to know."

"I think he's having sex."

"Why'd you say that?"

"You didn't see the hickey on his neck?" Lorraine pulled her head back into a double chin and raised her eyebrows, the way she did when she'd scored a point.

"A hickey?"

"I don't know what kind of modeling he's going to be doing for the next couple of weeks with that baby."

"Oh, my God. Do you think he and Joseph—?" Janna's hand flew to her mouth.

"You think I care?" Lorraine said, ever practical, ever unexplained. "I don't even know if that matters nowadays. I'm not asking the man to marry me. Hell, I wouldn't even want to be married to a man that good-looking. I'd never sleep at night, and you know I love my sleep. The only thing I care about is that I don't catch the big A from him, but I brought my supply of gloves, so that should take care of that."

"You're willing to hang out with him?"

"Are you kidding? Just to be close to the man is good enough for me." She started unpacking again, this time a blouse that Janna recognized, a brown one with a low beaded neckline. "Make sure you take some photographs of us together, though, they could be worth a lot one day. I want to show them to my sister. Jamaica—and a man like that? She'll be totally green."

She hung the blouse up in the closet and took out a little peach sweater, which she held in front of her.

"Do you think I should wear this to the bonfire thingy tonight?" she said.

CHAPTER FORTY-SEVEN

"Dadda! Dadda?" Joella's voice rang through the house.

"Right here," Shad said, "in the kitchen." He was making a Spam sandwich with thick slices of hard-dough bread. From the bedroom the roar of the sewing machine erupted again.

Joella appeared at the kitchen door. She was trying to control her mouth, trying to hide a smile. "Winston want to see you, Dadda."

"Tell him to come back here," Shad said, and raised his voice, leaning in the direction of the bedroom door, "*because certain people don't have time to make my lunch.*"

A couple of minutes later, Winston stood slouching in the doorway, a floppy brown hat on his head. "Afternoon, suh."

"Afternoon, youth. What up?"

Winston glanced toward the living room as if Joella was hovering nearby. "I can have a word with you, suh?"

Shad finished buttering the bread and patted the sandwich closed. He took a bite and looked at the boy. "Remember is good manners to take off your hat when you come into a house," he said with his mouth still full. Winston grabbed the hat off his head.

"I meet you outside in fifteen minutes," Shad said. "Go talk to Joella, but keep the music down."

After he'd followed the sandwich with a glass of lemonade, Shad walked into the bedroom and stood beside the bed, where Ashanti was sleeping with her skinny knees tucked into her chest.

"I not taking a nap today, please notice," he said. He was trying to be civil, trying a new tactic.

"I not stopping you," Beth said, looking up from her sewing, today a white net thing.

"Tired of picking thread off my clothes." Shad straightened his shirt, unzipped his pants and tucked the shirt in, and zipped up his pants. "Yesterday Miss Maisie embarrass me. She take a string off my shirt and ask me if I sewing a dress. Solomon burst out laughing like a fool."

The machine roared again. "I leaving now," he yelled, waving his defeat.

"Walk good," his woman called back above the noise.

On the road outside his gate, Shad turned to Winston. "I have a present for you, son."

"Yes, suh?"

He handed the boy a deodorant stick in a red-and-black case. "After you bathe. You can't miss with the girls after that." Winston thanked him and pushed the stick into his pocket, his face more serious than usual.

"What happen to the radio?" Shad asked.

"The batteries run down, suh."

"So life go, man," said Shad. "One day you playing

music, next day your batteries gone. You say you have something to tell me?"

"Yes, Mistah Shad," Winston said, and slapped the hat back on his head.

"You hear something?"

"Something about what we was talking, suh."

Shad frowned at the boy, his patience used up for the day. "Well, cough it up, nuh?"

"I hear that Pastor's son come back to Largo."

Shad stopped walking, allowing a mongrel dog to cross their path. The dog looked at them and dropped its head before running off with its tail between its legs.

"How you know?" Shad said.

"My friend Lebert—the same friend who told me he was talking in the bar—he say that Kenneth—"

"Kelvin is he name."

"—that Kelvin talking in the bar again."

"What he talking this time?" They'd reached the corner, and Shad looked down the main road. Two taxis were racing each other through the village, occupying both lanes. Shad shouted after them as they flew past. "You don't see children—" He gave up and waved at the dust. "I hate those taxis, you see? They have no manners, and police don't even pay them any mind."

They started walking in the direction of the bar. "Talk to me, Winston. What Kelvin doing now?"

"He come into the bar two nights ago, Lebert say—"

"How come this Lebert know so much? He living at the bar?"

"No, suh. He a bartender, like you, at the bar in the

square. He say he know you, how you come asking for me one day. He have short hair, little dreadlocks."

"I know who you talking about," Shad said, remembering the two young men on the bridge near Winston's house, and the one with the spliff. "I never know he was a bartender, though. Okay, go on."

"So Lebert say that Pastor's son come into the bar two nights ago, like he excited. He start to drink right away and he buy two rounds for everybody in the bar, even the men playing dominoes outside. And he start talking about Mistah Eric's son, and he walking up and down in the bar, saying that he must be a batty man, because his Indian man-friend so pretty that he must be his lover, and he say that they bringing the devil to Largo, and he say that they have no shame, how they driving around in Mistah Eric's car like two lovebirds." Winston paused for breath, looking up uncertainly like he thought Shad would reprimand him. "He say we should teach them a lesson."

"What he mean by *a lesson*? What kind of lesson?"

"He never say exactly what, but he asking if anyone want to help him."

By the time they reached the bar, Shad's stomach was churning. In the parking lot, the bougainvillea hedge was rustling in the stiff breeze. He stopped just inside the hedge and placed his hand on the tall boy's shoulder. Winston looked down at him, startled, holding on to his hat to keep it from blowing away.

"We need to talk some more, star," Shad said. "You want some nice, cold coconut water?"

CHAPTER FORTY-EIGHT

T he road to the plantation tour twisted uphill between bamboo plants and towering trees that met
overhead. It had cooled since they left the main
road, and Raheem turned off the air-conditioning.

"I prefer the window open, if you all don't mind."
He rolled down his window and took a deep breath.
"I love the smells in the Caribbean." He was looking
around at the passing scenery, his face lit up. Examining the side of his neck, Janna noticed that the hickey
had completely faded and nothing had replaced it. The
skin of his satiny brown neck was now as unmarked as
his face. Despite her continuing uncertainty about his
relationship to Joseph, she did, somewhat reluctantly,
enjoy Raheem's company. There was something refreshing about the man, a simplicity and openness that made
him seem almost childlike, younger than his twenty-
seven years.

"I love this road," Lorraine said, turning down the CD
player. "It's like a cathedral."

"Are you sure we're on the right road?" Joseph asked.
"Raheem has a way of—"

"Raheem has a way of what?" his friend said, acting wounded, his hand to his chest. "I never get lost, man."

"Remember that time we went to Paul's, and you drove around for half an hour and came back to the same spot?"

"That was your fault! You got the directions wrong."

They bickered, besting each other amicably until they wound down. Janna opened her window. Whenever Joseph spoke to Raheem, his voice had an upbeat familiarity to it, a tone he never used with her, that made her want to gulp air.

"Did we turn off at Labyrinth?" Lorraine asked, looking at the small tourist map in her lap.

"I didn't see any Labyrinth," Janna said.

Half an hour later they were still driving, but now through rolling hills of red dirt and grasslands farther inland. Every few miles, it seemed, they passed a tiny community with a church, a grocery shop, and a bar, each with a gracious British name that the Brontë sisters might have used—Balmoral and Hobson and Wentworth.

"I'm telling you, we missed the turn," Joseph said, and his grip on Janna's hand tightened as he said it.

"Aren't you enjoying the adventure?" she asked, keeping her voice light.

"Some adventures I can do without," he replied. "I like to get where I'm going." His mouth was tightening up again. In the three days since Lorraine's arrival, he'd gained a new earnestness. He'd started coming up to the office again, working feverishly, foregoing his usual morning call and phoning government offices and Kingston companies instead, typing away at his laptop as soon as he hung up. He wanted to finish the report in time for his mother's wedding, he said, and he'd insisted that Raheem drive the girls around, suggested beaches and restaurants in the area, as if he wanted to get them out of his hair. The three had ventured out in Jennifer's car with Lambert's permission, dubbing themselves the Three Musketeers, taking photographs everywhere—usually of Lorraine hugging Raheem—and once going out in a glass-bottom boat on the Blue Lagoon near Port Antonio. Wherever they went, Raheem turned heads, greeted people with his slow smile and tried out a few patois words, and seemed totally at ease, as if he'd been here before.

In the evenings, Joseph joined them for dinner, once at the bar and once at Miss Mac's. They'd told him their latest adventures and he'd told them what government official had frustrated him that day, showing a funny side that Janna hadn't seen before, hamming it up sometimes when he imitated people, and they would laugh at his stories. The best part of the new scenario for Janna was that Joseph paid her attention in public. Even if there was no more sex—no time or place for it, apparently— he would put his arm around her waist when they were walking, sit close beside her, and even kiss her lightly on the cheek when she made a joke. He was doing all the little things she'd wanted, and she took it as a good sign. Emerging from the shower the day before, she'd realized that life with Joseph was like living in a play: she never knew what scene she'd be playing next and what costume she was supposed to wear. Today, Sunday, he'd decided to take the day off and join them—they were to be tourist couples sightseeing for the day, it seemed.

Still looking for the plantation sign, Raheem straddled the old Toyota across a wide pothole. The road was getting narrower and bumpier, the hills steeper, and there was still no sign of a plantation.

"Let's ask this guy," he said, and slowed down beside an elderly man walking toward them. Neatly dressed in a light cotton shirt, dark pants, and shiny black leather shoes, the man stopped and looked at them cautiously, his eyes narrowing.

"We're looking for the Peacock Plantation," said Lorraine. "Do you know where it is?"

"You are foreigners?" he said. Taking his time, he leaned into the car until he could see all the passengers, letting his eyes rest for a second on each. "You pass it long ago. Turn around and keep going until you see the sign that say 'Plantation tours ahead.' It's on the left. You can't miss it."

"Thank you," Lorraine sang out in a cheerful let's-get-going voice.

The old man smiled at Lorraine without pulling out of the car, the gray stubble on his chin a few inches away from her face. "I tell you what. I going that way. If you give me a ride, I will show you." Janna was about to make an excuse, when the man opened the back door and climbed in next to Joseph.

"I am Samson," he said, whistling on the *S*. Silence descended over the car while Raheem turned it around and started back.

"What are your names, please?" Samson asked after a while. Joseph introduced everybody.

"You come from far?" he said.

There was no limit to Samson's curiosity and, little by little, as the miles wore them down, they unwound from their resentment and began telling him about themselves. He was happy to share his own story, how he'd grown up in Kingston and traveled to England.

"I was a shoemaker in Birmingham," he said. "I could repair any kind of shoe."

"Why'd you come back?" Joseph asked.

"I like Jamaica," he said, and laughed. He was missing two teeth in front, and his top lip bent inward.

"What do you like about it?" Lorraine said.

"The food, the warmth, the sunshine. I always want to come back home." He'd made a little money in England, he said, and used it to build a house not far away.

The trip back seemed to go faster, and when they came to the bamboo arched across the road, Lorraine started laughing. "I can't believe we went that far out of our way," she said. "Trust my navigation skills! No sailing around the world for me."

Samson told them he would be getting off at the next intersection. They slowed down at a path that crossed the road and he reached for the door handle.

"I tell you what," he said, staying put. "Turn up here and you will see my house. I know you thirsty. I want to give you something to drink, a little thank-you for the drive, you know?"

He wouldn't take no for an answer, and they ended up

bumping a couple of hundred yards up the unpaved road to a small concrete house surrounded by a sugarcane field. The bungalow sat some four feet off the ground on sturdy columns and was topped by a shingle roof. A verandah stretched the width of the front, and blue curtains waved from the windows.

"Right here, right here," he said, and opened the car door. He beckoned them out, and they slowly acquiesced, Raheem stretching as he stood up.

"Yes, the sweet smell of sugarcane," he said, one of the only times Janna was to remember him laughing outright. "I could be at home in Chaguanas."

Samson was already walking hurriedly up the path. "Giddy!" he called as he approached the front door. "Giddy, we have guests." The four visitors trooped up the steps single file and onto the verandah.

"Come in," Samson said. He waved them through the narrow double doors, into a small, dark living room crowded with furniture. Three photographic prints of London—Buckingham Palace, Big Ben, and the Houses of Parliament—decorated the walls.

From inside came a voice, a musical voice almost singing the words. "Who you bring, Sam?"

"Some foreigners," Samson called, and smiled at the quartet. The odor of curry drifted from the kitchen. A tall, barefoot man in his midtwenties emerged between the nylon curtains leading to a corridor. His copper-colored face topped by short, wavy hair, the angular young man was wearing Bermuda shorts and a T-shirt that had been cut off, showing his navel. Janna froze between the coffee table and a straight-back chair and glanced at her friends: Lorraine was looking at the man with a puzzled expression on her face, Joseph was staring at Samson, and Raheem was wearing a strained smile.

"Hello," Giddy said, slipping on some sandals next to the kitchen door. He avoided their eyes and stayed busy getting drinks from the kitchen while the elderly host beckoned them to sit down in the living room. A fan buzzed in one corner, disturbing the heat.

"Four rum and Cokes, right?" Giddy said, delivering the drinks on a wooden tray.

"Come and join us," Samson said, and the young man sat down. They sipped their drinks in silence for a few seconds until Lorraine and Raheem started talking at the same time. Lorraine waved him to continue.

"Were you living in England, too?" Raheem's question was directed at Giddy.

"No, I never leave the island yet."

"He wouldn't have liked England," Samson interjected, "too cold." Giddy looked at him, and they laughed at a private joke.

"Do you still have family in England?" Lorraine said.

"Just a sister," Samson said. "I never marry." The narrow wooden bookcase behind the man displayed a collection of ceramic birds on one shelf, a dozen books on another. Janna read *Gone With the Wind* and *The God of All* on a couple of spines. Old photographs of people, all in faded color, were displayed on the other shelves.

"Was it hard to adjust to Jamaica when you came

back?" Lorraine said to Samson. She was shifting in her chair, smelling a story.

"I went back to Kingston, but I didn't like it. The only good thing was that I met Giddy. We decide to move to the country, and I build the house here."

"Why here?" Joseph said. "It's kind of out of the way, isn't it?"

"We left Kingston—" The elderly man stopped and lowered his head. Giddy reached out and put his hand on his friend's knobby knee and rubbed it.

"We moved," Giddy said, "after a good friend of ours drowned."

"They murder him," Samson said, his voice muffled.

"Some people chased him off the end of a pier," the graceful young man said. "He didn't know how to swim. He was in the market, and a woman and he start arguing, that's what we hear. Then she pick up a machete and called him all kind of names, and she started running after him. Other people came and join her and they chase him out of the market and down the road. When he ran out to the pier, they chase him right to the end and he jumped. And they watch him drowning and laugh after him." Giddy took a sip of his drink with eyes averted, and everyone watched him swallow. Joseph and Raheem exchanged glances, and Janna looked away.

"Sometimes you like to be out of the way," Samson said finally, looking up with tired eyes. "It quiet here, nobody to bother you."

"Isn't it too quiet?" Lorraine nodded to the younger man.

"Sometimes, but I sew," Giddy answered. "I like to sew things." He waved at the matching blue cushions and curtains.

"Giddy, guess where they staying?" Samson said. He didn't say it with a smile but heavily, like a warning.

"Largo," Joseph said. "Largo Bay, a little—"

"I know where Largo is," Giddy said. His narrow face got narrower for a second, withdrew and returned. "I born there."

"Do you know the Largo Bay Restaurant?" Joseph said.

"I don't remember that. I remember a hotel, Largo Bay Inn."

"That was my father's," Joseph said. "It's gone now. He has a bar."

Raheem crossed his legs, kicking the coffee table, and a little ceramic bird fell over. Giddy leaned forward to straighten it while Raheem apologized.

"Why did you leave Largo?" Joseph asked. His face blank, unreadable, had turned to Giddy. The only sound for a while was a dripping tap in the kitchen. Giddy looked wordlessly at Samson, who scratched his chin.

"Largo is one of them villages," the old man said, "where you have to watch the people, because some of them not so nice. They like to mind up in other people's business, you know. Giddy had to leave because they mind up in his business."

Eyes round, Lorraine leaned both elbows on her knees. "Forgive me," she said, "but I'm a very—curious kind of person. Are you both—are you partners? I'm just asking you," she gabbled on, "because I've been reading all kinds of things about Jamaica. My own cousin is gay, mind you, and I know he has a rough time in Antigua sometimes. I was just wondering—"

She broke off, and Janna closed her eyes for a second, not daring to look at Joseph.

"We don't talk like that in Jamaica," Samson said, almost sternly.

"I'm sorry," Lorraine said. "I didn't mean to pry, but I'm a reporter with an American newspaper, the *Miami Herald,* you may have heard of us, and I was thinking that I could write an article about the situation in Jamaica—"

"We don't want to be in no paper," Samson said.

"I wouldn't call any names," Lorraine said.

Raheem uncrossed his legs, clenching his jaw, the jawbone pushing out and in. "The man says—"

"I heard him." Lorraine tucked her chin in, chastened, and leaned back in her chair.

"Miss," Giddy said, extending his hand toward Lorraine, "is not that people outside shouldn't know what going on here, but we don't need to call *attention* to ourselves, understand? We been through a rough time in Kingston and we just looking for a little peace now."

"And you feel safe here?" Lorraine ventured, one last question.

"So far, so good," Giddy said. He looked at the curtain near him, tugged at its hem. "Although things change quick in this country."

Lorraine nodded. Janna knew her friend's mind was racing to another question, smelling a Pulitzer. She wasn't one to give up a good story.

"Time to go," Joseph said, standing. "We still want to make that plantation tour."

"You're right," Janna said. "Thank you so much for the drink."

When they were seated again in the car, Giddy waving from the porch, Samson leaned in for the last time.

"Watch your back in Largo," he said, looking straight at Raheem.

CHAPTER FORTY-NINE

S had had known Meredith McKenzie all his life, from kindergarten anyway, and he'd never seen the old lady so agitated before. She'd seldom come to the bar at night, either.

"Miss Mac? What happening?" he said after the woman had tapped him on the shoulder from behind, surprising him as he poured orange juice into two glasses.

"I have to talk to you," she said, twisting a handkerchief, glancing over her shoulder.

"Give me a minute and I come to you," Shad said. When he finished serving the drinks, he took her elbow and led her to the side of the restaurant.

"What the problem?" he said.

"I heard—I don't know—" She wiped her damp forehead with the handkerchief.

"Take your time," Shad said.

"I hear the men talking, Joseph and his friend. They were under my window, like they didn't know I was so close, because I don't like to listen to my boarders, you know?"

"I know, go on."

"Anyway, they say that—"

"When was this?"

"Tonight, just now. I hear them saying that they have to go somewhere, and that they taking the gun with them."

"Going where?"

"I never hear that. They never say."

Shad took a deep breath. "Are they back in the house?"

"I don't know."

Steering the woman to the bar, he patted her arm. "Miss Mac, I going to look for them. I know you don't know anything about no liquor, but you going to take my place tonight. Solomon couldn't come in, so you going to be bartender and cashier."

"But I—"

"Don't worry, I show you, and you have to learn quick." He tried to laugh. "I know you a good teacher, and now I want to see if you is a good student." He opened the fridge. "Ice in the freezer up here. Soft drinks down there, juices and beer and white wine here." Closing the fridge door, he pointed to the shelf behind them. "Rum, whiskey, vodka, gin, red wine up there."

"Where the glasses?" she said, wiping her forehead again.

"Over here."

"And the prices?"

"On the chalkboard over there. The customers can tell you themselves, most of them." He gave her a quick hug. "Tell them no food serving tonight. Just do your best, okay?"

Shad rushed past the kitchen to get Eric, who opened his apartment door in his boxers. "Draw on your pants, boss, and bring the car keys. We have work to do."

When they were in the Jeep, he explained. Eric scratched his scalp and combed his hair with his fingers. "Oh, fuck," he said. "Where do we start?"

"Let's see if they're next door," Shad said. "I'll drive."

"Suppose they've left already?"

"We cross that bridge when we come to it."

Shad screeched to a halt in front of Miss Mac's house. He jumped out, Eric behind him. The front door was open, and they stepped inside the dark house.

"Joseph? Raheem?" Eric called. There was no answer to their calls. Eric closed the door, and they ran back to the Jeep. Shad started driving toward the village.

"Where do you think they've gone?" Eric said, holding on to the door frame with both hands.

"I have no idea."

"Let's get Lambert," Eric said. "He has a gun."

They'd just passed Lambert's driveway and Shad jerked to a halt and reversed in the middle of the road, empty of traffic tonight. When they banged on Lambert's front door, the big man opened it with a magazine in his hand.

Eric stepped in a few feet. "Lambert, we need you, man—"

"Bring your gun," Shad said, nodding. "We have an emergency, but we need to use your car. Three of us can't hold in the Jeep."

Lambert frowned and set the magazine down on a

small table. "The Rover is gone. Joseph and his friend came up here asking to borrow it and I let them have it."

Janna walked into the living room in her pajamas, the pant legs too short. "What's the matter, Daddy?" she asked. "Was that Joseph a little while ago? I thought I heard his voice."

The three men looked at her. "Go back to bed, sweet pea," Lambert said.

"What's happening?" she said, crossing her arms. She looked from one man to another.

"I'm going out with Eric and Shad," Lambert said, and disappeared down the corridor.

"Where are you going, Uncle Eric? I know something is up. Daddy doesn't go out at night just like that."

"We have a little emergency," Eric said.

"An emergency that has to do with Joseph?"

Eric and Shad looked at each other. "We don't know exactly," Shad said. Lambert appeared again with a bulge in his pocket and urged her to go back to bed. He had the keys for Jennifer's car and waved the men out the back door, Janna trailing behind them to the kitchen door.

"Not the fastest car in the world," he said, getting into the driver's seat, "but it'll do."

In answer to a query from Lambert, Shad laid out the plan. "We going first to Winston's house, a young boy who keeping his nose to the ground for me. He supposed to know what going on."

They didn't have to go far. Winston was walking fast down the main road, toward the bar. They slowed down alongside and he peered into the unfamiliar car, looking relieved when he saw Shad in the back.

"You hear anything?" Shad said to him.

"Yes, suh," he said. "They planning something to-night. I was just coming to find you."

"Get in the car," Shad said, and moved over. "Tell us what happening."

The four men drove slowly down the road while Winston talked, staring at Shad the whole time. "I did what you said, suh. I pretend that I want to be part of the group that Pastor's son was getting together. Remember, I told you—"

"Yes, I remember."

"I been going to the bar in the square like you said, and when Mistah Kelvin come in tonight, I pretend that I was having a soft drink and talking to Lebert. I didn't order any hard drink, you know—"

Shad shot him a look and the boy focused again. "And he start to talk about Mistah Eric's son again, and he say he want to get some people together, people who don't want any nastiness in Largo, and I tell him, like you tell me to, that I ready to join up. He didn't know who I was, even though he told my father—"

"Time is life, boy," Shad said. "Talk quick."

"Anyway," said Winston, "he said he expecting the two batty—" He broke off and glanced at Eric. "He was expecting Mistah Eric's son and his friend to come to Mistah Cedric's house at the end of the bay, and we was to grab them."

"What time?" Eric demanded.

"He said we was to come at midnight."

"It's quarter to twelve," Lambert said, glancing at his watch. He sped up and headed toward the end of the village.

Shad put out his hand. "Wait, wait," he said. "We have to pick up another passenger."

CHAPTER FIFTY

"Lorraine, wake up," Janna said, and turned on the bedside lamp. Lorraine was sleeping, her open mouth dripping saliva onto the pillowcase.

"Wake up!" Janna said louder, and shook her friend's arm. Lorraine sat up suddenly, the sheet sliding off her bare breasts.

"What, what, what?" she said. "An earthquake?"

"More serious than that," Janna said.

Lorraine blinked and rubbed one eye. "What are you talking about?"

"Something's going on and we're going to find out what."

"Something like what?"

"If you get yourself decent, we can find out," Janna said, and went to her own room. She changed into jeans and a blouse, pulled her hair back into a ponytail, and returned to Lorraine's room.

"Will you please make a move?" she said. Lorraine was still in a daze, standing naked in front of her closet.

"I can't decide what to wear," she said.

"Shorts and T-shirt, that's good enough."

"What's all the hurry about?"

"Daddy has just gone out with Shad and Uncle Eric. And Daddy lent the SUV to Joseph." Janna put her hands on her hips. "Something is up, I'm telling you. They were all doing their we-can-handle-it dance, keeping it to themselves."

With one foot in her panties, Lorraine lost her balance, held on to one of the bed's posters. "What kind of something, do you think?" Her reporter instincts were waking up.

"Whatever it is, you're not going to write about it," Janna said.

"I'm making no promises this time," Lorraine retorted, and tugged on a pair of shorts. "Where are we going?"

When they were ready, they got a flashlight out of the kitchen drawer and jogged down the driveway, Janna ahead.

"And we're going to the bar because—?" Lorraine said.

"Because Shad must have told somebody something."

Miss Mac was sitting on Shad's stool when they approached. She looked uncomfortable but excited, her eyes wide.

"What are you doing here, Miss Mac?" Janna asked.

"Shad told me to mind the bar. I served three drinks already."

"Where did they go?"

"Who?"

"Shad and Uncle Eric."

"I don't know where they went." She was playing the innocent, spreading her hands.

"Miss Mac," said Janna, "something is happening. I know that much. Are Joseph and Raheem in trouble?"

Miss Mac puckered her dry lips. "All I know is that they were talking about going somewhere, and saying something about taking Joseph's gun."

"Joseph's—" Janna started.

Lorraine darted a look. "Joseph has a gun?"

"Yes."

"Why?"

"I don't know," Janna said. "Miss Bertha said something about duppies."

"Not real ghosts, I hope," Lorraine shot back. A man leaned on the bar counter and cleared his throat.

"Where were they going, Miss Mac?" Janna pleaded.

"Your guess is as good as mine," Miss Mac said. She looked at them for a second, biting her lip. "Check Cedric, the fisherman, like I just remember the voice—"

"Where does he live?" Janna said insistently, ready to shake the woman.

"I don't remember," she said, sliding off the stool and opening the fridge door. "Excuse me, I have to get a beer for the gentleman."

Outside the bar, Janna stopped and put her hands on Lorraine's shoulders. "It's you and me, girl," she said. "Are you ready?"

"Are you kidding?" her friend said. "You forget who you're talking to."

CHAPTER FIFTY-ONE

From the street it looked like the little house was in darkness, only a wind chime tinkling on the verandah. Shad mounted the steps and peeped through the glass louvers on one side of the door. A dim light was glowing inside, down a corridor, it looked like. Pastor must be awake, Shad thought, reading his Bible before bed, like he told them to. Shad knocked once, louder the second time. A murmur inside, then silence. Two voices started talking at the same time, a woman's and a man's.

"Who is it?" the woman called.

"It's me—Shad." More talk from within, the words low and unheard. Behind him, he could make out Eric's desperate face looking up at him from the car. Someone shuffled to the door in slippers, paused a second before opening, must have been looking through the side windows at him. Shad looked straight ahead. The verandah light snapped on and Pastor McClelen slowly opened the door. He was fully dressed in shirt and pants.

"Yes, Brother Shad," he said, his voice stiff. They hadn't spoken since the last time Shad visited.

"We have a situation on our hands, Pastor."

The minister came out onto the verandah and closed the door behind him. "What's so urgent you have to get me out of bed?" he said, not sounding like he'd just been reading the Bible, not looking like he'd gotten out of bed.

"Pastor, it look like your son doing something tonight—"

"I'm not responsible for my son," the man said, and started back to the door. "He's a big man."

A muffled voice called from inside. "What he wants, Manny?"

The minister stuck his head inside the door. "Nothing, nothing," he called. He turned back to Shad with an impatient flick of his head. "What you hear?"

Shad told him what he knew, that his son had gotten some people together to teach two men a lesson, two men he said were gay.

The minister shook his head. "I not responsible for Kelvin."

"But suppose your son kill a man?"

"Kelvin not going to kill anybody."

Shad beckoned to the three men in the car. They opened the car doors and climbed the steps.

"Who are all these people?" said McClelen, backing up a little. "What you want with me?"

Eric pushed forward. "It's my son in danger here, that's who we are."

"Mr. Keller, I know who you are. You don't have nothing to worry yourself about." His voice was still irritated but respectful, the way country people spoke to foreign people. "I don't know what my son is saying, but he don't mean no harm to your son, I'm sure."

"This is Lambert Delgado, his friend," Shad said. "He come with us because he have a gun, in case of trouble."

"Gentlemen, you don't need no gun." The minister gave a shaky smile. "Kelvin would never hurt a fly."

Shad pointed at Winston. "This is the youth your son told about the action tonight. He say he and some other people going to set up an ambush for Mistah Eric's son and his friend tonight."

Pastor turned to Lambert, his hand on the doorknob. "The boy has an active imagination. My advice is to go back to your beds."

Shad sighed loudly. "*Mistah* McClelen," he said. "You not listening. Your son get a gang of people together to hurt this man's son and his friend, maybe to kill them." Shad planted his foot against the door, kept it closed. "Pastor, we need you to come and stop him. If you don't stop him, we going to shoot him. You think your Sunday flock going to understand that one?"

"Give me a minute," the minister said, and slipped inside the door.

Two minutes later they were back on the road, Lambert following Shad's directions to Cedric's house, the holy man squashed between Shad and Winston in the back.

Eric glanced at his watch. "It's midnight," Eric said. "Hurry, Lam."

"Nothing is going to happen," Pastor said. "Cedric is only—"

"Is at Cedric's yard," Shad said, looking at his minister, "and you trying to protect him?"

"What else did he tell you?" Lambert said over his shoulder to Winston.

"He say to bring whatever tools we have, machete and so."

"Who else was part of it?" Shad said.

"I don't know all of them, but a couple men from the bar said they would help him and get some more people together," Winston said. The minister was quiet now, his face set, his hands clamped between his knees.

"Down this lane?" Lambert asked.

"Yes," said Shad. "Straight down."

They were now on the edge of the village, the beach behind them. The half-moon gave an anemic color to the passing trees and shrubs, a dull moonscape. Ahead of them the car's lights picked up an unpaved driveway to their right. The Range Rover was parked on the side of the road, parked at an odd angle with the back sticking out.

"Stop right here," Shad said. Lambert pulled the car over as far into the bushes as he could get, and the men climbed out. They could hear noises in the distance, someone shouting in a screeching voice, a woman wailing, then a lull. Eric started forward, leading the charge, and Shad touched his arm.

"Boss, let Lambert go first," he whispered. "Like how he have the gun."

Eric waved at Lambert impatiently. "Come on, come on."

They crept inside Cedric's fence, Lambert with the gun, followed by Eric and Shad side by side, Winston behind, and the minister in the rear. The shouting was starting again, and they could see the glow of a fire reflected off the trees and bushes behind the house. Shad signaled the group to get over, and they edged toward the back of the house, plastering themselves to the wall. In front with the gun drawn, Lambert stopped suddenly at the corner of the house.

"Oh, dear God!" he gasped, like he'd seen a corpse. Shad and Eric peeped over his shoulder.

"Oh, God!" Eric said. Behind the house was a towering mahogany tree, and under it a large bonfire, the flames shooting high into the air. A noisy crowd of about thirty people surrounded the fire, some with sticks and others with machetes. Between their restless bodies, Joseph and Raheem were just visible, seated on the ground beside the fire, back to back, their wrists bound behind them. Their hair and clothes were disheveled, as if they had been struggling. Raheem's sleeve was torn and Joseph had lost one of his shoes. A few feet away from the two men, Cedric held Joseph's Glock, pointed at the ground.

Above the commotion, Kelvin's voice rose in a wail. He was stamping his feet, reading, his high, nervous voice shouting quotations from the Bible, squinting at the words in the flickering light of the fire. Beside him was Sister Arida, shuffling from foot to foot and moaning to some hymn in her mind. Above the woman's head were two nooses hanging from the huge tree—and a ladder leaning against the trunk.

"What the *raas claat*—?" Shad whispered. He'd prepared himself to see a few people with machetes, but there was the crowd, far more than he'd thought, and there were the nooses, two larger versions of the one in the Jeep.

"Is he goddamn crazy?" Eric hissed.

Kelvin was raising his arm in the air. "'And thou shalt not let any of thy seed pass through the fire to Molech, neither shalt thou profane the name of thy God,'" he was saying in a nasal voice, a parody of his father. "'I am the Lord. Thou shalt not lie with mankind as with womankind. It is an abomination.'" He paused to let Sister Arida be his echo.

"An abomination," the woman wailed.

"And we must be strong, brothers and sisters, we must be strong against the foreign influence of nastiness, of sodomization in our community." Kelvin paused and pointed at Joseph and Raheem. "These men are *sinners*—"

"Just string them up and finish," a man shouted.

"Stop the chat, get it over with," a woman yelled.

Shad signaled Lambert and Eric to pull back, and they formed a small, tight circle, heads together, while Winston and Pastor moved forward to have a closer look.

"We need a plan," Shad whispered.

"I can fire a shot in the air and see what happens," Lambert said.

"No," Shad said. "Twenty machetes and a gun going to be hard to escape."

"He could fire at the guy with the Bible," Eric whispered, his eyes aflame.

"Then we'll really have the mob after us," Lambert said.

"We need a distraction," Shad said.

Lambert and Eric looked at each other. "A distraction?" they said together.

CHAPTER FIFTY-TWO

They had driven for at least fifteen minutes already, up and down every dark road in Largo, and they hadn't seen anything or anybody they could ask. On top of that, Janna still hadn't gotten used to the manual gears on Eric's Jeep. She'd forget to press down on the clutch when she changed the gears, and there'd be ugly noises that made her grind her own teeth.

"Will you stop doing that?" Lorraine snapped at her.

"Sorry," Janna said. "I'll get it eventually."

"Who can we ask?"

"No one that I know. Unless—"

"Unless what?"

"Unless Miss Bertha knows something."

"*Now* you think of it. Where does she live?"

"Near the square, I think," Janna said. She turned back to the main road and left at the square. All was quiet and dark. She stopped in front of a house that looked familiar, but it was the wrong house, and after many apologies from Janna, the sleepy occupant pointed to the house opposite.

"I'll go in," Janna said to Lorraine. "You stay in the car, in case of—"

"In case of what?" Lorraine said.

"Whatever," Janna said. "We'll have a quicker get-away."

"What do you think this is? A bank robbery?"

"No time to crack jokes, Lorraine."

"Point taken."

"Miss Bertha," Janna called softly at the front door of the house opposite. "Miss Bertha!" After a few knocks, the housekeeper opened the door in a rumpled dressing gown, her hair in twists and pins.

"Janna?" Bertha said. "Something happen to Mistah Lambert?"

Janna explained that Joseph and Raheem were missing, and her father and Eric had gone off to find them.

"Jesus, help us," the woman said, her hand to her mouth.

"Do you know anything, Miss Bertha? Anything at all?" Janna watched her biting her lower lip, struggling with possibilities, with passing comments.

"You check Shad?"

"He's gone with them. But do you know where a man named Cedric lives? Miss Mac said he may have something to do with it."

"No," she said, "but I know somebody who know." She pulled the door shut and started down the steps. "But how we going to fit in the Jeep?"

"Lorraine can sit on the brake," Janna said, and opened the passenger door. With a pull from Lorraine in front and a shove from Janna, the ample woman settled in the passenger seat, nodding to herself.

CHAPTER FIFTY-THREE

The front door was locked, and Eric crept around the side of the house, keeping low under the windows. He tried a window in a front room, but it was sealed shut. A rear window was open, and he slid it wider until he knew he could fit through. After a second's pause, his heart pounding like a hammer, he nodded, and what normally would have been unthinkable, that he should pull himself into a man's window, any window, drag his body across a gas stove, and fall to the floor, was done in less than a minute.

With pain searing through his left leg where he'd fallen, Eric struggled up and got his bearings. Cut through by the flickering light from the fire outside, the kitchen was small and crude, the main features being the stove and a sink. He patted the top of the stove, peered closely at small objects on a counter, knowing that the matches were somewhere. Whatever it took, he'd decided. The sight of Joseph, his son, his seed, tied like a pig, had sprung loose three decades of suppressed emotion, and Eric was suddenly thrown back beside the tousle-haired boy with chicken pox curled up watching television, and a rage had risen inside him that made anything possible, made any action forgivable.

His hand landed on a small box. When he shook it, he heard the familiar chinking of loose matches. Beyond the kitchen, he could just make out a single room. He felt his way around a dinette table to a window with a flimsy curtain. Opening the matchbox, his hand shaking, he extracted a match and lit the curtain at the hem. It went out quickly with his heavy breathing, and he lit another, turning his face away. The match caught, and he slowly placed it under the curtain, watched it catch and throw up a flame quicker than he'd expected. He stepped back to make sure the flame had taken hold, lit the curtain at the window opposite, determined now to burn down the whole house because the man deserved it and there was no time to lose. Back in the kitchen he found an old rag, which he lit and threw onto a sofa inside.

Outside again, Eric crept around the house to join the others. His body was aching and scratched from his second fall, this time out of the window, but he paid it no attention, kept looking back to see what damage had been done. Flames were licking the old curtains inside, he could see, but they were now smoking more than anything else.

"I did it," he whispered to Lambert, who was waiting for him near the front porch, still holding his gun.

"Good man." They tiptoed along the side of the house. From the open land in the back came the clatter of sticks being hit together, shouts about sodomy and fuckery. Shad was under a window, saying something to a stooping Winston with one hand on the boy's shoulder, gesturing toward the house with the other hand.

"Where's the minister?" Eric said to Lambert, and the two men looked around in the half dark.

"The fucker's gone," Lambert muttered.

Shad patted Winston on the back and the boy straightened. He started walking quickly toward the crowd while Eric, Shad, and Lambert tiptoed to the corner of the house for a better view. Winston was running now, calling out above the ruckus. Kelvin and a few others raised their arms in greeting, but Winston was pointing toward the house.

"Fire! Fire burn down Mistah Cedric's house!" he shouted.

He had to say it a few times before they understood, and then there was only the crackling of the bonfire while all eyes turned to the smoking house. Cedric started trotting toward the house, calling on Jesus, Joseph's gun still in his hand.

"What the *raas claat*—?" a younger man shouted, a man with the same bowlegs as Cedric. The two men rushed through the back door of the house, followed by Winston and a couple more men. For a few seconds Eric thought it might all be over, that they could run forward with Lambert's gun to free their captives, but the rest of the crowd had stayed behind, their minds still on the deed in front of them, the animals still to be skewered. There were new cries for the job to be finished. One of the men rushed toward Joseph with his machete raised, and Lambert aimed his gun at the man.

"Stop!" shouted Kelvin, raising the Bible. "We have to do this right. I told you, no blood! No chopping up, you hear me?" The man stopped and lowered the machete, glaring. Four men dragged Joseph and Raheem to their feet, and a skinny man in a green shirt climbed the ladder and scooted along the branch above the nooses.

"Quiet, quiet!" Kelvin was shouting. "We have to ask God's blessing first!"

"What blessing?" a woman yelled back. "You tell us already God say we to kill batty men."

"Kill them, yes! Hang them!" The cries went up, and the rest of the crowd dropped their weapons and surged forward to help the hangmen, and Raheem and Joseph were dragged toward the nooses. Suddenly, Raheem swung his bound hands at a man and missed, Joseph elbowed another, and more men jumped on them.

"We have to do something!" Eric whispered furiously.

"Now!" Shad hissed, and the three rushed out of the shadow of the house, Lambert in front.

"Let the men go!" Lambert shouted as he trotted forward, the gun pointed straight at the preacher's son.

"Let them go," Eric yelled.

The crowd stood still, trying to grasp this new development, their heads swiveling between Kelvin and Lambert. Kelvin had frozen on the spot. Joseph and Raheem looked up at the same time, and Joseph mouthed something to his father, something that wouldn't come out. Some of the men and women, reenergized, started moving toward the three invaders, waving their weapons.

411

"Go 'way! Go 'way!" a woman yelled. "Mind your business."

"Don't stop!" a man shouted. "If we going to hang them, then hang them!"

A fiendish man yanked the nooses over Joseph's and Raheem's heads with gritted teeth, while three men held them each in place. Others circled Lambert, Shad, and Eric.

"Shoot, if you think you so bad," a large woman said. She walked up to Lambert's gun and struck a wild-woman pose in front of the barrel, her hands on her hips. Lambert stepped back, his arm shaking.

"Let my son go!" Eric yelled, flinging out his arms as he started toward the group.

Lambert raised his gun above the woman's head and fired. Someone screamed. Someone rushed out of the house, shouting something. Kelvin ducked down, his head covered with the Bible.

"You next!" a man shouted at Lambert, grabbing his arm with the gun. Eric lunged at the man as two men held on to Shad. Then a woman and a man were struggling with Eric, and another man came to help them, all three pushing against him, pinning his arms down.

"Who are you people?" Shad wailed. "You go to church on Sunday and kill people on Monday?"

"Let me go, you motherfuckers!" Eric yelled. He freed one arm and swung at one of the men and connected. The man hit him on the side of the head and grabbed his arm.

"Kelvin!" Shad called. "You is a hypocrite, a murderer!" Kelvin looked at him with wild, questioning eyes.

"String the batty boys up first, then the father," screamed a woman into Eric's ear. He struggled to get free of his captors, cursing them, but they held on tighter, dug their fingernails into his arm.

"Let me go!" he shouted.

"You all going to prison," Lambert yelled, struggling and cursing. Still hanging on to the gun, he hit a man with the barrel and shoved the gun into his pocket.

"You can't kill all of us!" Shad said.

It was like the mob didn't hear, couldn't react to anything but a decision already made, some fate already sealed. They moved like inflamed robots about their business. The skinny man straddling the branch pulled both ropes until they were taut.

"Pass the ropes down!" shouted a man below.

"Stop that, you sons of bitches!" Eric screamed.

"Stop!" Lambert and Shad joined him, yelling to stop the craziness. But the men and women were chorusing scornfully, drowning them out, shouting that *batty boys must dead*. The man on the branch threw the end of each rope to two hefty men below, one standing behind Joseph, and the other, Raheem. The men started pulling, yanking at first, and then straining with the ascending weight of their much lighter prisoners. Joseph and Raheem straightened, the nooses and ropes pulling them upward until they were standing erect.

"Dad!" Joseph called, his face red and twisted in terror.

"Joseph!" Eric answered him.

The hangmen continued to pull, and their victims

continued to stretch up, trying to delay leaving the ground. Raheem was staring at his feet, now on tiptoe.

"Joseph, I'm coming!" Eric called out. He struggled to free himself, but four or five people yelled at him to shut up, pounded his arms and back.

Suddenly, a grinding sound shattered the night, the soul-piercing noise of gears being changed without a clutch, a sound Eric would have hated on any other night. The red Jeep was careening toward them, around the corner of the smoking house, Janna, a madwoman, driving, beside her a wide-eyed Lorraine and Bertha with her hair pinned up. The crowd darted out of the path of the car plowing toward them, screeching to a halt in front of the nooses. A huge man stood up in the flatbed of the Jeep with the largest machete Eric had ever seen.

Towering over the crowd, wobbling a little with his liquor, Solomon swooshed the machete up in the air. He cut both nooses with two quick swipes that sent the men holding the ends of the ropes tumbling to the ground. At the same moment, Joseph and Raheem crumpled to their knees, their hands still tied behind them. Raheem recovered first and stood shakily. He turned his back to Solomon, who sawed at the rope around the man's wrists until it came loose and did the same for Joseph after he scrambled to his feet. Raheem pulled himself up into the flatbed and helped Joseph up, the severed nooses still dangling from their necks. Joseph pulled Raheem's noose off and then his own.

"If any of you bitches come close, I kill you dead," Solomon boomed to the gaping mob, "because I is a chef and I like to—to cut up things." He raised the machete again, glaring at the man on the branch a few feet away, and the man shrank back. Below him, the two hangmen were still lying on the ground holding the severed ropes, their eyes huge.

"What you want with them?" one of the hangmen called. "They *faggots*!"

"They faggots, yes," Solomon shouted back, "but they Mistah Eric's faggots."

And with that, the worst was over—the frenzy, the retribution, the deception, the denial—made powerless by the drunken Solomon's words. Weeks later it occurred to Eric that by laying claim to Joseph and Raheem in the name of his employer, Solomon had wiped out years of bigotry in Largo. What he had said, and what the mob had understood, was that if they wanted to have a nice bar to have a drink—instead of the little rat holes in the square—wanted to have a place for their wedding receptions without driving all the way to Manchioneal, wanted a good meal for a birthday or an anniversary, a meal cooked by a real chef, then they better open their ignorant minds or at least close their mouths. And what his machete had said was that he wouldn't be afraid to use it if they ever tried anything foolish like this again.

Seconds after he said it, the crowd began to move back, lowering their weapons, and the skinny man scrambled down the ladder, falling the last few feet to the ground and tearing his green shirt. Kelvin started melting toward the fence with his Bible in hand.

"Kelvin getting away! Grab him!" Shad shouted, and

shook free of the men holding him, Eric and Lambert behind him. The three jumped at Kelvin, pinning him to the ground, while his followers shrank back. Lambert pulled his gun out of his pocket and stuck it at the man's head, and Kelvin, in the fetal position, closed his eyes tight.

"You almost killed two men, you know that?" Lambert shouted. Kelvin unrolled and tried to get to his feet, but Shad pushed him back down.

"Shoot him if you have to!" Eric cried.

Behind them, the house made a popping noise. It had burst into flames, fire pouring out of the windows, and the men and women still left in the yard started running toward it, shouting instructions to each other.

Kelvin writhed on the ground, pulling away from the gun at his temple. "You *bumba claat,* you going to jail!" Shad yelled at him.

"Leave me alone," Kelvin cried.

"Who start all this?" Shad said. "Who organize it?"

"Is not me," Kelvin whined. "Is not me."

"I know is not you," Shad spat at him, "you too coward. But it feel like a setup to me—all this hanging business—from the beginning. Nobody hang people in Jamaica except the government. Who responsible for this madness? Talk, or we going to shoot."

Kelvin was almost sobbing now, and Eric and Shad dragged him to his feet.

"Daddy!" Janna called from the Jeep. "Come on! We have to get out of here!"

"She's right," Lambert said. "Let's go."

They pushed Kelvin up to the back of the Jeep and clambered in behind. Janna reversed, then ground the gears into first, and headed jerkily toward the road. Raheem and Joseph, their faces still frozen in shock, held on to the roll bar in front beside Shad. In the middle of the flatbed, Eric clasped Lambert's shoulder for support, while at the rear a terrified Kelvin cowered beside Solomon, who sat smiling down at him, the machete across his knees.

"What about the young man, what's his name?" Lambert said.

"Winston okay," Shad said. "He a survivor."

The inferno that had been Cedric's house now loomed in front of them. It was engulfed in fire, spectacular orange and red flames licking the wooden walls and shooting thirty feet above the shingle roof. Noises that Eric had never heard before—crackling and whooshing and whistling—had turned it into a roaring hell. To the left of the house, a clear, narrow path between the barbed wire fence and the fire beckoned them on. Janna began steering the Jeep carefully along it, keeping the vehicle a few feet away from the flames, but the heat was ferocious and the men shrank from it as the car crept along the path. When they were almost past the house, a thunderous, tearing sound made them all look up.

"Holy shit!" Eric yelled.

The roof was breaking loose, sending a nightmare of fireworks into the sky around them. A ball of fire landed in front of them and one behind. The Jeep jerked to a stop, sending the passengers in the flatbed tumbling on top of one another, knowing they were trapped.

CHAPTER FIFTY-FOUR

"Keep going!" Shad shouted, bending over the driver's seat and grabbing Janna's shoulder. The girl swung around with a look of panic.

"I can't," she cried.

"Yes, you can! Gun the engine and hit it!"

"Stay low, everybody," Lambert yelled. Janna revved the motor for a few seconds, then tore up and over the burning wood and asphalt shingles, landing with a plop in front of it.

"Yes!" shouted Shad.

In front of the house, the former lynch mob had gathered at a safe distance, their faces contorted in sorrow, lamenting the hellfire before them. Sister Arida had her arm around Cedric; others stood in shocked silence with their arms folded. They didn't even look at the Jeep, as if it were past history. Shad stared at them, people he thought he knew, forever strangers to him now. Grinding the gears again, Janna started forward.

"Wait!" shouted Lambert. "The cars!" The Jeep stopped with a jerk. Lambert climbed down and ran to the Rover, followed by Shad, who jumped into Jennifer's car. They started the cars quickly and turned them around.

Ten minutes later, all three vehicles were parked in front of the preacher's house. The man's front room now as crowded as a startup church, the unwelcome congregation was made up of Eric, holding on to Kelvin's waistband, Joseph, Raheem, Shad, Solomon, still clutching his machete, and Lambert, standing with the gun close to Pastor and his wife. Outside the porch door, the three women peeked over each other's shoulders at the scene, Lorraine's eyes the biggest and Miss Bertha's pin curls twisting down the sides of her face.

Pastor had allowed his wife to answer the pounding on the front door, and, seeing the crowd of men pushing into his living room, his son in Eric's grip, he'd hung back, his face contorting. Now the parents stood in the corridor to the bedrooms, half turned to the men in their living room. Both husband and wife were dressed as if they'd been waiting up, waiting for news, or waiting to travel.

"You didn't expect us, eh, McClelen?" Shad said.

"What you want with us?" Pastor said. His face looked old and wrinkly in the lamplight from a side table.

"Your son tried to murder my son and his friend!" Eric shouted, and shook Kelvin by the waistband. "He and that mob had them hanging—"

"I didn't have nothing to do with it," the wiry little man said fiercely.

"Don't lie!" Kelvin said. "You told me to go to the bar and—"

"Shut your mouth," his father said.

"It was you all along, *Pastor,*" Shad pressed him. "You who call Miss Mac's house and left that message for Joseph."

"What message?" Joseph said, exchanging a look with Raheem.

"That wasn't us," Kelvin said bitterly. "It was Cedric. He get so work up that he said he couldn't help himself. He must have think he was a prophet or something."

"It doesn't matter who made the fucking phone call," Eric yelled, his face red as sorrel juice. "You were going to murder two innocent men!"

"Two *innocent* men?" McClelen said. He pulled his scrawny chest high and walked a couple of paces toward them. "They are *sodomizers,* sir! The country should be glad to get rid of scum."

"You would know scum when you see it," Lambert jeered.

"We are doing God's work, gentlemen," McClelen said, his head high.

"Which God?" Shad said. "A God that tell people to kill other people?"

"Jesus's own disciple say—" started Kelvin.

"Say what, Kelvin?" Shad said with a dry laugh. It suddenly made sense, all the nodding in church. "Like how you is an expert in what the Bible say about batty men? And like how you is a batty man who go to Kingston to find other batty men, you mean?"

Kelvin winced. "I not no batty man."

"And you was the youth with the high voice who

come to kill Sister Elsa's son. You think I don't know? Talk the truth, the reason you so against gayness is because you gay yourself."

"You have a dirty mind!" Kelvin shouted.

Pastor raised one hand, the fingers straight and glued together, itching to hit somebody. "My son is *not* a homosexual! How dare you? He has studied to be a man of the cloth, a messenger of God!" His wife reached out and clutched his arm, hushing him.

"You mean your wife didn't tell you, Pastor?" Shad smiled. "Your wife didn't tell you that with all that seminary business, all that Bible beating, that your anointed son, who supposed to take over your church, that he is a batty man?"

"I tell you I not gay," the anointed one insisted. "I is a man, a real *man*."

"Well, talk the truth, then," Raheem said sharply, and everyone's eyes swung to him and the red bruise around his neck. "A real man will talk the truth."

"I not gay," Kelvin said, and pointed at Joseph, "but I knew Mistah Eric's son was gay from the first time I see him. He was walking to the beach the first day he come, his head high, and he didn't even say a *good morning* or nothing to me, just snobbish like. He don't even notice me."

"And you liked him, right?" Lambert said with a flourish of the gun. "That's why you started the whole thing, because he didn't—"

"Leave him alone," Pastor sneered. "Nothing wrong with him. He not no sodomizer. I knock it out of him already." His wife looked down at her stubby toes in their slippers.

"He beat me, yes," Kelvin said. "Beat it out of me."

"But you still think about men, don't you?" Joseph said.

Kelvin glanced from his father to Joseph, the Bible still clutched in his fingers. "What you think about don't—don't make you a sodomizer."

"Stop!" his father commanded. "Those are the *devil's* thoughts."

"I will think what I want to think," Kelvin barked back. "I too old now for you to whip me with the tamarind switch. You think I forget how you take off my pants and whip me beside that table?" He pointed to the oval mahogany table in the dining alcove. "Whip me like you was going to kill me because I walk home with Gideon? You think I don't remember?"

"He was the devil's child, that's why! You play with the devil—"

"He was my *friend,* that was all he was. My friend! And you made me go with Sister Arida and Cedric and all of them, when they was going to—"

"Shut up!"

Mrs. McClelen stepped forward and held out her hand to her son. Her face looked pained, the eyes sorrowful. "Kelvin, you not no devil's child, you hear? You not no sodomizer, son. God created you through me, and you are a blessed child."

"If I was a blessed child, why you didn't stand up for me? You let the man beat me raw, and you never said anything. When he said the only way I could take over the church was to fight the demon of sodomy in my soul, where were you? Answer me that!" His mother looked at him with no words for her cowardice, and Shad looked at Eric, staring at the guilty mother.

"You know how it feel to be different in Jamaica?" Kelvin shouted. "You know how it feel? Heavy in my heart every day—*that* how it feel."

"Hush, son," his mother said, still extending her hand.

"I shame for you," his father mocked.

"McClelen," said Shad, "you ever know a homosexual?"

"Of course not."

"I knew a man, he was my cell mate in the Penitentiary for three months. His name was Freddy and he told me how he never attracted to a woman yet, and how his life been hell from the beginning." He paused for a second, enough time to see Joseph and Raheem glancing at each other. "People ridicule Freddy, call him a batty man, and he never feel safe except when somebody take care of him. And he got a lover, a professor man in Kingston at the university, and he lived with the man and the man take care of him. One day the man tell him he done with him, and Freddy got crazy and kill the man, and he got twenty years in the Pen. He happy, he said it was better than going home." When the man said nothing, only stared at him blankly, Shad thought of all the people who'd been different in Largo, who'd been chased out because they were gay or because they were mentally ill or because they were dwarfs, or who'd been

423

hidden away in back rooms because they had big heads or clubfeet.

"Enough talk," Eric said, and started pushing Kelvin toward the door.

"Time to go." Joseph nodded, and he and Lambert held on to the minister's wrists.

"You riding in the back with me," Solomon said, swinging the machete loosely at his side and opening his eyes wide at his wife's pastor.

"Off to jail with you," Lambert said, his gun trained on McClelen's chest. "Straight to Port Antonio."

Mrs. McClelen sucked in her breath. "Oh, dear Jesus," was all she could say.

"I want a lawyer," Pastor squealed while Joseph was lifting him down the front steps. He looked like a scrawny doll, his legs dragging beneath Joseph's muscular arms.

"And, Pastor," Shad said, laughing, behind them, "like how you little and skinny, they going to love you in the Penitentiary, nuh? You better start praying."

CHAPTER FIFTY-FIVE

Janna turned on the hot water as soon as Joseph entered the house, his familiar footsteps the signal to start her new ritual. After pouring bubble bath under the tap, she sat on the side of the tub, watching the bubbles coming to life, listening to him walking to Jennifer's office. He must have been wearing sneakers today, his footsteps muffled and the wooden floor creaking only now and again. Janna removed her shorts and shirt and placed them on the toilet lid. She stepped into the bath, ran some cold water to cool it down, and slid into the tub. The water closed in on her, seeping into her crevices, the bubbles sending off little sprays of water near her face.

"You look like Ophelia, drowning herself in the river." It was Lorraine, standing with arms folded beside the tub. "I always thought she should have drowned Hamlet, not herself."

Janna groaned. "I need my privacy."

Lorraine removed the clothes and sat down on the toilet lid. "I'm tired of your privacy. You've been moping around for days now since the—the whole drama, and I've had to stay in this house. I'm getting cabin fever."

"I thought you were writing."

"I need a break."

Janna closed her eyes again. She wanted to think about the dream she'd had last night. She'd been standing in the middle of a wide boulevard, in Miami maybe, with skyscrapers on both sides. The street was empty of cars, but up its center walked a line of sad women, about twenty feet apart, each in a white bridal gown. And the gowns were sad themselves, *thrift store* written in their crumpled sleeves and torn hems. None of the women carried a bouquet or wore a veil. Some were barefoot. All looked tired and hopeless, walking up the center of an empty street, going nowhere. Placing her washrag over her face, Janna leaned her head back on the edge of the tub.

"I have nothing to say."

"Janna, you're in love with a man who's in love with a man, and you have nothing to say? You saved them from *death,* and you have nothing to say?"

Janna removed the cloth and looked wearily at her friend. "Lorraine, just let it go."

"You had sex with the man, girl," Lorraine said, leaning forward, pressing. "You exchanged bodily fluids. That's *big* for you."

"I'll get over it."

"Then when are you going to get out of this bath and get over it?"

"I'm waiting for him to leave."

Lorraine sighed and examined her charm bracelet. "Let me put it another way, you're acting like a fucking

426

child, all this hiding in the tub. And when are you going to start eating? You'll be dead in no time if you keep this up."

"I'll live."

"That's the thing. You're going to live, and you're going to have to face him. Suppose he comes to visit his father again and you're here. What are you going to do? Hide in the tub with a false white beard again?"

"I just need a rest."

"A rest? You didn't need a rest when you jacked me out of bed in the middle of the night and went roaring off to save Joseph and Raheem."

"A temporary state of insanity."

"I'm telling you, you were like this—crazy lioness all of a sudden. I didn't know that Janna. That's how you should be the rest of the time, girl. You can't keep ducking your head down and running from stuff. You can't keep being a daddy's girl, running when you don't get what you want. I'm telling you, you're a runner. If you'd stayed at the *Herald,* you would probably have gotten into reporting, we don't know. Instead you quit, because you weren't being *challenged enough,* and you ran off and did something entirely different. It's time to turn around and take some freaking responsibility for your own life, Jan. You need to step up, like you did the other night, you know what I mean?" Lorraine rubbed the back of her neck and grimaced. "Besides, we need to get out of this house. I've been writing up the story and my eyes are crossed."

Taking a deep breath, Janna braced herself against

the sides of the tub and got to her feet. Globs of foam dripped down her body. "You're right. I hate to admit it, but you're right. I saved his fucking life and he owes me an explanation." She grabbed the towel that a speechless Lorraine was handing her and stepped out of the bath.

Dressed in black, from jeans to T-shirt, Janna walked slowly down the corridor, feeling the grain of the planks under her bare feet. He was sitting at the desk as usual, and she knocked on a pane of the open door.

"Yes," Joseph said, and looked up from his laptop. He had a black-and-blue around his neck and under his chin, and she tried not to look at it.

"There you are," he said, smiling, looking a little shy. "You just disappeared." He was giving her that look with the curl dangling in front of one eye. It looked different seen with a hollow stomach, and she no longer wanted to reach out and tuck it behind his ear, felt the wall between them.

"I've been around," she said, and leaned on the door frame, folding her arms.

He stood up. "I've been wanting to thank you. I spoke to your father—"

"He told me." She looked down at her feet with their long toes.

"If it hadn't been for you—"

"I'm just glad the keys were still in the Jeep."

"Janna," he said. "I know it must seem as if—"

She shook her head, wishing she had something to hold on to other than her own thin arms. Be strong, she reminded herself. Get the questions out of your head and over the wall.

"Are you in love with him?" she blurted out.

He opened and closed his mouth, then nodded, looking at the ring on his right hand that had been absent for a while.

"You were never in love with me, were you?"

"Let's go sit on the verandah," he said.

On the far end of the porch, he sat in a rocking chair and she in a straight chair beside him. She looked out to sea, to the island, and suddenly understood why the woman had been there, far from people.

"This is difficult for me," he said. He exhaled and leaned back. There was a steady, centered manner about him now that spoke of balance, like he'd brought all his warring parts together into a peaceful whole. She examined the verandah balusters opposite, seeing but not seeing them, knowing that someone else had done this for him.

"Janna," he started, "my whole life has been about trying to be what other people wanted me to be. My mother wanted me to be—well mannered, so I went to ballroom dancing. My father wanted me to be a man, so I went fishing." She knew he wanted her to look at him, and she refused to look, needing to stay apart.

"After they split up, I went into middle school in Virginia, and, like everybody else, I avoided the gay students like the plague. I became the brainy, cute guy with lots of friends, none of them really close. The boys didn't bother me, unless they wanted help with a paper or something, and I had lots of girlfriends, so I had a date when I needed one."

He paused and took a long breath. "Then I went to college and I had to face the truth. It started when I was a freshman. I studied with this guy called Aaron, a really bright guy. I thought he might be gay, but we never discussed it. One day he started asking me what I was, gay or straight, and he made me think."

By his second year in college, he said, he started hanging out with gay friends, but he still felt guilty, so he worked even harder, worked his butt off for good grades. Only later did he realize it was to stop his parents asking questions.

"When I graduated I started working for this financial firm with a great reputation—not a big firm, but a respected one in DC. My boss was this macho type, you know, very athletic, and he'd make cracks about homosexuals. So I started working out, and I started dating girls again. I had this cool apartment, this very cool Alfa Romeo—a black convertible—and I would date women and break off after a few dates if they got serious. And on the side I was going to gay bars, feeling split down the middle.

"Then I met Raheem a couple years ago, and all of a sudden I knew it would be all right. He was very secure in his sexuality, and it kind of affected me. I'd changed jobs the year before and started working with this big company, and there were other gay guys there." He gave a short laugh. "It was cool to be queer all of a sudden, but I still couldn't come out, tell everybody, my mom and my dad. It's taken me two more years, but I'm ready." He added quickly, "Not here, of course."

While his words seemed to strengthen him, they were leaving her weak, all the energy draining out of her body and into the chair.

"You don't want to hear this," he said. "I don't blame you."

"You should have told me," she said, so softly it was almost a whisper.

"Told you what, that I'm gay?"

"I defended you."

"You know the funny thing, Janna? What I discovered with you was that, yes, I'm still gay and I love a man, but I can be with a woman, too. I can have sex with a woman and enjoy it. True, I don't get that real passionate—connection, whatever it is—like I do with a man, but I can have fun with a woman, even sexually. And you knew how to turn me on. You really did. Does that make me gay, straight, bisexual? I don't know anymore. I don't know if it matters."

"But you're gay!" She gave up fighting the tears, letting them flow down her face, giving her strength to say what she had to.

"Yes, I am, but I wanted to know what it would feel like to sleep with a woman. It was fun, relaxing. Wasn't it for you? I thought we'd have a fun time and go our own ways after."

"A *fun time*?" The words stung her lips.

"Yeah. I thought—you got that, that we were just having a good time. The kite flying, the swimming, the vision board thing, it was all fun. And I had to be straight here. This is a crazy country, Janna, but I wanted to be here. I wanted to show my father that I could write this report—do something he couldn't do—and do it better than he expected. I wanted his respect, I guess."

He snorted, like it was a reality check. "And I'd run out of money, so I had to come, but I wasn't going to announce I was gay. Not in Jamaica! When I was here last time, people looked at us funny, whispered stuff. Ron and Dave didn't always see them, but I did. I know this place, and it's not just Largo, it's the whole fucking country. I had no choice: I couldn't be queer here."

"I wouldn't have told anybody," she said, wiping her eyes with her sleeve.

"You mightn't have meant to," he snapped at her, "but—"

"If you were going to sleep with me, you should have told me."

"I wanted to sleep with you."

"Don't you get what I'm saying, Joseph?" she snapped back. "You're a gay man and you didn't use protection. You should have told me before we had sex." Head to head, don't back down, she reminded herself.

"You told me you were on the pill, and for the last two years I've only had—I told you, I'm clear, I get checked every six months." The words were loaded, separating them even more.

"You used me as a cover. You wanted everybody to think you were straight. I just became this—this—mask you could use. You said so yourself—you had to be straight here."

"But I liked hanging out with you. You were easy

to talk to. You mightn't believe me, but that part is true."

"We could have just been friends." Even if she'd wanted more. "When did you decide to sleep with me?"

"When I realized there were people counting on me to write the report—Dad, Shad, everybody. The hotel is the only straw they can hang on to." He snorted again, louder this time. "And it really changed when I knew I could be killed."

Janna rubbed her arms, suddenly chilled. "What happened?"

"Some really fucked-up guys—" He leaned forward, his nostrils flaring. "They almost dragged us off, Shad and me, because they thought we were a couple. It scared the hell out of me, I'm telling you. I was going to leave Largo after that, but Shad talked me out of it.

"Then Raheem came down. That was crazy. I'd told him not to come, but he said he couldn't sleep worrying about me. He tried to talk me into going back, but I wouldn't leave. And then whenever we went out together, in Ocho Rios or wherever, people would look at us in this weird way—it reminded me of the time before—and he noticed it, too. We decided it was best if you and me—and him and Lorraine—you know, looked like couples." He turned red, suddenly embarrassed by his opportunism. "We could go out in public without people staring at us."

"Then how did you end up—?"

"After we dropped you girls off after dinner that

night, this little boy came running by with this—this note, telling us to go to that house."

"Why'd you go, Joseph?" she said angrily. "We could have all been killed!"

"The note said they were going to burn Dad's bar down if we didn't go, and I believed it. I had the gun and we thought that would be enough. Shad had said there were probably only one or two guys involved, and I thought—but as soon as we got out of the car, all these people started swarming us, pushing us around, tying us up. The whole thing was—was totally bizarre."

His face and body had gone rigid at the memory, and she knew she should soothe him, should reach out and touch him. Instead, she scratched the letter *J* with her nail in the white paint of the chair's arm, focusing her breathing, pinning her hurt down to one letter.

"What did Raheem say—about us sleeping together?" she said when she had finished scraping.

He rocked twice in the chair and stopped. "He was angry, of course, maybe more in pain than angry, but he understood—after a while. He even told me I shouldn't hurt you."

"I can't forgive you," she said, staring at the *J* on the chair, seeing the jilted and the jealous in the letter.

"Maybe you'll never forgive me, but I want you to know that I care about you. A lot. You're a beautiful woman, inside and out. I felt like you accepted me totally, like you knew I was gay and you still accepted me."

"But why did you act so weird, so moody?"

"I was confused about what I wanted, and I had all

this stuff going on, with my father, with the new sister, with the report, and I was worried about being killed." He took a deep breath and exhaled slowly. "And I felt guilty about being unfaithful."

Janna spread her fingers over the arms of the chair, covering the *J*. "I guess that says it all, then," she said, and stood up, hurt but vindicated. "A person only feels guilty when they love someone."

He reached for her hand when she turned to walk away. "I wondered what it would be like—you and me."

The warmth of his hand spread from the back of hers, into her palm, and up her arm, forcing her to listen for any fragment of hope. "And?"

"We'd have amazing-looking kids." He smiled up at her, the crooked tooth making her heart ache. "But I'd be unfaithful, and you'd be miserable."

"There's nothing more to say, then," she said, and tugged her hand away.

Walking back, trailing the hand he'd touched along the corridor wall to wipe off his warmth, she knew that the numbness within her, even the bitterness, had been worth it. She had risked loving him despite the warnings of others. It had been *her* decision, no one else's, and despite her grief, there was a prickly, new feeling inside her, as if she were standing on the edge of a vast, unknown land. And part of the armor she was wearing in that land was the knowledge that she had, without a thought for her own life, saved two men, no, five men, from death. She had done what many men couldn't have done, had driven the Jeep right up to the mob so Solomon could cut the nooses down, had told them all to get into the back when they were dawdling, and made the Jeep vault over the fire to safety, and no one, *no one,* would ever accuse her of being milquetoast again—not even Lorraine.

CHAPTER FIFTY-SIX

December 2011

Almost everyone was in place at the table when Shad rushed out, stumbling over the suitcases next to the bar.

"What you having to drink, folks?" Shad said, straightening. "It's on the house."

"It's too hot for rum," Joseph said, his eyes darting to Eric. "A ginger ale, Dad?"

"That'll work," his father said. He was sitting back, arms folded tight across his chest. It was the first time they'd assembled, almost the whole cast—the rescuers and the rescued—from that night they'd never forget. The attempted hanging was still an ugly subject everyone tried to and yet couldn't avoid discussing, even the villagers. It was different from the attack on Gideon, everyone agreed, because it had involved the very white and very American Joseph (who had bedded Janna, after all) and his model friend from Trinidad. And the drama had been heightened because of the arrests of the pastor and his son, quickly followed by the rare appearance of a police car sent to arrest Cedric and Arida, causing no end of gossip and hearsay. It had become a shameful thing, a social disgrace, to be named among those who'd taken part in the event, and a few of the more prominent participants were known to have left town already.

Shad circled the table. "Drinks for anybody else?"

"I'll take a Carib," Raheem said.

"A coconut water, Shad," Lambert called.

"And a piña colada for me," Lorraine said, "since I'm to stay put and cover the story for another week, according to my boss. God, I love that man."

"Is Janna coming over?" Joseph asked.

"I don't think so." Lorraine flicked her bangs back. "She wasn't feeling too well. Some little stomach thing, nothing serious."

"I have something to show Joseph," Shad said, breaking the awkward silence. "But let me get the drinks first."

When he returned with his tray, Eric pulled out the chair beside him. "Come sit with us, Shad." The bartender nodded his thanks and distributed the drinks. It was a small gesture but big in Largo, for a man like Eric to invite a poor man like Shad to sit and eat with him. But that was Eric, and the way he'd done it—his eyes grateful and his twitching smile teasing his bartender turned detective—left nothing unsaid between him and his future partner.

"Just a minute," Shad said, and rushed off. In the kitchen, Solomon was frying chicken and fanning himself. Winston was helping out, laying the dishes on the counter, looking at Solomon nervously, probably still wondering what it was going to be like to live with him and Maisie. He was to move in with the couple that weekend and help them with cutting grass and weeding the vegetables, whatever they needed, in exchange for room and board. All three would benefit, Shad had convinced them. It would give the old people young legs and give the boy a home.

A solid boy, Winston, Shad had decided, who would make a good assistant one day. Slipping into the bar the day before, the young man had reported that his friend Lebert had confessed that he was responsible for the note and the noose hanging in the Jeep. Soon after Joseph's arrival, Kelvin had started his ignorance in Quality Bar, Winston had said between slurps of grape soda. Lebert had found out from Shad's friend Frank that Shad was going to Maurice Barnett's party at Marlin Bay and using the Jeep. He'd asked a security guard friend who was working at the party to hang the noose in the car with the note. It was supposed to be a warning for Shad to look out for Joseph, Lebert said, because he'd had a bad feeling about Kelvin's comments from the start. Yes, with a little training, Winston would make a good sniffer and snuffer, but in the meanwhile he needed a mother, and the childless Maisie had jumped into the role already. She'd cleaned out their back room and moved in a bed and a small desk. Last night she'd asked Shad what Winston liked to eat.

"Food," he'd answered. "Plenty hot food."

The afternoon trade wind was blowing into the kitchen, sending the smell of fried chicken through the restaurant. "I going to sit with the boss," Shad said. "When you serve everything, why you both don't come and sit with us? The table can hold eight."

Winston looked at Solomon, who grunted, "Not today." He always preferred to eat in the kitchen with his glass of white rum beside him, but he would have grumbled for days if Shad had been invited and he hadn't. The boy would keep him company today, and maybe the chef would do some mentoring of his own, although you never could tell with Solomon, who could be a grunter or a gossip, depending on the day.

When he got back to the table, Shad slid into the vacant chair. "I know you guys talking about what happen the other night."

"No," Lambert said. "We were talking about the report."

"It's all finished," Joseph said. His voice was clear and satisfied, and even the way he nodded was strong. "I'll print it out when I get back to DC, three copies. I'll mail one to you, Dad, and one to the investor, like we promised. I'll keep one for the record."

Eric unfolded his arms and sighed. "The whole enterprise is going to take years, I see it now." Shad narrowed his eyes at Eric for a second and pursed his lips.

"The figures are looking good," Joseph said, turning to the island. "I hope the investor hasn't changed his mind, because everything looks great for a hotel, man, and a campground on Simone Island. I called Horace like you asked me. He's definitely on board."

"Everybody counting on it, boss," Shad said. "We can't back down now."

Eric peered at the island for a second, pulling his hair back. "If it gets off the ground, maybe I'll call Simone to let her know. She might want to come out for the groundbreaking or something."

"I don't know how you finished that report," Lorraine said to Joseph, "with all the—" She stopped and looked down at her drink.

"I had to finish it," Joseph said. "I'd promised Shad."

Eric shook his head at the vase of bougainvillea in the center of the table. "You have guts, boy. I take my hat off to you." When he looked up quickly at Joseph, his glance carried a new respect.

"I still can't get over it—the whole thing," Raheem said, hitting the edge of the table with his long fingers. He had on a nice brown cowboy shirt, expensive-looking but not one a real cowboy would wear.

"Have you told your family?" Lambert asked him.

"Yes. They're still in shock. My mother said I was to call as soon as we get back to DC. I'll call them tomorrow after we get Joseph moved in. We have to get his stuff out of storage." The silence that followed reminded Shad of when Beth dropped a five-dollar coin into her jar on the kitchen shelf and everyone in the house stopped what they were doing to listen.

Lorraine took a sip of her piña colada and licked her top lip. "Hey, I'm almost finished writing my article for the *Herald*. I'm emailing it in tonight. My editor will be thrilled, he's a pushover for a scoop. Then I'll write up the feature and send that in, too." She nodded at Joseph. "Thanks for talking Samson and Gideon into the interview—once they knew there'd be no names called. I just hope—"

"Samson and who?" Shad said, thinking he may have heard wrong.

"Gideon," Lorraine said. "We didn't tell you? We met the guy Kelvin was talking about, the guy who—"

"—was chased out of Largo ten years ago?"

"That's the one," said Joseph. "We met him and his partner earlier that same day, when we were driving around about fifty, sixty miles from here. Is that a coincidence or what?"

"And you know where he lives." Shad twisted his mouth and nibbled the inside of his cheek, wondering if he should find out or not, thinking of Sister Elsa, what she would do if she knew where her son was. Probably start harassing him for money to support her in her old age. Some sleeping dogs were best left alone, yes.

Joseph waved a hand in front of Shad's gaze, bringing him back. "Hey, man, you had something to show me?"

"Yeah, yeah," Shad said. "I have a surprise for you." Out of his pocket he drew the chunky Glock and laid it next to the vase of bougainvillea. It looked like a hard rock under the soft purple blossoms.

"Oh, my God," Joseph said. "How'd you get that back?" He didn't pick up the gun, just kept looking at it, his hand still on his glass.

"Winston found it during the fire. Cedric must have thrown it down." Shad rubbed his hands together. "I can take care of it if you want."

"I can't take it on the plane anyway, man. You can have it."

"True?" Shad said, and quickly slipped the gun into his pocket, aware of five sets of eyes on him, knowing that no one would say anything more about it, because now there would be two guns in town on the side of justice—his and Lambert's—even if there was no chance of getting it licensed with his record. He'd have to find a good hiding place for it, out of the children's way.

Eric swirled the ice in his glass. "So do you still think you're going back to Trinidad to live, Raheem? I mean with what you've just been through—"

"I think I'm going to let my sisters take over. They've been running it for years, anyway."

"A women's auto parts business." Shad chuckled. "I must tell Beth."

"Sounds like another feature article in the making," Lorraine said, her face lighting up. "Hey, I could go down at Carnival time to write the story! That could work. But I'm going to follow up the story here, shine a light on this whole homophobia craziness—I've been thinking about it." Her little body was full of energy, pulsing forward while she talked. "Maybe some record producers in Atlanta will give me their take on the dancehall lyrics. And I want to interview some of the guys who write this gay-bashing crap and ask them why they do it."

"Can you send us the articles?" Shad said. It would be worth struggling with the big words to read them.

"Of course."

"Do you think they'll call us to testify?" Lambert said.

"I'm sure we'll have to," Eric said. "They have our statements from when we brought in Kelvin and his father. Joseph and Raheem will have to come back for that."

"Are you kidding?" his son said quickly, and Raheem nodded, their decision already made. "We'll do it by deposition from DC."

"It's going to take a while, though," Shad said. "Neville said it would be a year or so before it come to trial, could be longer. It take a long time."

"The whole thing is like a dream," Raheem said. He put his hand up to his throat, to the fading black-and-blue mark encircled by the fish necklace.

"And Pastor was behind the whole thing," Shad said, rolling his eyes up at the thatch roof, which was finally turning brown. "His days done in Largo. *Thank you, God.*" He shook his head. "Yes, boy, he look pale like a sheet when we went back to get him." Standing up, he started to do what he did best, playacting the Pastor's wife opening the door to Kelvin's knock, her mouth a big O. The group smiled nervously at first, then tittered, then laughed outright at Shad's clowning, needing to be released from the memories, needing to find humor in it.

"He almost peed in his pants when he saw me with the gun on his beloved Kelvin," Lambert said in mid-guffaw.

The bead curtain in the kitchen doorway clattered. "Lunch," Solomon said. He shuffled toward them and started plonking the cooked dishes down on the table, mixing up the orders as usual, leaving the sorting to the hungry.

"Am I in time?" said a quiet voice behind them. There was Janna, smelling of talcum powder like she'd just had a bath. Her yellow strapless dress looked festive, but her face and upswept hairdo looked sedate. She placed a package wrapped in brown paper beside Joseph without looking at him.

"Miss Bertha sent this for you. Banana bread, I think."

"Please tell her thank you," Joseph said, eyebrows raised.

She pulled up a chair from another table and placed it between Lambert and Lorraine, and her friend smiled at her.

"What you want to eat, Miss?" Solomon said.

"I'm not hungry, thanks," she said.

"Let me get you a drink," Shad said, rising with a fork in hand.

"I'm good, honestly."

They all started in, chewing, moaning, commenting. The fried chicken was the best Joseph had ever tasted, needed a little salt, according to Lambert, but after fifteen minutes, all plates were clean. Solomon cleared the dishes, enjoying the compliments, and followed up with stewed guavas and ice cream. Janna nibbled at Lorraine's dessert, and all the men polished theirs off and complained that they'd eaten too much.

A screeching sound in the car park turned everyone's head. "The taxi is here," Shad called. He hoped Xavier had fixed the hole in the backseat by now.

"I guess it's time to go," Eric said, looking at Joseph. He stood slowly, and Joseph did the same, both big men, rising to the same height, their noses thin and straight, the same kin. Eric looked uncomfortable, started fidgeting with his shirt pocket.

"Wait, wait," Joseph said, signaling the stirring group to stay seated. "I just want to say—guys, where do we start? Thank you, thank you for everything." He swept his hand around the table. "You folks, you saved our lives. How do you thank people for that?" He turned to his father. "Dad, I want to tell you, in front of your friends—"

"Don't embarrass him, now," Lambert called out.

"I just want to say, you're a hell of a father," Joseph said. "Riding in with your posse—"

"Thank Janna," Eric said, blushing, holding out one hand to the girl, and all eyes went to Janna.

Joseph's voice dropped. "Janna, what would have happened without you, I—cannot—cannot even imagine."

"It was a team effort," Janna said, looking around the table.

Lorraine rubbed her friend's back. "She's being modest."

"And Solomon." Joseph cleared his throat and waved toward the chef, loitering with Winston near the bar. "You were on fire with that machete, dude!" Everybody laughed, and Solomon nodded and smiled, his lips clamped tight.

"It seems almost funny now," Joseph said, "but it was ugly and serious. Deathly serious." Silence fell over the group for a few seconds, *like angels passing over,* Granny would have said. "Raheem and I—my partner and I—will never forget what you did. You saved our lives, risked your own, no less, and we wouldn't be here without you."

Eric, pink to his earlobes, smiled a wobbly smile like he was having indigestion. "You're my son. What do you expect?"

"I love you, man," Joseph said, and threw his arms around his father. Caught off guard, Eric raised his arms helplessly in the air. Then he placed his hands on his son's back and closed his eyes.

"I love you, too, buddy," he said at last. "Always know that—that I'm here for you." He patted Joseph's back with his big, square hands and pushed away. "And you're going to call Shannon, right? You have her number. Tell her hello when you call, and tell her I want Eve to come out next summer. Tell Eve I love her and I'll call soon."

"Right." Joseph gave a quick nod, then shook his head, smiling. You didn't have to be a mind reader to tell he knew his father would never change, Shad thought.

"Time to get the show on the road," Raheem said, standing up, as tall as Eric. "Thank you, Mr. Keller." He reached out his hand and Eric looked down at the young man's hand and shook it, flushing again, needing more time. Everyone stood up and there was a hubbub of hand shaking and hugging.

"Good-bye, Joseph," Janna said. She'd walked up quietly beside him, her face ironed flat.

"Come here, girl," Joseph said, and pulled her toward him. At first she stood stiffly, and it looked for a second like she wouldn't respond, would keep her body rigid in the pretty dress, but she placed her hands on his shoulders and he held her for a long time, stroking her back while the others went on chatting and smiling, pretending they didn't see. When she pulled back, there were sparkles of water on her eyelashes.

"You're a good man, Joseph," she said softly. "I have no regrets, I want you to know that."

"Keep in touch, I mean it," Joseph said. "I want to know where you're working."

She allowed him a smile. "There's a job opening up at the *Herald* in the online department. I'm going to apply. I want to know if I can be as committed to something as you've been. Maybe I'll end up as an online reporter after all. What about you?"

"Keller Consulting, my own business," he said, "thanks to you and your vision board. I've decided I'm going to work with small businesses, writing business plans to get them started."

She turned to Raheem. "Take care of him," she said, and behind her sadness there was a weariness, Shad told Beth later, as if she'd aged ten years. Something about her looked like a woman, he said, not a girl anymore.

Raheem reached up and removed his necklace. "I want you to have this," he said, folding it into her hand. "I got it in Hong Kong. They say it brings good fortune—prosperity, love, whatever you want." The diamond winked from his earlobe when he nodded. "That's what we both want for you."

"Thank you—you two," she said. She opened her fist and looked hard at the fish.

Lambert walked over to his daughter and put one arm around her shoulders. She turned into his arms and hugged him, holding him tight so he couldn't escape.

His eyes shut tight, his face showed that he knew he wasn't always going to be able to protect her, even when he wanted to, because his baby girl made her own decisions now. They were a sight to behold, the teddy bear of a man with his great arms wrapped around the stalk of a woman, rocking a little—without tears, without words. The hug any father would want from a child, and any child would want from a father, and every man and woman around the table was blinking hard, connecting with some long-lost parent, some wayward lover.

Shad dashed the tears out of his eyes and rushed for the suitcases. The gun swung heavily in his pocket when he bent over, and he could hear the soft scrunching sound when it hit the bag with Granny's grave dirt. A suit bag in each hand, he sang out above the last-minute words that had started again.

"People, people, listen up," he called. "Just one message. Like Master Marley say, we are all one. Let we not forget—one love and one heart." Leaning on the bar, Winston swung his fist up and grinned at Shad.

"Preach!" said Lambert.

"Amen," Lorraine said, and everyone clapped and cheered.

EPILOGUE

Miami Herald
December 12, 2011
NO PLACE FOR OLD GAYS
By Lorraine Harrington

JAMAICA—The elderly man takes the hand of the thin young man beside him and lets out a long, deep sigh. A sigh that comes from knowing that time is running out.

"If I ever knew Jamaica was terrible like this," he says in his Jamaican-British accent, "I would never have come back here to live."

Patrick Henry (not his real name) is a 67-year-old gay Jamaican who has been shaken by his latest discovery—that the country he loves could also be the country that kills him. Named by *Time* magazine in 2006 as "the most homophobic place on earth," Jamaica's murder rate of gays (30 deaths between 1997 and 2004, and counting) makes it a retirement hell for gay men.

Henry left the country of his birth 47 years ago to seek his fortune in Great Britain.

"To tell the truth, I didn't even know I was homosexual until I was in England. I didn't know what homosexuality was when I left home!" What Henry describes is a different Jamaica, one that didn't single out young men who weren't socially active with the opposite sex.

"When I was a boy, I was always busy, no time for the ladies, you know, helping out at home, doing my schoolwork, learning my trade, playing cricket, that kind of thing. Nobody never thought anything of it. I never thought anything."

A year after settling in Birmingham, Henry was invited by a friend to a private gay bar.

"I was so shocked—men with men! But it was nice. I could relax and be myself, and I began to accept that I was different, that I preferred men to women."

Henry eventually took a long-term lover, kept it quiet from his employer, but lived undisturbed for most of the time he resided in Britain. Only a few bad incidents occurred, he says, usually with drunken people making comments after the pubs had closed. When his partner died of cancer, Henry started thinking of moving back home.

"I hate the cold," he says, and manages a smile. "England is wet and cold all the time. The house stays dark, and I never got used to that. I wanted to come back home and live out my days in sunshine."

But another shock awaited Henry when he returned to Kingston. Not being a man who keeps up with the news, he says, he had no idea that being gay in Jamaica would endanger his life.

"Jamaica don't have nothing for a gay man. I don't know how it is for the women, but they treat us men bad. Even though I had the money to buy a nice town house in Kingston, I couldn't find no peace.

"I started to make friends, gay like me, and when I invited them over, the neighbors would talk about me, right to my face. One woman told me I was a sodomizer and I was 'going straight to hell.'"

A chance encounter one evening led to Henry meeting his current partner, David (not his real name), a man in his twenties from a small rural community. He, too, had suffered at the hands of judgmental Jamaicans, having narrowly escaped being murdered at the age of 16 by a group of villagers who came to his house.

"They used to tease me from young, you know," he says. "Then one night they came with all kind of stick and machete. If I hadn't been by a neighbor lady learning to sew, I would be dead now. She gave me money to take a taxi, and I never gone back."

After they became partners, the couple always felt under threat in Kingston, seldom leaving their home.

"If I walk on the road with him," Henry says, "my friend and me, we can't touch, can't even walk close. People looking for any opportunity to taunt you, call you a batty man. And like how (David) here look more different to me, look more like a girl, they always calling him names."

Homophobia will continue to plague Jamaica, according to Henry, until the country's political and religious leaders take a united stand against it.

"They have to come together and speak out with a strong voice," he says, "and they have to pass laws to stop that terrible music telling people to kill us, like we some kind of animal. But they not going to do that."

He shakes his head hopelessly. "They afraid of their followers. They don't have the courage. They too weak."

When asked how they have protected themselves thus far, David says that they look for other people to warn them. "You need straight friends around you. They form like a wall, you know. When you don't have that, you dead."

In their search for a location where they could live undisturbed, the couple moved to a home that Henry built in the countryside two years ago. However, he reports, their presence is starting to attract unwanted attention.

"We hear that some people in (a nearby town) saying they coming to *visit* us," Henry moans. "That only mean that we not going to have no peace, even here. That is all we want, little peace."

When asked what they plan to do next, David pats his partner's hand. "We going to England. I going to take care of him, keep him warm." He adds with a broad smile, "And I going to learn dress designing."

Time, however, is not on their side. While they wait the three to four months for David to get a British visa, danger lurks.

"You don't know who you can trust," says Henry. "You don't know who going to lift the machete against you or burn down your house. So you pray a lot."

ACKNOWLEDGMENTS

This second volume in the Shad Series was not an easy one to write. Even while I felt passionately about the subject matter and knew the book had to be written, it was clear from the beginning that it was going to be difficult. But, as so often happens, synchronicity stepped in to solve the problem. During a two-week writing excursion to San Francisco, when all I was anticipating was a struggle with a challenging topic, I met three people who magically appeared to make my struggle disappear. Not only did they warm my chilly July by feeding me hot tea and cake, but they also gave me suggestions that contributed greatly to the plot and character development in the novel. The appearance of this book says as much for these three friends, who later became expert readers, as it does for me. My deep gratitude, therefore, goes to Amy Donovan, Eileen Cristin O'Keeffe, and Eric Peterson for their invaluable assistance.

Thanks go, too, to my stalwart experts and readers: Larry Chang—my former business partner in Jamaica; Cathryn Davini, objective friend and reader; and my keen-eyed daughter, Lauren Baccus. All three gave me honest and sometimes painful feedback on this novel that helped me in its final drafting. Numerous friends and family members offered advice, places to stay, and willing ears to my frustrations.

I cannot give enough praise to my editor, Malaika Adero, who has served as my main supporter, my sometime therapist, and the experienced hand that held mine throughout. I am also deeply grateful to Atria and to its publisher, Judith Curr, who had the faith to believe that I could tackle this topic with the sensitivity it deserved.